DECEIVED BY BEAUTY, DRUNK
WITH PASSION

Alex inhaled sharply. Nichole looked so innocent sitting there wrapped in the blanket. Reaching for her, he put his hands under her arms and drew her out of the chair and against him. Looking down into her eyes, his voice husky, he murmured, "A husband can hold his wife, Nichole. He can caress her." He started running his hand gently up and down her back and across her shoulders. "And he can kiss her, too."

Alex bent his head and touched her lips very softly with his.

The blonde French girl was in turmoil. Never in her short life had she experienced anything that would compare with the feelings that were threading their way along every nerve of her body. His warmth and his touch were driving her to distraction. She clung to him, wanting his touch, wanting his kisses, wanting to make him continue to stroke her. She arched up against her husband, and whispered, "Let me love you as a wife, Alex."

Suddenly there was no more embarrassment, no mention of deception, no quarrels of arranged marriages . . . until the splendor of the moment was over. . . .

Satin Seduction

Allison Knight

ZEBRA BOOKS
KENSINGTON PUBLISHING CORP.

ZEBRA BOOKS

are published by

Kensington Publishing Corp.
475 Park Avenue South
New York, NY 10016

First printing: December, 1988

Printed in the United States of America

Dedication

*To Marlynn, my special lawyer
who was always there when
I needed her.*

Prologue

September 1777

The crack of a pistol split the early morning mist. The two boys crouched in the tall marsh grass of the bay and watched as a tall dark figure whirled and staggered to the ground. "First blood let," came the call. The duel had ended.

Alexander Dampier nudged his French cousin. Silently he led the way to the small boat hidden in the cattails, and together they shoved the skiff onto the river heading north, their destination, Manor House. They had slipped away from the plantation before dawn, and now they were returning.

"Do you think anyone was killed?" Charles asked quietly after they had raised the tiny sail and settled back to man the tiller.

"No!" Alex answered. "But now do you see how important it is to learn how to use pistols?"

Alex hunched forward in the sloop. "Why don't you ask Father about the pistols one more time? He'll be returning tomorrow afternoon." Alex watched as Charles seemed to slide down into the sloop, his shoulders slumping forward. He could tell that Charles clearly remembered Henry Dampier's rage the last time they'd asked to try the guns.

Charles stared at Alex, his blue eyes widening. The last time he had asked, Uncle Henry had shown him the same treatment Alex said he had received for years. His uncle had cursed and shouted and finally stomped out of the room, his face dark red in rage.

"I'm not saying another word to him about those pieces. If we are going to learn to shoot, we'll have to sneak them out," Charles snapped.

Alex frowned in the early morning sunshine. He liked his cousin, really liked him, and Charles had made such a difference in his life. His father had left him alone for the first time in four years. He didn't have to rise before dawn to work in the tobacco field like one of the slaves, and he didn't have to spend the evening hours with the tutor. In fact, his father hadn't screamed at him for weeks.

Alex watched Charles, who sat staring out toward the mouth of the river and the open sea. He's getting homesick, Alex thought, and with Father tiring of his visit of three months, he'll be going home soon. A grim expression crossed Alex's face. If he was going to teach Charles how to use the weapons it had to be soon.

"We have the rest of this morning, this afternoon and all of tomorrow morning to get the guns and try them," Alex said quietly, watching as Charles brightened considerably.

"But how will we get the pistols out of the house? Your housekeeper watches us like every thought we have is immoral."

"Don't worry, I have a plan," Alex assured the blond boy.

When Catherine, Alex's baby sister, started screaming, Charles left the kitchen and hurried outside. He made his way through the woods to the place where he had agreed to meet Alex, far enough away from the house that the sound of the gunshots would be muffled. He flopped

8

down on the grass and leaned against the old oak tree at the edge of the woods. The minutes drifted by slowly as Charles waited quietly. Then he spied Alex running toward him waving the rosewood box.

It took a while for Alex to show Charles how to prime and load the pistols. Alex described each step, and Charles's eyes glistened as he watched and listened. Finally, Alex commented, "I think you understand enough now. We'll start by trying to hit the center of that old elm tree. I'll go first."

He pulled the trigger. The pistol exploded and Alex found himself staring at his hand, the gun hanging loosely in his numb fingers. How could anything so small make so much noise, he wondered. Looking over, he explained to Charles, who had paled considerably, "I didn't expect a little gun like this to have such a kick."

Alex reloaded the weapon and handed the pistol to Charles. He braced himself and fired at the target. Grinning, he handed the weapon to Alex, who reloaded and fired again. A half dozen times Alex reloaded the gun and they each fired. Finally, Alex removed the second gun from the box. He loaded the second gun, paying little attention to Charles, who primed the first pistol. Alex announced with authority, "We'll shoot together at the target. Just like a real duel. On your mark, get ready, fire at the count of ten. One . . . two . . . three . . ."

At the count of ten Alex fired. The explosion at his side covered his own pistol shot. He glanced at where his cousin had been standing, and then down at the body on the ground. Alex stared in horror. Charles was lying perfectly still. Alex knew something was terribly, frightfully wrong. He leaned over his cousin and shuddered. A wave of nausea flowed through him. The left side of Charles's face was gone. A deep hole in his neck had severed his blood vessels, and the royal blood of Charles duPres was soaking into the warm Maryland soil.

Alex dropped the pistol, fell to his knees, and clasped

9

the still warm hand. In the distance he heard the shouts. His father was home! He fought the desire to run far and held the limp hand of his dead cousin. It had been an accident. Surely, his father would understand that it was a terrible accident.

Chapter One

June 1789

Henry Dampier chuckled and shifted his weight in the saddle. He had been in Baltimore for a week, and had spent a delightful time with his mistress of five years. The Paris-bound letter to Ma Mere Thomas, mother superior of the convent of St. Mary Magdalaine, was on its way, and Jacques had been notified. All was in readiness. Now was the time, he thought, the time to tell his son. He grinned in anticipation.

As his horse traveled south over the muddy road, Henry let his thoughts drift back to that day twelve years ago. Something—he had never figured out what—had driven him back to the farm a full day ahead of schedule. He remembered being furious about something. He smiled as he recalled that that was the day he had found his then current mistress in bed with the landlord. He shook his head; that was not why he had raced back. Something else had forced him back. If only, he groaned, he had arrived an hour earlier.

Once again, the rage that he had felt that day bubbled up and threatened to consume him. He could feel the terror he had felt when he had looked at the lifeless body of his sister-in-law's oldest son. They had buried the boy, and Henry had made the arduous trip to France to tell Charles Philipe and Catherine duPres about the death of their firstborn. His own son had been responsible—if not by his own hand, then through his carelessness. The du-Preses had both been gracious, even in their sorrow. He clenched his teeth. His only son, who would produce the heirs that he had been unable to have, had started his adult life by destroying Henry's connection to the courts of France.

Henry recalled his own bleak youth. He had been a poor boy, born of dirt farmers in the colony of Maryland. He had worked and stolen and cheated until he had a magnificent home and farm. As the market for tobacco increased, so did his profits. When he felt he was rich enough, he went to France in search of a wife. Through his agent, he met Marguerite Claudine Maison. He fell in love with her immediately, or at least with her titles. And the beautiful girl returned his love. Catherine, the older sister, had already been betrothed to a duke, and because her Russian mother was a romantic, Marguerite was permitted to marry her first love, the landed Colonial.

They were married and sailed for Maryland only days after the royal wedding of her sister. At first, he and Marguerite had been delightfully happy. Marguerite had loved the farm, and in her broken English she had described it as a house in the Manor Grande. Henry had liked that and named it Manor House for her.

Henry's face was now a black scowl. The reason for a marriage in the first place was a family, a huge family. He had told Marguerite often enough. He wanted heirs. But, after a year and a half of marriage, Marguerite had only succeeded in losing their first baby.

Alexander was not born until they had been married for over three years. Already thirty-three years old, he had wanted more children and quickly. In the next six years Marguerite had lost five more children. The doctor and

12

then the priest had come. They demanded that he stay away from her! How dare they tell him to stay away from his own wife! He clenched his teeth in anger all over again.

Unfortunately, both the priest and the doctor had talked to Marguerite. After that, Marguerite and he started to quarrel, and for a while, he did stay away from her. But then, just as he did now, he had felt cheated. Alex, even as a babe, looked like the Maison side of the family. He wanted another child, a boy, who looked like him!

As the days turned into years, Henry grew more and more incensed that Marguerite would not at least try to give him another son. As Henry watched his only heir, he grew more and more distressed. He once more insisted that Marguerite try again. She was reluctant, Henry remembered, but he was persuasive, and once again she lost the baby.

Finally, one last time, Henry forced his attentions on her and she conceived. Catherine arrived nine months later. He screamed, oh, how he had raged, when the doctor told him that the child was a girl. He still wondered just when he had realized that the doctor had also told him about Marguerite's death.

At first he had suffered from remorse, but it hadn't lasted long, and thank God, Catherine, named by Marguerite moments before she died, looked like his family. Catherine was a sickly child. Within two months, Henry had found Peter and Priscilla Bentley. Peter eventually became the property overseer and Priscilla took over the job of housekeeper and all of the care of Catherine. Henry devoted himself to the raising of his only son.

Henry's grimace deepened. His son! He was as stubborn and arrogant as Marguerite's family. The brat blamed him for the death of his mother. He had been twelve when she died, and when Henry had told him about her death, Alex had glared at him and announced, "I don't understand why she's gone, but I know it is your fault!"

When Henry hit him hard across the face that day, the battle lines were drawn. No son of his was going to speak to him that way. He had decided right then that he would force Alex into becoming the kind of son he could be proud of.

Just when he had hopes of succeeding with Alex, the business with Charles duPres happened. After he had explained as best as he could to Charles and Catherine, he had sailed home to the Colonies. On the slow voyage home, he imagined all the things he was going to make Alex do. His son would be a man worthy of his name even if he had to kill him to see it accomplished.

"Damn that boy!" Henry yelled out loud, startling the horse. Alex had not waited for his father to return; instead he had run away to serve in the Colonial army. Briefly, after the war, Alex returned. He was even something of a hero. Henry remembered his delight. Now Alex could begin the task of producing the heirs to the plantation that Henry could never have, but he felt, deep in his heart, he deserved.

At Jacques's insistence, he had gone to France in 1780 to meet a young woman Jacques had found. Her mother, described by those who knew her as an attractive woman, had been a distant relative to the sister of the king. The child was untouched by the world. Her father, a poor chimney sweep, had given her into the care of the nuns when she was four. Jacques had learned that the girl's father had just died. That meant the girl had no one to care for her, but the reason Henry was interested was because Jacques reported that the family was rather slow. Henry smiled; it fitted into his plans so perfectly.

He liked the convent, and he liked the mother superior. What better way, he reasoned, to control his grandchildren

14

than through their governess. With her training in obedience and the gratitude she would feel for his care, Nichole Ramoneur would be a perfect choice. He made arrangements with Mother Thomas and made it clear that the girl was to have no contact with the outside world. Each year, he sent Jacques Manage to see for himself how the child was faring. He sent instructions and received apologetic letters from Mother Superior. The girl was slow and was having a hard time with her studies, but she promised to try harder. Henry's lips turned into a leering smile.

Once more, the edges of his smile turned down into a scowl. His damn ungrateful son. Well, he smacked his thick lips, this time Alex would have no choice. He had him right where Henry knew it would pain him the most: Catherine. He laughed out loud with pleasure. Just let him try and wiggle out of his father's plans this time.

He stopped for lunch, and after a satisfactory repast he continued on his way. Alex should be waiting at the house by the time he got there. Henry chuckled. Alex was about to become a married man. He laughed out loud as he thought of Alex's rage. Knowing that he was going to thoroughly enjoy the evening, he pushed his horse even faster toward home.

Alex Dampier had burst into Manor House the evening before, and he was as angry as his father predicted he would be. While he waited, he spent the day asking the servants what they knew about Catherine's plans. He begged and pleaded, but no one knew anything. "That old man better get here soon," Alex muttered as he made his way to the study. Pouring a brandy, he threw himself into one of the leather chairs that stood beside the large oak desk that occupied the place of honor in the center of the room.

"Why? What does he hope to gain?" Alex mumbled as he took the crumpled note from his pocket. He stared at the words his father had written. He had memorized them. "Come immediately, if you ever want to see Catherine again!"

Alex's thoughts turned to Catherine. His expression softened, and he thought, Poor little imp. How could he have done the things to her that he did as a boy? He had never forgotten the summer Charles had come, and how, when he wanted out of the house with Charles, he would take away her toys, or even her food. It had always worked: Catherine would start to scream and Priscilla would always arrive and order him from the house.

His thoughts jumped from Catherine to Charles duPres. It wasn't until that fateful summer that he accidentally found out why his father treated him the way he did.

Charles had grinned up at him one afternoon. "Has your father ever mentioned the Black Russian?" Alex had shaken his head; he had never heard of anyone called the Black Russian.

"Well, you should know about him. You're related." Charles started to explain: "Catherine, my mother, and Marguerite, your mother, are sisters." Alex wanted to choke him. He knew how he and Charles were related. Charles grinned, knowing that he was irritating his older cousin. "Did anyone ever tell you about their brother?" Once more Alex shook his head; he was losing patience with Charles. "Well, they have a younger brother. I guess from what little I've heard that he was a devil. Tall, dark hair, dark brown eyes. His name is Dennis Ivan Maison, but even when he was really young, nobody called him Dennis."

Alex interrupted, "Dennis Maison is my godfather."

Charles nodded his head. "Now he's usually called the Black Russian. He sails the warm Caribbean seas and goes by his pirate name. He's a real pirate, and he has aided the Colonialists by capturing British vessels. Why do you think they let me travel here during a war?" Alex just shrugged; he had never given it much thought.

16

"The Black Russian guaranteed my safety, what's why!" Charles's next words were never forgotten. "He may be your godfather, but you look so much like him, he could be your father."

As he remembered all the times his father had shouted about making him into a son he could be proud of, Alex realized that his father was ashamed of Dennis Ivan Maison. He must also be ashamed of a son that looked more like his uncle than his father. Even after all these years, Alex grinned, it still pleased him that his father had never been able to shape his son into the kind of a man he wanted as a son. Alex was his own man!

Alex took a sip of brandy and shivered. Just the thought of Charles brought the scene of his death back vividly, as if it happened only yesterday. Henry had screamed so many words—that he was guilty of murder, that he had killed his cousin, that he had destroyed his father's connection to the French court. Alex knew it was his fault. He didn't need his father screaming at him and telling him the same thing over and over.

His father had threatened him with the press-gang and then something about working from dawn to dawn, but he had been too distraught to remember all his father said. Peter and Priscilla Bentley had cornered him and tried to talk to him, but it wasn't until Henry left for France that Peter got his attention. He had pulled Alex into the stable and stated simply that his father was sure to work him to death if he stayed at the farm.

As he recalled the arrival of Peter and Priscilla, Alex smiled fondly. They had come to the plantation shortly after his mother died; Priscilla had taken over the care of Catherine and the house and Peter had started working the farm. Over the years his affection for both Peter and Priscilla had grown. How many times had they tried to spare both children from the rages of their father?

After Henry had left for France, Peter had talked and

Priscilla had pleaded, but Alex had stood tall and announced that he was no coward. He would stay on the farm and work as his father wanted. But Peter had not been about to give up, and he had told Alex that Henry was a cruel man. He had told Alex about seeing Henry beat more than one slave to death just for stopping to rest. When Peter had told him about witnessing the brutal chopping of fingers that Henry had ordered when he thought his bondservant had stolen some hay, Alex began to consider leaving. Finally, Prissy, as she was called, had explained quietly that she and Peter were afraid that Henry just might take out his anger on Catherine. Alex realized he must go. He had already caused his little sister a great deal of pain.

Peter had made the arrangements, and Alex had ridden off for Pennsylvania before the first snowfall. When he had arrived at Valley Forge, Alex was assigned to Friedrich von Steuben. The German spoke little English and Alex knew less German, but Alex could read and write, and the German had insisted that the boy become his aide. Alex chuckled; they had communicated in little more than sign language for months.

Alex had liked the Prussian. He was a soldier and he took his job very seriously He had made the tiny army at Valley Forge into a group of fighting men. Alex shivered as he remembered standing knee-deep in the snow with hot coffee, waiting for the colonel to stop drilling the men in his broken English.

When the army had moved on, Alex, now a man, had gone to serve with General Gates. He had managed to get into some of the thickest parts of the fighting and had been given two awards for his bravery. Alex had honed his ability to observe, and he had been sent to deliver messages behind enemy lines, several times. He rubbed his side as he remembered the Redcoat who had tried to run him through at Jamestown. The bayonet had caught him n the side, and although he had been weak for a while, he had recovered completely. He frowned. Because of that wound, he had missed the surrender. After Jamestown when most of the men went home, Alex stayed on, primarily to stay away from his father.

Alex chuckled. It was a good thing he did remain in the army. It was late that spring when he played cards with a German sergeant. He had won fair and square. When he had picked up the paper the German had bet, Alex remembered how astonished he had been. The sergeant had bet the title to a 6500-acre farm, land which was rich and forested and next to a river. It was prime farmland, the sergeant assured him. It was a half day's ride east of Frederick. Alex remembered his sinking feeling at the mention of Frederick. Alex had stuttered, "Frederick is in Maryland!"

"Zat's right, ze land, she is in Maryland," the sergeant had explained.

Alex had left the army soon after that. "I want to see my land," he had told his commanding officer. He had traveled through the countryside, trying to decide if he really wanted to farm the land or sell it. But after he saw the small one-room log cabin and the acres that had been cleared, he had been elated. He had wanted to shout! He was free of his father. He didn't have to go home ever again, he didn't have to endure his father or Manor House unless he wanted to.

Alex wondered if, perhaps, he had decided to go home because he didn't have to go. In August, five months after the Treaty was signed, Alex had left his farm and traveled to Manor House. He chuckled. Even the servants had not recognized him. Peter had told him it was because he was taller and had filled out completely, but Prissy had said plainly that he had changed. His dark brown curly hair was neatly confined to a queue at the nape of his neck, and his face was thinner. His thick eyebrows and round brown eyes dominated his face. He was strong and he carried himself with pride, his dark eyes gleaming in his round face.

The meeting with Catherine was something he would never forget. She had looked up at him for a long time and then shyly told him she was delighted to have him home. It was love at first sight. He had grinned sheepishly and even apologized for all of the tricks he played on her as a child.

His meeting with his father had taken place just before dinner, and it had not gone nearly as well, he mused. The first thing the man had said to him was, "I thought you would be home in April. Where were you?"

Alex had ignored his father's question and asked Catherine about her life now that she was a grown up lady of eleven. Catherine had giggled and looked up at Alex with adoring eyes. Henry had scowled and started slamming things around on the table. He had even gone so far as to shriek at the poor black girl serving the meal.

After dinner, Henry had glared at Catherine and demanded that Alex meet him in the study, "Where we can discuss your future without interruption." Alex had said nothing more then, but the yelling that was to characterize all of their future meetings had begun shortly after Alex went to the study.

The old man had poured himself a glass of brandy and failed to offer a glass to his son. Alex had pointed out the oversight immediately and poured his own glass. Henry had scowled as he looked Alex over.

"What do you want to discuss with me?" Alex had asked quietly.

"I want to talk about your future."

Alex snapped, "My future?"

"I want to know what you plan to do. In fact, I demand to know what your plans are. If you are finished playing soldier, I need help here at the farm. It is time that you settled down, took a wife and started a family. Children take time, and if you are ever going to have any, you had better get started."

Alex had sat back in the chair and sipped his brandy. He could still see the look of disbelief on Henry's face as he had his say. "I just got home, damn it. I'm not ready to settle down yet. And you might as well know. Father, I have my own farm now. It will require most of my time and I intend to become a profitable farmer. I have no time for marriage, and certainly no time to look for a wife. I will decide when that time comes, not you. I'm no longer a frightened little boy that must wait on every word you say. I'm a man now, and I will make my own way in life. However, if you need my help, when I have the time, I will help you with this farm."

Henry had turned red with rage. "Get out! Get out of my house. You are no son to me." Henry had moved toward Alex, and Alex had been afraid for a second that his father was going to strike him.

Standing, Alex had gazed at the man with contempt. "Father, I have come home to meet my sister. I want to get to know her a little. Then, I will leave."

A grim smile played across Alex's lips. At that moment he had thought his father was going to have a seizure, but suddenly, the man had turned and rushed out the door. Henry was gone the next morning and didn't return until Alex left Manor House.

He had spent a delightful two weeks with Catherine. She was bright and witty and full of fun. The pre-teenage awkwardness had been there, but there had been an inward sense of self-worth that was grace in itself. And he idolized her.

Alex had also spent a great deal of time with Peter. He needed to know as much about farming as the overseer could tell him in the few weeks he was at Manor House. Together, they had found two local men who needed work, and Peter had insisted that he and Alex travel to several farms to meet those men that were making their farms pay.

Alex snarled as he thought of the times his father had tried to manipulate him and his farm. That first year had been bad. The money had gone out faster than it had come in, and Alex had had little money to pay the men. They had told him that they would be willing to stay and work without pay if Alex agreed to share in the profits their first good year. Somehow his father had found out about the lack of cash. First, he had tried to buy Alex's men, and when that didn't work, he had tried to buy the farm. After that, Alex only traveled to Manor House to see Catherine, and he tried to make those trips only when Henry was in Baltimore.

He couldn't escape his father completely, however, and this was one of those occasions. When Henry demanded to see his son, there wasn't much that Alex could do but put in an appearance. It was always the same thing. Why, Alex asked himself for the thousandth time, did the old man want him married so badly? The crumpled note, held tightly in Alex's clenched fist, would lead to another confrontation about his unmarried state, Alex was sure. But what had the old man done with Catherine?

Alex grew weary of just sitting and waiting. That was all he had done for two days, he thought in disgust. He left the study and went in search of Prissy. He would try once more to jog her memory; perhaps she had forgotten something that would tell him where Catherine was, or what his father had done to her.

Prissy was in the kitchen, taking time from her busy schedule to sip a cup of tea. "Prissy," Alex interrupted her conversation with Mrs. Barber, the plantation cook, "would you mind telling me again just what Catherine told you before she left?"

Prissy's blue eyes flashed annoyance. "How many times

do you want me to tell you? She didn't say a thing! She told me that her father said if she told anyone, she wouldn't be allowed to go. Knowing Catherine, I'm certain that it must have been someplace she really wanted to go. And, Alex, I said this before, it could have been a hundred places."

Alex gazed at the rawboned woman. She's as concerned as I am, he thought. "What did you pack for her? That might give us a clue." Alex wasn't willing to overlook any possibility.

"Why, I never thought of that." Prissy glanced past Alex at the open door of the big room. "Let's see. I packed most of her party dresses, and the blue cotton, and several day dresses. In fact, I packed most of her summer wardrobe. We loaded two trunks."

Alex stared at the woman, who was at least a score of years older than he. Her graying hair peeked out from under her thin linen cap and curled in soft wisps next to her lined face. Didn't she realize, Alex wondered, at being asked to pack so many of Catherine's belongings?

"Now, don't you go thinking she might not be coming back." Prissy read his mind. "She usually takes that much when she travels. She has clothes for two, or at the most, three weeks. She'll be back."

Alex sulked from the kitchen. Prissy was simply no help, no help at all. He ambled back to the study and his unfinished brandy. There was nothing he could do. He had to wait for his father. There was nothing more he could do.

Before dinner, Alex heard the crunch of stones on the drive. His father had returned. Now he would get some answers! he thought.

As Henry burst through the study door, Alex bellowed, "All right, Father! Where is Catherine? What have you done with her?"

Henry looked at his red-faced son and tried to hide the

pleased expression that teased the corners of his mouth. He walked over to the small table by the window and reached for the decanter of brandy. Without looking at Alex, he said quietly, "She's tucked safely away, and there she will stay, at least for the time being."

"Have you harmed her? If you have hurt her . . . I'll . . ."

"You'll what? She is my daughter! If she is hurt, and it won't be physically, it will be your fault." Henry finally looked at his arrogant son. Alex was standing directly in front of him now, his hands resting on his hips. Henry moved over to one of the leather chairs in the room. "I'm not, despite what you might think, that kind of a monster."

Alex wanted to argue that statement, and he wanted to denounce the man sitting comfortably and sipping his brandy, but, he decided, now was not the time. He would have to control his temper, and at least keep his mouth shut until he heard his father out. Glaring into the steel gray eyes that were so much like Catherine's Alex threw himself into the chair across the room. Alex gazed into his father's eyes. The only difference between Catherine's eyes and the eyes that were looking at him now were the tiny little laugh lines that Catherine had around her eyes when she laughed, which was most of the time. Alex stared at his father in surprise, for he couldn't remember when he had last heard his father laugh. Henry had no lines around his eyes.

He forced himself to ask in a reasonable tone of voice, "What do you want this time, Father?"

"Would you like a drink? Some brandy? Rum? Perhaps a glass of wine?"

Alex could feel his jaw tighten. "I've already had a brandy. I don't want a thing, not a damn thing! Just get on with it. Where is Catherine? What do you want this time?"

24

"Son." Henry smiled and let the words roll off his tongue. His time had come. "I suggest strongly that you take a glass of spirits. I think you will need it." Henry smacked his lips in anticipation.

Chapter Two

June 1789

When the bell rang, Nichole Ramoneur glanced up from her translation. Everyone in the drab, gray stone building that was St. Mary Magdalaine's convent looked up when the bell rang. The great brass bell announced someone at the front gate. It seldom rang.

Nichole lowered her eyes and began her task once more, Virgil this time. Did Frere Francis never run out of Greek and Latin passages for her to translate? she asked herself. She would so much rather have been in the rolling orchards behind the building with Soeur Clare. Ripening on the trees were dark sweet cherries, and they were ready to be picked. She could almost feel the sticky juice between her fingers and taste the dark burgundy fruit.

A quick rap on the study door interrupted her labors, and she sighed as one of the new novices peered around the door. "Yes, Marie! What is it?"

"Ma Mere wishes to see you, Nichole. She sent word that you should freshen up and come to her office." Marie gazed at Nichole with a concerned expression. To be called to Ma Mere's own office meant that you had done something, something for which hours, perhaps even days of penance were required. As she closed the door behind her, the novice shuddered. Then she remembered. Nichole was not at the convent to become a nun. She was there to learn to be a governess, and eventually she would leave.

Nichole watched the door close, and she shook herself. The last time she had been summoned like this to Ma Mere's private office, she had been told that her father was dead. Nichole brushed at the tears that still came after all these years. How long had it been? She had just turned one and ten, then. Almost ten years had passed since that fateful day. Nichole could never forget the words, even though Ma Mere had tried to be kind. "I'm so sorry, child. He died in his sleep. Now he will be happy with your dear mother." She had patted Nichole on the head.

"But I have good news as well. God is taking care of you, little one, so that you will not be a burden to any of your brothers and their wives and families. A gentleman from the Colonies with family here in France approached me. He wants us to train a genteel young woman to become governess to his grandchildren. He is very interested in you. He will be here this afternoon to meet you. Now, go to your room, and thank God that you have a patron. Remember also your own dear parents in your prayers. Go, go now and pray." She had pushed Nichole toward the door.

Desperately, Nichole brushsed the tears from her cheeks as she remembered. She had raced back to her room, but she had not prayed. Instead, she had wept, deep, bitter tears. Her whole life had been devastated, first by the death of her mother, and then with the passing of her father. She would never get to go home.

Once more, Nichole rushed back to her tiny cell. She brushed her thick golden hair and poured a bit of cool water from the pitcher into the plain white bowl on the table. Dipping her hands into the water, she splashed some onto her face, her mind whirling with the possibilities her summons represented. Could the Colonial have returned for her as he had promised? Would she finally be leaving the only place she could call home? A part of her rejoiced, and another part of her wanted desperately to turn and run. Run where? she asked herself. She had no place to go.

She patted her plain brown dress and started for the door. Ma Mere did not believe in tardiness. As she hurried down the long dark corridor, she thought back to that afternoon, so long ago.

It had been late afternoon when Ma Mere sent word for her to come to the office. Nichole had poked her head around the door, and Ma Mere had stepped up and urged her into the room. Nichole had stood, gazing up at an enormous man. He had been pleasant-looking, not too old, and he had explained quickly what he wanted. His French had had a strange accent, but Nichole had been too concerned about the news of the day to ask him about his speech. "I have a son and a daughter. There is little education, quality education, in the Colonies. I want to be assured that my grandchildren have the kind of education that my own children did not receive. You will study hard, and I will provide clothes and food and pay for your training. When the time comes, you will journey to my home and will begin the task of teaching my future heirs."

Nichole had lowered her eyes. "How many grandchildren do you have, sir?" I'm little more than a child myself, she thought. Before she could wonder how she could be a governess to children like herself, his answer had thrown her into a state of shock.

"Oh, my son is not married yet," he had smiled at her, "but, when he does marry, I want an educated, genteel woman, convent-trained, ready to take on the task of training my grandchildren. My son is eighteen now, so you will stay here and learn. I will expect you to learn everything the good sisters can teach you. In five or six years,

28

when my son has decided on a wife, I will send for you."

Nichole couldn't help but wonder if this was the way governesses were educated. She knew nothing but the life of the convent, and that knowledge gave no hint about the hows of life. But that episode had been over nine years ago. She had given up any hope that she would ever leave the convent.

As Nichole's shoes clicked along the cobblestone floor of the hall, she wondered if at long last, the son had married and the grandchildren of her benefactor, Monsieur Henry Dampier, were ready for their governess. She was certainly ready for them.

Moving down the corridor that led to Ma Mere's businesslike office, Nichole smiled as she passed two of the new postulates, girls much like herself, who had only been at the convent for a few months. Nichole almost giggled out loud; there was nothing different in her dress to distinguish her from the other young girls, a dark dress of simple lines and a lighter brown veil that covered her dark golden curls almost completely. At first glance Nichole knew she looked no different than either girl, plain of feature and full of religious zeal. Nichole could only guess how soon it would be before the new girls wondered how she could be a postulate for so long. Next, Nichole grinned, they'll worry that there is something wrong with me.

As she hurried by, the taller of the new girls watched her pass. She glanced at her companion. "Surely, she has not renounced the world." She stared as Nichole raised her head. This girl was truly beautiful, and her remarkable features were not soon forgotten. Her face was oval, and her skin was clear. Her complexion was like pale cream, and her golden hair, just visible around the edges of her veil, complemented her fair skin. Her small nose flared out slightly at the nostrils, and her lips were full and pink. Long ago, Nichole had adopted the habit of biting her lips as she studied, so their natural color was frequently more like the sweet strawberries that grew in the garden behind the convent. The girl continued to stare as Nichole moved down the hall. If only she had looked like that, perhaps her father would have tried to find her a husband, instead of sending her into the service of a demanding God.

Nichole tapped on the office door, and Soeur Bernard ushered her into the small anteroom to wait for Ma Mere. "Is Ma Mere alone?" Nichole whispered.

Her constant companion for these fifteen years past leaned toward her. "A message came." She glanced at her charge, startled once more by her innocent beauty. Her large round eyes were her most striking feature, Soeur Bernard decided. They were green, a deep green like the sweet grass of summer, and they were fringed with long dark gold lashes that lay against her cheeks when she lowered her eyes properly. Her plain muslin dress hung around her slim frame, but it did not hide the full high bust or the narrow waist of her tall figure. Even in her convent garb, she was a lovely young woman. Soeur Bernard flushed with pride at the beautiful young lady, hoping that the Lord would forgive her for feeling that she in part was responsible.

"Soeur Bernard." The stern voice of Mother Superior shook the nun from her thoughts. "Is Nichole here yet?"

"She has just arrived."

"Send her to me." The voice had mellowed.

Soeur Bernard pushed Nichole toward the door. "I will wait for you in the study."

Nichole nodded and straightened her dress once more. Why, Nichole asked herself, did she still shake when she approached this door? Reluctantly, she tapped on the inner door to Ma Mere's sparse office, just as nervous as she had been that first time so long ago.

Nichole edged her way into the room and stood before

30

the desk. Unwanted memories came flooding back to her. Suddenly, she was not a young woman of twenty-one, but a child of four. Her own father had brought her to the convent, and she could see herself holding onto his shaking hand. He came seeking the sisters' help with his only daughter, he had said.

"My wife"—his voice had broken as he tried to explain—"is gone. I have ten sons; there are eleven children. There would have been twelve, but . . ." He had brushed the tears from his eyes, unable to continue.

"I understand," a much younger Ma Mere had consoled. "You cannot care for this child."

"It isn't that we don't want her. But there is no one, no relatives. And she is so lost without her mother."

"We will care for her." Ma Mere had pulled Nichole from her father and guided her into the tiny antechamber. "Soeur Bernard, your first duty as a new novice is to care for this child." Soeur Bernard had taken her charge in hand and together they had faced the future.

"This is not the time for daydreaming, Nichole." Ma Mere's sharp reprimand broke through Nichole's reminiscences.

"Oh, I'm sorry, Ma Mere. I was only remembering the other times I have stood in this office."

"Sit down, child. I will order tea." Ma Mere's tone forced Nichole to glance over at the tiny little woman covered in brown and white. She was angry about something, Nichole thought, but then she usually was angry. Nichole sank into the straight-backed chair across from the desk as Ma Mere disappeared into the adjacent room.

With Ma Mere gone from the room, Nichole's memories came flooding back again. After the Colonial, Monsieur Dampier had left, Frere Francis had been summoned and Nichole had begun the lessons that were to consume all of her time. Her green eyes darkened as she thought of the long hours each day that she was forced to spend learning Latin, Greek, German and the language of the Colonies, English. She had struggled through History, Mathematics and Literature. As she glanced at her long fingers, she once again felt the twinge of pain from the blisters that had developed as she learned the harp and the guitar. She sighed; even the long hours she spent learning the gentle art of needlework for which the convent was famous had never been much more than a chore. Always, no matter how hard she tried, she mused, Ma Mere or Frere Francis were never satisfied. She remembered Ma Mere's not too gentle pushes: "Now, Nichole, I know you can do better!"

Frere Francis had not been any nicer at first. "Nichole, you really must try harder. Monsieur Dampier will think that you are a poor subject for a governess. Then you will have no place to go, and there is no one to provide for you." Shuddering, she remembered her nightmares, in which Monsieur Dampier rose from a dark fog to point an accusing finger at her. He never said anything in her dreams, but she knew that he was furious that she had not done better with her studies.

Shaking her head, and trying desperately to forget the painful moments, she muttered, "I was just a child. No one ever remembered that I was just a child. I wanted to play, like other children." A solitary tear streaked down her cheek as she tried to pray for forgiveness. Surely, the good Lord would understand. She tried to be obedient, tried to be a good student, tried to pretend that she lacked nothing.

Suddenly, she leaned forward in her chair, thinking about her one act of defiance in her fifteen years in the convent. Trying to stifle her giggles, she remembered the face of Soeur Mary Margaret, the laundress. She had arrived at Nichole's small bedroom door carrying Nichole's two chemises, a look of horror on her face. Nichole smiled again in spite of herself. She had known the minute she started embroidering the tiny pink rosebuds on her chemises just exactly what Soeur Mary Margaret would do. The poor woman had been scandalized, Nichole remembered with a snicker.

Once more, Ma Mere's arrival broke into her reverie. "The tea will be here soon." Ma Mere settled her thin frame into her chair, heaving a sigh as she picked up the parchment on her desk.

"We have a letter here from Monsieur Dampier." She glanced up at Nichole. "Do you remember Monsieur Manage? Jacques Manage?"

Nichole nodded her head. She had been forced to entertain the ugly little man when he came to check up on her for Monsieur Dampier. How could she ever forget him?

Ma Mere continued, "In a few weeks, Monsieur Jacques Manage will arrive. This time, however, you will be married by proxy to Monsieur Dampier's son, Alexander. You will leave here and travel to Maryland, where this young man lives."

Nichole gasped, "Married? No, it is not possible. I am to be a governess." She trembled. How could she marry? She had never thought about marriage. She knew nothing about marriage! She was a teacher! Nichole stared at Ma Mere, her green eyes clouded with confusion. Why, she didn't even know anyone who was married.

"Nichole," Ma Mere bean gently, "this is no more of a shock to you than it is to me. But I have checked with Frere Francis, and in extreme cases, a marriage by proxy is permissible. With France in turmoil, Monsieur and his son do not feel that it is safe for them to travel here for the wedding, not with the name Dampier and their royal relatives here in Paris."

Nichole trembled, and tried to stand. *"Non,* I am to be a governess." Then she turned pleading eyes to the superior. "Why me? Why can't he marry someone from his own country? Oh, Ma Mere, it is not possible!"

"Sit down, child! It is not impossible. It seems that this Alexander can find no one that suited both him and his father, and Monsieur Dampier has received such glowing reports from Monsieur Manage that he has convinced his son that you would make an admirable wife." Remembering her duty, she glanced at Nichole sternly. "I can assure you that you will be married, and let me also assure you that it is a real marriage, binding in the eyes of God. When Monsieur Manage arrives, you will be married to Monsieur Alexander Dampier!" More gently, the old woman added, "Nichole, today most young women of substance do not know the men they marry. Some of them are not much different from you, because they have not met their betrothed until the day of their wedding. You will meet yours several weeks after the wedding. That is the only difference."

As she rushed back to the study, Nichole tried to ignore her tears. Why, she questioned, did she always leave Ma Mere's office in tears, with her heart breaking? Why couldn't she stay right here at the convent, and learn to be as happy and as peaceful as Soeur Bernard always seemed to be? Stumbling toward the study, she tried desperately to compose herself. Silently, she screamed, I don't want to marry!

Minutes later, she was pouring out her agony to her only friend. Soeur Bernard listened patiently; then she shattered Nichole's limited composure. "Why don't you want to marry, little one? What are you so afraid of? Marriage is often very fulfilling. You will have children of your own, and you will learn to love your husband. He will love you and together you will have a happy life."

Nichole sobbed, "I don't know anything about marriage. I don't even know any men."

"Nichole," Soeur Bernard enfolded the frightened girl in her arms, "I know that you have met very few men . . ." She laughed when Nichole held up her hand to indicate four. "All right, you have met four men, and the convent has not been the best preparation for marriage, but obviously this young man needs you. I'll ask Frere Francis to find some books about marriage and about this Maryland, and when you get the books, you will see that being married has it own rewards."

Soeur Bernard was true to her word, and before the week was out Frere Francis had presented her with a book on marriage and several about the Colonies, about the revolutionary war that had just ended, and about tobacco farming in Maryland.

Greedily she absorbed the books. As she read, she knew that she liked the principles that these Colonials had fought and died for, and farming intrigued her, but the book on marriage completely confused her. As she studied the carefully worded sentences, she asked herself what on earth all the references to oneness were about. The more she read the more confused she became, and she promised herself that at the first opportunity she would ask Soeur Bernard for a clarification.

The days moved swiftly, and one afternoon, a week after Nichole's meeting with Ma Mere, Soeur Bernard arrived at the study with her arms full of bolts of fabric. "Monsieur Dampier sent funds for these, Nichole. We are to make a suitable wardrobe for the wife of Alexander Dampier. Look, there are cottons and silks, even several wools. There is fabric here for chemises and petticoats, and this" — she lifted up a luxurious cream satin — "this is for your wedding dress." She dumped the fabric on the table. "We must start immediately. We do not know how much time we have."

As they sewed, Nichole asked Soeur Bernard about the book of marriage Frere Francis had given her. As Nichole listened, Soeur Bernard explained, "You will, in essence, belong, mind and body, to Monsieur Dampier. You must obey him in all things. You must bear his children and

35

. . . and submit to him." Soeur Bernard smiled. She felt like patting herself on the back. She had managed to tell Nichole the whole of it.

Nichole just stared at her. She thought, Those are almost the exact words of the book. She still knew little more than before she had asked for an explanation. She frowned; submit must mean to obey without question.

Soeur Bernard noticed Nichole's slight frown. "Marriage to a man, Nichole, is not unlike the sisters here. You will belong to this Alexander Dampier just as we belong to God."

A tantalizing smile lifted the corner of Nichole's mouth. Now she understood. To submit to the man meant to be completely dedicated to the man. Nichole voiced her other concern. "Why do you think the women of his own country did not want to marry him?"

Soeur Bernard chuckled at the girl. "Did it never occur to you, Nichole, that the women of that country might not have appreciated the man? Perhaps he is not a perfect specimen. Women who live in the world can be most selfish. But you know that what is inside a person is so much more important that what is on the surface, don't you?"

Nichole only nodded, but that night as she lay on her narrow cot waiting for sleep that would not come, Soeur Bernard's words kept repeating, again and again. Suddenly, she remembered that Alexander Dampier had been in the war between England and the Colonies. What if he had been injured? A shudder ran through her, and she jerked to an upright position. What if he had been left maimed by the war? What if he was disfigured or had suffered some deformity? No wonder the women in his country did not want him as a husband.

She smiled to herself. She remembered the soft, tiny kitten she had nursed back to health after it had lost its leg in a furious fight with a dog. It had lived and managed quite well on three legs for several years. The fact that it had had only three legs had not affected Nichole's love. She could love something that was not perfect. Surely, she could love a man who had suffered an injury, even if he was disfigured. Satisfied with her new feelings, she eased back down on her cot and drifted off to sleep.

Chapter Three

"I will ask you once more, and then, if you choose not to answer, I'll be taking my leave!" Alex shouted. Trying desperately to calm himself, he asked softly, "What do you want?"

Henry started in a soft voice. "I want what I have always wanted. I want to see you married and I want a houseful of grandchildren. And I want it before I die."

Alex couldn't believe his hearing, and he snapped in disgust, "Is that what this is all about? We have been over this before. I have no time to court and woo a woman. I'm not ready for the responsibilities of fatherhood. And I may never be. I have had such a good example, you see!" Alex strained to keep the sneer off of his face.

"Oh, but you are ready, and you will be married. You will also begin a family. It is all arranged." Henry grinned at Alex, who stood before his father, stunned.

Alex fought against the shock; his father would use Catherine to force him to do what he wanted. Could Henry be mad? Slowly the rage began to swell up within him. For a second, Alex Dampier's expression was an exact copy of his father's face. Both men were drawn so tightly into the drama unfolding in the study that Henry didn't notice, and Alex would not have believed it if he had seen his own face just then.

"Just how do you think you are going to accomplish this feat, Father?" Alex snarled as he sank into his chair.

"I have a story to tell you, but I insist that you have a glass of rum." Henry rose from his chair and splashed a good portion of liquor into one of the glasses on the tray at the edge of the desk. He grinned as he handed the glass to Alex and returned to his chair. This felt even better than he had thought it would.

"Several years ago, while you were busy playing soldier, Jacques Manage found a young girl for me, a distant relative of the queen. She was in a convent in Paris. How he found her is unimportant. She was the last of eleven children and the only girl. When she was only four, her mother died, and the father and brothers could not care for her, so she was placed with the nuns. When her father died, I took over her expenses. At first, I'll be honest with you, I thought to make her the governess for your sons. She has been training for that occupation for ten years."

Henry stopped long enough to take a deep drink from the glass he swirled in his fingers. "With the trouble in France, it is imperative to get her out of the country. She will not be safe in the convent, if the rumors about the church are correct. With her background, she will be arrested. That rabble over there look unkindly on the church and the aristocrats. Can't say that I blame them!" Henry lifted up his hand to indicate that Alex should join him in a drink.

In defiance, Alex slammed the glass down on the table next to his chair. "What has all of this to do with me? I have no children. I don't need a governess, nor does Catherine. Now, where the hell is Catherine?" Henry's rages Alex could deal with, but the soft tones his father was using were making him very nervous. Why wouldn't his father just tell him where Catherine was?

"Let me finish! I know you have no children." Henry's face turned red and he began to shout. "Damn it, that's what this is all about. And I'll tell you where Catherine is and what will happen to her, when I'm ready."

As Alex stared at his father, a sudden chill crawled down his back. The old man was planning to do something to Catherine! He knew it!

Henry smiled at his son. "I have checked with the authorities and the priest. You can marry this girl. It will be by proxy and that is very legal. I can't have you going to France. You might do something foolish, even play soldier over there to avoid this marriage."

Speechless, Alex glared at his father for several minutes. He was so angry, he could not get the words out. Finally, he bellowed, "Marriage! Proxy! I WILL NOT!"

Henry's rage was a tangible thing now, as he screamed, "Oh, yes, you will! That is, if you ever want to see Catherine again."

"I will not! What has Catherine got to do with any of this? Where is she? What have you done to my sister?" The questions hissed from Alex's lips. He felt the heat of his red face and forced the words over a hoarse throat. Never had he been so angry, or so frightened.

"At the moment, Catherine is enjoying herself in the south." Henry thought, If he wants to tear the countryside apart looking for her, he can start looking in the wrong direction. "She knows nothing of our conversation, nor will she ever—at least, not during my lifetime. I doubt that you will ever tell her, for it would undoubtedly destroy her. However, if you do not sign the papers I have here, Catherine will be sent to Mexico. I have already made arrangements for her to be accepted into a convent there, a cloistered convent. You will never see her again."

Alex felt the blood drain from his face. He sank back into his chair. "You can't do this. No convent would take a girl who didn't want that life. You are insane!"

"My dear son, when will you learn that money will buy almost anything? It has been arranged! And Catherine will go willingly, if you do not sign these papers. Your life will depend on it. Catherine idolizes you. She will agree to anything to prevent you from death." Henry smiled into Alex's pale face.

"You won't kill me and you know it."

Henry chuckled. "I know that, you know that, but Catherine does not know it. She believes that I am a cruel and heartless man. She will believe me when I tell her that I have had enough of your defiance and that I have arranged for you to be handed over to a press-gang. Catherine will be told that at the first sign of trouble from you, the overseer is to hang you. All legal and tidy, if I don't say so! Catherine will believe every word. She will do exactly as she is told just to prevent your certain death."

"You are a monster! You would force your only daughter into a convent just to see me married? You're not even human."

"No, my dear son. I am simply tired of waiting for you to do what every other normal man does. I had hoped to let you choose your own wife, but since you will not, I had to take matters into my own hands. I have chosen for you. It is not an unusual practice, a little outdated perhaps, but still not that unusual."

Alex jerked himself from the chair and strode for the door. He needed to get out of that room before he strangled his own father.

"You have one week," Henry said to the back of Alex's head. "If you have not signed the proxy papers by then, Catherine will go to that convent."

Alex spun around and faced his father. "You aren't as smart as you think. I will follow you! I can steal Catherine from you easily."

"Don't you give me credit for any intelligence?" Henry laughed, a hard, cold laugh. "I'll be right here. I have no intentions of looking into her tear-filled eyes as I describe

41

what I plan to do to you. Someone else, someone you don't even know, will talk to her, and explain my ultimatum. That same person will then escort your sister to her own prison."

Alex turned away, fighting the violent urge to wrap his hands around his father's neck and squeeze his deranged head from his shoulders. Instead, he said quietly, too quietly, "I have one week?"

Henry purred, "Yes. One week! And don't think that you can see to my demise. If I don't send word to the person in question, Catherine will be on her way. Do I make myself clear?"

Alex knew there was no answer, at least not one that he could think of himself. Robert! He had to get to Baltimore and Robert Patterson. Robert was a lawyer, he knew the law. Robert would help him. He rushed from the room.

He found himself going through the motions of throwing clothes into his travel bag and heading for the stable. It was dark now, but Alex told himself it did not matter. He had to get away from the plantation and his father before he destroyed the old man. He led his big stallion from the stables, only slightly aware that Peter was asking him something. He waved his friend away, mounted and took off as rapidly as he could. By morning, he had to be in Baltimore, he had to see Robert!

As he pushed his horse over the dark road, he thought back to the first time he had seen Robert Patterson. He had been at Valley Forge and there was snow on the ground. The white stuff was inches thick, making each day a fight for survival. He spotted Robert among the new recruits, shivering from the cold. Alex had never figured out what drew him to Robert. He was poorly dressed, and hung toward the back of the group. Robert was nearly as tall as Alex, and he had looked hungry. Alex made it a point to introduce himself and ask Robert if he would share his rations.

That day, Robert seemed to be bewildered. Alex didn't find out why until several months later. Robert and his father also had argued because Robert supported the idea of independence for the Colonies. His father had thrown him out of the house, and Robert had left to join Colonel Washington at Valley Forge that same day.

Alex and Robert became almost inseparable. Together, they served with Gates, and Robert shot the Redcoat that stabbed Alex at Jamestown. After the battle, Robert returned to Baltimore, to study law with his uncle. Alex saw him several times before the end of the war, and was pleased when Robert told him that he and his father were at last reconciled.

The most important thing, Alex told himself, was that Robert was first and foremost an excellent lawyer. His uncle saw to his education and had also introduced him to the men of law in Maryland and in Virginia. Alex smiled grimly. If Robert knew anything, he knew who to ask about the law.

In less than ten hours, Alex confronted Robert's clerk. "I'll wait until Mr. Patterson is available. Just tell him I must see him."

In minutes the apologetic clerk was ushering Alex into Robert's tiny office. The men clasped hands as Alex tried to explain his dusty appearance. "I rode all night. Father has Catherine and I only have six days to find her."

Robert grinned at his friend. "It's not the end of the world. Catherine is his daughter."

"It may be the end of my world!" Alex grimaced and sank into a chair before Robert's desk.

"You better tell me what's happened." Robert sat down in his desk chair and faced Alex. By the time Alex finished his explanation, Robert was shaking his head. "I'll say this much for the man, he is determined to see you wed. Well, first things first! I think you had better sign the papers he wants you to sign."

Alex was out of the chair before Robert finished. "I have no intention of wedding some slow-witted French governess to please my father. You figure something else out." He shouted, "I'm not marrying the girl!"

"Don't go yelling at me! Now, hear me out. Your father is a respected man of business and he has friends up and down the coast. He could have Catherine hidden right under your nose, or traveling from friend to friend. You could search for months and still be a step or two behind her, if she is visiting. We must let Henry Dampier think he has won. He'll release Catherine and then you can set the marriage aside."

Alex stared at Robert. Was he serious? "I don't understand."

"Look." Robert toyed with the quill pen on his desk. "Any court of law, and even the church, will annul a marriage that has never been consummated. If you stay away from the girl, you could easily have the marriage set aside just as soon as you have Catherine back. First, you must determine if your father will release Catherine when you sign the papers. Then, you take Catherine with you to Frederick. Tell your father that you and Catherine intend to redecorate the farm for your wife. Once Catherine is safely at the farm, you have only to sign the necessary petitions and that will end the marriage."

"And what about this French girl? I can't let my father bring her here and then turn her from my door. He did tell me that she has been in a convent since she was four years old." Alex groaned and dropped his weary head into his hands. "He's planning to ruin my life, Catherine's life and this poor thing from France, as well. She spent all those years learning God knows what to please my father, and for what purpose?"

Robert gazed at Alex in surprise. "That's the answer, my friend! After she arrives we will arrange a position for her as a governess with a family here in Baltimore; or better yet, let me see what I can arrange in Virginia. I'm sure, if your father had her trained to be a governess for his grandchildren, she must have an excellent education."

"I must be a great deal more exhausted than I thought. You're making good sense," Alex muttered quietly.

Robert smiled. "It's settled, then. There are several things you must do. First we will hire several men to check on Catherine. I doubt seriously they will find out anything, but we must make your father think that you are going along with him. In three days, you will have to return to Manor House. Find out all you can about this girl, and—this is important—make sure that you know where Catherine is before you sign those papers. Once Henry has told you where Catherine can be located, then sign the papers."

Alex snarled, "You make it sound so simple. I may not be responsible for my actions, if he makes me as angry as he did yesterday."

"Alex," Robert cautioned, "you will have to stay calm! Now, your father will have to deliver the papers, and when he does, you can get Catherine and take her home with you. Just leave word with your overseer. Say that you have taken her to Frederick to see to your house. He might be so pleased with what he's accomplished that he'll send his blessings. The important point here is that you must know Catherine's location before you sign. Do you understand?"

Alex could only nod; he was exhausted. He hadn't slept well for days, and he had traveled all night to get to Robert.

Robert seemed to understand. "Now, you go get some rest. I'll get my clerk to send someone to my town house. Jason will have a bath and something to eat ready for you. Then, my friend, have a large glass of brandy and go to bed. I'll get the men together and send them out to start looking for Catherine." Robert started to laugh. "We can't have the bridegroom fainting from fatigue."

Alex couldn't hide the look of panic that surfaced, nor did he try to disguise the rage that replaced it. "I'm not married yet!" he growled, as Robert called the clerk into the office.

"And you won't be married for long," Robert assured his friend, as he pushed Alex toward the door. "I'll see you tonight," he added as Alex walked wearily out of the building.

As Alex worked his horse through the morning traffic, he speculated on Robert's advice. If anything went wrong, he could end up tied to a woman he had never seen, didn't want to see. He scowled. Robert's idea did make sense. Robert was probably correct when he suggested that Henry would be so delighted over Alex's capitulation that the old man would indeed let Catherine return to Manor House. Alex stopped his horse and stared off into space. Robert's plan seemed so simple. Had Henry thought of it too? Surely Henry must know that Alex might appear to be giving in when in truth, he was not at all. Alex jerked on the reins so suddenly that the horse almost reared. What if Henry would not release Catherine until a child was on the way? No, his father could not do that! That was out of his control. Still . . .

Chapter Four

As Alex made his way toward the address Robert had given him, he shook himself. There was no way his father could hold Catherine until an heir was apparent from the union between him and this French girl. Henry Dampier had absolutely no control over something like that. He was getting morbid, Alex reminded himself. Surely, his father was not as smart as Robert. Everything would be all right, just as soon as he had Catherine at Frederick.

Alex couldn't believe how tired he was. When he finally arrived at the town house, he was extremely grateful that the messenger had arrived before him. Robert's man was waiting for him with a hot bath and a light lunch.

After he bathed and ate, he fell into the guest bed that had been prepared as he bathed. As he drifted off to sleep he wondered about the French girl his father was forcing on him. What did she look like? Was she thin and plain, or fat and decidedly ugly? Well, he thought, she would only be his wife for a short time, only as long as it took to sail across the Atlantic.

When the valet woke Alex for dinner, he stretched and smiled. He felt better now that he was rested. Robert's man told him that Mr. Patterson had arrived and was waiting for him in the study. Alex was to join him for a drink before dinner. Alex dressed hurriedly. Perhaps

Robert already had some news of Catherine.

In the study, Robert explained, "I have five men looking for Catherine. I sent them south but I seriously doubt that they will find anything. She has to be at a friend's home if your father said she is enjoying herself."

Alex hesitated, but confided his fears that Henry might keep Catherine confined until a child was on the way. Robert laughed. "I doubt that your father plans to keep her hidden that long. I don't think you need to worry that she will be secreted away until the French girl is pregnant. That would have to be at least six to eight months. There is the sea voyage to deliver the papers, the return voyage for the girl, and my sister tells me that you can't be sure that you're pregnant for three months, at least. Only relatives could be asked to keep your sister for that long, and you've told me often enough that you have no relatives in this country. I don't think you have to worry about that. No, your father believes that once he has forced you to marry, your basic male instincts will take over."

Robert scowled and then glanced at Alex. "I suspect that she is quite attractive, but don't you touch her, or you will be permanently married."

After dinner, Alex discussed his plans for the farm, and Robert told him about some interesting cases he had taken in the last several months. They talked late into the night. Before they retired Robert once again returned to Alex's problem. "Why don't you stay here with me for the next several days? After we have the reports from the men, then you can return to Manor House. At least, if you're here, I'll be able to tell you what we find without sending someone to the farm, or Manor House."

Alex ran his fingers through his dark hair. "You're afraid that I'll do something I'll regret, aren't you?" Robert's grim face was Alex's answer.

The afternoon of the second day, Robert dragged Alex to see the bishop's assistant, a wiry little priest who glared uncomfortably at the reluctant young man. "Father, tell my friend here what you told me this morning."

"If a marriage is not consummated," the priest frowned at both men, "then you do not have a marriage. It is null and void. Of course, if the couple has agreed, before the vows were spoken, to remain," he cleared his throat, and continued with authority, "virginal, then the vows are final. If you sign a proxy marriage agreement, if you are both willing to sign the agreement, but the marriage is never consummated, then there is no marriage."

The priest looked at Alex with concern. "My son, are you being forced into a marriage? Is that why your friend is asking these technical questions?"

Alex wanted to tell the priest exactly what was going on, but Robert grabbed him and yanked him from the office before he could reply to the man's questions. "Your father is not holding a gun to your back!" Robert told him angrily.

"Oh, no," Alex sneered. "What do you call it then?"

Robert gave him a look that could only mean, "Act your age!"

By the end of the next day, Robert reported that it was as he expected: Catherine was not to be found. "It will take months to do a house-to-house search for her." He told Alex quietly, "You must go back to Manor House now. And only after he has told you where Catherine is do you sign the papers. I want you to take my young houseboy with you. If you need to send me some word, Jon can rush back in half the time."

The next morning, as they were preparing to leave for Manor House, Robert gave him a pep talk. "Alex, I know how irritating this is for you, but you must promise me that you'll follow my direction. Your father thinks he has everything figured out, and if you tip your hand, he may try another tack. Keep your head on your shoulders and your mouth shut, no matter what the temptation."

As they started back to Manor House, Alex watched the tall, gangling teenager, and wondered what Robert had said to him before they left. The effervescent youth appeared rather subdued.

As they traveled, Alex kept running the events of the last several days through his mind. They had missed something. He was sure of it. But what? Henry had Catherine, and unless the papers that wed him to the French girl were signed, Catherine would be sent to a convent. Cut and dried, or so it seemed. But Henry must know that the church would set aside a marriage never consummated, unless his father thought he had less willpower than he thought he had. They had overlooked something that Henry Dampier knew. What was it? Robert was a lawyer, he knew the law, he had talked to other lawyers. He seemed confident that Alex was safe from this unwanted marriage. Then why couldn't Alex feel the same. He muttered as they rode, "We've overlooked something. Somehow, this isn't going to work." The closer they got to Manor House, the more tense Alex became. If he were his father, what would he do? Alex had no answers.

Henry was waiting when they arrived. Alex was certain that his father had had him followed. "He knows that I've been to see Robert, and that we have men out looking for Catherine," he told himself as he pushed Jon into the warm kitchen. "Feed him," he told Prissy, and then he went into the study to talk to his father. He still could not shake the feeling that he had overlooked something.

"All right! You win," Alex mumbled as he sank into one of the leather chairs in the room. "After you tell me where Catherine is, I'll sign those papers."

Henry looked over at his son from his chair at the desk. His expression, Henry chuckled, was funereal. Victory was so sweet, he thought. "No, first you'll sign the papers, before witnesses, especially the paper that declares that you are doing this willingly. Then, and only then, will I tell you where Catherine is. Peter can leave to get her immediately."

Alex looked up suspiciously. "Does Peter know where she is?"

"Not yet," Henry said quietly.

"Father, I have no intentions of signing anything until I know where my sister is." Alex stood to leave.

"All right," Henry snapped. "Before you sign the papers, I'll give Peter a note that will tell him where she is. Satisfied?"

"How do I know that she will be where you say she is?" Alex snapped.

Henry drew himself up to his full five feet eleven inches and sneered at his son, "I have given my word!"

"Before I sign my life away," Alex mumbled, "I would like to know what I'm getting. What does this girl look like? How old is she and is she agreeable to this . . . union?" Alex almost choked on the word "union."

Henry's upper lip curled into a typical half smile. "I've only seen her once, and that was when she was a child. Every year, though, Jacques Manage has gone to Paris and visited the convent. She is just twenty and according to Jacques she is quite attractive. I'm afraid that she is a little slow, but she is educated, perhaps overly so for a wife. She knows nothing of the outside world, so she should be content, even if you don't spend much time with her. She should be able to have a dozen children. That's why I chose her! She is the last of eleven and the only girl. I'm sure she'll give you a dozen sons."

"Has she agreed to this marriage? Or is she also being forced?" Alex snapped, not at all happy with what his father had just told him.

"I don't like to hear you say that you are being forced, Alex. You are doing this of your own free will. Your life is not being threatened. You choose to do this because you think Catherine will be unhappy in a convent. That is not being forced!" Henry pointed out quietly.

"I have only one more question," Alex muttered. "Just who will witness this . . . this contract?"

"Why, Peter and Priscilla Bentley, of course!"

Alex's mouth fell open, and he could only gape at his sire. This man was going to make him swear before his two friends that he was willing to marry this girl and that he was doing so of his own free will. What would Peter and Prissy think when he refused to honor his agreement with the girl and had the marriage annulled? He sighed. He would have to cross that bridge when the time came. Sometimes ships coming from Europe did not make their American ports, he thought. There were pirates and storms — not that he wished the French girl harm, but she wasn't here yet!

"Let's get the Bentleys in here and get this over with. I want to get Catherine home," Alex snapped.

Henry yanked open the top drawer in the desk and pulled out a packet of parchment. Turning to his son, he asked quietly, "I have your word that you'll sign these after I give Peter the location of your sister?"

"You have my word." Alex felt like he was signing his own hanging order.

Henry took up his quill pen and began to scratch across a piece of paper, which he then folded and laid aside. Then he took the pieces of parchment and wrote on them. Alex watched as he laid them out on the desk, smiling broadly. Henry walked to the door and called for the housekeeper and the overseer. While they waited, Alex poured himself a healthy brandy and sat across the room from his father, staring off into space. Something was wrong, he told himself, but what?

Arriving together, Peter and Prissy glanced first at Henry and then at Alex, looking very concerned. Alex had already mentioned to Peter that his father was up to his old tricks, but Alex wished now he had been more explicit. How could he make them both understand that he was doing this to get Catherine away from his father, that he had no intentions of taking a wife?

Henry addressed the overseer and his wife. "You have both been with us for sixteen years now. You know Alex well, perhaps too well. But I think it is only right that you both witness Alex's signing the papers that will wed him to Mademoiselle Nichole Clarissa Ramoneur of Paris."

Alex felt the stares of both old friends and heard Prissy gasp as he turned away. He could not look either of them in the eyes.

Henry was now grinning from ear to ear. "Alex has even insisted that he sign a paper that he is doing this of his own free will, that no one is forcing him to sign these papers." Alex spun around and glared at his father. How could he lie like that?

As Henry watched his son carefully, he asked, "Isn't that so, son?"

Alex could not say a word. He nodded in agreement. He felt sick to his stomach. As he watched, Henry lifted the folded paper from the desk and handed it to Peter. "After these papers are signed, you and Alex can go get Catherine. Alex has said that he wants to tell her the good news himself."

Suddenly, Alex realized just how well his father had planned all of this. He had forgotten that Peter could not read. There was no way Peter could have been able to tell him where Catherine was until the papers were out of the way.

Henry read the first document, passed it to Priscilla so that she could read it and tell Peter that it was what Henry said it was. The paper was handed to Alex who read the statement carefully. It said in simple terms that Alex was signing the marriage contract of his own free will, that he was not being forced to do so, that he understood what the proxy meant and that he knew it was binding.

Alex glanced up at his father, then walked to the desk and dipped the quill pen his father handed him in the ink and put his name on the bottom of the parchment.

Peter stared at him, and Priscilla blinked tears back from her eyes. "You are doing this of your own free will?" she whispered.

Alex's grim expression belied his words. "Yes!" was all that he could manage, and he couldn't look at her when he replied.

Priscilla took the pen, looked at Alex once more very closely and then signed her name. Peter affixed his "X" and Henry set the paper aside.

As Henry read the marriage contract out loud, Alex realized that the contract amounted to the same promises that he would have spoken in church. Henry informed him that he had to sign the words "I will" after each promise as well as his name. This paper was witnessed, and Henry even proposed that they drink to Alex's new bride.

Alex thought at first that he would tell his father to go to hell, but at a knowing glance from Peter, Alex accepted the glass of wine and toasted his wife, Madame Nichole Dampier. Alex set his glass on the desk and said quietly, "I'm going for Catherine now."

Henry was busy rolling the two parchment documents into a long roll and putting them in a leather case. He glanced up at the tall young man before him. "Yes, you do that, SON!"

Alex and Peter heard him laughing as they left the room. Once they were outside the study, Peter and Prissy turned on him. "How did he do it? Why did you do it?" Peter asked him quietly. Alex just shrugged. He had, only minutes before, sworn before his friends that he was not being forced. He had too much pride to admit to them now that his sworn word was no good.

"It was time" was all Alex could say. Trying to disguise

his emotions, he moved toward the kitchen. Well, it was done. He was committed at least for several months, he thought. He scratched out a note for Robert and gave instruction to Jon. Then he turned to Peter. "Where is that note?"

Peter offered the note and Alex exploded, "Philadelphia!" He jammed the paper in his pocket and glared at Peter. "It will take three or four days to get there and that many more to get back."

Peter studied Alex carefully. The events of the last hour had confused him, even more than he wanted to admit. The questions swirled around in his head. There had to have been a reason why Alex had agreed to marry some Frenchy. And there was the paper he had signed that he was not being forced when both he and Prissy knew better. Now he was hell-bent on getting to Catherine. The possibility that Catherine might have something to do with the situation entered his mind. Something was definitely not right, but Peter decided that this was not the time to talk to the man. First, he needed to talk to Prissy. Watching Alex carefully, he asked quietly, "You want to leave now, or wait until morning?"

"We might as well wait until morning. The trip will be tiring enough as it is. We might as well start fresh." He started for the kitchen. He wanted a sizable lunch packed so they didn't have to stop for meals the first day or two. He stood rigidly for a moment. "Hell, we'll have to take the carriage. Catherine took her trunks."

He frowned. He might as well tell his father that he was taking Catherine right to Frederick. He would give him the excuse Robert had suggested; he would tell Henry that he would need Catherine's help with the house. He would hint that he wanted to make it ready for his . . . wi . . . Nichole. "Damn," he muttered; he couldn't even think wife.

Alex went in search of his father and was surprised to

find him preparing to travel as well. Alex thought he seemed too pleased to hear much of what Alex told him, shaking his head in agreement when Alex explained his plans. He surprised Alex when he suggested softly, "You might even want to take a day or two in Philadelphia and see to some furniture, something more appropriate for a married man."

Alex wanted to wipe the smug grin off of his father's face, but he kept his hands tightly clenched at his side. "You don't seem to be disturbed about Catherine going to Frederick with me."

"The matter is finished. Catherine is no longer of any use to me," Henry stated deliberately as he filled a carpet-bag with a change of clothing. "I have things to see to, and I will be gone for several weeks. When I return, you can bring Catherine home. We will also have to prepare rooms for you and your wife. There is no need for her to spend all of her time at the farm. She can spend time here with Catherine and me." His lazy grin bothered Alex more than any of his rages ever had.

Alex watched as his father turned and left the room heading for the stable. Alex stared at the empty space and his mind raced. Henry Dampier seemed so sure the matter was finished. There was something else involved here, Alex was positive. He stumbled from the master bedroom and raced for the kitchen, praying Jon had not started back for Baltimore. He had to alert Robert. His father had something else up his sleeve. Robert would have to figure out what it was.

Alex found Jon in the kitchen, helping Mrs. Barber, the cook, fix a lunch. The boy jerked around, looking guilty. "Mrs. Bentley says I'm to wait until tomorrow. It's too dark now. I don't know my way that good."

Alex smiled, trying to relax the boy. "I agree, and I'll have a much longer note to send back with you. You can leave at first light, when Peter and I leave. I'll give you my note to Mr. Patterson then." Alex left the kitchen, only slightly relieved. Perhaps Robert could figure out what they'd missed.

Chapter Five

Henry headed for the stable, chuckling as he went. It was time to put the rest of his plans into motion. This first part had been almost too easy, he thought. His son thought he could outsmart his father. Even the young lawyer that Alex had befriended wouldn't be able to do a thing. Of course, it would take some time for his arrogant son to admit defeat and start living with the girl, but if Jacques was correct, she was attractive enough to intrigue Alex. And she would be available.

Reaching the stable, he carefully placed the leather case in his saddle. Then he started for the home he had provided for his mistress. All through the night, as he rode northward, he chuckled. He would have heirs, finally. Just let his son try to keep him from his grandchildren.

By early afternoon, Henry had bathed and rested. When Jacques Manage arrived, he said to the short round woman at his side, "Leave us. I have business with this man."

An hour later, Henry stood in the doorway of the cottage hurrying Jacques along. "You know what to tell the girl? I don't want any slips. You know what to do?"

Jacques's grin was answer in itself. "I understand completely. My ship leaves tomorrow afternoon. If the weather holds, and it should this time of year, I will arrive in Paris by the middle of August. We should arrive here by late October, or at least by the first of November."

Jacques held the precious case all the way back to Baltimore. He was more than satisfied. Henry Dampier had taken every single suggestion he had made. Not only was he going to be paid well for his efforts, he thought, but he was truly going to enjoy this visit to France. He smirked as he thought of the satisfaction Henry would have when he told Alex about Jacques's part in this drama.

Someday he would tell his cousin how much he appreciated the information she'd given him. Jacques had listened as she told him all about her husband's little sister in the convent. Jacques remembered that his cousin had been so afraid that her husband was going to have to help pay for the child's care that she told him everything she knew. Now that child was going to Maryland, where she would serve as a rich man's wife. But, first . . . Jacques laughed so hard that his sides hurt.

Just as dawn was lighting the sky over Manor House, Alex was readying the carriage that would take him to his sister. He checked the large basket of food Mrs. Barber had fixed and then turned to see the boy, Jon, on his way. "Here's the note for Mr. Patterson. Take your time and take care."

Satisfied that Robert would give his questions and fears some consideration, Alex left Manor House, riding on the top of the carriage with Peter. For the entire night, Alex had imagined the things that his father might do, but Catherine always figured into the schemes he thought his father might devise. He was worn out trying to think as his father thought.

They were on the road less than ten minutes when Peter asked, "Well, are you going to tell me what this is all about or do I have to guess?"

Startled, Alex glanced at his companion. "I am getting married. That's all there is to it."

Peter let loose with a string of expletives, and Alex couldn't help but grin. Peter and Priscilla Bentley knew his father well. Still, Alex was not going to admit to Peter, at least not for many years, how Henry planned the whole of it. "He can stew, just like I have been," Alex told himself.

"Peter, damn it," Alex shouted after three hours of badgering, "I'm not going to tell you anything. Why don't you just mind your own business!" Alex sighed. He couldn't even be honest with his oldest friend, the man who more often than Alex cared to remember had saved him from his father's wrath. Alex glanced over at Peter sitting stiffly on the carriage seat, his lips thin and unsmiling. I've hurt his feelings, Alex scolded himself.

Peter was too angry to be hurt, not so much with Alex as with the situation. He thought through his conversation with his wife, both last night and again this morning. Prissy could add nothing to what they both knew to have happened. How did Henry Dampier convince his son to do something so ridiculous as marry a French girl that Alex had never seen? Peter scowled. Alex wasn't going to say a word, and that was for sure! Peter could badger him the whole three days to Philadelphia, but he doubted that Alex would admit anything.

Peter remembered some of Prissy's wild speculations, but perhaps they weren't so wild. Prissy wondered out loud if Catherine didn't have something to do with the situation. She had offered, "It just might have something to do with Charles duPres. I'm sure there's more there than we were told. Could Mr. Dampier have made the decision about this Nichole creature when he went to France in eighty?"

Peter glanced over at his grim young friend. There was no question in Peter's mind. Alex was not a happy man, and no matter what he had signed, somehow, Henry Dampier had forced his son into an arranged marriage, arranged against Alex's will.

Peter thought back to the beginning, when they had first come to the Dampier home. Marguerite had been dead for eight weeks when they arrived. Prissy had picked up the miserable, motherless baby, and it had been love at first sight for both of them. Peter frowned when he thought of their first eight years of marriage. As much as they wanted children of their own, they had never been lucky enough to have any. Catherine and Alex had become the children Prissy could never have. Peter wiped at the sudden mist that blurred his eyes; they had almost become his own children, too. And whenever her children were in trouble, some second sight told Prissy there was danger.

Peter remembered that day in September when the pistol exploded, killing the heir to the French estate. Somehow, she had known that something terrible had happened, even before Henry returned, carrying the lifeless body of Charles. He remembered the night Prissy pulled him from his bed. She had been up for hours, and her eyes were red from her tears. All she would say was that Alex was in trouble, he was hurt, and she had been right! Word came that Alex had been wounded at Jamestown. Peter shuddered.

How many times had Prissy demanded that Peter prevent Henry from hurting *her* boy? All through the years, especially those times when Peter himself had wanted to apply the strap to the boy's behind, Prissy had tried to protect the lad. Why, she had even screamed at him not to hurt the boy.

Perhaps it was best if this French girl was going to live at the farm. If she made Alex miserable, Prissy would have her clawing and screaming her way back to France. And, from the look on Alex's face, there was no doubt in

Peter's mind that this marriage was nothing more than a farce and Alex was going to be very miserable.

Alex glanced over at his companion. Peter had been scowling and frowning, and once Alex was sure that he had tried to wipe tears from his eyes. Alex leaned forward. "Peter, I'm sorry, I just don't want to discuss yesterday with you. It really is none of your business. If I decide to talk about it, you'll be the first to know."

Peter grinned at the younger man. "You can't blame me fer bein' a mite curious, now can you? The subject is closed."

By the time they stopped for the night, Alex and Peter were sharing memories and discussing the joys and problems of farming. The next two days were equally pleasant, and late in the afternoon they arrived at the large brick home of Joshua Beal. Alex's face twisted into a cold sneer. Well, at least now, he thought, Mr. Beal would have to look elsewhere for someone to wed his daughters.

Henry Dampier and Joshua Beal were lifelong business associates, and Mr. Beal had not one, or two, but five daughters that he must find husbands for. He of course had turned to his business associates who had sons. Coldly, Alex thought back to the first time his father suggested he might consider one of the Beal girls for a wife. Alex had choked at the thought. The four older girls were all plain, dim-witted, flat-chested shrews. Martha, the youngest, was only a child at the time, but Alex grimaced; she too, fit the pattern. Marry a Beal! Never!

Henry had insisted several times that Alex accompany Catherine and him to the Philadelphia residence. Twice Alex had been tricked into escorting Catherine there, but he never even hinted that he would consider offering for any of those girls. Unfortunately, Martha and Catherine had become true and close friends over the years. "I should have remembered how close they are," Alex mumbled as he dragged himself down from the carriage.

Catherine heard the arrival of the carriage, and when she spotted her brother she threw herself out the front door and into his arms. "I thought you would be here a week ago," she scolded.

"Aren't you having a good time?" he laughed as he hugged her to him.

Remembering that she was supposed to be a young lady, she wiggled out of his arms and scowled up at him. "Of course, but I do miss you, sometimes." Alex laughed. Arm in arm, they walked back up the steps Catherine had descended only moments before.

After dinner that afternoon, Alex pulled Catherine away from Martha. "How would you like a nice long visit at the farm? I have a lot of work to do, and I thought we would go there for several weeks. Would you like that?"

Catherine grinned, her soft gray eyes twinkling with mischief. "You just want to have me all to yourself. You're a jealous big brother, that's what you are."

Alex laughed at her teasing. "Want to come?"

"I'd like nothing better!"

Early the next morning, brother and sister bade a tearful Martha farewell as they took their leave of the elegant brick home. Catherine seemed more than willing to depart, and Alex commented to Peter that perhaps the girls hadn't gotten on as well as they had in the past.

Peter kept waiting all day long to hear Catherine's reaction to the news that Peter felt sure Alex would relate. But by the end of the second day of travel, Peter looked at Alex with astonishment. "He has no intention of saying a thing to her." He rubbed his chin in confusion. What would his Prissy make of this?

Even traveling slower for Catherine's sake they arrived at the farm by midmorning of the third day. After he had seen to his sister's comfort, he took the carriage to the barn. Peter, his confusion clear, followed Alex, watching him carefully.

When they got to the barn, Peter asked softly, "What did Catherine say about the marriage?"

Alex glared at him but continued to work at unharnessing the big draft horses.

Peter stood quietly as realization dawned: Alex was not even going to tell his sister. He blurted out the question almost before he realized he had thought it. "You're not going to tell her, are you?"

"Leave it be!" Alex shouted. Peter stared as the young man surged from the barn, leaving the horses before he had finished his work.

Alex slammed into the house and sank into a chair at the big wooden table in the kitchen. Propped up against an empty tankard was a message from Robert Patterson. Alex tore it open and read Robert's words. The papers that would declare the marriage as annulled were already prepared and were awaiting his and his new wife's signature. Alex sighed in relief. He read on. Robert repeated that there was nothing Henry could do that would force Alex to complete the marriage. Robert felt sure that Alex's apprehension was only nerves. "Forget it!" Robert had advised.

Alex relaxed and spent the rest of the day seeing to the chores that had been left unfinished when he raced to Manor House with Henry's note about Catherine. Toward evening, after a filling meal of turkey pie, Alex asked Peter, "Do you think that Prissy might come for a visit, too? Father said that he would be away for several weeks, and with Catherine here, there is really no need for Prissy, or you for that matter, to stay at Manor House. I must return the carriage and get my own horse, and I could bring Prissy back, if you think she'll come."

Peter frowned; there was no doubt in his mind that Prissy would relish a week or two at Alex's farm, if for no other reason than to pry the information out of Alex. Would she learn anything that Peter had not been able to drag from him? Peter shook his head slightly; he was sure she would come up as empty-handed as he had. "I think she might like that," Peter offered skeptically.

Two days later, Alex was once more on the road. He reviewed his instructions to Peter. He did not trust his father, no matter what the man had said. Peter and his five men were to watch every move Catherine made. If there was even a hint of trouble, Peter had his instructions. Alex knew that Robert would help protect Catherine, and Peter had been told to take her there immediately if Henry Dampier or any of his hirelings turned up in or around Frederick.

He traveled back to Manor House relaxed, and for the first time in weeks, he felt almost content. Catherine was safe, his father was away on business and Robert had all of the paperwork ready that would dissolve his ridiculous marriage. He took his time, enjoying the countryside in full bloom.

When he arrived just after sunset on the second day, he turned the horses and carriage over to the bondservant and checked on his own horse. He chuckled; he would have to take the carriage back, for Prissy traveled no lighter than Catherine, Peter had told him.

As he walked up the steps to the house, he felt good. His father had not beaten him, could not win in this game. He would select his own wife, if and when the need for one ever arose. As he opened the front door he bellowed, "Prissy?"

Henry Dampier rushed out of the study. "What are you doing here? Why aren't you at the farm? Where is Catherine?"

Alex stood stunned. Questions swirled around in his head. What was his father doing back? He was supposed to be away on business. Was there something else Henry planned that was yet to be revealed? Sweat broke out on Alex's strained face. "I must stay calm," he told himself.

"I see that you have come to your senses. You have decided that you and your wife will live here, isn't that right?" Henry demanded in cryptic tones.

The expression on Henry's face and the tones he used destroyed Alex's resolve to keep his temper in check.

"Catherine will not be coming back for quite a while, Father," Alex snapped.

Henry looked surprised. "Did you say anything to her? What did she say about your wedding? She's angry because she knew nothing about it?"

Alex hand snapped up and he glowered at his father. "What are you afraid of, that she will never speak to you again for what you tried to do to me?"

"What I tried to do to you?" Henry shouted. "Don't you mean, what I did to you?"

Alex sighed; he should have been more careful with his choice of words. But Catherine was safely away from the man. Henry Dampier could no longer use Catherine. Alex asked himself, "What does it matter if he knows that the marriage will cease to be the minute the girl steps from the ship?"

Alex smiled. "Father," he said softly, "I haven't told Catherine about the marriage, I have no intention of saying a word to her. She's going to stay at Frederick with me, and there's nothing you can do to her now. And, this farce you call a marriage—you can forget that too. The marriage will be declared null and void just as soon as 'my wife' arrives from France."

Alex grinned, starting to enjoy the bright red that was mottling his father's face. Rarely did he get the better of the old man, and this time he surely had.

"The marriage will stand!" Henry shouted. "You signed a paper stating that you were not being forced. You swore before witnesses that you were not being forced. You cannot back out now!"

"I have been informed by the best of authorities, the

66

bishop's own man, that to be a marriage, the marriage must be consummated. Father," Alex stated quietly, "I have no intention of bedding the girl. She can stay here with you for a week or two and I'll stay at Frederick. She won't warm my bed." Alex's soft, calm words were slowly turned into deep, loud snarls. "Don't worry, I'll find her a respectable position as a governess and if you insist, I'll repay you for all of your expenses for her transportation. I'll even pay for whatever you have provided over the years, but I'll be damned if I BED THE WENCH!"

Alex stood in utter amazement. Henry was laughing, deep, satisfying laughter. Had he pushed his father too hard? Had Henry lost his mind?

As Henry smiled at his son with that half smile of his, Alex knew, he just knew, that he and Robert had missed some small point. "Don't you think that I prepared for just this eventuality?" Henry sighed deliberately. "Oh, I know you, and I know the way your mind works. There will be no annulment." Henry was chuckling again.

Alex stared at his father. Somehow the man had beaten Robert and him, but how?

"I did tell you, didn't I, that the girl is a little slow? She knows absolutely nothing about marriage, or the laws, I made sure of that. Jacques Manage had promised to explain everything to the girl, very carefully. She will understand the the marriage is not complete without the bedding. The girl will not arrive a virgin. Jacques will see to it."

"That won't matter," Alex mumbled, his confidence very shaken; "as long as I don't touch her, the marriage will not exist."

Henry snarled, "The question is not what you do, but what the girl believes. She will think that the marriage has been consummated. She will tell any authorities that you or your friend Robert might drag up that the marriage has been completed. If an examination is forced, the matter will be proved." Henry started to chuckle again. "The girl will think and SAY that the marriage has been consummated. You cannot get out of this marriage. I will have my way."

Alex shook his head to clear the fog. Surely, his father would not spoil the girl just to make a point. Alex's upper lip curled up as he clenched his teeth. Why not? He would have confined his own daughter to a cloistered convent to see the contract drawn. A sheltered French girl meant nothing to the man.

His father was still speaking. "But even I know that just the girl's word, in itself, will not be enough. I hadn't planned on it being enough." Alex's head snapped up at Henry's words. He had been right, there was more to his father's plan.

"My dear son, you can't outsmart me. By now, every one of my dear friends and associates, from here to Williamsburg, have been informed that my heroic son asked my help in finding a wife for him, just like his dear departed mother. They have been told how you married the girl I chose for you, by proxy, and only after YOU insisted that you sign a statement that this was your will. In fact," Henry said chuckling, "there's many a father that wishes he had such an honorable son. Why, I have even been approached as to what would make a suitable gift for you and your bride."

Alex could only stare at the man he called father. This plan was even more diabolical than having the poor thing abused on the way to Baltimore. But Henry wasn't finished. "We must consult on plans for a Christmas Ball. You must introduce your new wife to society. And I figure by then you'll have come to your senses."

Alex gazed at the shorter man. He could taste his anger. His father was inordinately pleased with himself, Alex thought, as he stood beaming at Alex. Spinning around, his one thought was to escape before he lost control, but he was stopped short by his father's final words. "Alex, my dear son, you are married. Face it! Squirm as much as you like, but you have a wife. Relax, enjoy your wife, get her with child!"

With those words ringing in his ears, Alex was out of the house in seconds, racing for the stable. Robert must be told immediately. Somehow, Henry's plan must be thwarted. In minutes, Alex was galloping toward Baltimore. His mind was busy churning over this turn of events. He and Robert had not analyzed the strength of Henry's commitment to seeing his son married and a father himself. There had to be a way out of this latest scheme. If they could figure nothing, then he was well and truly trapped. He jerked the horse to a stop. Dear God, he was probably married!

Chapter Six

As Alex raced toward Baltimore, his father's words played through his mind. Very late, he stopped for the night, but there was no way he could relax enough to sleep, so the next morning with the sky beginning to lighten he saddled his horse and was back on the road. He arrived in Baltimore just before noon.

He made his way to Robert's office rehearsing over and over what he would tell Robert of the conversation he had just had with Henry Dampier. Surely, Robert would have the answer. He knew the law. He would be able to tell Alex what to do.

When Alex arrived at the small building, tucked away from the street, he gazed at the locked door in surprise. Where was Robert? he asked himself. Looking around, he realized that there was a very limited amount of traffic. Stunned, he tried to remember what day it was. "It's Sunday," he gasped. How could he have lost all track of time?

As he rode to Robert's town house, he admonished himself for not remembering that it was Sunday. Surely Robert would be at church or away from the city with his family. But Robert was at the town house when Alex arrived.

"I was afraid you wouldn't be here." Alex hurried into

the parlor where Robert waited.

"Those who deal with the law are much like doctors. When we are needed, we are there, no matter what the time or the day," Robert laughed.

"I'm sorry to have to disturb you again. I'm afraid I'm becoming a nuisance."

"Come, have a drink and a good cigar. You look like you can use both. If I didn't enjoy your company, or your father's antics, you would be disturbing me. Now, tell me, what has he done now?" Robert led the way into the cool study.

"Catherine is fine," Alex commented, settling back in one of Robert's soft leather chairs. "She is at the farm. But I'm afraid I lost my temper with my father. However, it may have been for the best."

Alex took a deep breath and told Robert exactly what his father had disclosed. Alex watched Robert as he described the argument for some sign that all of Henry's plans were in vain. Robert said nothing at all, but the frown on his face deepened with each word. Alex felt his stomach twisting and turning as he watched his learned friend. "I'm not stuck with her, am I?" Alex asked in a bewildered voice.

Robert got up and made his way to the shelves in the room, pulling first one book, then another down from their resting places. Once more Alex tried to apologize. "I didn't mean to destroy your day of rest. This can wait until tomorrow," he mumbled.

Robert looked up from the book he was studying. "I may have to wait until tomorrow. I need to talk to a few more authorities."

Alex rose to leave, his face pale in the early afternoon light. "I better be going."

"Do you have someplace to stay? You should stay here until I have an answer of some kind." Robert glanced at his friend with more concern than Alex wanted to see.

Halfheartedly, Alex muttered, "I hadn't given much thought to where to stay. I was so angry and concerned that I just took off."

"Catherine is at the farm? She has protection?" Robert asked softly.

"Peter is with her and five of my men are watching out for her. My father won't be able to touch her there."

"Thank God for that. As to the question you asked, Alex, I just don't know. We may have problems. I must check with better, older legal minds. I may not have an answer for a week. I insist that you stay here."

"No, I think not," Alex replied, "I will stay the night, but, if it's all right with you, tomorrow I'll leave for Frederick. I want to tell Peter and my overseer not to let Catherine out of their sight. And I need the work of the farm to keep me busy. I would go mad if I stayed here waiting for word from your friends. You wouldn't get any work done at all. No, it's best if I return to the farm."

Robert asked Alex to repeat everything he had said and Henry Dampier had said, and as Alex talked Robert sat writing furiously. "I'll send word as soon as I have an answer," he added as he put the paper in a leather satchel. "It should take no more than a week."

Early the next morning, Robert and Alex broke their fast together and Alex rode west toward the farm. As he rode, Alex considered the men that Robert had mentioned as possible sources of information. Several of the names Alex recognized. They were outstanding men of letters, and surely, he thought, they would understand the law. If the law needed to be interpreted, any one of those men could do an excellent job, he consoled himself.

When he got back to the farm, he called his men together. "I want word immediately if any of you see or hear anything that would indicate that Henry Dampier or one of his men is within ten miles of this place. And Catherine is not to be allowed out of your sights. One more thing," he cautioned. "She is not to know that we are watching her."

Alex waited anxiously for eight days before the message from Robert arrived. "Damn," Alex muttered as he read his friend's sentences. Robert would tell him what he had learned if Alex would come to Baltimore without delay. Alex groaned. Robert had even underlined the words "without delay."

When Alex walked through the office door in Baltimore, he knew the information Robert had for him was not something he wanted to hear. Mutually, they decided to postpone an explanation until that afternoon. "You go to the town house and wait until I can wrap things up here. I should be there in two hours." Robert pushed Alex back toward the door.

"Can't you tell me anything?" Alex sighed.

"We have problems!" was all Robert would say.

After the evening meal, Robert pulled a book down from the shelf of the library and handed it to Alex. "This is what we go by."

Alex looked over the title, smiling slightly. At least the title was impressive: *English Law, In the Manner of Marriage in the Realm.* Alex glanced at Robert, a frown spreading across his face.

"We have adopted the English law with regard to marriage. The law is very hazy on something of this matter, and the proxy contract only muddies the waters. As far as I can determine, the crux of the thing seems to be what this girl believes. If she believes that the marriage has been consummated, then I guess it has."

Alex stuttered, "You . . . you mean, that . . . that I will be properly and truly wed, even though I never touched the wench?"

Robert shook his head. "Unfortunately, there is nothing specific in the book and the men I discussed the problem with are divided. We could press the issue and I'm told we would probably win, if the jurymen believed you. However, all three men agreed that the scandal that would accompany a situation like this would destroy the girl. It wouldn't do your reputation any good either. Alex, remember, we live in a very tightly controlled social order. No one, not a soul, would hire Nichole if this thing became public. You would lose your social standing and even Catherine would be affected. I'm sure your father would fight it, and it is so unusual that there would be all kinds of gossip." Robert paused and glanced nervously at the tall man sitting across from him. "I have been advised to tell you to leave it alone. You could establish the girl in Manor House and then find yourself a nice mistress."

"But what about a family? What if I want to have children? What then?" Alex asked in a daze.

"Something will work out," Robert mumbled.

Alex glared at his counselor. "How could I have gotten myself into this mess," he snarled. He lifted his head and stared at the silent hearth. Slowly, his eyes hardened into dark brown coals of rage. "My father will not win. SHE will stay at Manor House with my despicable parent and I will live at the farm. She will have my name, but nothing else. And I intend to tell my father exactly that!"

"Now, Alex," Robert cautioned, "don't make any rash decisions. This girl just might be lovely."

Alex gave Robert a scathing look. "I'm for bed. I want to leave for Manor House first thing tomorrow. I have words to say to my parent!"

"Don't jump the gun," Robert pleaded. "At least wait until the girl arrives. Maybe Jacques's ship will be lost on the way to France; maybe the girl will never arrive."

"I can hope," Alex responded. He consumed his brandy without pleasure and left Robert in the study.

Alex left Baltimore before dawn and several hours before Robert would awaken. He slept very little the night before and the quality of what sleep he had was poor indeed, he thought to himself. It wasn't Robert's fault, he admitted, but he wanted desperately to place the blame someplace. He had been truly trapped by his own father, he scowled. For once, the old man had worked everything out to his own satisfaction, even before hinting at his plans, and now Alex was left to pick up the pieces.

Alex reached Manor House by midafternoon, and as he yanked the front door open he bellowed for his father. Peter stuck his head out of the study. "Your father left five days ago. I sent word to the farm that he was on his way to Williamsburg. I even had one of your men follow him. Didn't you get my message?"

Alex shook his head, confused. Why had Henry taken off for Williamsburg? None of this made any sense at all.

"I think he'll be gone for a month or two. It sounded like he wanted to stay away from you until he was sure Jacques had arrived in France and you and the French girl were officially joined." Alex winced at the choice of Peter's words. "He'll not be back until the end of September. I'm sure of it."

Alex stared at Peter. He was enraged. When had his father learned to read his mind? There was nothing he could do but return to the farm and prepare for the harvest. Perhaps he could gather enough courage to tell Catherine what had transpired in the four weeks since she left Manor House. "You'll send word, just as soon as my father returns," Alex begged Peter. "I must talk to him before this girl arrives."

He left for the farm, angry, frustrated and more than a little confused. His father had never run from a confrontation before. Did that also mean something? Alex didn't know, and what was worse he couldn't guess.

Weeks passed and Alex stayed busy, keeping his mind active with the problems of the farm. Peter sent an occa-

75

sional note, penned by Priscilla, to inform him that his father had not yet returned. Alex and Catherine spent the August and September days in easy camaraderie. They rode together, and while Alex spent a good part of his time directing the work of his men, Catherine spent time in the big sunny kitchen. She fixed many of the meals she and Alex shared, and he let her help with the small garden just outside the kitchen door.

One afternoon, while she was waiting for Alex to finish his work and return for the evening meal, she admitted to herself, "I'm bored. It's time I returned to Manor House."

She voiced those same thoughts to Alex when he came in for dinner. Alex wanted to explain that she was to stay with him until he found a worthy man to be her husband, but he couldn't. If he told her that, he thought, he would also have to explain why she was at the farm in the first place and why she had to stay there. But he couldn't do it. Try as hard as he might, he still could not bring up the subject of his own marriage. He argued with himself long into the night. Catherine had to know. He had to tell her something. But he couldn't, not yet.

September was no longer a young month when a messenger arrived from Peter with the information Alex had been anticipating. Henry Dampier was finally at Manor House. Catherine and Alex had just returned from the village, and Alex took her by the arm and solemnly led her into the house. His time had run out. He had to tell her now.

When they were seated in the parlor, Alex explained, "Catherine, I don't want you to return to Manor House." He told her about their father's plans for Alex, and then he carefully detailed the role Henry had planned for her.

Catherine was incensed. "Oh, Alex, how could you sign that paper? How could you have done anything so foolish? I could have gotten away from the convent. It would have been several years before I said final vows and I could have left any time before that. Alex, how could you?"

"It no longer matters. I have been truly snared, but you and I will remain here, until you wed yourself, and this French girl will stay at Manor House with Father."

Catherine stared at him in disbelief, her soft brown eyes confused. "You mean you are not going to sleep with the girl?"

Alex grimaced. He had not even considered that she might understand the facts of life. "Well, Father planned for grandchildren, but I will not be the one to give them to him. I will not sleep with the girl!" he winced. Such a thing to say to your younger sister!

Alex left for Manor House the next morning. In two days' time he was handing his horse's reins to Peter. "I suppose he's still gloating over my misfortune?" Alex paused; he should have softened his remarks, for Peter really had no idea what had transpired.

Peter seemed to understand and nodded his head. "He was chuckling when he left the stable the day he returned. Prissy says he's being so pleasant in the house, the cook and the two house slaves are sure he's lost his mind."

"He won't be so happy in a few minutes. Better warn Prissy."

Peter admonished, "Now Alex, don't do anything foolish. You're the one to suffer if he gets too angry, you or Catherine," Peter amended.

"Sorry, but I have to have my say." He strolled toward the house, trying to calm his bitter emotions. He was certain his father would rage and scream, but Catherine was safe and in two or three years she would be married. What did he care how his father reacted?

Alex greeted Prissy as she asked, "Where is my father?"

"He's in the study," she answered, looking him over carefully, concern etched in her face. "Alex, don't argue with him! For once in your life, try to talk to him without

77

making him angry."

Alex walked away without another word. How did she always know when a storm was brewing with his father? This was certainly not the first time she had cautioned him to talk instead of shout.

He knocked on the closed door, and then, without waiting for an invitation, he threw open the door and stalked into the masculine room. He glanced around the room. This was the only room of the whole house he really hated. The dark, heavy furniture was not to his taste, but that was not really why he disliked it so. The room radiated his father's personality. He detested this room.

Alex threw himself into one of the heavy leather chairs before the tall graying head had invited him to sit down. Raising his head from the paperwork sprawled across the desk, Henry glared at his son. His voice heavy with disgust, he reprimanded the man, "You refuse to show me even a tiny bit of respect, don't you? You think nothing of barging into my rooms without an invitation. What are you doing here, anyway? Your bride has not arrived yet."

"Father, I have decided to explain a few facts of life, my life, to you. You may have arranged a marriage for me and cleverly managed to make it impossible for me to get out of it, but you will not have your way. It matters not at all to you whose life you destroy in your desire for grandchildren, does it? I have had several months to consider this situation and *I* have decided that there will be no grandchildren. I may be married to the wench but I will not bed the girl. And I won't be around here often enough to have any interest in her. She will not conceive by me, even if I must live a celibate life!" Alex stopped his tirade to glare at his parent.

Henry's face was mottled red and white, and his lips curled up in his usual half smile. He shouted, "How do you expect to avoid her? You will be living with the woman!"

Alex watched his father with fascination. Was the red receding slightly in his father's face? "Oh, there you are wrong. I have no intention of ever living with her. You cannot throw her out of this house, for she will be my wife in name. But, you see, I won't be here. I'll be at the farm, and both you and the girl will not even be allowed to visit. Catherine, by the way, will be staying with me. I'll have some female companionship. Perhaps not the kind that is appropriate for a man my age, but I can easily make other arrangements as you have done. This Nichole may be my wife, but she'll never know me." Alex grinned at his father, delighted that Henry seemed speechless for the moment.

Henry stared at his son, the shock beginning to register. Suddenly, he sat upright and the white pallor of his face was repalced by a scarlet so bright Alex wondered for an instant if a blood vessel had ruptured. Henry rose from his chair like a stone statue. Slowly he raised his hand and pointed at Alex. "How dare you attempt to thwart my plans! Get out! Get out of my house!"

Henry lunged at Alex, almost as if he had no control, Alex thought. Sputtering, he grabbed at his chest. "No son . . . to . . . me. A . . . dis . . . grace." Alex stepped aside and watched as his father sank slowly to the floor. At first he thought the man might have fainted, but the red in his face faded so quickly, too quickly for it to be a common swoon. Alex glanced at the man who was his father. His eyes were open but they didn't seem to see, and Alex couldn't tell whether he was breathing or not. Suddenly, instinctively, Alex knew that his father was dying.

For a fraction of a second, Alex couldn't decide if he should go to his father or get help. Then he stepped to the door and yelled for Peter, even before he had the door open. Both Peter and Prissy arrived in seconds.

Peter rushed to the prone heap on the floor. He turned to look up at Alex. His eyes were dark blue and he looked up with a mixture of relief, anger and pity. Then, from his kneeling place on the floor, he glanced first at Prissy and then at Alex. Softly, he murmured, "Alex, your father is dead!"

Chapter Seven

The carriage swung through the gates of the city and Jacques Manage sighed. Paris! Finally, he had arrived. The long voyage, uneventful as it was, was over, and the three days of travel from the coast were behind him. He could relax and enjoy his favorite city. Even the unpleasant odors from the piles of garbage baking in the warm fall sun didn't bother him.

He made his way to the inn close to the west bank. Once a year, he came to Paris, and he had chosen the inn long ago as comfortable and cheap. Henry Dampier gave him money for the rooms, Jacques sneered, but over the years he had managed to save a goodly portion by selecting much cheaper accommodations than his boss's money would have provided.

The innkeeper greeted him enthusiastically. "Oh, Monsieur, you have arrived early this year. Did our problems here in France bother you?"

Jacques groaned, remembering the talent the innkeeper had for long-winded conversations. The innkeeper launched into a description of all that had happened in the last several months, and Jacques wondered if he would get to his room before sundown. "Damn," Jacques muttered under his breath when the innkeeper continued. Several prisoners—the innkeeper swore the number to be eight, but gossip said a hundred — were released from the Bastile in July by an angry mob. The committee was meeting, and things looked bad for the clergy. As for the queen and king, the innkeeper assured Jacques, "The mobs are interested in blood. I doubt the royalty will escape. Many of the nobility have already rushed off to Spain and England, carrying what they could. Paris is a hotbed, my friend. I would see about my business and leave as quickly as I could if I were you."

Jacques frowned at the innkeeper, remembering that years before he had explained his reasons for returning to Paris every winter. He wondered if he would regret having told the innkeeper about the little French girl at the convent who was being provided for by the rich American. He tried to remember if he had mentioned that she was a distant relative of the queen.

The innkeeper sensed Jacques's concern, "Sir, I would not tell a soul about the girl, but I implore you, take her to America now. She will not be safe at the convent. She may not be safe anyplace in Paris."

Jacques had no intentions of disclosing any of his plans to the talkative innkeeper, and he muttered, "I'll see." He headed toward his room, his eyes laced with concern. It was apparent that he must get the girl out of the city and on a ship bound for Maryland just as soon as arrangements could be made. He would have no time to enjoy Paris this trip, he thought grimly.

Early the next morning, Jacques Manage presented himself to Mother Thomas and handed her the all-important document signed by Alexander Dampier. "Mother," he began, "I don't mean to sound difficult, but I propose that this wedding take place today or tomorrow at the latest. I must get the girl back to Le Havre quickly. The journey from Paris to Le Havre will take three days as it is. We must leave France soon. I hope that you'll understand."

Mother Thomas forced herself to smile at this agent of Monsieur Dampier. She had never liked the little man, although she could not quite put her finger on why she harbored such a dislike. Watching him carefully through lowered lids, she once more tried to decide what there was about him that she distrusted. He stood straight and proud; perhaps he had too much pride, the woman thought. His clothes were a little too stylish, his hair was a bit too dressed and powdered. He was barely two inches taller than Mother Thomas, several inches shorter than most of the men she knew, and he was thin. But there was something about his dark blue eyes and the way he looked through her and then quickly shifted his gaze away from her that made her leery. Instinctively, she knew he was a dishonest man, a man she could not completely trust. At the moment he was looking down his slightly pointed nose at her as she studied the parchment he had given her.

"I do hope everything is in order," Jacques interrupted her. "The girl knows why I have come, does she not?" Jacques squirmed uncomfortably. This woman has always made me uncomfortable. Perhaps the destruction of the church will not be such a bad idea, Jacques pondered silently.

Distracted for the moment, the mother superior frowned. "Yes, she knows and she can be ready to depart day after tomorrow. We had hoped that the Bishop, himself, would be able to perform the ceremony in the cathedral, but that is out of the question now. I will see that Frere Francis, our confessor, agrees to perform the ceremony here. And, I do agree that it is imperative that the wedding take place immediately. We will arrange for the vows to be spoken tomorrow afternoon, following Mass. Nichole will be packed and ready to travel early the next morning. Is that satisfactory?"

Jacques sighed in relief, nodding his head. The sooner he got the wench out from under the control of the convent and this woman, the sooner he could convince her to complete the wedding. He grinned as he thought of the voyage home. Henry Dampier never had indicated how often he was supposed to bed the girl, but he intended to enjoy the trip.

After Jacques left the office of Mother Superior, she sent word to Nichole to come to her office once more. The note to Frere Francis had already been sent, informing him of the change in plans. She paused briefly, wiping a tear from her tired eyes; she too, had grown very fond of the young girl who would be leaving them in just two days. As she waited for Nichole, she wondered just what her life would be like. She offered a quick prayer that the child would find happiness in her new world.

A timid rap on the office door broke into Mother Thomas's thoughts. "Come in," she called.

Nichole opened the door and stuck her veil-covered head between the door and the doorjamb. She glanced around the room, half expecting to see the disgusting little man waiting for her. Except for Mother Thomas, who sat at her desk, the room was vacant. *"Oui,* Ma Mere," Nichole murmured as she opened the door wide and glided into the room.

"Nichole, sit down. We must talk." Mother Thomas waited for Nichole to sink into the chair across from the desk before she began. "Jacques Manage, Monsieur Dampier's agent, has arrived. The papers are in order, and I have already informed Frere Francis that the ceremony will take place after Mass tomorrow afternoon." Mother Thomas noticed the color fading from Nichole's cheeks. The older woman took a deep breath. "Soeur Bernard has told me that she already talked to you about the role of a wife. I would feel that I had neglected my own duty if I did not also speak to you."

Nichole raised her shocked eyes to Mother Superior. Was there more to marriage than Soeur Bernard had told her? Would Ma Mere straighten out some of the confusion that still existed in her mind? She leaned forward, intent on every word Mother Thomas spoke.

"A wife belongs to her husband," Mother Thomas explained softly. "She must do as he says, obey him in all manner of things. She must bear his children willingly. Many young women do not know their husbands when they marry, so your situation is not unique. But those same young women have had some acquaintance with men; fathers, brothers and friends of the family. You know nothing of the world, or the kinds of men that inhabit that world. Some of them are not to be trusted."

She watched Nichole's eyebrows raise slightly. "I must have your promise, child, that you will let no man touch you except your husband. No man but your husband has that right! The pain of betraying the man you will be promised to tomorrow will place you in the fires of hell. Do I have your promise?"

Nichole was speechless. Soeur Bernard had never mentioned the fires of hell. Nichole felt even more confused, but as she sank back in her chair she told herself that Mother Superior knew a great deal more about the world than either she or Soeur Bernard. Perhaps, in time, she would understand what Ma Mere was talking about. She sighed. "You have my promise, Ma Mere."

"There is one more thing. Ann Margaret Saint James has asked to leave the convent. She has only been here for four months, and we both feel she is not ready for a commitment to our way of life. She is from Le Havre herself. I will ask Monsieur Manage if she may travel with you to that city. You will leave here the day after tomorrow, and in three days you will be in Le Havre, where you will board a ship. That ship will then take you to this Maryland and the man are to marry tomorrow. You do understand the proxy contract, don't you?"

Nichole nodded her head; everything was moving too

fast for her.

"Good!" Mother Thomas stated in a tone of finality. "Soeur Bernard will help you pack and also bathe and dress you for your wedding." Mother Superior rose from her desk and took several steps toward Nichole. To her complete surprise, Mother Thomas put her arms around Nichole and hugged her for a brief second. "Little one, I wish things could be different, but I have faith in the Good God. He will give you a happy life and much joy." She released Nichole and pushed her toward the door. "Go! Get your things together. Tomorrow is a very special day for you, my child."

Nichole stumbled back to her cell. She was frightened. She didn't understand why Ma Mere was in such a rush to see her married. Surely, the wedding could have been postponed for several weeks. Suddenly, she jerked to a stop. She could not be married tomorrow. She and Soeur Bernard had finished only one of the dresses for her wardrobe. With her wedding dress and only one other traveling dress, she could not leave. For a certainty, she was not expected to wear her wedding dress on the ship.

Starting toward her room once more, she calculated the amount of work needed on the pale gray traveling suit that was almost complete. They would have to wait for her to finish that garment and her pink and white striped day dress. She clenched her fists. They must wait. For an instant her eyes filled with tears. No, she was not going to cry, she told herself. She could finish her dress and make the others on board the ship. For many years now, she had been schooled in obedience, and this was not the time to begin questioning Mother's orders. She would do as she was told.

To her delight, Soeur Bernard was already in her tiny room, sorting through the fabric and Nichole's clothes. Another sister was busy wrapping the fabric for the other garments in plain cloth along with the thread and trims she would need to complete the gowns. Nichole breathed the words softly: "You know?"

Soeur Bernard raised her head and nodded. Nichole did not miss the glimmer of tears in her friend's eyes. "Nichole, I will miss you, and I will pray for your happiness every day." Soeur Bernard rushed from the room, and Nichole stood quietly with tears streaming down her face. She would dearly miss her friend.

The rest of the day passed in a daze for her. Even Frere Francis came to offer his prayers, and he gave her several books carefully wrapped in oilskin so that the dampness of the ship would not affect them. She worked hard, and the emotional trials of the day left her exhausted. She fell into a deep sleep that night.

The next morning flew by as her companion sisters offered her their own personal gifts for her wedding and her home. Soeur Clare, the cook, gave Nichole a collection of recipes for the fruit Nichole loved so, and Soeur Martin, who was in charge of the gardens, brought Nichole a box of strawberry plants for her new home. Even Soeur Mary Margaret, the laundress Nichole had shocked with her embroidered chemises, had stitched a beautiful quilt for her bed. Nichole found herself continually brushing away her tears. She sighed; leaving was so much more difficult than she had thought it would be.

Before a light lunch Nichole bathed and tried to rest. Emotionally she was spent. Never in her most frightening dreams had she thought that leaving the cold gray building that had been her home for these many years could cause such depression. She did not want to go. How could they force her to do this thing? Couldn't they understand that she wanted to stay? She could not leave them and sail away across the seas to belong to a man she had never even seen. She sobbed against her cot in the corner of her tiny room.

She had just gotten herself composed when Seour

Bernard came to help her dress. Even before she was ready the bell rang at the front gate. Nichole froze. She stood as still as the granite column in the back of the churchyard. It had to be Monsieur Manage. She thought for a moment that her heart had stopped. Was this really what she had to do? She was leaving everything she had ever known, and for what? For the first time in her life, Nichole questioned the word of Mother Superior. She did not want to marry, especially a man she did not know, and then travel to a place that was only printed words in a book she had read.

Soeur Bernard gazed at Nichole's troubled expression. Poor child, Soeur Bernard thought, her emotions are plainly written on her face for anyone to see. It's a shame there is no mirror for her to see herself. She would feel better about everything if she could only know how truly beautiful she is.

A pleased smile curled Soeur Bernard's lips up, and she had the look of a proud mother. She sighed. Nichole was breathtaking in the cream gown of silk and satin. The square neckline of the fitted bodice and the sleeves, fitted to the elbows, were constructed of fragile silk. The neckline itself and the flounces of the sleeves below the elbow were trimmed with rows of delicate lace. The lace matched the lace veil that covered her shimmering dark blond hair. The full skirt was held out on all sides by four large circles of wire sewed onto a half petticoat of linen and tied around her tiny waist. The cream-colored petticoat of matching silk was trimmed with the same lace, and an overskirt of heavier satin was drawn up on each side in large puffs. Her slippers matched the cream-colored satin. She looks like a princess, Soeur Bernard thought.

As Nichole stood next to Soeur Bernard, she was afraid to move. She waited to be summoned to the small chapel where the ceremony would be performed. Fighting the panic that threatened to make breathing impossible, she tried to swallow, but the lump of terror that stuck in her throat made even that mundane task a battle. Without a doubt, she knew she would not be able to utter a sound, let alone promise herself to an imagined man.

Soeur Bernard touched her arm. "It's time, Nichole." The girl moved from the tiny room in a daze. She remembered nothing of the walk to the chapel, but she was aware that she was standing next to the despicable little man during Mass. After Mass she heard herself make the proper responses, in spite of her fear. Soon it was all over and she was no longer Nichole Ramoneur, but instead Madame Alexander Dennis Dampier, soon to be of Maryland, in a new land far from her home.

After the ceremony, Frere Francis, Mother Thomas, Soeur Bernard and Nichole were joined by Jacques for some rich red wine and tiny cakes. No one in the small parlor had much to say, and Nichole wanted feverishly to ask Mother Thomas to let her return to her room. She was still frightened and confused. In spite of the ceremony, she did not feel even a little bit married and she did not like the way Monsieur Manage was looking at her.

Frere Francis toasted her happiness, and then Mother Thomas took pity on her and excused her to finish her packing. Soeur Bernard asked to be excused to help with the task of putting the remaining garments into Nichole's trunk. The priest left also, and Mother Thomas glanced over at the thin little man still sitting comfortably in one of the parlor chairs.

"Monsieur," Mother Superior began, "there has been a slight addition to your entourage. There was no time for us to arrange for a maid for Nichole, and you said nothing about securing one. However, one of the novices has changed her mind about joining our order. Since her family lives in Le Havre, she will accompany Nichole to the ship."

Jacques sat stunned, trying to still the scream he felt

bubbling to the surface. The old witch was going to ruin all of his plans. Carefully, hoping not to alert the woman, he phrased his objections. "Oh—oh—Mother. I . . . I am so sorry. She cannot come with us! The ship leaves in only four days! I . . . I mean that there is no time to see the child home. It will take three days to get to Le Havre. We will just barely make the ship as it is."

"Oh, I'm aware that you have no time, so I took it upon myself to send word to her brothers. They will meet her at the dock in Le Havre. It is not a problem, nor should it cause you any additional delay, because both men work near the docks."

Not ready to give up his carefully prepared plans, Jacques responded, "I have only a small carriage. I will not be able to carry much in the way of luggage. I fear that I will not even be able to carry all that Madame Dampier will want to bring with her. There is no way I could carry the luggage of another."

Mother Thomas scowled at the little man. He was protesting too much. She murmured, softly, "Surely, Monsieur, you cannot refuse to take the girl with you? It will be dangerous for her to stay here. Then, we cannot have the new Madame Dampier traveling without a lady's maid, can we? You sir," Mother raised herself up to her full five foot two inches, "are not her husband!"

"I . . . I . . . was only . . . concerned for Madame's comfort." Jacques backed down, knowing that he had to travel with the unwanted baggage or incur the Superior's wrath. "Of course the girl can come. I know that I am not Madame's husband and I meant no disrespect. I have been so concerned over the young woman's safety that I saw the other girl as a delay. You must forgive me!"

Mother Thomas looked at the man standing before her. She didn't trust him at all. Somehow, she had to ensure Nichole's safety on the way to that ship. Ann Margaret was an intelligent girl and she could follow orders. Mother would see that Nichole was not alone with Jacques Manage until they reached the ship. She breathed a sigh of relief. Thank goodness Ann Margaret's brothers did indeed work on the docks. She would give Ann Margaret a message to be delivered to her older brother. He would take the note to the captain of the ship that would take Nichole to her husband. Surely the captain of the ship could be made to feel responsible for the naive young woman. She smiled grimly. It was the only thing she could do.

her about their Nichole was her sister Soer. The boys
all talked of her until her recess tomorrow to turn a
as the number of many of those experiences than Nichole
as she could know. Because she was not than the maker of the
by Anne had never felt the pressed of Nichole an get
two days were to the custom of the another's would read
children to any part of all the lives dream of the sad
to it seemed to. At home working for the glove come
warmly and eager pleasant and through though she would
so that

Chapter Eight

As the coral sky lit the cathedral spires, Nichole finished her morning prayers. There was no more time. In
minutes, she would be leaving the convent to begin a new
life. Her heart sank. She wanted nothing more than to fall
back onto her cot and pretend that the whole summer and
early fall had been nothing but a bad dream.

The evening before, her trunk had been placed in the
room next to the front gate and now, her bag and the box
of gifts were ready to be carried to the waiting carriage.
Soeur Bernard had already told her that Jacques Manage
had arrived with the sun. There was nothing to be done
but to say good-bye.

Ann Margaret helped Nichole take the last of her things
to the carriage, and these were quickly loaded. Amid tears
and promises to correspond, Nichole was briskly ushered
from the convent. The day was warm even for late September, but the sky was overcast. I suppose it will rain,
Nichole thought. Even the heavens cry for me.

Ma Mere's direction to Ann Margaret had been to entertain Nichole on the trip and to keep her attention. As
the carriage wound through the streets of the city, Ann
Margaret pointed out to Nichole things her brothers told

her about when they first came to the city. The young girl had traveled to Paris with her brothers a number of times, and she shared as many of those experiences with Nichole as she could recall. Before they reached the gates of the city, Ann Margaret's enthusiasm infected Nichole and the two girls were talking, pointing and giggling at the things they saw.

They left the city and Nichole was shocked at how quickly the day was passing as she discovered the world outside the city of Paris. Both girls leaned out of the windows of the carriage as Ann Margaret pointed to first one thing and then another.

Shortly after dark they pulled up before a small inn. Jacques had already made arrangements on the way to Paris, but he was not pleased that he had to inform the innkeeper that he had two women, not one, with him. The evening meal was served and the two girls were shown to a tiny, plain room. Jacques decided that since Nichole knew only convent life, there was no need to spend much money on accommodations in their travel to the ship. He watched for a reaction from the girls when he showed them their room. He looked at both girls when he explained that he would be next door if they needed anything during the night. They nodded as if he was of no concern to them. Well, he said to himself, at least that nun said nothing to them about accommodations. Still, this was not the kind of a night he had planned. In disgust he slammed his door shut. Damn Mother Thomas!

The next day was almost a repeat of the first. On the third day, Jacques had both girls up and ready to travel before the sun had risen. His one desire was to get to the ship and take possession of what he felt was his. Late that afternoon they arrived in Le Harve, and Ann Margaret and Nichole sat in the carriage waiting for all of Nichole's bags and her trunk to be loaded onto the ship.

While they were waiting to leave the security of the

93

carriage, they were approached by a sandy-haired man of indeterminate age. Ann Margaret screamed out loud, "Jean, oh Jean! You came!" Quickly, she introduced Jean to Nichole and Jacques Manage, who was suddenly smiling and gracious. Then she dragged her brother a short distance from the carriage.

As Nichole watched, Ann Margaret hugged her brother and she saw them whispering, their heads together, as if they were planning a conspiracy. Ann Margaret handed Jean something and then she rushed back to say good-bye to Nichole.

After their good-byes Nichole's attention was drawn to the vessel that would carry her away from France. It was very much like the drawings she had seen in some of the books Frere Francis had given her to study. There were three long poles rising straight up from the ship, one in the middle, one short one toward the front and another one as tall as the middle pole in the back. They were strung with a crisscross of ropes, and each had several arms extending into the air almost like ladders. Around each of the arms were puffs of gray fabric that would be unfurled to collect the wind and send them on their way.

It was much bigger than Nichole had thought it would be, and in her amazement, Nichole forgot all about Jean and his sister, Ann Margaret. Jacques told her he would take her aboard when all of her luggage had been delivered to her cabin. Once they were aboard he introduced her to the captain and then dragged her down to the second deck and her cabin.

Nichole would have much preferred to stay on deck and watch the fascinating activity, but she never thought to question Jacques's direction. She spent the rest of the afternoon rearranging her things and pulling the gray suit from her trunk. She made a mental note to request an additional lamp from the captain so that she could work on her sewing during the voyage. She sighed. It was going to be a very long voyage.

Jacques rapped on her cabin door. "Nichole, I must talk to you."

Nichole stood quietly as he explained about meals, and then he told her he would bring her meals to her. "I'll be back in about an hour with your evening meal, and we'll talk about what you can and cannot do on board a ship."

Nichole grimaced. Was she to be trapped in this small room for the duration of the trip? She was certainly not going to enjoy being forced to endure Monsieur Manage's company for two months, of that she was sure.

When Jacques brought Nichole's meal he watched her carefully. Quietly, he told her that she could not go up to the main deck of the ship unless he accompanied her. She seemed nervous, and he caught her looking at him strangely, then lowering her gaze. He was growing angry. Had that damned Mother Superior told her more than Henry Dampier wanted her to know? And why had he seen the brother of Ann Margaret and the captain of this vessel in close conversation? He would have to bide his time and wait until they were well out to sea before he attempted to take her. Damn, damn, damn! Why were things getting so complicated?

For three days, Jacques had to content himself with bringing Nichole her meals and accompanying her for a stroll around the deck. The girl seemed more relaxed and comfortable with her surroundings. The captain had personally seen to another lamp for her even before they sailed that first night, and Jacques knew she had spent the mornings working on the costumes Henry Dampier had provided for her. However, by the fourth day he was sick of his role of guardian. It was time. During their morning stroll, Jacques leaned toward her. "I thought perhaps we could dine together tonight. I'll bring my own dinner to your cabin when I bring your meal."

Nichole smiled up at him. He had been most gentlemanly, seeing to her comfort without hesitation. She quelled the uneasy feelings that accompanied his words. "All right. I think that would be pleasant."

When Jacques arrived at her cabin that evening with their meal, the sun was just beginning to set. Nichole put her sewing away and made room for the two of them at the tiny table. Jacques brought fish and rice, and small biscuits with jam and fruit. He proudly displayed a bottle of white wine from the basket, saying it was to finish the meal.

They ate the meal in silence and while they were drinking the last glass of wine, Jacques cleared his throat. Now he could begin his lecture on the importance of completing the marriage agreement. He smiled at Nichole and opened his mouth.

A sharp rap on the door forced his attention away from the girl. Nichole left the table and opened the door.

"I thought Madame Dampier might care for some tea. Good evening, Monsieur Manage. I have meant to inquire, how does Madame like the sea voyage so far?" The captain stood in the passageway holding a tray with a teapot and mugs on it.

Jacques wanted to scream. Smiling pleasantly, the captain stepped into the tiny room, placed the tray on the table and pulled up a bench. It was obvious to Jacques that he intended to watch out for the French girl, too. Why? Jacques wondered. He felt his anger rising to the surface, and he excused himself as quickly as he could.

By the time he got back to his cabin, Jacques was in a black rage. What was the captain doing bringing tea to the girl? Why was he intent on inquiring after her comfort? His head shot up. Had that witch of a Mother Superior asked the captain to watch out for the girl? Just in case, he decided that perhaps he needed to explain the facts to Nichole out on the open deck where they would be surrounded by people. Belowdecks, it appeared, she was going to be watched by the good captain. He scowled. His time would come. The captain couldn't watch the wench every minute of the voyage.

For three days, Jacques uttered curse after curse, this time at the weather which also seemed to be conspiring against him. The sky was dark and the rain cold and he knew that he could not take Nichole to the upper deck without raising every eyebrow on the ship. So he waited. The weather would have to break eventually.

The fourth day dawned nearly perfect. The sun was bright, the sea calm, and although there was a chilly wind blowing from the west, no one seemed to want to stay in their cabins. Most of the other passengers, about forty in number and a good number of the crew, were out in the fresh air when Nichole and Jacques made their way to the rail. Jacques looked around him in disgust. Now there were simply too many people milling about. Someone could easily overhear what he had to say. He consoled himself by assuring himself that he could wait until later in the day.

For most of the day Jacques waited, while the travelers strolled the deck, sat in the sun or stood at the rail watching the sailors perform their duties. In disgust he went back to his cabin. Not once the whole day did he get a chance to talk to the girl.

They were at sea for two weeks before Jacques managed to get Nichole on the deck without the other passengers nearby. The day was clear, the sun was shining, a brisk breeze was blowing, but the sea was not as calm as it had been. The waves were building, and walking around the deck required careful stepping. And they were on the deck because Nichole had insisted.

Nichole had been sewing steadily for the two weeks they had been at sea. Her rose gown and her gray suit were finished, and she had started working on the small rosebuds with which she had decided to decorate the top of one of her chemises. But she was tired of sewing, and even though the sea was getting rough, she couldn't stay in her cabin, not a minute longer. She was bored.

Jacques maneuvered her into the forward part of the vessel. They stood by the railing with the spray wetting their faces and their clothes. Despite his own misery, Jacques made up his mind that today he would tell her. This might be the only chance he got.

He smiled at her. "I don't know what the nuns told you about the marriage contract, but the wedding is not complete."

Nichole glanced at the man beside her. What did he mean, the wedding was not complete? She opened her mouth to ask him, but he interrupted her.

"You will not be truly wedded to Alexander Dampier until you are — uh — bedded."

Nichole gazed at Jacques, her confusion clear. "Bedded?"

"Yes." Jacques cleared his throat in his nervousness; she had to understand. "Why don't you tell me just what the dear sisters told you about being married."

Nichole froze. An alarm went off in her head. For some reason this conversation made her deathly afraid. Why was he looking at her with that peculiar leer in his eyes? Suddenly, she wanted nothing more than to be back in her cabin, working on the rosebuds she had found so boring. But his question, in itself, was a simple one. She would answer and then demand to be escorted back to her room. She glanced at the rolling waves. "The sisters told me that I must obey my husband, bear his children and submit to him." She glanced back to see if that was the answer he wanted.

Before Nichole could demand to be taken back to her room, Jacques continued, a smile playing across his face, "There is also the matter of consummating the marriage. Until that is done, you are not truly married. As Mr.

Dampier's agent and the proxy groom, I must complete the vows." He tried to look sincere, but he failed miserably.

Nichole felt cold chills travel down her spine. His words did not sound right. Surely, if there was something more that required Monsieur Manage's attention, Ma Mere would have mentioned it. A sudden thought struck Nichole. "Will this completing of the marriage require that you touch me?" she asked innocently.

Jacques almost choked. She knew nothing. She was not only slow but completely naive. What luck, he wanted to shout. He tried not to laugh. "Touch you? Why yes, I must touch you. But you will enjoy it, I assure you."

"No!" she shouted, "no! You will not touch me." She turned and ran quickly for the stairs, not waiting for him to escort her. She got to the door of her cabin just as she heard his footsteps on the stairs. Swinging open her door, she rushed inside and slammed it shut. She stood breathing heavily, from fear and from her efforts. He would not touch her.

She sensed that he stood before her door, and she tried to quiet her breathing. Standing frozen in place, she wondered if he could hear her heart pounding in her chest. At first, she thought the rapping on the door was her heart, but she realized quickly that he was trying to get her attention. "I do not want to talk to you," she muttered softly.

She heard his fading footsteps, but she could not believe that he had truly left. "I'll have to see if the captain will send my meals to me," she thought. She had no intention of finding herself alone with the little man again. Whatever he wanted from her, she instinctively knew was wrong. Ma Mere had tried to explain. But why hadn't the dear sisters been more explicit?

She stayed in her cabin for the rest of the day, ignoring Jacques when he pounded on her door with her meals.

She nibbled on some fruit she had set aside from her dinner the evening before and tried to ignore the pangs of hunger that attacked her as the dinner hour came and went. She sewed quietly and prayed that something would happen to keep Jacques Manage away.

As she sewed she became vaguely aware that the ship was rolling more than usual. Putting the fabric away, she crawled into bed. She drifted off into a restless sleep. Much later that night, Nichole was awakened by the force of the storm as it hit them. She grabbed onto her bunk, as she was almost thrown to the floor. As the ship creaked and groaned, she fought her panic. She rolled first one way and then another as the ship bobbed in the heavy seas. In the distance, she heard splintering wood and a crash. Dear God, was the ship breaking apart?

For over an hour, she fought with herself. She wanted to run to the door, fling it open and race up the stairs to the open deck. She imagined the turmoil above her and hung onto the edge of the bunk for dear life. Even if she could get to the door, however would she maneuver the stairs? This small room was really the safest place for her, at least at the moment.

For a second, above the roar of the sea, Nichole thought she heard a noise at the door. She gingerly made her way to the portal, hanging onto the heavy furniture as she went. "Is someone there?" she shouted, trying to be heard above the noise of the storm.

"It's Jimmy, Madame. Capt'n sent me down with some food and he wants me to talk to you. You'll have to open the door, ma'am, my hands is full," the young male voice shouted back.

She unlocked the door and intended to open it just a crack, but the motion of the ship threw her across the room. The latch jerked from her hand.

Nichole sighed in relief as the young cabin boy lunged into the cabin, holding a bottle of wine and a basket of food. "This storm won't last too long, ma'am. The capt'n says to tell you, except for some broken yardarms, everything is secure. Might be scary, but we'll make it. Got some biscuits and jam, and some dried meat here. When the weather breaks and it get's a little calmer, I'll bring ya something warm." He turned to go. "Oh, there's one more thing. Capt'n says ya to stay down here. He don't want no pretty little thing like ya flying over the rail."

Nichole thanked him, and as he turned toward the door, her curiosity was aroused. She asked, "What happens when someone goes flying over the rail?"

Jimmy looked at her in surprise. "We can't very well turn around and go look for them, now can we? If someone sees 'em go, sometimes we gets 'em back, but usually, they're gone. We lose one or two mates in every bad storm. And, Capt'n, he ain't a-wantin' to lose you, so ya stay here."

Nichole stared after the boy as he stumbled from the cabin and fought his way toward the stairs. She shivered. She would stay in her cabin, no matter what she heard.

Through the long hours of the next day, Nichole lay on her bunk. In the morning, she had tried to move around the room, hanging onto the heavy furniture, but she was continually thrown against the table or the bunk. In desperation, she gave up and stayed in bed. She couldn't sew or read, and she was afraid to light her whale-oil lamps the way they swung.

Jimmy's words, spoken so matter-of-factly, came back to haunt her. If she went up on deck and was thrown into the sea, no one would even try to rescue her. What a terrible fate!

Later that evening, when she was sure that the waters were calmer, she was very tempted to go up on deck. The ship wasn't lurching as badly, and there were no more splintering sounds. She wanted desperately to leave the cabin for a little while. A loud rap on her door drew her attention, and remembering Jacques Manage for the first time in twenty-four hours, she asked hesitantly, "Who is it?"

When the young male voice answered, "It's Jimmy, Ma'am," Nichole breathed a sigh of relief.

Nichole moved to throw open the door, and Jimmy handed the basket to her. "We're through the worst of it. The seas will be a little rough, but you shouldn't be tossed about like before. I'll be back for the basket later. Oh, there's hot tea on the bottom." He grinned at her.

Nichole thanked him and watched him move to the stairs; then she turned and locked her door once more. This would be the perfect time for Jacques to force himself into her room if he was of a mind to do so, she thought. "But I won't let him in," she muttered as she spread the contents of the basket on her table.

After she ate and drank every bit of the tea the captain had sent, she waited for Jimmy. Finally, she admitted that he wasn't coming, at least not tonight. She crawled into her bed and sleep came quickly. She never finished her prayers for the ship and the crew.

A noise awakened her, and she realized that it was lighter than it had been, but the ship was still moving up and down now. There was a slight sideward roll that she hadn't noticed before. Again, a rap on her door drew her attention, and Jimmy once more answered her question.

"Capt'n says you're not to try to come topside, not yet. It is still too rough, Ma'am," he told her after she opened the door.

"What time is it?" Nichole asked as she handed him the empty basket and took the full one he held out to her.

"It's after ten," he answered, and then he was gone.

Nichole grinned as she examined the contents of the basket. She had just lived through her first storm at sea. She lit her lamps and sat down to enjoy her breakfast. Grabbing her sewing basket, she decided that in spite of the motion of the ship, she would sew. She made a game of trying to get the needle into the fabric with each dip of the vessel. Married or not, she laughed at herself, she was still a child at heart.

Chapter Nine

When the knock on her door came, she set her sewing aside, grabbed the basket and the empty teapot and took several steps to the door. She was smiling happily when she threw open the door, prepared to thank Jimmy and insist that she go above to thank the captain.

The words died on her lips. Before she could protest Jacques Manage was in her room. He pushed her aside, then closed and bolted the door.

"What are you doing here?" Nichole whispered. "Get out, before I call the captain."

"We must complete the contract," Jacques sneered at her. "I have come to do so now. Don't bother to cry for the captain. The seas are still rough and the deck is too noisy for anyone to hear your screams. Save your breath!"

Nichole backed away from him. "You will not touch me!" she muttered through clenched teeth.

Jacques was laughing at her. "Oh, but I will." He made a lunge for her and grabbed her arms. He held her tightly with one arm and with the other, he reached up and held her head still in an iron grip. His mouth descended on hers in a painful bruising kiss. She could feel her lips cracking under the pressure. Struggling violently, she tried to free herself. For an instant he released her. She backed away from him, screaming as she went. He grabbed at her, but she had moved away just enough that his hand caught in the bodice of her new green dress. As she yanked away the bodice split, exposing her breasts.

She froze, staring at her torn dress, and in that second Jacques was on her again. He wrestled her toward the bed as he untied his breeches. Nichole fought and pushed until she at least had gained some freedom for her arms. She swung at him wildly, trying to push him away from her. He is so strong for such a little man, she thought. Her hand grazed the sewing basket above her head on the edge of the bed, and she tensed. Her scissors! She managed to get her fingers into the basket just as Jacques knocked it from the bed.

In that instant her bare leg touched the flesh of his thigh. She realized that he had nothing on from his waist down. Her own dress and petticoats were no longer any protection. As she struggled, they had worked up to her waist, and she was as naked as Jacques.

As Jacques forced her legs apart she clenched her hands. Her right hand gripped the pin cushion that must have fallen from her sewing basket as it was pushed from the bed. Her fingers grabbed for one of the embroidery needles that she had been using. Without a thought, she viciously stuck the needle into his arm.

He bellowed in pain and jerked away from her toward the wall. Nichole could feel the flesh tear, and she watched the crimson stain ooze through his shirt. He raised his hand to hit her and some of the sticky red stuff dropped onto her thighs, then ran down her flesh, staining the sheets.

The blow she thought inevitable never came, and she looked up, trying to locate the pounding that had stopped Jacques from smashing her senseless. Even before Jacques got clear of the bed the door came crashing in. When Nichole realized that someone else was in the room, she jumped up from the bed and tried to pull her dress closed about her. She was too ashamed and embarrassed to say a word to the captain of the ship, who stood in the doorway. Instead, she backed into the corner of the room and lowered her eyes.

The captain stood and glared at Jacques; then slowly he took in the disordered room. He had seen the blood on Nichole's legs as she leaped away from the bed, and as he glanced at the bed, his eyes were riveted to the stains on the white linens. Seething, he grabbed Jacques by the ruff of the neck and led him from the room. The mother superior had been right. This worm was nothing but trash.

Nichole heard the captain shouting as he dragged Jacques out of the room. He was saying something about working on the deck where he could be watched until after the storm. Suddenly, Nichole felt her legs turn to limp rags, and she knew she was going to be violently ill. She rushed for the chamber pot in the corner of the room.

Out of nowhere, a woman appeared at her side. "I'm Nellie Hutchinson, my dear. Here, let me help you." She held Nichole's head and murmured soft meaningless phrases, and Nichole was sick again and again. The woman who called herself Nellie led her to the bed, and then Nichole felt what was left of her dress being pulled from her shaking frame.

Reality seemed to fade in and out, and Nichole knew she was being bathed, and dressed in one of her own soft gowns, as the woman mumbled soft words of endearment and encouragement to her. As she floated in and out of consciousness she thought she heard male voices. Was she dreaming? Her senses returned slowly, and she started to cry. For some reason, she couldn't stop sobbing. Nellie held her just like she remembered her own mother holding her. She blurted out, "My husband won't want me now! Another man has touched me . . . I will burn in hell!" But Nellie continued to pat her and murmur soft English phrases to her.

Finally, she fell into an exhausted sleep, and there were no dreams. She had no idea how long she slept, but when she finally woke, Nellie was there. Did I dream myself a nightmare? she wondered as she struggled from the bed. She glanced down at the soft gown she wore. Vaguely, she remembered that the woman sitting at the table had bathed and then clothed her. And there were bruised marks around her wrists. Her new green gown was folded and lying on her trunk. She shook herself. It was no nightmare. It had really happened.

Nellie mumbled, "After ya eat, the captain wants to talk to you."

Nichole sat down at the table and asked in French, "How long did I sleep?"

Nellie looked at her quizzically and Nichole asked the same question in English.

"You do speak English! The captain said ya did. I was afraid we'd never talk. All your mumbling was in yer own tongue. And, ya been asleep about sixteen hours now."

Nichole stared at the woman in surprise. Nothing Nichole had said did the woman understand. And she had slept away the better part of a day.

Nellie interrupted her thoughts. "Do you think you could talk to the captain now? He has been waiting since late last night to see you."

Nichole glanced at her, her expression guarded. She was not sure she wanted to talk to any man, captain or no. Nellie seemed to sense her thought and commented, "I'll stay right here with ya, if ya want me to."

Was she so transparent? Nichole wondered. She nodded her head. Nellie sent for the captain and then seated herself on the small bench the captain had used himself, two weeks before. Nichole paced the room, nervously clutching her hands together until a short rap sounded. Nellie rose and ushered the captain into the small room.

"I'm glad to see you up and about, Madame," the captain murmured quietly. "Please, can we sit down?" He waited until Nichole sat in one of the chairs at the table and then he sat down himself. Nellie returned to her bench, and Nichole noticed that the captain did not seem to mind in the least that Nellie was still in the room.

"After your, ah—attack"—the captain watched as all color drained out of her face—"I took Monsieur Manage on deck to help clean up after the storm. The sea was still heavy and I was too upset to notice that the man had no shoes." He paused, watching Nichole. "I regret that I must inform you that he slipped and was lost at sea."

Nichole's breath caught in her throat. The man had become a victim of the storm.

"The sea was still running so heavily that we could not search," the captain offered in a whispered tone. "Somehow, I think you will be better off without him. I have placed you under my protection. No one else will bother you." Nichole sighed at his last words. Would she be truly safe?

As if to answer her question the tall, soft-spoken man said quickly, "I have arranged for the widow Hutchinson to stay with you for the remainder of the journey. She has graciously agreed, especially when I told her that you can understand and speak to her in her own language, English." The captain rose and turned to her once more. "I have all of Monsieur's papers in my cabin for safekeeping. I have your marriage papers there as well. When your husband comes to get you, I will present the papers to him. Do you have any questions?"

Nichole shook her head, lowered her eyes and whispered *"Non,"* softly. The captain strode through the door, leaving Nichole with Nellie still perched on the bench. Nichole shuddered. Jacques had been lost at sea. She glanced over at Nellie and smiled at her confused look. The captain had conducted his interview in French, and Nichole understood the Widow Hutchinson's confusion.

She quickly explained what the captain had told her, watching Nellie's look of satisfaction when she mentioned Jacques's fate. She had been right. His plans for her were not honorable. "Did you truly agree to stay with me?" Nichole asked hesitantly.

"To my way of thinking"—Nellie grinned at her, nodding her head—"a young lady of quality should never have been allowed to travel without a maid. Your attack would never have happened if you had a maid."

Nichole's smile faded as she remembered the implication of what had occurred. She had been touched by another man. She tried to remember what Mother Thomas had said. The Superior had never mentioned what would happen to her if she had not wanted to be touched by someone other than her husband. She had fought him; surely that counted for something. She glanced over at Nellie, wondering if she should discuss it with her. *Non!* she thought. She could not discuss her situation with anyone.

Trying to erase her troubled thoughts, she asked the older woman, who was still seated on the bench, "You must know a lot about me, but I know nothing of you. Tell me," she pleaded in her soft lilting English, colored by her accent. Nichole gazed at the woman as if she were seeing her for the first time. Nellie was short and slightly rounded with a small round face and light brown hair sprinkled liberally with white. She had warm brown eyes and a short turned-up nose. She was shorter than Nichole by at least four inches, but Nichole remembered the soft comforting arms that held her as she cried.

Nellie beamed. "What would ya like to know? I've been a widow fer eight years now. We had no children of our own, and I been trying hard to find work, but it is difficult. My younger sister and her husband left for a place called Pennsylvania two years ago. They have five young'ens and she sent word that she needed me. Since I

109

ain't found a position, there weren't nothing for me in England. So I packed my things and here I am."

Nichole grinned. The widow Hutchinson seemed to be a pleasant person, and she also was concerned with other people. She would be a wonderful companion, she decided. "What should I call you? Widow Hutchinson, Madame Hutchinson," she questioned.

"How about Nellie?" The older woman grinned up at Nichole and the friendship began to flower. The next day the two women got acquainted. Nichole was stunned when she discovered that Nellie could not read or cipher. "I'll teach you," she offered, deciding that she could return Nellie's assistance with a skill she could surely use.

Nellie was delighted. "Nobody in my family can read," she confessed.

Nellie was bright and she quickly learned to read and write her name. Nichole discovered that the woman was talented with a needle as well and together the two women tackled Nichole's remaining wardrobe. Each morning they sewed. After lunch the fabric was stowed away and a book and a small slate were drawn from Nichole's trunk. After the reading lesson, the women crawled up the ladder and walked around the deck, always under the watchful eyes of the captain.

The next several weeks passed happily for Nichole, and she almost forgot about her attack. Once in a while she dreamed, and the dream would become a nightmare, with Jacques once more ripping her gown from her body. When she cried out in her sleep, Nellie would instantly be at her side, comforting her and holding the frightened girl.

Nichole was shocked when one afternoon as they strolled around the deck, the captain approached them. "I expect to sight land in a day or two." Instantly, Nichole was filled with apprehension. What would happen when she met her husband? All of the fears that had bothered her at the time of her attack came flooding back. Would the captain tell Alexander Dampier what had happened? Would her husband still want her now that she had been touched by another man, or would he set her aside?

That evening Nellie helped Nichole pack her trunk with the new gowns and delicate underdresses they had stitched together. As they worked Nichole kept wiping at the tears that formed.

The next day, Nellie took her aside and handed her a small piece of paper on which she had laboriously lettered her name, her sister's name and the area of Pennsylvania where she was going. "If you and your husband ever come to this Carlisle, you'll know where I am. If you ever need me, you send for me and I'll come," Nellie assured her.

Nichole nodded her head, trying hard to hold back her tears. Of late, her life seemed to be one long series of good-byes. She was overcome with a deep sense of desperation. At least Nellie knew that her sister and her husband wanted her. Nichole had no idea what waited for her at her husband's plantation.

Nichole took a slip of parchment and wrote her name and the name of the plantation on it; then she handed it to Nellie. "I'll be there. If you have a need, if you ever want anything, and it is in my power, I will see that you have it." She took the scrap of paper Nellie had lettered and carefully placed it in one of the books Frere Francis had given her. It was a connection to the only friend she had in this new land.

The next morning, Nichole stood on the deck with Nellie at her side. Together they watched the ship glide into the wharf. They had arrived at the port of Baltimore.

Nichole looked out over the town spread out before her and the hills in the distance. The town was much bigger than she had thought it would be, and even from the ship she could see carriages and people moving rapidly. There was a vitality about the place that amazed her.

She pulled herself up to her five feet, five inches and squared her shoulders. Somehow, she thought, I'll be able to survive here. No matter what her new husband thought, she told herself, she would enjoy the activity of this place. Surely, if he set her aside she could make her own way. Even on the surface she sensed the calm confidence of the people, just by watching them move. She smiled grimly. No matter how her husband greeted her, she would find her place in this new world.

Nichole waited for the rest of the day, but her new husband did not come. At first she didn't give it much thought, but as the day wore on, she grew more and more concerned. Before the evening meal, the captain told her that the storm had brought them into port two days early, and she should not become too concerned if her man did not arrive for another day.

She saw Nellie on her way, then ate the first meal she had taken alone in weeks. That night, as Nichole tossed restlessly in her sleep, her nightmares returned.

She arose with the sun the next morning, and when she glanced in the mirror to arrange her hair, she noticed the dark circles under her eyes. He'll know when he looks at me, she thought. Will he pity me? she wondered. Sitting at her tiny table she tried to eat some of the hard dry biscuits that were available for breakfast. She was too nervous, and she found that she could barely swallow. While she sat in her chair, sipping her tea, she tried hard to get a grasp on her emotions.

Peter Bentley had just arrived in Baltimore when he saw the ship that carried Alex's young wife. He hurried to the gangplank and identified himself to the first mate. He asked about Monsieur Manage and the mate responded, "The captain wants to see you."

Peter frowned. Where was Jacques? Perhaps the man was with the captain, or could it be that he was ill? Peter followed the sailor, his brow wrinkled in a frown. Where was the girl Jacques was bringing from France, the girl Alex would not come to Baltimore to see?

Peter was met at the captain's quarters by the man himself. Peter had to look up at this man, too. He was almost as tall as Henry Dampier had been. He was clean-shaven and pleasant as he insisted that Peter come into his cabin and have something to drink.

After both men were seated the captain handed Peter the papers that had been in Monsieur Manage's possession, including Nichole's certificate of marriage. The captain nervously cleared his throat. "I have bad news for you, several counts." He explained what he believed had happened to Nichole.

Peter's shock silenced both men for a moment. When Peter found his voice he could only murmur, "You must be mistaken. The man was a leech but he was not completely immoral. I cannot imagine him forcing himself on another man's wife." He said no more.

"I assure you, I heard her screams. It was necessary to break down the door to her cabin. I saw myself the damage the man did," he went on and explained in detail what he had seen: the stained sheets, Nichole's appearance and the guilt Jacques exhibited.

Peter was more shaken than he had ever been. "Is the girl all right?" he whispered.

The captain told him about Widow Hutchinson and how he had given Nichole his protection for the remainder of the voyage.

"You have given Monsieur Manage up to the authorities." Peter's question sounded more like a statement than a question, even to him.

"That won't be necessary," the captain stated quietly. "Monsieur Manage was washed overboard during the storm we encountered."

Peter could not help but wonder, Had the man indeed been washed overboard, or was he conveniently pushed?

He didn't press the issue; instead he asked softly, "I would like to tell this Widow Hutchinson how much we appreciate her help. I would like to thank her in Mr. Dampier's stead."

"The widow has already left for the wilderness and to meet her family. If there is nothing more, then I would like to send for Madame, for I know that she is most anxious to leave the ship. Have you seen the girl?" As Peter shook his head the captain grinned. "You are not aware, then, that she is a most beautiful young woman." The man grew quiet as he gazed out over the sea.

Peter grinned; perhaps this might work out, in spite of the fact that Alex was making noises about setting her away from him. "Please, send for the girl. I am ready to go as soon as her things are loaded into the wagon."

A knock on Nichole's cabin door brought her fear to the surface again, and she tried desperately to calm herself. She wasn't very successful, she thought, as her voice broke, *"Oui . . . com . . . come in."*

Jimmy opened the door and grinned at her. "Your husband's man is topside with the capt'n, an' they're waiting for ya. Time to go."

Nichole stared at him. She had no desire to move. Glancing around the cabin, she wondered if there was a place where she might hide. She sensed Jimmy's confusion; then she thought about her reflections only the day before. It did not matter what happened with her husband. She would be able to make her own way, if she had to. Throwing back her shoulders and straightening her back, she drew her head into the air and preceded Jimmy through the door and up the steps to the deck.

Chapter Ten

Nichole gasped. She didn't know what she expected, but the friendly, little man who greeted her was not it. His dark eyes twinkled as he looked at her appreciatively, and she couldn't help smiling back at him. She liked him instantly, and she couldn't say why.

"Madame Dampier, may I present Mr. Peter Bentley. Mr. Dampier has sent him to see you to his plantation," the captain said softly, drawing Nichole's eyes from Peter to himself, then back again.

Peter stepped toward her. "Are you ready, lass? We've a good day of travel before us."

Nichole nodded her head and then turned to thank the captain for bringing her safely to Maryland. As Nichole stood exchanging pleasantries, she caught sight of her trunks being carried down the gangplank to a waiting wagon. In minutes Peter escorted her down that same gangplank and into the wagon.

Peter took the reins and guided the horses around the massive confusion that littered the docks. He started telling her about her new home and about his own wife, Priscilla. "I'm afraid I must tell you some bad news. Before you arrived, Henry himself passed on." He groaned as he noticed the tears filling her eyes. He was not going to be the one to tell her how her benefactor

115

died, even if she asked. But, to his surprise, she said nothing.

Once they had left the bustling port town, they passed the first of the large plantations that marked their passage to Manor House. He tried to explain to her what the plantation system was all about. When she started asking intelligent, thoughtful questions, his mouth dropped open, and he shook his gray head. She seemed to have an excellent grasp of tobacco farming and some of the more important problems facing farmers. He stared at her in disbelief. There was nothing slow about Nichole Dampier, in spite of what Henry and then Alex had said. Peter could hardly contain his enthusiasm; this girl was beautiful, bright and quite a lady. If he knew his Alex at all, this young woman was a perfect mate. He would not be immune to her charms, Peter chuckled. He glanced over at the young woman poised on the seat beside him; she was charming.

They stopped for lunch, and Peter's delight grew. By early afternoon, Nichole had another champion. They had talked about farming, plantations, colonial history, music and France. Nichole confessed to Peter her astonishment watching the citizens of Baltimore as they rushed to their daily tasks. Her apparent appreciation of what she saw endeared her to Peter even more. He was grinning broadly. This young woman would do, she would do nicely.

They were only two hours from Manor House when Peter began to tell her about Prissy. Suddenly, Peter remembered his conversation with his wife the day before. "Have you seen Alex, really looked at him lately? He is despondent. The lad is angry and terribly hurt. That French girl is to blame! He would be happily working his own farm, if it weren't for the likes of that girl! I hope she turns around and goes back where she came from. We don't need her kind here!"

116

Peter lost his happy grin. Prissy had already made her mind up that she wasn't going to like this girl. Maybe, after he explained what had happened to her, Prissy might reconsider. Peter scowled. Prissy seldom changed her mind about anything, even when she was wrong.

Nichole watched Peter's smile dim and change to a scowl. What had she said to affect him so? Had he remembered what the captain had told him? He had been talking about his own wife when his mood had changed. Grimacing, she wondered if he had just realized that Alex would have to set her aside because of what Jacques had done. Her own smile faded, and they rode the last two hours in complete silence.

The sun was setting rapidly, as the wagon bearing Nichole and Peter pulled into the drive that led to Manor House. Speechless, Nichole stared at the huge house. With the sun coloring the sky a bright pink directly behind the building the house looked a fire-breathing demon. The many closely set windows of the lower level glowed with a dim light, reminding Nichole of a picture she had seen once of the mouth of a monster. The long drive, lined with enormous trees, appeared like a dark tunnel leading right to the creature's mouth. Nichole shuddered, then tried to tell herself that it was only a house.

As they got closer, Nichole looked closer at the brick structure and the two smaller wings jutting out from the main section. A cold chill ran down her spine, and Ma Mere's words about burning in hellfires screamed from her memory. The house looked ready to devour her instead of welcome her.

Standing on the crushed-stone walk, she stared up at the door, waiting for someone to come out and welcome them. Peter had come for her, they knew she was coming. Where was someone, anyone? And where was her husband? A feeling of foreboding washed over her, and something told her that she was not welcome. The color faded from her cheeks, and she followed Peter reluctantly up the steps to the large door. She wanted to run away to someplace, anyplace; instead, she stood waiting for Peter to open the door.

Peter pushed the door open and stepped aside so that she could enter. As Peter led the way, Nichole glanced around. The entrance was aglow with candlelight, and she noticed the soft green flowered paper and mirrors hung on either side of the wall to catch the light. There were several closed doors that led from the entryway. Peter moved toward one, opened the door and indicated that she should wait in the room. "I'll find Prissy, you wait here!" Then he was gone.

Nichole couldn't move. Where was everyone? Why was there no one there to welcome her? It was as if they were pretending that she did not exist. Suddenly, she was terrified. What would she do if Alexander Dampier didn't want her? What if no one wanted her?

Peter left to find Prissy. He scratched his head. Where was Alex, and why hadn't anyone come to meet them? The poor girl was already frightened; now she was bound to be panicky. His lips thinned. Sometimes that boy didn't think!

Peter found Prissy in the kitchen. She seemed surprised to see him. "We didn't think you'd arrive until tomorrow. Is the girl here?"

Peter couldn't help but notice the tone of her voice when she slurred the word girl. Prissy was going to be difficult, Peter thought. "She's here," he mumbled. "Prissy, there are some things you need to know. After I've talked to Alex, you and I better have a talk. That girl is not what you think!"

Prissy snarled at her husband, "Where did you leave her? I better take her to her room. I suppose she'll want a full-course meal. I don't have time to wait on her hand

and foot, and you better tell that to Alex when you see him." She wiped her hands on her large white apron and left him standing in the warm, firelit kitchen.

Peter stared at her. Something must have happened while he was in Baltimore. Prissy was bristling like a bantam rooster. He scratched his head. Alex must have let his feelings be known to all of the staff. That spelled trouble for the French girl. Damn, and he had counted on Prissy to make the girl feel welcome, because, for sure, Alex wouldn't.

Prissy opened the door to the parlor, and greeted Nichole without enthusiasm. She led her up the stairs to the room that had been made ready for the girl several weeks ago. "This is your room. You can freshen up in here. There's water in the pitcher." She pointed to the pitcher and bowl in the corner. "I'll be back for you in fifteen minutes; then I'll take you to the dining room so that you can eat."

"I'm not hungry. Please, don't trouble yourself," Nichole answered curtly, trying to hide her fear. "If it is not too much of a problem, I would like some tea. I could have it up here. I don't want to upset the routine of the house."

Prissy snorted. She had already upset the routine of the house. Her lips thinned. This lady, she thought, was already trying to change things. Tea in her room! Never! Food was taken in the dining room. In that instant, Prissy knew that the girl standing before her was going to turn her well-run household into chaos. Prissy glared at Nichole. Why doesn't she just go back to France? she thought. Instead, she snapped, "As you will!" As she marched down the stairs, she mumbled to herself, "That one is a troublemaker, if I've ever seen one."

Peter found Alex in the study. Alex stood quietly staring out the window, and Peter cleared his throat several times before Alex turned around. Peter was startled; the man's mood was beyond gloomy, he thought. He was even less enthusiastic than Prissy. Peter scowled. Was no one going to give the girl a chance?

Peter handed Alex the marriage certificate, and then he quietly explained everything that the captain had told him. He watched the tall young man for some sign of sympathy or compassion. There was none! It was almost as if Alex had expected the news, Peter decided in amazement. "Don't you even care if the poor little thing's been violated? Aren't you concerned about what she's been through?"

Alex just stared at him. Peter turned to leave the room in disgust.

"I want you ready to ride with me to Baltimore, after I've talked to the girl," Alex announced quietly as he turned back to the window.

Peter couldn't keep the shock out of his voice. "Tonight?"

Alex turned back to smile at him grimly. "Yes, tonight. There are things that need to be done."

Peter still couldn't believe his ears. "Tonight?"

Alex lost his patience. "Yes, Peter. Tonight!" he snapped. "Get yourself something to eat and saddle up the horses. There's plenty of moonlight. It's not too cold yet. I want to be in Baltimore by tomorrow morning."

Peter's shoulders slumped forward. The girl didn't have a chance. Just as he reached the doorway, Alex added, "Tell Prissy that I'll talk to the girl as soon as she's eaten."

Peter made his way toward the kitchen. Had Alex lost his mind? he wondered. He wasn't going to consider the girl at all. He had hoped . . . Given enough time a romance might bloom—one could never tell. Peter smiled grimly. Alex couldn't set her aside, not after all the gossip that Peter had heard up and down the coast. Before he died, Henry made sure everyone knew that his son had married the French girl, and that Alex insisted on signing a statement that he was doing so of his own free will. Peter wondered if Alex knew about that.

While Peter was seeing to his own dinner, Nichole was washing up as best she could; then she waited for her tea. After what seemed like hours to Nichole, a young girl with dark skin arrived with a tray. There was tea, a cream pitcher, lemon and sugar and a small plate of tiny cakes. Nichole poured a cup of tea and nibbled at the cakes, even though she found that she had trouble swallowing. Her thoughts spun around in her head.

Certainly, there was no welcome here. She had not even met her husband yet. If he rejected her, she asked herself, whatever would she do? There was no place to go and no way to get back to France. She admitted that she was no longer frightened, she was terrified.

Nichole was jolted out of her thoughts by a soft knock on her door. She looked at the same small serving girl who had brought the tea. "Yer wanted in the study, Ma'am. I'll show ya the way." The girl led Nichole down the stairs, through the swinging doors and into the main part of the house. Nichole glanced around at the rest of the house. She had first been ushered into the parlor to the right, and now the servant was pointing her toward the left. "It's the last door, there, Ma'am," she hissed. "Masta Alex be in da study."

Nichole glided toward the doorway the girl had pointed out. The door was open, and Nichole glanced at the room quickly before she entered. "It's the library," she thought with relief. The wood was dark and the walls were covered with shelves of books. Instantly, Nichole felt some of her tension ease, for here was at least one room she could enjoy.

At first, she didn't notice the man standing in the shadows before the dark window. But as he started to turn she glanced in his direction.

When Monsieur Dampier had first visited her in

121

France, she had wondered about his height, but this man was taller still. Slowly, as he turned around, his hands still clasped behind his back, Nichole gasped. She was stunned, as if someone had punched her in the stomach. Before her stood the most perfect specimen of maleness she could have imaged.

She stared at his dark brown hair curling ever so slightly around his round face. Dark brown eyes seemed to bore into her soul, and his straight broad nose was lifted slightly, giving her the distinct impression that he was arrogant and very stubborn. He was clean-shaven, his full lips were not smiling, and he looked tense. She told herself that his clothes must have been sewn on him, they fitted so perfectly. His shoulders were wide and covered with a coat of dark blue velvet, hanging just past narrow hips.

She glanced at a frill of white lace that covered the neckline of the light blue silk vest he wore. Then she let her gaze drift down his legs, which were covered with breeches of the same light blue as the vest. The breeches were fastened just below his knees, and pure white stockings covered his calves. His thighs and calves were strong, muscular and well formed.

Slowly, she brought her gaze back up to meet those eyes. A deep red colored her cheeks as she realized she was staring at him. She wanted to lower her eyes, but there was something magnetic about him. She couldn't look away, she just couldn't. She felt her knees go weak, and she wondered if she should sit down before she floated to the floor. This surely was not her husband. No woman could ever be so fortunate as to claim this man for her own.

Alex was as stunned as Nichole. Before him stood the most beautiful woman he had ever seen. She was taller than most, and her golden hair hung in soft curls around her face and down her back. It looked like spun silk in the candlelight. Her face was a perfect oval, accented with large, dark round eyes. The small nose above full pink lips was narrow and flared out slightly at the nostrils. Her skin was clear and pale in the soft light. Her neck was long and she was thin, but her full bustline was high and made her small waist look even thinner.

She was gowned in a gray traveling suit that made her look almost fragile. Alex fought an overwhelming urge to protect her. He wondered how she had managed to survive Jacques's savage assault. Suddenly, he was filled with rage over what had happened to her.

He jerked back to the window, angry that he was allowing her visual charms to unman him. What was wrong with him? he asked himself. He had seen beautiful women before, he had even bedded a few. However, he reminded himself, he could not sleep with this woman, and he could not afford to want her. If he so much as touched her, he would be committed to her forever. He did not want to be committed to any woman forever, he repeated silently.

Nichole glanced from Alex's rigid back to the chairs in the room. She was exhausted and not yet ready to deal with the effects the man was having upon her. "May I sit down, sir?" she asked in a soft lilting voice with just a trace of an accent.

Alex whirled around in embarrassment. His second glance was as stunning as his first. She was too beautiful, he thought. "Please, sit down," he murmured in a deep, husky voice. Nichole almost swooned. His voice was as perfect as the rest of him.

Her question reminded him that he needed to offer the amenities of the house. "Have you eaten, is there anything I can get for you?"

She shook her head. "I'm not hungry, thank you. And there is nothing I need."

Alex had rehearsed his conversation with this girl for weeks now, but he admitted there was no way for him to deliver his speech if he had to look at her. He began to pace the floor. He tried three times to start the conversation by clearing his throat. I'm a coward, he berated himself. Somehow, he knew that what he had to tell her would hurt her. He stopped pacing and stared out the dark window. He simply could not look at the lovely creature who according to Robert was his wife.

Finally, he got the words started. He had promised himself that he was going to be honest with the woman, at any cost. "Nichole, my father had some very specific ideas about what his children should and should not do. When we did not agree with him, and that was often, he took things into his own hands. He arranged this wedding." He turned around to look at her pale face in the soft gleam of the candles. Did she understand what he was trying to say? "I did not want a wife; I still don't want a wife." Her gasp stopped him, for a second.

He took a deep breath, for he owed her the truth if nothing else. "My father selected you because you came from a large family. He hoped that I would have a large family also. What he tried to assure was that my heirs and therefore his heirs would be numerous." He glanced over at her, wondering if he was imagining that she had turned very pale. He mumbled as if to himself, "I would never take a wife just so that she could bear me children."

Nichole glared at him. His words belied the fact that he had married her. Perhaps the wedding was not legal. "Are we married, sir, legally married?" she whispered in a confused voice.

Alex turned back to the window. "Yes," he snapped.

Nichole stared at his back, her thoughts bitter. She had left the only home she had ever known to come to this place to be his wife. And now for some reason he no longer wanted her. She had come through too much to be dismissed so easily. If he didn't want her, he could see her returned to France. She stood up and moved toward the door, her voice brisk. "Sir, you feel that you no longer want a wife. Perhaps you were forced to wed. Whatever! You do not want me. I do not believe that I care to stay where I am not wanted. Please, make arrangements for me to return to France!"

Alex was beside her in a second, stopping her movement toward the door. "I've handled this very badly. I'm sorry. I didn't mean to hurt you, but you are my wife, and you cannot return to France."

"Why can't I return to France? You do not want a wife. Set me aside. It has been done before."

Alex grasped her arm tightly. "I can't set you aside!" His temper was flaring. "Such a thing would be scandalous. My father made sure that every creature from Virginia to New York knew that I was willing to wed you. If I set you aside, your reputation, as well as mine, would be ruined. And, France is in the middle of a revolution. It is not a safe place for you."

Nichole raised her chin in the air. "And who are you to worry over my safety?"

Alex glared at her. He was furious. "I'm your husband!" He stomped from the room.

Alex stormed his way into the kitchen. Prissy was sitting with her Peter while he ate his evening meal. "Have you finished talking to the girl?" she asked quietly.

"At least for the present," Alex snapped. "I'm leaving for Baltimore. I should be back in about ten days. Peter is going with me and then on to Frederick. When I have finished in Baltimore, I'll ride on to Frederick and Peter and I will bring Catherine home." Thank God, he told himself, he had had the foresight to send Catherine to the farm for several weeks. "I want you to see that my . . . my . . . that Nichole is kept busy. Give her something to do while I'm gone. And keep an eye on her."

Peter couldn't keep quiet. "Alex, why are you running away from your bride? You don't know anything about her. She is . . ."

Alex interrupted, obviously attempting to control his rage. "I do not want a wife," he answered through clenched teeth. He shouted at Peter, "She was my father's idea, not mine. I'll not live with her. I don't want to know anything about her. As far as I'm concerned, she is little more than hired help. Oh, don't look so shocked, I'll feed her and clothe her, but that's it! I will not live with her!" Alex looked at Peter, wincing at the shocked expression on his face.

Nichole had just left the library, intent on finding the kitchen. What she needed, she told herself, was a hot cup of milk or at least a cup of tea. Perhaps, she thought, the warm liquid would calm her tense nerves. She was close enough to the kitchen to hear every word Alex yelled at Peter. In the gathering gloom, Nichole's shocked face was even more telling. Whirling around, she moved through the swinging doors in a daze. She was nothing but a servant. If that was not hurt enough, the fact that Alex would yell that same information to the other servants was more than she could take.

She staggered up to her room, hurt, confused and frightened. He did not want a wife, but he had married her, and he said she couldn't go back to France. He thought of her as his wife, but she was going to be his servant. She fought the tears that threatened to spill. She would insist that she be sent back to France. That was the only possible solution. She shed her gray traveling suit and pulled her gown over her head. Was all of this misery part of the punishment Ma Mere had mentioned for allowing the little Frenchman to touch her? She wiped at her bitter tears. Of course it was.

Chapter Eleven

Nichole woke up very early the next morning. Struggling from her warm bed, she wandered to one of the two tall windows and looked out over the plantation. It was a cold gray day, a day to match her mood, she thought. She slumped down in one of the chairs in the room and looked around her. It had been too dark last night to see very much of the room.

She gazed at the fine furnishings, her head whirling in confusion. She had never seen such a fine room. This was not the room of a servant. This was a lady's room! The walls were covered with a soft cream-and-yellow floral print. The bed was of very dark wood and was the largest bed Nichole could ever remember seeing. Four people could sleep in it comfortably, she decided. A sudden thought made her panic. Was she to share this room with someone else? A dark matching armoire stood in one corner, and two small chairs faced the fireplace opposite the door. The washstand with the pitcher she had used last night was of fine china, and it repeated the floral design of the walls.

Nichole looked closely at the blinds hanging at the windows. They were wooden slats hanging one above another, and attached to each side was a string. Standing up, she walked back to the window. She played with the cords

127

on either side of the blind. Giggling, she watched as the slats moved up and down as she twisted the cord. Grinning, she turned back to view the room once more. It was a pretty room, much prettier than she expected, but it obviously was a woman's room. This room was not a man's room, she decided. Where did her husband sleep? she wondered.

Slowly, she dressed in one of her new day dresses, brushed her hair and made her way down the stairs, through the swinging doors. She wanted to make a good impression on any of those in the family who might still be present. Waiting for someone to approach her and tell her where she was to go, she looked around. She stood quietly for a long time, and when no one came, she started in the direction of the yelling she had heard the night before.

A short, fat little woman was busy at a long table in front of the fireplace. Her blue eyes twinkled, her hair was completely covered by a plain linen cap, and an immaculate apron covered up most of her dress. She glanced up at Nichole and smiled. "My, don't we look glum this morning. I'm Mrs. Barber. I'm the cook here at Manor House, and you must be Nichole. Where is your fine husband this morning?"

Before she realized it, the words were out of her mouth. "He is not fine and he is definitely not my husband!" She clamped her hand over her mouth and ran from the room. Mrs. Barber stared after the girl, her own mouth hanging open.

"Well, I never," she muttered and went in search of Prissy. "What on earth is going on? What could the girl mean, he is not her husband? Prissy?" she called. "Prissy?"

She found Prissy behind the house, in the shed where the laundry was done. "I want to know what is going on. Nichole ran in and out of my kitchen, shouting about

128

Alex not being her husband. You said . . ."

Prissy interrupted, "Come into the house, we'll have some tea and I'll explain." She glanced over at the black girl who helped with the laundry. "I'll be back in a bit."

As the tea steeped in a big pot, Prissy told Mrs. Barber what Alex had said the night before, adding, "I'm sure it has something to do with Charles duPres. You do remember him, don't you?" When the cook nodded her head solemnly, Prissy continued, "Although he's said nothing, I'm sure Alex didn't want this marriage, and now he's regretting it. You can tell just by looking at him. He said last night the girl is to be a servant. He didn't wait around to explain things to her either, but left last night to get Catherine. He told both Peter and me that he doesn't intend to have a thing to do with her. He expects me," she stressed the "me," "to keep the wench busy!"

Prissy leaned toward the cook and whispered, "I'd sure like to know what she's holding over his head to force her way into this house."

"You mean, Alex didn't want to marry, but you said . . ."

"Oh, he's not admitting to anything, but you only have to look at his eyes to know that he is furious. I tell you, he did not want to marry!"

"He's not happy, you're sure?" she questioned, the concern thick in her voice. She was as devoted to the children as Prissy was. Anything that hurt them or angered them, she was against. Shaking her head, she remembered all the times she had hidden them from their father's rage and the times she had deliberately served meals late to get even with Henry for the trouble he caused.

"If you could only have seen him last night. Why, he could barely talk!"

Mrs. Barber's skin prickled. "Why doesn't he just send her back?"

Prissy leaned her head toward the cook once more.

They had been good friends since the Bentley's arrival sixteen years ago. "She must have a hold on him. There can be no other reason. Perhaps he's waiting for her to ask to be sent back."

The cook smiled slightly. "Do you suppose we might be able to force her hand?"

"What do you mean?" Prissy gazed at the cold gleam in the cook's eyes.

"She obviously came here to be the lady of the house. After all, she was in that fancy French school. The nuns knew she was to be the wife of a wealthy Colonial, and they probably waited on her hand and foot." Prissy nodded and Mrs. Barber continued, "You said you were to keep her busy, didn't you? Well, if we work her hard, convince her that she'll never get the attention she must want while she's here, why, she might insist on going back to France. All we have to do is to give her lots of work and by the time Alex returns, she'll be begging to go back."

Prissy looked a little skeptical. "I'm not sure it will work. Alex might not like it if we work her too hard!"

"I thought you said . . ."

"I did! I just don't want my boy upset more, that's all." Prissy stared off into the fire for several more minutes before she answered, "No, she must go. You're right, of course. I'll put her to work this morning. Christmas is only three weeks away, and the house could use a good cleaning. If she's supposed to work like a servant, Alex can't object if she helps with the work that must be done." Prissy stood to leave the room. She looked back at the cook. "What brought all of these questions about?"

"She marched into the kitchen, very unhappy this morning. She is not at all happy with Alex," the cook repeated Nichole's statement. Both women nodded their heads. Nichole's words confirmed their suspicions. "Alex must have told her he was not going to act like a husband.

If we put her to work, she might even be on her way back to France before the holidays," the cook chuckled.

Prissy made her way up the stairs, to Nichole's room. She knocked on the door and then threw it open. Nichole looked up, her expression one of anger. I'm right, Prissy thought. The girl thinks she is going to be mistress of this house. Well, we'll just see about that. She studied Nichole carefully. "Don't you have anything simpler? That dress is too fancy to clean in." She continued before Nichole could comment, "Alex said I was to keep you busy. Christmas will be here soon, and this house has to be cleaned good before the holidays. As soon as you've changed, come down for your breakfast and we'll get started."

As Prissy left the room, Nichole hurried to the armoire. If she was busy, perhaps she wouldn't have time to think, she told herself. As she hung up the rose silk she had donned, she stopped for a fraction of a second. Christmas was soon; maybe she could convince Alex to send her back to France as a Christmas gift.

She pulled out the dark brown convent dress and remembered how she had insisted Soeur Bernard pack both of her old dresses. She sighed; little did she think she would be wearing them so soon. Buttoning the bodice, she hurried down the stairs. She could use something to eat this morning.

As she walked into the kitchen both Mrs. Barber and Prissy glanced up at her. The amazed look of both women surprised Nichole. She asked softly, "Is this dress not suitable for cleaning?"

"Where did you get that dress?" Prissy asked quietly.

"This is what I wore in the convent," Nichole offered, as she fingered the pleats of the skirt.

The two women looked at each other. The dress was old and worn, but it fit the tall girl too well to have been a hand-me-down.

Prissy asked the question that both women were thinking, "How long were you in the convent?"

As she poured a cup of tea, Nichole breathed softly, "Forever." Busy with the tea, Nichole missed the shocked expression that registered on the face of each woman as they exchanged surprised glances. No one said another word as they ate their meal.

After they broke their fast, Prissy gathered the cleaning supplies and led Nichole to the library. "You'll start here," Prissy told her, handing her the supplies and a list of instructions. Prissy glared at the girl. "Do you have any objections?"

Nichole wanted to object. She didn't want to start in that room, not in the library. The humiliation was still too fresh in her mind, but she said nothing. She took the supplies and the instructions and prepared to begin her role as servant.

All morning, she scrubbed and polished and dusted. She refused to look at the titles as she dusted each book. Perhaps, someday, she would have a chance to read some of them. Two dark-skinned boys showed up after she had started moving furniture, and she gave them the red and green rug to hang on the clothesline. They carried the rug back to the room when she had beaten it clean to her satisfaction. They helped her move the furniture back into place. She thanked them and stood back to look at her work. It was midafternoon, and the library sparkled. She leaned back against the doorjamb and smiled with satisfaction.

Prissy stood in back of her, amazed. The room was perfect. The girl had not stopped except to have a bite of lunch. And she had not complained once. I'm not going to compliment her; I'd lose the advantage. It would defeat our purpose, Prissy thought. As Nichole turned around and spotted the woman, Prissy snarled, "We can't tarry. We have plenty of time. You can start on the parlor yet today."

Nichole breathed a weary sigh and followed Prissy to the parlor, listening to Prissy chant the list of things to be done in this room.

That night, Nichole sank into bed aching from her labors. She had been too tired to eat anything of her dinner. It had been many months since she had cleaned so hard, and her muscles were not accustomed to that much work. Smiling grimly to herself, she thought, "I certainly didn't have any time to think." She closed her eyes and drifted off to sleep immediately.

For the next five days Nichole was up at dawn and after a quick breakfast she started her tasks. She cleaned, polished and scrubbed whatever room Prissy had assigned for the day, frequently working through lunch. Each night she sank gratefully into her bed, not even aware of her hunger, and fell asleep almost before her head hit her pillow. During the day, with little time for adequate meals and with the strenuous work she was doing, she noticed that her dress was getting very loose. She was losing weight and her hands were rough and cracked. She hadn't had a bath since she had been in the house, and she felt filthy and grimy. At least at the convent the good sisters had thought of cleanliness in the same vein as prayers.

She had been at Manor House for a week and a day when everything went wrong. She overslept, and the little dark-skinned girl had to bang on her door to wake her up. "Miz Prissy say ya better be up, Miz."

Nichole shot up out of bed and grabbed her dark brown dress, ran the brush through her hair quickly and struggled into her stockings and shoes. She rushed down to the kitchen for a quick snack and a cup of tea. Both women looked up at her in surprise. For a week, they had paid little attention to her, for she was in and out before they had time to really look at her.

Prissy looked at Mrs. Barber. She's as stunned as I am, Prissy thought. Nichole, Prissy realized, looked haggard.

There were dark rings under her eyes and she was thinner, noticeably so. Her hair even looked stringy, and as she reached for the teapot, both women stared at her raw, red hands. As Nichole grabbed her cleaning materials and rushed to finish the music room she had started the afternoon before, Prissy spoke her concerns out loud: "I don't think Alex is going to like this. She looks like she might be ill. Do you suppose we are working her too hard? She has never complained. I think, tomorrow, she had better help you here in the kitchen. She can clean silver or something."

Mrs. Barber just nodded. She had been even more shocked than Prissy by Nichole's appearance. Why was the girl working so hard? According to Prissy, she had only to scrub the front hall to have cleaned the entire downstairs, all seven rooms, and mostly by herself. Prissy had mentioned yesterday that the girl never complained. The cook wrinkled her forehead in thought. "Do you suppose she is trying to win us over? You know this doesn't make much sense."

Prissy looked over at her perplexed friend. "Something isn't right, but I can't figure it out."

Just then a muffled crash sounded from the music room, and both women rushed in that direction. Nichole was kneeling on the floor, picking up pieces of a small figurine. "I'm sorry. I knocked it over when I moved the table. I don't think it can be fixed. I . . . I . . . can't replace it. I . . . I . . . don't have . . . any money."

Prissy answered first. "Accidents can happen to anyone. Just be more careful." Prissy stared at the girl. Her vivid green eyes were wide with fear and they stood out like dark lamps in a small room. Her whole face radiated alarm. Prissy felt terribly uncomfortable; no, Nichole wasn't trying to win them over.

Mrs. Barber glanced over at Prissy. "I insist that you stop and rest. It's lunchtime, and it's obvious that you've worked too hard. Come on out to the kitchen and I'll fix you something to eat." She took Nichole by the hand and led her toward the kitchen. She tried to catch Prissy's eyes but the woman was still busy picking up the remaining splinters of pottery from the broken figurine.

In the kitchen, Mrs. Barber watched the girl as she fixed a bowl of soup and buttered several pieces of thick bread. Just after she served Nichole, Prissy came to the kitchen table and she and Mrs. Barber sat down across from Nichole, sipping tea.

"Do you have family?" Mrs. Barber asked, trying to draw the girl out.

Nichole sighed, "Yes."

"Are they still living in France?" Prissy took up the questioning.

"I don't know," Nichole murmured.

To each of their questions she softly murmured a yes or no, or an I don't know. She was too tired to carry on any kind of a conversation. And she still had the front entry-way to scrub.

Prissy frowned at her friend; the girl was exhausted. It was a good thing Alex wasn't returning for several days yet. Nichole would have to rest, she thought. "Nichole, with the main floor finished, I think you can rest a day before we start the upstairs. You can sleep in tomorrow. The silver must be cleaned tomorrow and you can do that here in the kitchen with Mrs. Barber."

Nichole picked her head up and gazed at Prissy, her eyes dull and lifeless. She sighed. At least, she thought to herself, I'll be able to sit down to clean silver. Gathering her dishes, she excused herself and grabbed the bucket, with more energy than she felt.

"When you finish the foyer," Prissy said softly, "why don't you rest?" Nichole stared at her, not sure she had heard her correctly. Breaking the figurine should have been an unforgivable offense.

She shrugged and looked down at the pail of warm water in confusion. Grabbing the scrub brush, she trudged back to the hall. She started at the back and worked her way forward. Scrubbing and rinsing, scrubbing and rinsing, then emptying the dirty water, over and over again, she kept her mind busy with her task. She refused to allow herself to think about Prissy, Mrs. Barber, the figurine, or her husband. She worked without a break, trying desperately to finish the loathsome task so that she could rest.

Her face was streaked with dirt, and wisps of hair had fallen down around her face. She brushed them back with her wet hands. The lower half of her dress was soaked and she was tired, oh, so tired. Her hands were red and raw, and at the moment they stung from the hot water she had used to rinse the next to last section of the floor. Sitting back on her heels, she looked at the hallway. There was a section about four feet square to finish, and then she would be able to rest, she told herself.

Grasping the scrub brush, she leaned forward and attacked the last section of wood. Suddenly, the front door was thrown open and Nichole looked at polished black shoes with silver buckles. As her eyes drifted up the tall male form standing before her, the breath caught in her throat. Alex Dampier stood in front of her, and he looked angrier than a man should look. For a brief second, she wondered if she was the source of his rage.

"What the hell?" he muttered as he sidestepped the bucket of water. "What's going on here? And what in God's name are you doing?" he yelled.

Nichole bristled. He had no right to yell at her. She was only cleaning his house. Servants were hired to clean and that's what she was doing. And he was keeping her from finishing the job she wanted done at all costs. "I'm scrubbing your floor. If you will get out of my way, I will finish!" Nichole glared up at him from her knees.

In a voice of deadly calm, Alex said, "My wife does not

.scrub floors!"

Rage shot through Nichole. First, she was his wife, then she was a servant, and now, again, she was his wife. "I wish you'd make up your mind," Nichole barked at him, getting up from her knees. "What do you want from me?" She folded her arms in front of her, the scrub brush still in her hands.

Alex stared at the bedraggled figure before him. If it was possible, she was thinner. She had lost considerable flesh, but why? She was wearing a dirty dark brown dress that hung from her shoulders, and her face was streaked with dirt. Her beautiful hair was stringy and lifeless, and it was straggling from a bun at the back of her head. What on earth had been going on? She couldn't meet Catherine looking like that! "Go to your room and clean yourself up," he snapped.

Nichole felt something in her snap. "Oh . . ." she screeched and threw the scrub brush at his head. Then she stomped off up the stairs as she heard Alex yell, "Prissy!"

137

Chapter Twelve

"Oh, Good Lord," Prissy grimaced, "Alex is home!" She dropped her teacup and ran toward the front of the house. She rushed up to him to explain. "I didn't think you would be home for several days yet. Where is Peter? Didn't you get Catherine?" She looked over his shoulder.

"Catherine is right behind me, Peter is waiting for me in Baltimore. Now, what is going on here? I brought Catherine back to meet my wife!" He glared at his house-keeper, "Why was she down on her hands and knees, scrubbing the floor?"

Prissy stuttered, "B-b-but, you said I should keep her busy."

"Keep her busy? Good heavens, what did you tell her to do? She looks terrible."

Prissy bristled. Was he blaming her for the wench's appearance? "She has only been cleaning. The holidays are almost here, and we cleaned the house. This floor was the last thing to be done." She pointed to the wooden floor of the entry.

"She looks like she cleaned the whole thing herself," Alex snapped.

"Well, she did have a little help." Prissy glared at the young man towering over her. He had told her to keep the girl busy, hadn't he? He said she was to work as a servant.

It wasn't her fault that Nichole worked like a demon.

Alex looked suspicious. "How much has she done?" he asked a little more quietly.

"Nat and Samuel did some of the heavy work," she explained, "but she did the rest of this floor by herself." Thinking that Alex would be pleased, she added, "She has done a fine job, too."

Alex stared at the woman. "Every room?" He didn't bother to keep the surprise and amazement out of his voice. Prissy nodded, and Alex fought to keep his anger under control. "I know you meant well, but my WIFE is not a slave. You've treated her like one. She looks like she might be ill. How can she meet Catherine looking like that? She is to do no more of this kind of work. Is that clear?"

Prissy looked up at him in surprise. "But you said she was a servant. What was I to think? You don't want her, send her back!"

Alex clenched his fists and glowered at Prissy. Ignoring her comment, he ordered, "Have Maude take up the tub and hot water so that she can have a bath. I suppose I'd better go up and apologize." As he headed for the stairs, he mumbled, "My wife, and she's down on all fours, scrubbing the floor."

Mrs. Barber had followed Prissy at a discreet distance, and as she turned to do Alex's bidding, Mrs. Barber asked, "What do you make of that?"

Prissy took her anger out on Mrs. Barber. "This whole thing was your idea. I should have told him that. I won't take the blame for your plan."

The cook glared at her friend and folded her arms over her heaving chest. "Oh? You were very agreeable when we first talked. You were the one who said she wasn't wanted. You are more at fault than I!" In sixteen years, this was the first time Mrs. Barber could remember that she and Prissy had argued. She'll not force me from my position, she told herself, then pointed a plump finger in Priscilla Bentley's face and jeered, "And you can just stay out of my kitchen!"

Alex was on the way to his room and never heard the women arguing. He decided to wait until Nichole had a chance to calm down and take a bath before he talked to her. He threw himself into one of the chairs before the empty fireplace and stared at the pile of ashes left from the last fire. He tried to recall just what he said to Prissy before he left. For the life of him he could not remember the conversation. He knew he mentioned something about not wanting a wife and that he was very angry, but had he truly said she was a servant? He would have to talk to Peter when he got back to Baltimore.

He made his way down the hall to Catherine's room. He checked to make sure all of her things had been delivered to her before he went back downstairs to his study for a large glass of whiskey. After he took a deep drink, he smiled to himself. The whiskey got better as it aged, and it was all his. He had made a batch after the harvest last year, and the quality was surprising. If the tobacco and cotton ever gave out, he chuckled, he could always sell his whiskey.

He settled himself in his chair and looked around the room. It was sparkling. Nichole had done a nice job with the cleaning. Then he frowned. Whatever would he say to her to undo the damage Prissy had caused? He sighed as he took another swallow. For the last seven days he had thought of little else but Nichole. He had not expected her to be such a beautiful woman. And he couldn't understand his reactions to her. He wanted her! But of all the women he knew, this was one woman he couldn't afford to want. Perhaps, he told himself, he felt the way he did because she was out of bounds. He took another sip from the glass and sighed loudly.

Sitting on the edge of her bed, Nichole realized that she

was as close to tears as she had ever been in this house. He had screamed at her for scrubbing his floor and then ordered her up to her room like a small child. Alex must hate her to speak to her like that. The housekeeper and the cook had also made their feelings very clear; they didn't like her at all. She choked on a sob.

A loud knock startled Nichole, and she took a wavering breath before she called out, "Yes? Who is it?"

"Miz, I's got yer bath water," Maude shouted back.

Nichole opened the door and stared at the dark-skinned girl holding two full buckets of steaming water. "I didn't ask for a bath," Nichole muttered, as she looked at the girl. Maude, she had learned, was a slave. At least, she thought, she knows she's a slave. I'm being treated like one, but no one seems to know just what I'm supposed to be. Another sob stuck in her throat.

One of the boys who had helped Nichole with the heavy furniture when she cleaned followed Maude into the room with the tub. In less than five minutes the large brass tub stood misting before the fireplace, but Nichole just sat on the edge of the bed. She had no strength to take a bath. As she sat staring at the mist rise, tears coursed down her cheeks. She couldn't help the tears. That glorious bath of steaming water was hers and she hadn't the energy to use it. It was as cruel as waving a chicken leg before a starving man.

After a half an hour, Alex decided that Nichole had had time to finish her bath and change, and he moved toward the stairs reluctantly. He would have to keep his temper in check, he told himself as he strode to her door. It wouldn't do, he reasoned, to yell at her anymore, not when he was supposed to be apologizing. He stood outside her door for several minutes, listening for any sounds that might indicate she had not finished her bath. The only noise he heard was from his sister, singing, happily helping Maude put away her clothes. He frowned; if he had let Peter bring Catherine back as he had originally planned, he would not be in this position now.

He knocked gently on Nichole's door and waited for the door to open or an invitation to be offered. When there was no response, he called softly, "Nichole?" and tapped on the door once more.

A soft muffled voice pleased, "Go away."

He tried the door and pushed against it. It opened and he stood in the doorway directly across from the empty tub. Thank God, she was finished with her bath, he sighed. Stepping into the room he glanced over at the the bed. Sitting on the edge, still clothed in that filthy dark dress, was his wife. Her face was still dirty and her expression was of such sadness that he felt his heart twist in his chest. What had they done to her? What had he done to her? He closed the door and moved toward her. Something was wrong. She seemed dazed, almost as if she were in a trance. She must be ill.

When he moved to stand directly in front of her, she glanced up at him, her enormous dark green eyes sparkling with her tears. He could see some of the sparkling bits of moisture resting on her incredibly long golden lashes. Fighting an overwhelming urge to take her in his arms and beg her forgiveness, he looked away. From somewhere deep inside, he could almost taste a desire to promise her the world if she would forgive him. He straightened his shoulders. What on earth was wrong with him? He didn't want a wife.

"Nichole, there has been a terrible misunderstanding," he whispered in a husky voice. She looked away, almost as if he hadn't spoken. Was she too tired or too sick to make any sense out of what he was saying? he wondered. He glanced over at the full tub of clear water. The soap and sponge rested on the floor. She hadn't taken a bath, and the water was probably cool by now. Once more, he glanced at her; she was obviously too exhausted to bathe.

For a moment he stood in indecision. She had to have a bath, and if she couldn't bathe herself, someone else would have to do the scrubbing. But Mrs. Barber was the cook, Prissy didn't seem to like the girl, the slaves were too young and he certainly couldn't ask his sister to wash his wife. No, if she was too tired to bathe, he would have to see the job done himself. After all, some of her condition was due to misunderstandings he had created. And she was still his wife.

He left the room and moved to Catherine's door. "Sis," he called affectionately, "open the door." When the door was pulled open, he said quietly, "You'll have to wait until tomorrow to meet your new sister-in-law. She's cleaned the house and she is too tired to talk right now. I'll introduce you two tomorrow."

Catherine looked at Alex, amusement twinkling in her steel gray eyes. Peter had spent several days at the farm with her before he left for Baltimore. He had told her all about Nichole. She mumbled, "That's fine," and turned quickly to keep from laughing in his face. Her marvelous brother was really not too bright. He was really taken with the girl, only he didn't want to admit it to himself or to anyone else, yet. It was perfectly obvious to her that he wasn't ready to share Nichole. Catherine felt bubbly with excitement.

Alex turned to leave and added, "I'll need Maude for a few minutes." He walked back toward Nichole's room, giving instructions as he moved. "Maude, fetch more hot water and take some of the cold water out of the tub. I'll need several towels, and bring the decanter and two glasses up from the study," he ordered.

The black girl ran off to get the buckets and the decanter. She, too, was grinning as she went. Catherine had asked lots of questions about Nichole, and Maude had offered her opinion. She liked the French girl, no matter what Miz Barber and Miz Priscilla said. She was nice to work for and she worked harder than any of the slaves. She'll make a wonderful mistress, Maude clucked to herself as she went down the stairs. She might even need a lady's maid. Miz Catherine shore didn't want one. Maude grinned; that was her secret desire, to be a lady's maid, and if she made herself invaluable to Nichole — well, time would tell.

In minutes, Maude was back with the empty buckets and the whiskey; then, after she ordered more hot water, she returned to Catherine's room. The two girls, only several months apart in age, whispered and giggled about what was happening in the room down the hall.

Pouring a small amount of whiskey into one of the glasses, Alex handed it to Nichole with the order to sip it slowly. She took the glass without a glance at him and raised it cautiously. While he watched her sniff the liquid, he poured himself a glass, and raising the glass, he said softy, "Go on, try a bit."

Nichole took a sip, and as she started to swallow her eyes snapped open wide. She gasped, then choked and sputtered before she pushed the glass toward him. "No! Are you trying to poison me?" she whispered in a husky voice.

Alex tried not to sound hurt. "No, only fortify you for your bath."

Nichole finally looked at him with recognition. "I'm too tired to bathe. Go away."

Nichole, you are filthy, and you need a bath. I know you are tired and that's why I'm going to bathe you."

Startled, she glanced away, her facing turning a delightful scarlet as she blushed from her head to her toes.

"It's all right," Alex tried to reassure her. "After all, I am your husband."

Nichole's head was spinning and she glared at him. He had already told her he didn't want a wife, but every chance he got, he reminded her of his relationship to her.

144

Her chin came up ever so slightly, and with a little quiver she muttered, "You don't want a wife!"

"Well, I may not want one, but I have one, and right now she needs a bath, and she's too tired to bathe herself."

Alex sat in his dark study, glaring at nothing. How could he have been so stupid? He had wanted to help her, take care of her. He had forgotten how really beautiful she was. There was something about her that caused the most insane reaction in him. It had happened the first time he saw her. He had forgotten that as well.

He had never been through such a torturous experience in his life. He was still aching with desire. How on earth he had kept himself out of her bed, he would never know. And she had had the effrontery to drift off to sleep just as soon as her head touched the pillow. He doubted if she even remembered the soft kiss he had placed on her lips before he left her.

How could she torture him like that? Surely, she knew what she was doing to him. There was no way he could stay to see her in the morning. He had to get away before she awoke. He would probably not stop hurting for weeks as it was. Taking another deep drink from his glass, he made his plans. He would tell Catherine that he had to leave first thing in the morning, at dawn. She would have to introduce herself to Nichole.

Trying to force the thoughts of Nichole out of his head, he took another long pull from the glass. There was no help for it. What had transpired in her room would haunt him for days, weeks, perhaps years. Suddenly, he was reliving the minutes after he had insisted that she take another sip of the deep amber liquid. She took several small swallows then refused to sip any more. After he laid out the towel and soap, he moved to her bed to undress her. She had not cooperated, but she had not fought him either. It was as if she no longer cared if he removed her filthy clothes.

Had it been when he removed the chemise, or when he picked up up in his arms to carry her to the tub, that the wave of indescribable desire staggered him? She had a perfect figure, those high, full breasts, a tiny waist and long graceful legs. He tried desperately to ignore the golden triangle of soft curls between her thighs. He wanted her, he wanted her so badly he was in pain. He tried to keep his mind a blank, he really tried. He groaned as he remembered.

Washing her face and hair had not been too difficult. He had regained some of his control by that time. He remembered that he had been all right as he washed her graceful arms and her back. When he worked the warm sponge over her breasts and saw the nipples distend—oh, God, why was he torturing himself?

He had finished as quickly as he could and lifted her from the tub. She clung to him, and as he dried her carefully, he tried to ignore her softness, her feminine curves. He got a chemise on her as quickly as he dared and nearly dumped her in her bed. For some reason, he had not been able to resist brushing a soft kiss on her lips before he left her. She was fast asleep before he left the room.

He cursed himself as he mounted the steps to his own bedroom. He was a grown man, surely he could deny himself one French girl, even though she was perfection in itself and legally his wife. He had vowed not to touch her and here he was drooling over her like some young whelp. Why? he questioned as he moved toward his door. Why this girl and no other?

He slept poorly and was up before dawn, dressed and ready to leave. As he slipped into Catherine's room to explain, he noticed the sky growing pale in the east.

"Catherine, Catherine," he shook her gently until he heard her groan. "Catherine, are you awake?" he whispered.

Raising herself up on one elbow, she glared at him. "I am now! What are you doing here? Why aren't you in bed where you belong? It isn't morning yet!"

"Catherine, I have to leave now. Nichole will probably sleep very late. Let her sleep! When she wakes up I want you to introduce yourself and see that she's comfortable. Will you do that for me, please?"

Catherine grinned up at her brother. So, Nichole would be sleeping late. She giggled. Her brother must have kept her awake all night. Sighing, she thought about an entire night of love in a man's arms. I'm a hopeless romantic, she said to herself. "You go on, I'll take care of Nichole. Hurry back though. Christmas is coming," she said softly.

Alex left quietly and made his way to the kitchen. Mrs. Barber was busy banging pots and pans. She is certainly in a disagreeable mood, Alex thought as she snapped at him, "Your lunch is packed." He poured a cup of coffee for himself and left the kitchen to find Prissy. Prissy was at the other end of the house, giving orders to a group of sleepy slaves. The slaves were never up this early. He turned to glance back at Prissy.

She's as upset as the cook, Alex decided as he watched her scowl at the servants. "Prissy, don't let Nichole do any more cleaning. Just let the two girls, Nichole and Catherine, get acquainted while I'm gone," he stated. He glanced at the woman he had known for sixteen years. The glare she sent his way would have frightened the average man. Alex retreated to the kitchen, left his coffee cup and made his way to the stables. "Women!" He would never understand them.

Riding away, he tried to push Nichole and the other two disagreeable females that lived in his home from his mind. He and Peter were to clear up his father's business endeav-

147

ors that remained in the office and apartment of Jacques Manage. Concentrating on the job at hand, Alex urged his horse forward.

Minutes after Alex charged from the house, Catherine was out of bed. She dressed quickly and hurried downstairs. On her way to the kitchen, she passed Prissy in the hall. Prissy refused to look her way. "Well, my goodness, what is wrong with her," Catherine mumbled. In the kitchen, Catherine decided that Mrs. Barber seemed angrier still. Catherine glanced at the cook. Both women were certainly disagreeable this morning. She wondered for a second if Nichole had made them angry; then, remembering what all Peter had said, she grinned. She knew that Nichole couldn't upset anyone, not and be the sweet, intelligent girl Peter claimed she was. No, Alex must have said something to spoil their day.

Catherine waited impatiently for Nichole to rise, but when she was still abed at lunchtime, Catherine decided that the French girl had slept long enough. Maude had already told her how hard Nichole had worked, but noon was long enough to sleep, she thought. Surely, she didn't need that much sleep to recover from a night of loving. She fixed hot chocolate and some of the tiny cakes that Mrs. Barber had baked that morning and headed up the stairs to the guest room. Gingerly, she knocked on Nichole's bedroom door.

Nichole was already awake when Catherine knocked. She had stayed in her warm bed, trying to remember all that had happened the night before. She knew that she had been too tired to bathe, but Alex had come to her room and insisted. He had mentioned a misunderstanding and then had given her the bitter liquid that burned when she tried to sip it. She was sure that she had denied being his wife once again, but he had said that she was. Had he undressed her and bathed her, as if she were a little child? Surely not. She blushed at the suggestion. Had he kissed

148

her, his lips brushing hers, or had that been her imagination? When had he left? She couldn't recall. Glancing over at the big bed, she realized that there was no indication that anyone but her had been in the bed. Alex must have put her to bed and left the room. How on earth was she going to face him now? And who was this Catherine that she was supposed to meet?

The knock on the door frightened Nichole for a moment. She glanced at the mantel clock. Prissy was probably angry because she had slept so late. She remembered that she was supposed to clean the silver. Yes, the cook and Prissy were probably furious with her. She jumped out of bed and rushed to the door.

Standing at the door with a tray in her hands was a tiny girl about three or four years younger than Nichole. She seemed completely at ease.

Nichole looked at her, sure that she had not seen the girl at Manor House before. Nichole stared at dark gray eyes and light brown hair. The girl was not beautiful but quite attractive with a smile that lit up her whole face, especially her eyes.

"Hello, I'm Catherine, Alex's sister. I've brought hot chocolate so we can get acquainted. I couldn't wait a minute longer for you to wake up."

Chapter Thirteen

Nichole just stared at the girl. His sister? Vaguely, she remembered that Henry Dampier had mentioned that there were two children, but no one had said a word about Catherine since she had arrived.

Catherine giggled. "No one even told you that Alex had a sister, did they?"

Could Catherine tell how surprised she was? Nichole wondered. Why hadn't someone told her about the girl before now? Nichole shook her head and stepped back so that Catherine could enter. She bounded through the door, and Nichole gasped. What energy she had!

Catherine set the tray on the table, turned around and looked at Nichole critically. "I can see why he changed his mind. You're gorgeous."

Nichole blushed. "Why, thank you. But who changed whose mind?"

Catherine giggled again. "Well, Alex of course. He originally said he wouldn't have anything to do with you, but he brought me back to meet you and he stayed the night with you, didn't he?"

Nichole turned scarlet. "He . . . he . . . doesn't want a wife and he did not stay the night with me," she whispered.

"Oh, I'm sorry. Really, it's none of my business."

Catherine looked truly dismayed. "I'm such a romantic. He seemed to want to spend the night with you." Realizing that she was only making matters worse, Catherine turned back to the tray. "I should have minded my own business. If you want me to leave just say so."

Nichole looked startled. "No, please, I would like for you to stay." She glanced at the door. "But I have work to do. Can we talk later?"

Catherine smiled. "Alex said we were to get acquainted and you are not to do any more work. Do you know, Nichole, I have always wanted a sister. I think I'm going to love having a sister." She poured the hot chocolate and handed Nichole a cup, grinning, her embarrassment forgotten. "I'll tell you all about me, if you'll tell me all about you."

Nichole laughed. "I think I'm going to like having a sister. But there isn't much to tell about me. Let's start with you."

And Catherine did. She and Nichole spent the day talking. Catherine told her about growing up in Manor House and the return of her brother. She described the farm in Frederick and told Nichole some of the things that Henry Dampier had tried in his attempt to control Alex's life.

Nichole had a hard time reconciling the father that Catherine described to the man she remembered. Ma Mere had often painted Monsieur in the most glowing terms, not the selfish man that Catherine was characterizing. Nichole whispered softly, "He was a generous man to me. He paid for my education, my clothes, everything I needed. He brought me here."

"And did you have a choice? Weren't you told that you would first be a governess and then that you had to marry Alex?" Catherine snapped as she watched Nichole's stunned expression, "See what I mean?"

By the end of the week, Nichole and Catherine were

good friends. Catherine found that she adored Nichole just as she idolized her brother, and she decided that Alex and Nichole were perfect for each other. She discounted everything Alex hinted at and the things Peter told her of his conversations with Alex.

Nichole was enchanted with Catherine, and as they became better acquainted she told Catherine about the convent, the trip to Maryland, even about the night Alex gave her a bath. The only thing she didn't relate was the attack by Jacques Manage. For some reason, Nichole found that she couldn't talk about that.

Catherine spent just enough time with both Prissy and Mrs. Barber to determine that they both disliked Nichole to an extreme. She spent time with each woman and got them to admit their plans and why they were no longer talking to each other. "I can't believe it," Catherine mumbled. "When Alex gets back, I'll give him a piece of my mind. Nichole almost killed herself cleaning his house and he rides off to Baltimore without a word. A wife should not have to clean the way she did. She should direct the cleaning." The more Catherine thought about it the angrier she became, but she held her tongue. Alex should be the one to tell Nichole what the women had done and why, when he apologized to her. "And he will apologize. I'll see to it," she muttered.

Catherine insisted that Nichole practice her music, and she personally accompanied Nat and Samuel up to the attic to bring down the fairly new harp that was purchased with Nichole in mind. Catherine even dragged Nichole out to the stable. Nichole, Catherine said, had to learn to ride a horse.

There were some tense moments the first time Nichole got up on a horse, but by the end of the second week, Nichole was not uncomfortable in a sidesaddle. She liked animals, and Catherine had chosen a gentle creature that sensed Nichole's affection. They got on quite well.

152

Nichole, in return for the riding lessons, spent time helping Catherine reconstruct several of the dresses that Catherine described as childish. An expert at embroidery, Nichole showed Catherine how to trim her own chemises with the tiny rosebuds that she admired so on Nichole's undergarments. As the days sped by, both girls developed a genuine affection for each other. Anxiously, they waited for Alex's return.

Two weeks before, Alex had raced for Baltimore, more frightened than he had ever been. By the time he arrived in Baltimore, he admitted that he was infatuated with the girl. For one thing, he couldn't get her out of his mind. He relived that bath over and over in his head. Placed in that same situation again, he would be guilty of raping his own wife, he was sure.

When he arrived at the Three Corner Hat Inn late that first afternoon, Peter was supposed to be waiting for him. But Peter wasn't at the inn. He had, though, left a message that he would be at Robert's town house and Alex was to come there as soon as he arrived. Why the town house instead of the office? Alex wondered as he headed across town. Had Robert found out something that required immediate action? Part of him prayed that that was the reason, and another part of him, something deep inside, argued, Leave things as they are.

When Alex arrived, Robert's man met him and directed him to the library. Peter and Robert were sitting in front of a warm blazing fire, enjoying brandy. Robert's foot was heavily bandaged and propped up on a footstool. He glanced up at Alex with laughter in his hazel eyes. "I may be a good lawyer, but I don't believe I'm much of a horseman. I got trampled last Friday. She was the sweetest filly." Alex joined in the laughter, glad to ease some of his tension.

Peter excused himself and went to see to the horse,

leaving Robert and Alex to their discussion. He had answered Robert's questions about Nichole, but despite the temptation, he told the lawyer very little. He chuckled; Robert had asked his opinion a dozen times. Pausing, he grew more serious. Alex would want to offer his own comments without Peter's words to confuse the issue, of that he was sure.

Alex wasted little time telling Robert about Nichole and the work she had done the first week she was at the plantation. He avoided telling Robert what he thought of the girl and chose to discuss what Prissy had said and what kind of condition the girl was in when he arrived with Catherine.

Robert smiled to himself. He wondered if Alex realized that he was as taken with the girl as he seemed to be. Robert made a mental note to get Peter alone so that he could talk the older man into offering more information than the scant amount he had given when he first arrived.

Robert grinned at Alex and thought, I'll test the waters a bit. Quietly, he said, "If you still want me to pursue an annulment, I will." Robert was delighted with Alex's stunned expression, then added, "Of course, the scandal would ruin you and the girl. I still have to advise against it, but I'll do whatever you want." Robert wanted to laugh at the relieved look on Alex's face. Robert chuckled to himself and thought, You've met your match, my friend.

Alex gazed up at the ceiling for a time, trying to drag the correct response from the beams. "I'm not sure what I should do. I don't want a wife. The girl is exquisite, but I don't need that responsibility just yet. Besides, she was my father's choice. However, Jacques must have hurt her and she hasn't fared too well at my house either. I hate to hurt her any more."

Robert took his cue from Alex's hesitation. "Well, you certainly can't send her back to France. The news from

154

there is looking worse each day. Many of our people are for the peasants, but those same peasants are taking over the castles and chateaus of the nobility and destroying whatever remains. I have a friend who just returned from a visit, and he feels that it's more like mob action than a revolution. There's talk of nationalizing all of the church property, and he expressed the opinion that the queen and king are not safe, not safe at all." Robert waved his brandy glass in Alex's direction. "There is no question. Nichole cannot be returned to France, not now! Perhaps never."

Alex stared at him and Robert suggested softly, "Why don't you wait for a bit. She isn't going anyplace. Neither are you. You can afford to wait for several months before you make any decisions."

Alex groaned. "What if . . . I . . . I can't stay away from her? What then?"

Robert's eyes flew open wide. For Alex to even consider such a possibility was staggering and more telling than he knew Alex was willing to admit. He answered softly, "Alex, she is your wife!"

Robert changed the subject and told Alex about the judicial system that the new congress had established. Alex teased him about becoming a new judge and moving on to New York. "Not until I learn more about horses," Robert laughed.

Their conversation drifted to the holidays, and Robert admitted that his parents had gone to Philadelphia to spend Christmas with his sister and her family. "I'll be staying here with this foot."

Immediately, Alex insisted that Robert accompany Peter and him back to Manor House for several days. "You shouldn't have to spend Christmas alone," Alex murmured.

"I wasn't asking for an invitation," Robert mumbled. It

occurred to him suddenly that Alex might be afraid to face Nichole by himself. He wanted to chuckle. Just the thought was ridiculous. Alex was a grown man and in control of himself. Surely, he would not be timid around an educated french mademoiselle.

"Will you, perhaps, be having a New Year's Eve party to introduce Nichole?" Robert asked. Alex only glared back at him.

"I take it you will accept my invitation?" Alex snapped. "We'll return on the twenty-first, if Peter and I can clear up the mess Jacques left of my father's affairs."

Robert grinned. "I've no place else to go and I can't wait to meet your young wife."

Alex spent the next week trying to sort out all of his father's dealings with Jacques Manage. One afternoon, Alex came upon a small piece of paper. "Peter?" Alex looked up from the massive secretary. "Did you know that Monsieur Manage changed his name?" Peter looked up from his packing, but shaking his head, he said nothing. Alex paused. "His name was Menace. He changed the 'e' to an 'a' and the 'c' to a 'g'." Peter only shrugged his shoulders. "It's no wonder: Menace in French means threat," Alex volunteered. "I wonder if this is legal," he mused aloud.

They had been in Baltimore for almost ten days when Alex had dinner with Robert. He asked him about the name change. Robert laughed. "It might mean something, and then again it might not."

"Oh, you lawyers," Alex laughed. "Is nothing ever black or white to you?"

By the twentieth, Alex had closed most of Jacques's books. The man, it seemed, had worked exclusively for Henry Dampier and himself, and although he kept poor records, Alex wondered at the large deposit of moneys Jacques Manage had received just before he left for

France. In the rush to close all of the accounts, Alex forgot about the name change.

The day before he planned to leave Baltimore, Alex left the meager office of his father's former employee and traveled to one of the better jewelers. He purchased a small broach for Catherine and a long strand of matched pearls, something she reminded him of almost daily while they were at the farm. He had failed to buy them for her birthday and she told him that pearls were the only thing she wanted for Christmas.

Alex noticed a set of emeralds nestled on a bed of white satin. There was a pair of earrings, a broach and a ring and they were just the color of Nichole's eyes. The jeweler assured him that if the young woman for whom they were intended needed a smaller or a larger ring, it could be adjusted. Alex purchased the emeralds, and even as he made arrangements to pay the proprietor, he felt foolish. Why was he buying jewelry for a woman who he insisted was not going to share his life?

Alex was more than ready to return home. He told himself that he was melancholy because of all the digging and searching he and Peter had done at the office, and that everything they had touched reminded him of his father. The last night, back in his bed in the Three Corner Hat Inn, Alex knew he had been lying to himself. He wanted to see Nichole. She and Catherine would be well acquainted by now, and he wondered what Catherine thought of the French girl. Visions of Nichole, wet and warm from her bath, invaded his thoughts, and once more he found he couldn't sleep. He fought the desire to rush home, take her in his arms and hold her, protect her, care for her. "My God," he mumbled, "what has the vixen done to me?"

The next morning, Peter and Alex descended on Robert's town house. Alex was disgusted to find that his friend was not ready to travel, but he was more disturbed when he found that Robert and the luggage would require a coach, something he hadn't even considered. There was no way that Robert could sit a horse with his foot bandaged as it was. Damn it all, but a coach meant all kinds of delays. And it would take hours longer.

Peter managed a carriage and they had everything loaded by noon. Alex grudgingly admitted that they would have to stop for the night, for there was simply not enough time to travel the distance in the few daylight hours left. As Alex fumed, Robert and Peter glanced at each other often. He was too anxious to get home, both men silently agreed.

Early the next morning, Alex sent Peter on ahead. He could reach Manor House before lunch and warn Catherine, Nichole and Priscilla that they would be having a guest for the holidays. Alex mumbled instructions to Peter about a guestroom being prepared, and a goose with all the trimmings, and sent Peter on his way. Struggling to keep his own emotions under control, Alex rode silently beside the coach.

Peter arrived at Manor House before lunch, as Alex had estimated. But Nichole and Catherine, waiting impatiently, were disappointed when they heard one horse head for the stables. Catherine raced out to see what had happened, and Nichole tiptoed up to her room. It was evident, at least to Nichole. Alex would not be there for Christmas. Catherine would be so disappointed, Nichole thought, and she blamed herself. "Poor little sister, she'll even lose the brother she loves so dearly, all because of me."

Nichole sat quietly on the edge of her bed, wondering how she would explain to Catherine that Alex had deserted them when she heard Catherine's happy squeal. "Nichole, Nichole! They're coming! They'll be here soon!"

Nichole opened her door and watched Catherine dash up the stairs. "Who's coming, who will be here soon?"

"Alex is coming and he's bringing his friend, the lawyer from Baltimore. We have a guest coming for Christmas." Catherine grabbed Nichole's hand and pulled her down the hall. Nichole laughed at her exuberance. Catherine chattered happily, "We have only three hours to see to the guestroom and the food, and . . ."

Nichole backed away ever so slightly. "I'm sure Peter has already told Prissy. She will see to the room and the food."

Catherine stopped and turned around to look at her sister-in-law. "Oh, Nichole," she sighed. She clenched her fists and placed them on her hips. "When are you going to start acting like the mistress of this house?"

"Like the mistress of the house? What do you mean?"

Catherine clucked her tongue and led the girl toward the study. "Come on! I think we need to talk about Madame Dampier!"

For the next hour Catherine outlined the duties and responsibilities of a plantation mistress. Only once did Nichole object. "I can't tell Prissy what to do and Mrs. Barber what to cook!"

"Oh, yes you can!" Catherine snapped. "Are you madame Dampier or not?"

"I'm not sure who I am," Nichole mumbled, but Catherine continued as if Nichole had not uttered a sound.

After the lecture, Catherine went with Nichole — for moral support, she said — as Nichole faced Prissy. "Catherine tells me that Peter says we have a guest arriving with my hus . . . husband." Catherine gave her a reassuring push, and Nichole asked softly, "Is the guest room pre . . . prepared?"

Prissy stood, stunned, before the questionable mistress

159

of Manor House. She could only nod. Whatever had gotten into the girl? Prissy wondered. Had Catherine decided that the wench should begin to take her place as mistress? Well, we'll just see about that! Prissy thought to herself.

Nichole was so pleased with her meeting with Prissy that she felt confident enough to tackle Mrs. Barber by herself. While Catherine waited for her in the study, Nichole went into the kitchen. Her greeting from Mrs. Barber was anything but cordial. The woman glared at her, and Nichole felt her confidence starting to slip. She smiled and attempted to explain what she was doing in the kitchen. "Mrs. Barber, Alex is bringing a guest for the holidays. I . . . I . . . might want to look at the menus."

Mrs. Barber bristled. "You've liked the meals so far, ain't ya."

Nichole tried, "Yes, but, I . . . I . . ."

The woman snapped, "Well then, get out of my kitchen. You can be sure that I ain't gonna shame Mr. Alex."

"I tried to assert myself," she told Catherine a few minutes later, "but she pushed me out of the kitchen."

Catherine bristled. "We'll wait until the lawyer has gone, then we'll talk to Alex. He'll make them listen to you."

Nichole wanted desperately to tell Catherine that Alex would not approve of her interfering with the routine of the house. Certainly, he would not back her against the servants. Dejected, she followed Catherine up the stairs to her own room, so that she could freshen up before Alex and his guest arrived.

As she changed into her rose dress with the rose-and-white petticoat, she asked herself what the arrival of Alex's lawyer meant. Were they good friends, or were there still things about the wedding that needed the con-

160

cern of a lawyer? Or was he going to take her advice and set her aside? After she had brushed her hair and adjusted her cap, she let Catherine lead her from her room and down the stairs to wait for Alex.

A light dusting of snow had covered the ground as the front door was thrown open. The master of the house had returned and with him a man of the law. Nichole shuddered. She had never felt so inadequate in her life as she stared up into the critical face of Mr. Robert Patterson. The questioned burned in her mind: Why had Alex brought a lawyer to Manor House for the holidays?

Chapter Fourteen

Alex performed the introductions as his cloak and Robert's were taken away by one of the servants. Catherine beamed and grabbed one of Robert's arms. She offered in a teasing voice, "I'll be happy to function as a crutch," as she led him toward the parlor. "Good sir," she laughed, "you will have to tell me how you came by the bandage you wear on your foot."

Robert chuckled and followed her, limping more than was really necessary. "In the telling, you will discover what a poor horseman I am."

Nichole was left standing next to Alex. She looked at him and then glanced away. His warm brown eyes seemed to be smiling at her, but he had a scowl on his face. The hallway crackled with tension as they stood next to each other. Nichole broke the silence first, offering softly, "I hope you have been well."

"And you?" Alex asked for want of anything better to say. To himself he added, you are absolutely beautiful, and you are doing it to me again. He could not think of another thing to say and in desperation offered his arm. "We should join the others."

The evening meal was delightful, and afterwards Nichole followed Robert, Catherine and Alex to the study. As the evening continued, Nichole began to feel a deep appreciation for Robert Patterson. The man was more than sensitive, she thought as he sought to draw her out with his comments about French art, which he insisted he loved. They discussed at length some of the newer artists as well as some of the older Italian geniuses. Robert was charming, and Alex listened and watched his wife display an insight and appreciation that stunned him.

When the conversation turned to politics, Nichole held her own there, too, grateful for the hours she had spent studying everything Frere Francis had given her on the American Revolution and the cause of it. When they began discussing France and the threat to the monarchy there, Nichole pointed out some of the transgressions of the current royal family. Alex could not believe what he was hearing. Not only did she have a grasp of the whole volatile political situation in France, she also understood a great deal about the philosophy of freedom preached in the cities of his own country.

He shook his head in disbelief. His father had insisted that the family was slow, that indeed, even Nichole herself was not too bright. Alex chuckled; it was a shame his father had not lived to listen to this conversation. As it was, Henry was probably turning over in his grave. Alex wanted to laugh, for his father would never have been able to control this woman. She would have figured out his moves even before he made them.

The next afternoon, after another elegant meal, Catherine insisted that they retire to the music room. The harp was sitting before the window, and both Alex and Robert were surprised when Catherine insisted, despite Nichole's reticence, that she play for them. She's embarrassed, Alex thought as she sat before the harp and played several French Christmas carols. Catherine clapped, delighted, then grabbed the guitar that sat on the bookshelf in the corner. "Now, Nichole, play something on the guitar."

Nichole blushed becomingly and gave Catherine a strained look. She pleaded, "It has been a busy day. I'm sure that Alex and Robert would like to spend some of the evening discussing things of interest to themselves. As it is, I find that I'm very tired. I must ask to be excused."

Alex jumped up. "Let me escort you to your room."

Nichole smiled sweetly. "Oh, that won't be necessary. You must stay and entertain your guest."

Robert and Catherine exchanged a knowing look, and Catherine chuckled as she rose to leave. Robert called after Nichole, "I'll expect a guitar concert tomorrow after dinner."

Nichole made her way through the swing doors and up the stairs without responding to Robert's request. I must say something to Catherine, she thought. She's not going to push me off on anyone, and especially not my husband.

Four days rushed by but Nichole never found time to talk to Catherine. She's making sure there's no time, Nichole thought to herself. For one thing, Nichole noticed that Catherine spent almost all of her time with Robert, leaving Nichole at the mercy of her husband, and he seemed as confused as Nichole. Although she enjoyed the hours she spent with him she refused to admit that he might be enjoying her as well. She knew her husband was not pleased with the situation because, often, when she glanced his way, she would find him watching her, and he would be scowling.

Two days after Christmas, Robert announced that he had to return to the city. "My clients will think that I have deserted them." Alex insisted on accompanying him back to Baltimore, to finish the remaining work on his father's estate. After the two men left, the household returned to normal. And Catherine began once more to give Nichole instructions on how to run a plantation home—that is, when she wasn't extolling all of the virtues of Robert

164

Patterson.

Nichole watched Catherine as she talked about Alex's young lawyer friend. She's set her heart on that man, Nichole thought. Frowning, she reminded herself that Alex had brought him home. It was really Alex's problem. Nichole listened with one ear as Catherine described a conversation she had had with Robert, and she worried: Alex had a problem, whether he knew it or not.

Nichole had not dared to question Alex about the length of his stay in Baltimore, but Catherine had, and Alex had explained that he would be gone for a week to ten days; then he would return. Catherine met with Nichole each morning to outline what she had to tell Prissy and the cook. But each time Nichole tried to carry out Catherine's directives, Prissy or the cook, and usually both, resisted with a vengeance. After each attempt, Nichole retreated to the study to tell Catherine how she had fared. The harder the two women resisted Nichole, the angrier Catherine became, and daily she left the study muttering, "Just wait until he comes back. Just wait!"

Alex arrived late the afternoon of the third day of the New Year. Catherine was waiting for him, and she dragged him into the study even before he had a chance to shed his dusty clothes. Alex glanced at his younger sister. She was as mad as a hornet, he thought, as he gazed into her flashing gray eyes. He didn't want to talk to her, he wanted to see Nichole. And he was not in the best of moods, had not been since he and Robert had left Manor House after Christmas. Once again, he could not get the golden-haired vixen out of his mind.

As Catherine poured him a whiskey, he slumped into one of the study chairs. During the holidays he had been entranced with his wife. She was bright, could speak well on almost any subject, and was well read and very talented. The night she played the guitar they had all joined in singing Christmas carols and drinking songs. Because she had been convent raised, Alex knew she couldn't have been familiar with any of the songs they sang and yet she had played along with chords as if she had written the songs herself. He couldn't remember when he had had such fun.

All he wanted was to find her and bask in her gentle charm, and Catherine was standing above him, her mouth moving. Alex dragged himself back to the present.

"Alex? Alex! You haven't heard a word I've said! Quit daydreaming and listen to me!" Catherine's eyes were shooting daggers his way, and for a fraction of a second he wondered if his sister and his wife had had a falling-out.

In agony, Alex tried to listen to Catherine. "They won't pay any attention to what she says. She has tried so hard but they are mean . . ."

"Who are 'they'?" Alex asked. He wondered how much of Catherine's explanation he had missed.

"Why, Prissy and Mrs. Barber, of course. Nichole is trying to run your household, but those two are fighting her every step. You must do something. Talk to them!"

Alex started to chuckle. "Now, Catherine. Nichole doesn't know anything about running a house. Prissy and Mrs. Barber are much more knowledgeable. They are just preventing Nichole from causing everyone difficulties."

Catherine's eyes sparkled with unshed tears. "They both hate her. They want her to leave. They are trying to drive her away. You must do something."

Alex stood up; he wanted to find the object of their conversation. "Sis, everybody loves Nichole. Robert was enthralled with her and even Peter thinks she's a sweetheart. You're just imagining things." When Catherine glared back at him, Alex grinned. "I'll say something to Prissy and Mrs. Barber. Is that what you want?" Catherine nodded her head enthusiastically, and they left the room together.

Alex found his wife in the music room, paging through a large volume of world history. He wondered if she was thinking about the things happening in France. He sat down next to her and told her what he had heard while he was in Baltimore. She listened with her green eyes cloudy and her expression solemn, but she said nothing. Alex couldn't think of another thing to say to his young wife, and in disgust, Alex left her to her book.

Prissy saw him leave the music room and she saw his look of disgust. Peter had been trying to tell her for the last several days about how abused Nichole was, but seeing Alex's face was all she needed to know. Alex was the one being abused, not Nichole.

After dinner that afternoon, and with more of Catherine's prodding, Alex made his way to the back room. "Prissy, I want you to cooperate with what ever my wi . . . Madame Dampier wants. For the moment she is the mistress of Manor House."

Alex left the room, pleased with himself. He had let Prissy know that Nichole was indeed Madame Dampier, and therefore mistress of the estate. And, in the spring, he had every intention of taking Nichole to the farm. They would live there. He stopped, frozen. He was actually considering a life with the woman. He grinned. Well, why not? She was his wife. They would go to the farm, where they could become acquainted. His mouth curved into a huge smile, and he turned around and marched back toward his housekeeper. "If you can settle your differences with Mrs. Barber, tell her too."

Her thoughts tumbling over each other, Prissy wondered at his words. He had not said his wife but instead Madame Dampier. Was he trying to tell her that the girl would never be his wife? Perhaps he had forgotten his comments the day the girl arrived. He had had a lot on his mind, with the settling of his father's estate. And he had said in no uncertain terms that she was not going to be at Manor House for any length of time. She was going! But where? Prissy wondered.

For the next several days Alex and Peter spent almost every waking hour in the study, going over the remaining paperwork from the estate. Alex confessed his desire to work his own farm, and he and Peter began to make the necessary plans so that he could direct the operation of Manor House from Frederick.

While Alex and Peter were busy in the study, Prissy was apologizing to Mrs. Barber. "You were right, of course," Prissy told the cook over tea. "He is not going to live with her, Peter says he's planning on going back to Frederick in the spring. And he did say she would not be here for any length of time, so he must be going to send her back to France."

"But, she's trying to run things. She's been in to see about the meals every day."

Prissy smiled. "That's Catherine's doing. For some reason Catherine likes her."

"It would seem that we must convince the girl that she is not welcome here, in spite of Catherine," Mrs. Barber murmured. Both women agreed that Alex would send her back the minute she asked to go. They spent the day discussing the things they could do. That afternoon small annoying things began to happen to Nichole.

Her bathwater arrived from the kitchen cold, her morning chocolate had no sugar, and lemon and cream were missing when she asked for tea. At first Nichole said little, but Catherine noticed her long face and cornered her. Nichole mumbled, "Sometimes I think everyone in this house would be much happier if I left."

Nichole's words came back to her that night, as she crawled into her cold bed. Someone had scattered the coals of her fire and the room was like ice. "I'm not wanted here, and I can't stay," Nichole muttered as she curled up in the quilts. But where would she go? The things Robert told her that were happening in France frightened her more than she wanted to admit. She wouldn't be safe with the good sisters of the convent if Robert's information was true. It made little difference; she had no money of her own. There was no way she could afford the passage to France.

She tossed and turned in her bed, wondering if Alex would object if she asked to go into the city. Her dream of becoming a tutor loomed brightly in her mind. She could do that and do it well. Alex might not object, but Catherine would never let her attempt such a thing. No, she couldn't leave Manor House and set up a school in Baltimore.

That night, she dreamed about Jacques Manage and how he had tried to abuse her. She awoke in a cold sweat. Draping the quilt around her, she sat in the middle of her bed. Why hadn't she thought of it before? Nellie Hutchinson had said if she ever needed help, let her know. That was the answer. Nellie could help her. Perhaps the town where Nellie's relatives lived had a need for someone who could teach the citizens to read and cipher. It was far away from Baltimore, so no one need ever know that the French wife of Alex Dampier was a tutor. He could send her away, make up some excuse about her going back to France. Alex would be rid of her and she could get on with her life.

The very next morning Nichole found writing supplies and sat down to compose a letter to Nellie. She tried to explain that things had not gone at all well, and that her husband did not want a wife, but after a dozen attempts she wrote only that she was bitterly unhappy and wanted to do what she had trained so many years to do, teach. Could Nellie's community use a person with those talents? She dug out her Bible, addressed her note and asked Peter to post it for her.

Peter must have checked with Alex for that night, at

dinner, Alex asked her who she knew in Carlisle, Pennsylvania. "I wrote to one of the women from the ship. She and I were very friendly and I wanted her to know that I had arrived safely. You're going to post my letter, aren't you?" she asked in a whisper.

"I don't see why not," Alex reassured her. "I'm glad to know that you made some friends on that voyage." For some reason, Alex was a little nettled by her accusation that he might not see her letter posted.

Nichole waited for a response, but nothing came for her. When she questioned Catherine, her sister-in-law laughed. "Nichole, letters take weeks. If you're waiting for a reply to the note you sent, you have to give it time to get there first. You might receive an answer in two months, but that would be unusually fast." Nichole said nothing more. If Nellie had forgotten her lessons, it could take even longer. The woman would have to find someone to read the note to her and then write a response. Nichole tried to keep herself out of Prissy's and Mrs. Barber's way, and she avoided Alex as much as she could.

Alex noticed how withdrawn Nichole was becoming, and he watched as his sister tried to draw her out. They did seem to be very close. Sometimes, he actually felt a little jealous. Why could Catherine question her and he could not? Why couldn't she tell him whatever it was that was bothering her? While Nichole grew unhappier and her eyes more distant, Alex's scowl became more pronounced. Prissy and Mrs. Barber saw Alex's long face and they conferred. They decided they had to be more direct.

After dinner, a week after Alex returned from Baltimore, he asked Nichole to play for him. He escorted her into the music room and seated her at the harp. He intended to ask her to come with him to Frederick after she played for him. She played one of the songs used in church, and her second song was a tender ballad. When she finished, he asked quietly, "Are there words for that song?" She nodded and he whispered softly, "sing it for me, please."

She began to play again, singing the soft French words to her own accompaniment. The words described the attributes of a loved one, first the lover's warm lips, then the hands and their caresses. Nichole's face turned scarlet and she could not finish. She pushed the harp into its upright position and rushed from the room.

Alex was so surprised that he didn't even try to stop her. Had she realized what the words meant before she started to play or after she started singing? And why couldn't she finish the song? His plans for the evening were spoiled now, and he left the music room angry at himself and angry at Nichole.

As he was leaving the room, Mrs. Barber approached with the tea tray for Nichole and brandy for Alex. He snapped, "We won't be needing that," and slammed out toward the stable. Mrs. Barber hurried back to the kitchen where Prissy waited.

The next evening, Alex asked Nichole to play for him again, and when they arrived in the music room Alex seated Nichole at the harp. As she ran her fingers across the strings, several sections split, as if they had been deliberately cut. His glance was accusing. Would she cut the strings just to keep from playing for him? Nichole didn't miss the look he gave her and with her head held high she marched out of the room, through the swinging doors, up to her room. She would never destroy a musical instrument, but she wasn't going to tell him that, not when his eyes already judged her guilty.

The next afternoon, Nichole went back to the library and hunted for her book of history. She couldn't find it anywhere, and when Alex joined her before dinner she asked if he had seen it. He looked at her for a long time before he shook his head. It was clear in her expression that she thought he had taken her damned book.

That evening after dinner, Alex asked Nichole to pour him a glass of brandy and join him in the library. "We'll look for your book together."

She poured the amber liquid from the decanter on the sideboard and followed him to the room. He thanked her and took a quick sip, then spit the liquid out, spraying the rug. "My God, woman! Are you trying to poison me? You don't mix brandy and whiskey together. I said the brandy decanter on the sideboard." Once more, Nichole ran from the room, her eyes glistening with tears. Was he trying to make her life miserable? Did he hate her so much that he would do these things? She cried herself to sleep.

Alex slumped into the library chair. Was Nichole pulling these stunts so that he would send her back to France? Was she so unhappy that she would not even give him a chance? His expression turned to disgust as he considered his wife and her antics.

While everything moved along smoothly for two days, Alex spent a good deal of time trying to figure out if Nichole indeed was intent on returning to France. He came to the conclusion that that was what she was attempting to do. He prayed that she had changed her mind and would not try to force him to send her back. Robert sent word that he wanted to come for a visit and would arrive tomorrow. Perhaps, Alex thought, Robert could convince Nichole that it was not safe to go back to France.

Late in the afternoon, but before the evening meal was served, Robert arrived bearing gifts for both Catherine and Nichole. He brought Alex a special bottle of French brandy, one of the first of its kind, he told Alex. Dinner was a gay affair, and even Nichole seemed more relaxed. After dinner the two men retired to the study to consider the properties of the French brandy and Nichole told Catherine to give her excuses to the men. Catherine in-

172

sisted that she wait for Alex and Robert. Nichole whispered, "No, please. My head has been throbbing all day." She wasn't going to tell Catherine that someone had loosened her bed ropes and hidden the wooden key. There was no way she could tighten the ropes. All night she had tried to get comfortable but no matter how she turned she ended in the middle of the bed, almost suffocating under the feather mattresses.

The next morning Alex and Robert closeted themselves in the study. Alex wanted to increase the size of the farm, and he gave instructions to Robert to negotiate for several pieces of prime land close to the farm. The will that Alex and Robert had discussed while Alex was in Baltimore after Christmas was ready for his signature. After business they took a brisk ride around the plantation. Both men were looking forward to dinner as they discussed the evening ahead.

While the men worked Catherine and Nichole lunched together. Then Nichole excused herself. "I'm exhausted, and I plan to take a long nap this afternoon."

"Aren't you sleeping well?" Catherine asked sympathetically. Nichole didn't respond.

Later that afternoon, Catherine wasn't too surprised when Prissy whispered that Nichole had sent word with Maude that she would not be coming down for dinner. "She's not feeling too well." Catherine took the message to Alex.

He was crushed. All day long, he had thought about the pleasant meal the evening before, and he was looking forward to the same pleasant dinner again. Suddenly, he wondered if she was truly indisposed, or up to her pranks again.

Catherine took Robert's arm and led him into the dining room, leaving Alex to follow, his scowl getting deeper by the minute. They seated themselves and were almost through the soup when Alex rose from the table and apologized, "I'm sorry. I think I better go see if she is truly ill."

Long before dinner was served, Prissy stationed Maude in the hall with instructions that she was to distract Alex if he attempted to go to Nichole's room. The young girl did exactly as Prissy had told her and when she spotted Alex coming toward the swinging door, she started groaning from her place on the stairs.

"What's the matter, Maude?" Alex asked softly. "Don't you feel well, either? You go tell Mrs. Barber to fix you some mint tea." Alex patted her on the head, and when she just sat wondering what to do now Alex said sternly, "You tell Mrs. Barber I said so!"

Maude had no choice but to move so that Alex could climb the stairs. She groaned, "That man ain't gonna let no little ole slave stop him, not when he's a worryin' over his pretty miss." She scurried off to tell Prissy that her plan had failed.

Alex hesitated at Nichole's door for a second or two. If she was truly ill and in bed, he did not want to disturb her. He opened the door a crack and stuck his head inside. Both bedroom windows were open wide and Nichole was sitting at the dressing table huddled in her cloak. Tears were streaming down her face.

Alex quickly moved inside the room and shut the door, just as Nichole shouted, "Don't shut the door!" Alex glanced at Nichole, then at the closed door, then at the windows. What on earth was going on? He reached for the door latch but it wasn't there. He looked at the door more closely; the latch had been removed. There was no way to open the door from inside the room, and it was freezing. Alex walked over to one of the windows and started to close it.

Nichole whispered softly, "Please, don't close the windows." She blushed crimson.

Alex raised his head and sniffed. He looked over at

174

Nichole and then around the room, then back at Nichole. "What is that putrid smell?" He wrinkled his nose.

If possible, Alex thought that Nichole turned an even darker red. She stuttered, "Some one . . . d . . . d . . . dumped the contents of the ch . . . ch . . . cham . . . ber pot in the bed." Her voice trailed off so low, Alex had to strain to hear the last several words.

Alex stepped up to the bed, gagged, then turned and shrieked, "My God, Nichole! Why did you do this?"

She gave him a disgusted look, and snapped, "In my own bed, sir? How can you even think such a thing? I certainly wouldn't have removed the door latch so that I would be trapped in this room if I was going to pull that stunt. You did it, didn't you? I want to know why you are torturing me, for this prank is truly torture."

Alex stared at her. "Do you really think I did this?"

Nichole nodded her head but said nothing.

Alex looked at her in disgust and then went to the door. Even over his loud pounding he could hear Nichole's sobs. After several minutes Alex swore and strode over to one of the windows. No one on the first floor was paying any attention to his banging, probably, he guessed, because they couldn't hear. Outside the room was a maple tree that was more than three stories tall. If he could just reach one of the larger branches from the window, he could climb down and come back inside to release Nichole. Then he would get some answers.

He eased his way over the window ledge and grabbed for one of the larger branches. "Stay here. I'll be right back." Working his way to the main trunk section, he slithered down the tree and was soon gone from view.

Nichole watched until he disappeared around the side of the house. Please, let him come back for me, she prayed. Then she chided herself. He would not return! He was intent on torture—hers. She gathered her cloak more tightly around her shoulders and shivered in the chill wind. The warm days of January had disappeared, and the wind tonight cried loudly of winter.

After what seemed like an hour Nichole thought she heard the banging of the front door, and then, long seconds later, she heard the angry footsteps coming down the hall. She looked up in surprise when her door was swung open and Alex stood in the doorway. "Come on, let's get you out of there," he muttered.

Nichole followed him out of the room. "I don't think I can go down for dinner this evening," she mumbled.

He turned and glared at her. "Dinner started without you, and you are coming with me. We are going to get to the bottom of this." He led her down the hall to his room.

Chapter Fifteen

At first, Nichole followed Alex down the hall, and then she froze. She had never even taken a peek at the master bedroom, she had never expected to see it, but Alex was opening the door and standing aside so that she could enter. Self-consciously, she slipped into the room and stared in complete surprise at the large masculine space. Her eyes roamed around the walls. In front of her were two armoires against one wall, and on the next wall was a huge marble-topped washstand. The fireplace, where the dying embers of a fire burned, was on the same wall. Before the fireplace two comfortable chairs stood.

Nichole looked longingly at the warm embers, and she shivered again in the warmth. Alex took her cloak and threw it over a hat tree that stood as a silent sentry in one corner. He led her over to one of the chairs then poured a drink from one of the decanters on the table. He handed her the glass and ordered, not too gently, "Sit down!"

Nichole took the glass and sat down quickly. While Alex poured himself a glass of whatever he had handed Nichole, she looked at the other wall. Her eyes flew open wide as she gazed at the largest bed she had ever imagined. It could easily sleep six people comfortably, Nichole thought. The four wooden posts were at least six inches in diameter and went almost to the ceiling. They were decorated at the bottom and at the top with leaves and grapes entwined just above and below a pineapple design. A large wooden canopy was also curved in a fluted pattern, and dark chintz drapes were held back with brass leaves. The coverlet repeated the leaf motif in dark colors.

Alex turned to find Nichole staring at his bed. "I'm a large man," Alex offered quietly. Nichole blushed as he looked at her. He sat down in the chair opposite and took a long pull on his glass. Lowering his glass he studied the woman in front of him. She was his wife, but did she want to be? She had had no say in what had happened to her, but that wasn't that unusual in her social order. Was she now as anxious to get away from him as he had been originally to get away from her?

"Nichole," he said softly, "I had nothing to do with what happened here tonight. I thought," he lowered his gaze and fixed his stare on the glass he was holding, "that you were doing these things so that I would send you back to France. You said that was where you wanted to go."

Nichole swirled the glass in her thin, graceful fingers. "I would not destroy a beautiful musical instrument, nor arrange cold water for my own baths, or hide the rope key for the bed. I certainly would not—do what was done tonight, certainly not lock myself in a room with—with . . ." her voice trailed off as she stared at the fire.

"Surely Catherine—" Alex's voice also faded.

"No! Catherine is my only friend. She would not do anything like that to me."

At her mention that Catherine was her only friend, Alex winced. Were Prissy and Mrs. Barber responsible for all the things she had mentioned? Had she imagined some of then? Neither she nor Catherine had said anything about cold baths or lost rope keys. Alex rose from his chair and threw several logs on the fire. "I'm going downstairs for several minutes. You stay here by the fire and warm yourself." He walked to the door. "I'll be back soon. I want you to stay here."

Nichole nodded her head. She was cold and she was frightened. If Alex hadn't ordered the pranks, then who was responsible? Would they get more serious until she was actually hurt or made ill? Trying not to think, she laid her head on the back of the chair and closed her eyes.

Alex hurried downstairs. He had a very good idea who was responsible for the mischief that had been done that night, but at present his concern was only for Nichole. She was chilled to the bone and she was hungry. She had twice been abused in his house and he wanted to make certain that she understood he was not to blame before he descended on the culprits who were responsible.

He stuck his head into the dining room. "You both will have to do without my company for tonight. I'm afraid that Nichole is—not feeling well, and I must see to her care."

Catherine glanced over at Robert, and they both grinned at each other. Catherine was so excited that she wanted to jump up from the table and kiss Robert. Alex truly cared for his wife. She giggled, "Are you sure you want to go back to Baltimore tomorrow? It may be interesting here, very interesting."

Robert was laughing as well. "If I didn't have an important client to see first thing Monday morning, you couldn't drag me away."

Alex went out to the kitchen. Huddled in a corner were both Prissy and Mrs. Barber. If I needed verification of my suspicions, Alex told himself, I certainly have it now. Both women looked very guilty and almost afraid of him at the same time. Alex gritted his teeth. He would have to confront them in the morning. Tonight, he had to take care of Nichole.

"I want the bathtub and lots of hot water in my room in ten minutes," he barked. "I also want a supper tray sent up to my room in about half an hour." Alex stalked out of the kitchen without another word.

The two women looked at each other. Was he angry with them? He hadn't said anything. They scurried about to get the water and the supper tray he had ordered. This was certainly not the time to question the issue. Prissy glanced at the grim cook. "Maybe he doesn't even know she's locked in."

The cook stopped her hand in midair as she reached for plates. "You may be right! He might just be angry because she didn't come down for dinner. Maude didn't say that he had gone into her room. If she couldn't open the door—" The cook went back to her work. Suddenly, both women glanced at each other. He wouldn't have gone into her room unless she had opened the door for him. A smile slowly lifted the corners of Mrs. Barber's grim mouth. Prissy started to smile as well. Nichole couldn't open her door to him.

Alex slowly climbed the stairs to his room, his mind busy. Tonight, his wife would sleep in his bed. He discovered that thought was not at all disturbing; in fact, suddenly he felt alive, full of anticipation. He grinned as he opened his bedroom door and stepped into his room. Nichole was sitting in the chair she occupied when he left the room. Her head was resting against the back of the chair, and he wondered if she was asleep.

He walked over the chair. "Nichole," he said softly, "Nichole?"

She opened her eyes. "I'm not asleep."

Alex smiled down at her. "I've ordered a warm bath and after your bath, we'll have supper. Then, we'll talk."

Nichole looked up at him, startled, "I can't bathe in here," she whispered.

"Nichole," Alex said ever so gently, "I've already

180

bathed you once. You can bathe in front of me. After all, you are my wife."

She lowered her eyes. "I'll be too embarrassed." Her words were spoken so softly that Alex had to lean forward to hear her.

Alex laughed easily. "You've nothing to be embarrassed about. You're a very beautiful woman." Nichole blushed but said nothing else. Alex sat down in his chair opposite her. It was time; he had to know. As his heart pounded frantically, he leaned forward and asked, "Nichole, do you want to be my wife?"

Her eyes met his and for several minutes she would say nothing. His presence in any room disturbed her, and here in his room, she felt suffocated. The few times he touched her, the skin where he touched felt warm and her stomach seemed to turn over. The feelings frightened her. Did she want to be his wife and be bombarded by these sensations all the time? She really didn't know. She told him that: "I don't know!"

As if he could read her mind he replied, "Sweetheart, you don't have anything to be afraid of. I won't hurt you, you know. I only want to make you happy."

Nichole was almost tempted to remind him of all the pranks she had endured these last several days. That certainly did not make her happy. A knock on the door interrupted her thoughts. And, seconds later, the brass tub was being filled with bucket after bucket of hot water. Finally the door closed and Alex stood in front of her. "Time for your bath, my lady."

Nichole sank further back into the chair. "I cannot disrobe in front of you." Her voice shook as she glared at Alex.

"You are my wife! I have already seen you without your clothes. I took them off, remember." At the mention of that evening Nichole turned a ghastly shade of red. Alex looked down into her frightened eyes and whispered

181

softly, "It's all right for a husband to see his wife in her bath. Sometimes, he even joins her!"

"You . . . you . . . you wouldn't," she gasped.

"Not unless you asked me to," Alex teased her gently. "I'll tell you what, you get out of those clothes and into the tub and I'll go for your towel and chemise."

"From my room?"

"Yes, from your room. Don't worry. I'll not forget about that door." He left the room, laughing softly.

Nichole struggled as quickly as she could to shed her clothes. Just as she sank into the delightfully warm water, Alex returned. She wondered if he had been waiting outside the door until he heard her splashes. The thought made her feel a little warmer toward him. He was not going to intentionally embarrass her.

The steamy hot water did much to revive her sagging spirits. She was thoroughly enjoying the warmth when a disquieting thought entered her head. How on earth would she get out of the tub without exposing herself? She grabbed for the sponge and soap and began scrubbing herself as she looked around the room. Alex was sitting in one of the chairs before the fire, sipping from his glass. He wasn't paying her any attention, she thought. She spotted her towel and chemise across the other chair. There was no way she could get to either of them without leaving the tub.

Alex glanced her way and then stood up. She held her breath; would he leave for something else? Instead, he looked at her briefly. "I'll warm a towel, if you're ready to get out of the tub." With that he grabbed a blanket and held it before the fire with his back to her and the chair with her towel and chemise.

She pulled herself from the warm luxurious cocoon she had enjoyed, reached for the towel and rubbed herself dry. Wrapping the towel around herself, she reached for the chemise. Immediately, Alex wrapped her in the warm blanket, not allowing her to pull the chemise over her head. "You need to stay warm for a while. I don't want you to get a chill."

He guided her to a chair, and when she protested that she'd get it wet, he grinned, "You can sit in my lap. I won't mind getting wet."

Nichole slid into the chair without another comment. Alex's teasing was unnerving her. She was much more accustomed to his briskness, and this new attitude of his was alarming. She had no time to consider his remarks for there was a sharp knock on the door and immediately Maude was shown into the room with the promised supper tray. While she arranged the tray, Nat emptied the water and then removed the tub.

Alex set the tray in front of her and pulled his chair up across from hers. They shared the food on the tray. There was chicken, biscuits, sweet apple tarts and tea with lemon and sugar. Nichole was surprised at how hungry she was, and she and Alex ate everything on the tray.

Over her tea, Alex told her about his farm and how much he wanted to return there. As he talked, Nichole felt a knot in her stomach tighten and a lump develop in her throat. He was saying good-bye to her. But why did it bother her so much? He had honestly told her that they would share no life at all when she first arrived from France. Her heart floated into her throat when he leaned forward and asked, "Would you like to live on a working farm?"

She glanced at him, quickly, afraid to believe that he just might be asking her to go with him to Frederick. "Isn't this a working farm?"

"This is a plantation. There are lots of people here to do the work. My farm is much smaller. I don't even have a housekeeper or a cook. I have four men and they each have their own families. They have their own homes and they live on my property. They work my field and pay me rent in the form of produce from their own fields. Occasionally their wives come into my house and clean, but that isn't often, maybe every three or four weeks. If you came to Frederick you would have to do most of the cleaning and cooking by yourself, except what I help you with."

"I think I would like that," she murmured softly.

Alex watched her carefully. Did she understand what he was asking? She was still wrapped in the blanket from her bath, and all he could think about was the thin but full female form under that blanket. He hoped she didn't recognize the lust he knew he could not hide.

Indeed, Nichole could not draw her eyes from his. He was looking at her so intensely, and there was something in his eyes, something she had never seen before. That look made her warm and tingling inside. Why, she asked herself, could just his eyes affect her so? It was a delicious feeling one of anticipation, as if something wonderful would happen, but what?

Alex set the tray out in the hall and returned to stand over her. He looked down at her with such an anxious expression that Nichole wanted to reach up and touch his cheek. In the soft light of the fireplace, Alex reached out to trace her cheek. "I want to love you, Nichole," he muttered in a husky voice.

She frowned, confused but also puzzled, for Ma Mere had told her that a husband was supposed to love his wife. Didn't he know he should love her? Not knowing what else to say but needing to respond, she murmured, "I want to love you, too."

Alex inhaled sharply; did she understand what she had said? She looked so damn innocent sitting there wrapped in the blanket. Reaching for her, he put his hand up under her arms and drew her out of the chair and up against him. She tensed immediately. He wondered if she was remembering Jacques's brutal assault. Warning himself to go slowly, he let her pull away ever so slightly. Looking down into her eyes, his voice husky, he murmured, "A husband can hold his wife, Nichole. He can caress her." He started running his hands gently up and down her back and across her shoulders. "And he can kiss her, too." He bent his head and touched her lips very softly with his. He felt some of the tension leave her, and he wondered if she was reacting to his words or his kiss.

He sprinkled feather-light kisses on her forehead, on her eyelids, her cheeks, her chin over her throat, and then moved back to take her lips. This time, he applied a little more pressure, kissing her a little more firmly. He kept kissing her for a long time until she was leaning into his kisses. Experimentally, he touched her lips with his tongue, but she did not draw away. Then, he traced the edges of her lips and she sighed. Lifting his lips, he smiled down into her eyes. They were now glazed with desire. He was sure that she was no longer thinking about Jacques. Now, she was his!

Nichole was not thinking at all. For the first time in her life, she was experiencing desire. Not once in all of her twenty years had she been held, nor had she ever been kissed. She liked it. For some reason his kisses made her feel warm and secure. As far as she was concerned, he could go on kissing her forever. She felt no guilt, not like the shame she suffered when she fought with Jacques. Somehow, deep inside, she knew this was right.

When Alex probed between her lips with his tongue, a spark was ignited and she forgot everything, the tricks someone was playing on her, the mess in her room, even the blanket she still had clutched around her. She had to have him closer and as she raised her hands to pull him up to her, the blanket dropped to her feet. She never gave it a thought.

Even as he continued to kiss her, Alex started to remove his shirt. She didn't seem to mind at all. Her breasts pushed into his naked chest, and as she arched up against him he wondered if he would be branded for life. As he tasted the sweetness of her mouth, he trailed his fingers over her fullness, caressing her hips, her tiny waist. He worked his way across her ribs and traced the curve of her breast.

Suddenly, standing there kissing her was not enough. Swiftly, he picked her up in his arms and moved toward his bed. He let her slide from his arms and he pulled back the coverlet. Picking her up again, he laid her on the fresh white linens. Laying his hand over her full round breast, he brushed the nipple with his thumb. She sighed and closed her eyes. He reached down and released the waistband of his breeches and kicked off his shoes. In a fraction of a second he was in bed with her and holding her tightly against his naked body.

Nichole was in a turmoil. Never in her short life had she experienced anything that could compare with the feelings that were threading themselves along every nerve of her body. His warmth and his touch were driving her to distraction. She clung to him, wanting his touch, wanting his kisses, wanting him to continue stroking her and making her feel so good. Somehow she had to tell him, let him know how he was pleasing her. She arched up against him, pushing her body against his long length, and in her attempt at silent communication she nearly destroyed his control.

He breathed against her lips, "Slowly, love, slowly"; then he left her lips and worked his way across her chin, down her neck, across her shoulders. She shuddered in his arms and he lowered his head to her breast. He grazed soft butterfly kisses across the taut skin, avoiding the nipple which stood at attention beckoning him. He gave in to the temptation, twirling the tight nub around in his mouth as she writhed on his bed.

At the same time, he let his fingers trace her pearl

186

white skin, down around her waist, her hips, the outside of her legs, across her knees and up the inside of her thighs. Ignoring the throbbing nipple, he raised his lips and moved back to her mouth, where he played against her teeth, tasting the inside of her lips and stroking her tongue with his. Gently, he let his hand cover the center of her. She pushed up against him instinctively.

Nichole had never been told anything about lovemaking, nor did she have any notions about what nice women did or did not do. She was feeling with all of her own sensual nature and she was loving every minute of it. Unconsciously her hands were traveling across his firm muscular back, down his waist, over his chest, mimicking his own tracings. She cupped his face between her hands and pushed her tongue into his mouth, enjoying the groan he made, knowing somehow that he was being pleasured.

Nichole was beside herself. Her body was on fire. Tiny little flames licked at her wherever he touched her, and he was touching her everywhere. He moved around her and over her and she had no idea what he was doing or why. She wasn't concerned with what would happen next.

Alex knew he couldn't take much more. Her response to him and her innocent imitations of his caresses left him little air for his lungs. His heart was thumping rapidly in time with hers, and he dragged his mouth away from her lips. Staring down at her, he shifted his weight, and gently nudged her knees apart. She didn't even seem to notice. Aware that she had surrendered to his passionate overture, he probed with his rigid maleness for the opening he was seeking. He lowered his lips to hers once more, forcing his tongue deep into the sweetness he tasted there. Without a conscious thought he plunged into her.

She tensed as a white hot cutting pain between her legs forced a scream from her throat, but his kiss muffled the sound. Still, he held her, kissing her fiercely. She was stunned. What had happened, what had he done? He did not move away, but held her close and whispered endearments into her ears, tracing his tongue along the corded muscles of her neck. He kissed her again deeply and let his tongue trail over her shoulder and down to her breast. She realized that the pain was fading rapidly, and in its place were a heaviness and the feeling that the sensations she had been experiencing were just a breath away.

He held her tight, more confused than he cared to admit. Had she been truly injured when Jacques had taken her, or was she just frightened? Intent on reawakening her passions, tenderly, he sucked the nipple into his mouth again and again. He could feel the tension begin to leave her, and once more she arched up against him. As slowly as he could he eased from her slightly and thrust forward once more. Instinctively, as he moved she tried to move with him. He held her hips and gently showed her how to work with him.

Nichole had no time to wonder what was happening to her, for she felt like she was walking up a stairway of clouds. Was she going to heaven, was she going to die? Something was about to occur and she didn't want it to stop. She was moving up, up and higher still. Then, it happened!

She exploded and the clouds turned into stars. Serenely she floated and glided among them. Alex's gasp brought her a little sanity and she remembered her husband. For a fraction of a second she wondered if he had exploded too. As reality returned, she realized she was lying in bed and her husband was still holding her tightly and kissing her with such tenderness tears formed in her eyes. She has tasted a bit of heaven and the magnificent man lying next to her was responsible. Suddenly, she felt better than she ever had in her entire life. She was completely at peace with herself, with him, with the world.

She opened her eyes to gaze up at the marvelous man

who showed her such ecstasy. He was smiling down at her, and his eyes were full of tenderness and another emotion that she could only guess at.

He rolled to her side, keeping her in his arms. She whispered, "I have never experienced anything like that before. Is that what married people do? I feel . . . I . . ." She couldn't put it into words.

He kissed her so tenderly she clutched at him. "I know sweetheart," he whispered, his voice husky. "I have been a man for some time now and I have never been pleasured like that." He smiled down at her.

She grinned back at him. "I like this! Can we do it again?"

Alex laughed out loud. "I have a feeling we'll be doing 'this' all night and all next week and for years to come."

Nichole felt absolutely incredible. Instantly she knew something was missing. "Would you get up and light some candles? I want to look at you. You saw me when you bathed me, but I've never seen a man before." She put her hands up to her face, for she knew she was blushing.

Alex was so pleased with her request that he jumped up from the bed and began lighting all of the candles in the room. Nichole rose up to her knees and moved to the edge of the bed to inspect her naked husband. He was gorgeous. And he was actually strutting like a peacock. Nichole giggled as she smiled up into his face.

He gazed at her fondly. She was radiant. He started to turn around as she indicated with her hands, but something in the bed caught his eyes. The sheets were smeared with a dark stain. The smile left his face. He leaned over to consider the stains more carefully; then he glanced at Nichole.

Pushing her down onto the bed, he looked at her thighs. There were dark red streaks on her legs. He felt cold, numb. She had tried to scream, she had tensed.

Virgin! The word screamed through his brain. Damn, she had been a virgin. Something in him snapped. She had tricked him. Jacques hadn't touched her at all. The whole thing was a trick. A marriage wasn't necessary. He jerked away from her as if she were evil. He stepped back, staring at her, and then he started yelling, "Jacques didn't touch you. You tricked me. You lied to me. I didn't have to stay married to you. I could have set you aside. There wouldn't have been any scandal. You tricked me!" His voice was full of pain. Forgotten were the carefully laid plans of his father and the gossip up and down the coast.

Nichole stared at him in horror. Her heart split into a million tiny pieces. And she was confused. She had no idea what she had done. Why was he so angry? Jacques had touched her. The captain knew about it, he had told Peter all about it. She hadn't lied to him about anything. But the words he spoke struck her like the knife of death. He didn't want to stay married to her. As he moved to his chair and began throwing on his clothes, she begged, "What have I done? What have I done? Tell me what I have done!"

He looked at her coldly. "You tricked me! Well, you are Madame Dampier now, for sure, but you'll never see me here again. I'm going to my farm and I don't give a damn what you do." He stormed out of the room.

Nichole lay huddled in the middle of his bed, whimpering, tears streaming down her face. What had she done? She replayed the whole evening again and again. He had seemed so happy. She was so happy. He had made her feel so good. She thought she made him feel as good. He had said she had pleased him. Was it because of Jacques? She would never know. She would never see him again.

Chapter Sixteen

Catherine stretched and wiggled out of her bed. The sun had just begun its daily climb. She giggled when she remembered that Nichole and Alex had spent the night together. They would be oblivious to the things going on around them, she decided. Robert would be leaving soon, and she would have to do the honors for the family. Besides, she thought, and raised her chin a bit, Robert was everything she'd ever wanted in a man.

She took her time and selected her clothes with care, wanting to look more than her seventeen years. She was nearly dressed when she found the note on her dressing table. She read the note quickly, smiling as she read. Alex was not willing to leave Nichole's side. He wanted her all to himself for two days. She was to accompany Peter and Robert to Baltimore so that Peter would have company on the return trip, Alex wrote. A little strange, she thought, but then she chuckled; it was easily understandable when one considered that he wanted Nichole to himself. Still grinning, she went downstairs to inform Robert that the two dearest people in her world were madly in love with each other.

Robert joined her for breakfast, and they discussed whether Catherine should stay for the night with his parents since they were once again residing in Baltimore.

He assured her they would love to have an unexpected houseguest for the night. They whispered and laughed, as the two conspirators they were, over the turn of events with Alex and his wife. They were both so preoccupied with their own satisfaction that neither one of them noticed Peter's worried frown or the looks of elation on the faces of Prissy and Mrs. Barber. In less than an hour, Catherine and Robert were in the carriage on their way to Baltimore.

Even when they stopped for lunch, Catherine hadn't yet noticed Peter's grim expression. She spent all her time entertaining Robert. Finally they arrived in Baltimore, and they stopped so that Robert could give Peter the directions to his town house. It was then that Catherine noticed the glum expression he wore. Thinking to tease him, she joked, "Now Peter, it seems you are stuck with me. Don't worry about Alex. He's a big boy. In spite of what you think, I believe that Nichole can take care of him. From now on, you have only to take care of me."

He looked at her without a trace of a smile. "Nichole won't be taking care of him. He left for the farm, just after midnight. He said he wouldn't be coming back to Manor House, not no more. He said you could come and visit whenever you wanted to, but not to bring his wife." Peter managed to spit the words out.

Catherine blanched white. "You mean," she gasped, "that he left Nichole last night?"

Peter nodded.

Catherine grabbed at the older man. "Peter, we have to get back to Manor House now! Right away." Catherine felt panic greater than she'd ever known. Something was wrong, terribly, horribly wrong. A sixth sense told her Nichole was in trouble. She couldn't explain it. She just knew it!

"Miss Catherine" — Peter always called her Miss

Catherine when she had made an unreasonable request of him—"we can't travel with the carriage at night."

"No, but we can ride. Robert, you have horses, we'll use yours."

Robert frowned. "Catherine, you will have to wait until morning. I don't have two horses, not riding horses, and I wouldn't think of letting you ride off at night like that anyway."

Catherine turned on Peter once more. "We have to go back. Something terrible has happened. I just know it, I can feel it."

Peter ignored her, and they rode on in silence. Catherine's mind was churning. Nichole needed her, she was certain. Somehow she had to get back to her friend, before whatever was going to happen occurred. When they stopped at Robert's she would take one of his horses—and if he refused? She frowned. She had ridden since she could barely walk, and the carriage horses were not meant for riding. But if that's all there was . . .

When they finally arrived at Robert's town house, Peter helped Catherine from the carriage and Robert alighted and trudged toward his residence, refusing to pay any attention to her pleas.

Peter had just pulled the horses away from the carriage, when Catherine hitched up her skirts and climbed up on one of the draft animals. She yanked the long reins out of Peter's hands and started toward the street, yelling back over her shoulder, "I'm going back, with or without you."

Peter jumped up on the other horse. "Damn stubborn brat! I'll have to bring 'er back." He trotted off after the defiant girl.

Thank God, Peter thought to himself, it was Sunday and late enough in the evening that there were few people on the street to see her riding bareback, with her skirt hiked up to her knees. Catherine led the way, winding through the streets. Several times, Peter got close enough and tried to grab the reins, but she had always been a good judge of horseflesh and had grabbed the better of the two horses. She only had to urge her horse forward a bit faster and the animal moved away from Peter time and time again.

They were outside the city before she slowed enough to let him catch up. He glared at her. "Proper young ladies do not go riding off into the night. Your brother is going to have my head."

Catherine looked over at Peter with tears sliding down her face. "You don't understand. There is something wrong, very wrong. Nichole is in trouble. When we get back to Manor House, you'll see." Peter was stunned. She was genuinely concerned.

Catherine moved her horse along as rapidly as she could. They were still ten miles from Manor House when a soft cold rain started falling. Peter ranted about how she would get sick and it would be his fault. Then, Alex would kill him for sure. Catherine, anxious, but not knowing why, only urged her horse on, and Peter was forced to speed up as well.

In the woods next to the road, Nichole was resting. She heard the flying hooves of the big horses and saw the forms racing through the night. Praying that the horse she had tied to the nearby tree wouldn't make any noise, she stayed very quiet herself. She ached all over. Catherine hadn't told her that a long ride on a horse would result in tired, sore muscles, but it did. Rubbing her sore arms, she tried to get comfortable.

As she rested, she considered what she had done. Early that afternoon she had left Manor House, determined never to return. Even before she drifted off to sleep the night before, she knew that she would have to leave; the only question that remained was where to go. When she got up that morning, after Alex left, Robert and Catherine were already on their way to Baltimore with Peter. Maude told her that much. Prissy and Mrs. Barber were cold and said nothing at first. After she had breakfast Prissy had started whispering, "Why don't you go back to France, where you belong."

She had retreated to her room. The feather mattress was gone and the room had been aired out, so she sat down and stared at her few possessions. They had to be packed, for somehow she was going to leave this place of misery, or lose her mind. She thought about her note to Nellie. No response had come. According to Catherine the letter was reaching Carlisle about now. There was no time for a response, not now. She had to get away. She could not stay, and she could not return to France. There was the matter of the fare for passage, and Robert had told her some of the things that had been happening in her beloved country. No, she could not go back to France. Whatever it was that she had done, Alex had left and would not be returning. He would not want her at the farm now. And she couldn't stay at Manor House, not with the hate from Prissy and Mrs. Barber eating her alive. There was simply no other place to go but to Mrs. Hutchinson in Pennsylvania.

She slipped into the study and looked for the book of line drawings Alex had shown her of the states. She found Pennsylvania but almost had given up the whole idea when she finally found Carlisle on the map. It was a long way off, but she had no other choice. At least by now, Nellie would know that she was considering someplace other than Manor House as a home. Nellie would help her. She just had to help. Carefully, she tore out the page of the book and folded it up. Then she crept up the stairs to consider what else she needed.

She decided to enlist Maude's help, telling the girl that she had to leave. "Alex doesn't want a wife," she whispered after she had dragged the girl up to her room. "He has left for the farm, and he told me he was going to stay there. Prissy and Mrs. Barber want me to go back to France, but I can't do that. I have a friend that wants me to come stay with her."

Maude had always freely expressed her opinions with Miz Catherine, but this soft-spoken French girl was something else. After all, Maude thought, she is the mistress of the house, and Maude didn't try to argue with her.

Nichole made Maude promise that she would say nothing to Prissy or Mrs. Barber should they inquire. "And, if you say nothing, they'll never know you had anything to do with my leaving." Maude was given instructions to find some of Peter's old clothes and gather foodstuffs, then to leave the clothes and the food by an old oak tree well behind the barns, but out of sight of the house and the field. Nichole sent Nat to tell the stableboy that she wanted to go for a ride, and then she sat down to write some kind of explanation to Catherine.

"Catherine," she wrote, "I have to go. I told you once that everyone would be better off if I left. I have a friend in Carlisle, Pennsylvania. I beg you, please don't tell Alex. Please, please do not tell him where I've gone. I don't know what I did, but I have done something terribly wrong to him. It would be better for everyone if he never saw me again. You have been my only friend. Thank you. My leaving is for the best. Nichole." She put the note in Catherine's room on the dressing table, then went downstairs for some lunch.

After lunch, Nichole changed to her riding outfit and retrieved the horse from the stable. She rode off down the lane toward the woods where Maude had promised to leave the bag of food and the carpetbag she had packed with her one brown convent dress and Peter's stolen clothes. She changed into Peter's shirt and breeches right there in the woods, left her riding suit folded neatly under the tree. She glanced at the other things Maude had left. There was a large bag of food and two wool blankets. Nichole tied the bag to the saddle, got out the page from Alex's book and went over the plan she had quickly contrived that afternoon. She would ride close to the road, but out of sight perhaps by a mile or two, and check often to see if the road curved. Staying out of sight, she could travel north.

While she was at the convent, she had studied astronomy. She spent many evenings peering at the stars and thought that she could stay on a northern course without any other guide. It was winter and she knew the constellations well. She decided that she wouldn't have to ask for directions for weeks, and by then she would be far enough from Manor House that if Catherine organized a search, she couldn't be found.

Pleased with her plans and full of hope, she started north. When the rain started to fall, she stopped. It had been slow going. Needing to check on the curves in the road meant that she had to make continual trips back and forth, but she was making progress and no one would even care to look for her until Catherine returned late Monday evening.

The horses, speeding down the road late at night, frightened her, but she knew she could not travel any more that day. With the cold rain wetting her thoroughly, she lay on the wet ground and prayed that God would guide her path.

Angry, confused and feeling betrayed, Alex dashed

197

away from Manor House. He thought about the note he had left for Catherine. It probably didn't make a whole lot of sense, but what could he tell her that she would understand? Besides, he admitted a little sheepishly, he had intended to fool her, at least a bit. He was in no mood for one of her lectures about something she knew nothing about. And there was no way he could have explained it to her.

Alex turned his thoughts to Peter. When Alex stormed out to the stable and told his mentor that he was going back to the farm and would never return, Peter had been so dumbfounded that he had not uttered a word, for or against. As he raced along the road to Frederick, he kept hearing Nichole's pleading voice, "What have I done? Tell me what I did!" Trying to block the memories, he screamed to the wind, "You tricked me. You tricked me." And he rode into the night.

As his thoughts overwhelmed him he pushed the horse harder and harder. Dawn came and still he rode. Shortly after dawn, sanity finally returned as he heard his horse gasping for air. He stopped and led the beast back and forth on the road for over an hour. Then he let the horse rest for another hour. Once more, he was on his way, but more slowly this time. The cold January rain started late that afternoon, and when he was chilled to the bone he stopped at an inn for the night. They were serving a hearty stew, but he had no appetite and after making excuses to the cook, he sought his bed.

Exhausted, he fell asleep immediately, but it was a restless sleep, filled with nightmares. In his dream, Nichole was wandering through the forest, wet, bedraggled and hunting for food. Next, she was fighting a dark man who seemed intent on ravaging her. Finally, he saw her aboard a ship, fighting a man not unlike Jacques Manage. Suddenly, he was awake and covered with sweat.

What had she done? Any other man would have been thrilled that his wife was a virgin, that no other man had touched her. In spite of his father, Nichole was perfect for him. She was intelligent, well read, talented and a joy in bed. She could clean and sew and he wondered if she could cook. Puzzled, he asked himself, what had she done?

He had been forced to marry her, he admitted, but then the world was full of arranged marriages, and some of them were very happy. It was entirely possible that she had no concept of married love or for that matter, what rape was all about.

He sat at the edge of the bed, thinking about Nichole's training. The nuns who educated her would have spared her from any of life's sordidness. They probably told her nothing about being a wife. She couldn't have been expected to know what was happening to her, and hadn't his own father indicated that she had had no contact with the world or any of its ways? He wondered about the stains on the linens on the ship. Obviously, it was blood, but whose blood and why? He would have to ask her to explain in detail what happened when Jacques tried to force himself on her.

The only way he was going to be able to ask her anything was to turn around and head back to Manor House. That was where he wanted to be, he admitted to himself, sheepishly. Before dawn he gathered up his things, ate a hearty breakfast, and started back the way he had come. A thousand questions surfaced. Would she forgive him for what he had done? He would make it up to her, somehow. He hadn't presented her with the emeralds at Christmas, he could give her those. Maybe, he pondered, she would like another wedding. They could repeat their vows together in church. Catherine would like that.

He rode slowly, engrossed in his thoughts. As the sky lightened, he increased his speed. As it was, he would not get back to Manor House until very late that night. Then they could make a new beginning, if Nichole was willing.

Catherine and Peter arrived at Manor House well after midnight. Catherine angrily admitted that carriage horses were not the way to travel. The trip from Baltimore had taken them almost eleven hours. Usually with a good horse the trip took eight hours. Both horses were winded and had to walk the last five miles. Catherine looked at the big clock as she walked through the front hall. It was nearly three o'clock.

Catherine raced up the stairs and flung open Nichole's bedroom door. She was not there. Catherine smothered her concern and checked in her brother's room. Nichole was not there either. In agony, she ran to her own room. Nichole was not in her room either. Catherine woke up Prissy and Mrs. Barber and ordered the slaves up as well. Bit by bit, Catherine pulled the information from the sleepy servants at Manor House. Nichole had left about two in the afternoon. She had gone for a ride, and when she hadn't returned by six, several of the bondservants went looking for her.

About seven they found her neatly folded riding clothes, but there was no sign of a struggle or an accident. They quit looking.

Catherine was beside herself. She whirled on the men. "Who gave the order to stop looking? She could be injured, or she could have been abducted. Why did you stop looking?" Tears were streaming down her white face, and Prissy stepped forward to comfort her. Catherine shrieked, "It's your fault. You didn't like her. You made her leave. If she's hurt, Alex will do something dreadful to you."

Prissy visibly paled and glanced at Peter, who was obviously very angry. She stuttered, "She should have gone back to France, Alex didn't want her."

Catherine gazed at her nurse coldly. "She asked to go back to France, several times, but he wouldn't let her go!" she snapped.

Catherine turned on her heels and strode from the room. The gasp behind her didn't even slow her down. Maude ran after her. "Miz Catherine, Miz Catherine," Maude started to cry, "I done something bad, I jus' know it, something really bad."

As Catherine dragged the dark-skinned girl up the stairs to her room, she muttered, "We'll discuss it alone."

Catherine closed the bedroom door on herself and Maude and sank down in the chair before her dressing table. She spotted the note, and gasped. Tearing open the envelope, she read the note, and tears started rolling down her cheeks. "She's gone away." Catherine's voice broke and she stared up at Maude, who was also crying.

Catherine read the note and then read it again. Then she gazed at the slave in front of her. "Did you have anything to do with this?" she accused.

"Oh, Miz Catherine, she says not to tell Missus Barber of Miz Prissy, but she went away. I got her food and clothes. She asked me to help. I couldn't tell her no!" Maude wiped at her own tears. "She was so unhappy here."

Catherine sent Maude back to bed and read the note one more time. She paced the floor. Nichole was smart. She hadn't tried to leave without someplace to go. Catherine wondered if she knew how to get there. Catherine flew back down the stairs to the library and lit a dozen candles. She found the book that Nichole had torn the map from and went after Peter.

Peter was still very tired and sleepy. It was too late and he was much too tired to figure out what to do until he had some sleep. He was not too inclined to pay much attention to Catherine until she snapped, "She's traveling in your clothes."

Peter woke up quickly. "My clothes? How did she get my clothes?"

Catherine frowned. "She had help and I won't tell you who, so don't ask."

Peter was frowning himself. Somehow the idea of Nichole trying to pass herself off as a man irritated Peter more than her running away, and his mind started working. Suddenly he realized just what kind of danger she might have gotten herself into.

Catherine said quietly, "You'll have to go for Alex. She is his wife! I don't know what happened but you'll have to convince him that he must go after her. He was good at tracking in the army, he can use that skill now. She's traveling north." Catherine turned on her heels and went up to her bed to try to sleep.

Peter crawled out of his own bed. He would have to go for Alex, immediately. If she did keep to a northerly direction, they might have a chance of finding her before she got into trouble. But first, he had to get to Frederick and tell Alex into what he had pushed his young wife. Peter was on the road before dawn.

Nichole woke with that same dawn and had her breakfast from the food Maude had packed. Even though it was packed in oilcloth, the food was soggy, but it was food and Nichole knew it would have to do for the time being. She traveled all day. North a mile, then east a mile or two to check on the road. When the road curved she turned with it, forcing herself to travel through woods and across fallow fields, waiting in the gray day for the warmth of spring to turn them into something other than

202

mud. Still she made progress.

By late afternoon, she was exhausted. She hurt all over and she knew she had to find a suitable place to sleep that night, or she would make herself sick. Before the sun set, she stumbled on a small cabin that was unoccupied. Grinning happily, she discovered a bed and a fireplace inside. There was dry wood stacked in the cabin and coffee, tea and even a flint on a shelf by the fireplace. I'm far enough from Manor House, she thought as she laid a fire in the fireplace. Within an hour, she was sitting down before the fireplace to eat a hot meal and enjoy a steaming cup of tea. After she banked the fire, she stretched out on the bed and fell into a sound sleep.

About the time Nichole was enjoying her tea, Peter met Alex on the road. Alex was astonished to see Peter. "What are you doing? Are you following me?" Alex laughed, "Did Catherine send you here?" Alex frowned; Catherine and Peter should just be returning from Baltimore about now!

Peter glared at Alex, "Catherine sent me, yes! You have a problem, my friend, whether you want it or not! Nichole has run away."

"Ran away?" Alex's voice was full of surprise and something more, Peter noticed.

Peter nodded his head. "Catherine knows where she has gone, but she also doesn't think she'll make it."

"Where?" Alex snapped, a dozen thoughts running through his head. What if he couldn't find her? What if she hurt herself? What if someone hurt her? She had no knowledge of the countryside or the people in it. Could he find her before something dreadful happened? "I've been six kinds of a fool," Alex murmured as he struggled with a feeling of impotent fear. He looked over at Peter with something close to despair in his eyes.

"It seems she left Catherine a note. But you know how

your sister is. She won't show the note to anyone. In fact, she says she won't show it to you, either. We better hurry. As it is, you won't be able to start looking until morning." Peter was talking to empty space. Alex was already on his way, charging back to Manor House.

Chapter Seventeen

Minutes after ten o'clock by the porcelain clock by her bed, Catherine awoke to the crunch of horses' hooves on the stones in front of the house. She started from her bed, and then sank back to wait. It was simply too early for Peter to have found Alex and brought him back, not when Peter had to travel all the way to Frederick to get him. A sigh slipped from her tight lips. What would Alex say when he found out his wife had left? Would he be upset? More important, would he go after her?

She heard a door slam, then another, and she was driven out of her bed. Grabbing for her robe she dashed downstairs. It was Alex, and he was yelling at the top of his lungs, "Catherine, Catherine, get down here, now!"

She yelled back before she quit the stairs, "How could you? How could you? You're stupid! Dumb, dumb, dumb! You hurt her! You let Prissy and Mrs. Barber hurt her! You don't deserve her." She turned back toward the stairs. "I won't help you, if that's what you're yelling about! Not after what you've done. How can my big brother be so dumb?"

Alex caught her wrist and yanked her around so that he could look into her eyes. Nothing she said made him feel any worse than he felt already. He looked at his sister, his eyes wet with unexpected moisture. "You've got to help me, Sis. She can't survive out there all alone."

Catherine glared up at Alex. Now! Now, he was sorry, she raged silently. But, she saw something else in his eyes. "She asked me not to tell you where she went," Catherine said quietly. "I'm going to honor her request." She watched Alex's face fall. "She left me a note, and if you want it," she held the crumpled paper up, "you'll have to take it."

Alex grabbed Catherine around the waist and before she could blink, he had Nichole's note. "Don't play games with me, Catherine," he snapped.

"At least," she snapped back at him, "I can honestly tell Nichole, if I ever see her again, that you took the paper away from me. You may not care what she thinks about you, but I care what she thinks of me."

"Catherine, I have no time for your foolishness," Alex mumbled as he headed toward the candles of the study to read the note Catherine had forced him to take. His heart twisted as he read the words. No wonder Catherine wouldn't give him the letter. Nichole wrote that Catherine was her only friend, and his sister was trying to protect that friendship and help him find his wife, all at the same time.

He slumped down into a chair. Carlisle was hundreds of miles away. He didn't even know how well she could ride a horse. How on earth could she get across the mountains, find food, battle the elements and possibly predatory animals? She knew nothing about the rest of the world, there was simply no way she could survive. He would have to find her immediately, and she already had two days' start.

Catherine watched the play of emotions on her brother's face as she sat across from him in the study. She said quietly, "You really care for her, don't you?"

Alex looked right through her. He blinked back the

206

sudden wetness in his eyes and tried to focus on his sister. "I think I love her."

"Well, you better find her and tell her so. If you don't find her," Catherine stood up, "I'll never forgive you." She went stomping off.

Alex spent the next two hours talking to each of the bondservants involved in the search, and then he talked to Maude. He was stunned at some of the things the little black girl told him. Finally, seething, he went in search of Prissy and Mrs. Barber. He found them in the kitchen, huddled around the table. "Do you two have any idea what you've done?" he shouted. "My God, there's no telling what she's up against out there." He slammed his fist on the table, and both the teacups before the women rattled ominously. "She is my wife! I made her my wife. You had no right to assume anything! Never again will you try to send her away. And, if I can't find her, you'll both think my father was a saint." Alex slammed out of the room.

Prissy glanced at Mrs. Barber, her face white. "What have we done?"

Mrs. Barber, her shoulders sagging, stared ahead at the door through which Alex had passed. "He loves her. I didn't know he loved her." Her voice a husky whisper, she leaned toward Prissy. "We never gave her a chance."

Prissy wiped at the tears in her eyes. "She worked so hard and we never told her what a good job she did. She never complained. If he can find her . . ." Prissy was sobbing now.

Mrs. Barber's voice quavered. "We'll make it up to her. Somehow, we'll make it up to her."

Alex pulled Peter into the study before he went upstairs. "I'll leave at dawn, have things ready for me." He made his way up the stairs to the room he had shared so briefly with Nichole.

Sleep came slowly, and when it finally came, terrifying dreams filled his subconscious. Nichole was mixed up with the memories of his days with the army and a dozen times he sat up in his bed, shaking in fear for her safety. Long before dawn, he was up and dressed. He went down to the kitchen and packed a bag of food that would last him for at least a week. Before long, Peter was in the kitchen with him, and the two men discussed Alex's plan of action.

"I think I'd better go, too," Peter spoke softly. "We can cover more ground between the two of us. If she has been abducted by savages . . ." He watched Alex pale considerably. "Well, damn it, man, it could happen! I can return to Manor House or go to Frederick for help if there's a need."

There was no answer for Alex to give. And he knew deep inside that Peter was right. Before dawn both men had their horses saddled, their supplies tied to the back of the saddle, waiting for the sky to lighten. At least, Alex thought as he finished his twentieth cup of coffee, they knew in which direction to look. Just as the first streaks of light could be seen in the east, they were off.

Nichole awoke just as the first light of dawn streaked across the sky. The sky was clear, and she was sure that it would be a nice day to travel, but she felt terrible. She was hot, and her head ached. Momentarily, she wondered if the afternoon she had spent in that cold room at Manor House, with the contents of the smelly chamber pot, had made her ill. After she fixed herself a hot breakfast, she packed up her supplies, then left the cabin. As she traveled, she would alternate between being much too hot and then chilled to the point where she was actually shaking. What is wrong with me, she wondered.

By late afternoon, she began to wonder if she would live to leave the forest. When she could stay on the horse no longer, she made a small fire and wrapped herself in her cloak. She had no energy to eat and although she was very thirsty, she had no strength to find water. Desperate now, she admitted she was ill and she prayed for deliverance.

She slept poorly and the next morning, she realized she was so ill that she would only be able to go a little farther. Her chest ached and she had trouble breathing, but she raised her head and glared at the trees. "I won't die, not in this desolate place. I'll survive! Somehow I'll leave this place of misery," she told the forest. With near superhuman strength, she pulled herself up on the horse. As she lay against the filly's neck she willed the horse to find help.

Nichole fought to stay in the saddle, but by the end of two hours, Nichole conceded that she had reached the end of her limited strength. Slowly, she sank into a black void. She was not even aware that she had slipped from the horse and lay unconscious at the base of a centuries-old oak tree in a soft pile of leaves. Her horse stayed close by, grazing on the winter grass that was easily available under the pile of leaves.

All day Tuesday, Alex and Peter tracked Nichole. She was heading in the direction of the cabin that once had been occupied by a family of settlers north of Manor House land. Alex prayed that he would find her there. They reached the cabin that evening, just as the winter sun was setting. Signs that someone had been at the cabin a day or two before did not ease the ache that Alex felt. He had been so sure that she would be at the cabin. He glared at Peter when the man refused to go on. "We can track her at night. I'm good at that," Alex argued when Peter pulled his blanket from the back of his horse.

Peter stated quietly, "You could miss her in the dark. I'll wait until first light, then I'll start out. You'll do whatever you want, no matter what I say," he grumbled.

Alex went on without him. He lost her tracks continually, and in frustration he returned to the cabin. Peter handed him a plate of food. "We'll leave at first light," the older man assured him.

Alex slept that night from near exhaustion, and he did not dream. Before dawn, both men were up, and once more, as the sky was streaked with light, they were on their way, following the trail that Nichole had left.

They had been traveling only two hours when Alex turned to Peter. "Something's wrong. She is no longer checking the road and the horse is moving in an erratic manner. Could she be hurt?"

Peter nodded gravely. "That, or she's sick." Both men moved forward a little faster. In less than two hours, Peter spotted her horse. As if by design, they separated. Alex was so filled with fear that speech would have been impossible for him.

In minutes, Alex found her, curled up at the base of an oak tree, and before he dismounted, he knew she was gravely ill. Her breathing was labored, her complexion was ashen, and as he reached to smooth the golden curls from her face, he felt the heat radiate from her body. He yelled for Peter, anguish in his hoarse voice.

Before he could assess her condition more, Peter was beside him, and together they wrapped her in the blankets Alex had brought. "I have to take her to the cabin," he whispered, "I can't force her to travel to Manor House. She'll never make it."

Peter sensed the urgency. "You take her to the cabin, I'll go get Prissy."

"No!" Alex said sharply. "Get blankets, medicine and food, and I'll care for her myself." He handed Peter his precious bundle and mounted his horse. As soon as he had her in his arms, he coaxed the horse into motion.

Peter mounted his own horse and glanced up at the sun. Riding hard he might be able to get to Manor House and back to the cabin before midnight. "I'll get back as soon as I can," he yelled at Alex's departing back.

Alex prayed all the way back to the cabin, "God, don't let her die." In a husky voice, he whispered into her ear, "Fight, Nichole, fight. We have our whole lives ahead of us. Don't give in, don't. Stay with me, so I can tell you how much I love you." Her only response was an occasional moan.

When he got to the cabin, he stripped Peter's clothes off of her, wrapped her in blankets and put her to bed. Then he set about building a blazing fire. Using the two kettles that were in the cabin, he filled each with water from the nearby stream and hung them over the fire. Next, he closed up the cabin. The stream would help her breathe, he reasoned. He trudged back to the stream for another bucket, and forced some cool water down her throat; she roused for a second, but her glazed eyes stared up at him without recognition. Through the long hours he bathed her with water from the stream, fed the fire, added water to the kettles and prayed. A half smile curved his lips slightly, for even when he was facing the British at Germantown, he had not prayed.

Darkness came and Peter had not returned; still Alex kept the fire going and the water steaming as he worked over her. She tossed and turned and tried to push the blankets away, fighting with him when he wrapped her up again. Whenever he lifted her to try to get some water down her throat, she struggled against him as if he was hurting her. Could she be hurt as well as sick? he wondered, and part of his heart twisted in pain.

Before midnight, Peter arrived with blankets, broth and herbs Prissy said would help. Peter fixed food for both of them and then saw to the horses. As he watched Nichole toss and turn, he suggested, "Why don't you get some sleep. I'll watch for a while."

Alex only shook his head and continued to fix tea from the herbs Prissy had sent. As Alex tried to spoon some of the tea into her mouth, Peter asked softly, "How is she? What do you think her chances are?"

Alex refused to answer Peter's questions, so Peter rolled up in a mat on the floor and tried to get some sleep. He was vaguely aware that Alex was moving about the cabin, but he forced his wild speculations from his thoughts. He would have to care for Nichole when Alex collapsed. He needed his sleep.

The next morning, Peter fixed breakfast, once again trying to get Alex to sleep. "I forgot to tell you, Robert arrived yesterday. He and Catherine will want to know how she is." Alex refused to answer. Peter grumbled, "I'll go chop some wood, and then you're going to rest."

Alex glared at him, but for once Alex realized his friend was only trying to help. When the woodpile was once again replenished, Alex stretched out on the mat Peter had used the night before. But every time he dozed off, Nichole grew restless. Her moans and the creaking of the cot brought him off the mat in seconds and to her side. He did sleep a little, and Peter fixed him something to eat. When Peter was certain there was nothing more he could do, he left for Manor House, with the promise to return in two days.

Through the afternoon, Alex continued to bathe her with cooling cloths and spoon the herb tea into her. Alex noticed that she seemed to be breathing easier, but she was growing more restless as the day wore on, and her fever was still high, much too high. As darkness crept through the woods, Nichole began to cry out. "Damn," Alex muttered, the fever was driving her out of her mind.

Nichole was once more at home with her father and

her brothers, but they were all crying. "Why are you crying, Papa?" Then she was at the convent. "Papa, don't go, don't leave me like Mama did. If you leave me, Mama will miss me when she comes home. I don't like it here, Papa. These women are all dressed in black. Papa, don't leave me!" Tears steamed from her sightless eyes.

As Alex lifted her to force more tea through her parched lips, she scolded him, "I don't want to drink the tea, Papa. Please don't leave me. I'll drink the tea if you will take me home."

She raised her hand and Alex wondered if she truly saw the hand above her face. "Why won't Soeur Barbara hold me? I cut my hand, and all she does is wipe up the blood, and tell me to be brave. I can't be brave, I want my mother, she won't know where to find me. Papa has forgotten me, he won't•remember where I am. Please, Soeur Barbara, hold me. Hold me, like my mother did."

Monsieur Dampier came toward her. "I don't want to marry, I want to be a governess. Frere Francis, why must I learn Greek and Latin? No one uses it anymore. I didn't do well on my mathematics test, did I? Monsieur Dampier won't like it. Why can't I go help Soeur Clare in the garden? All I ever do is study. Frere Francis, I can't remember the name of the king. Will Monsieur Dampier quit sending the money?"

"Why must I marry, Ma Mere? I was to be a governess, not a wife. I don't know about being a wife."

"You must not touch me, only my husband can touch me. Monsieur Manage, if you touch me, Ma Mere says I'll burn in hell. Mother Thomas, I fought him, but I couldn't stop him. He held me down, he ripped my dress, my brand new dress. I couldn't stop him, I couldn't make him stop."

As Alex bathed her with the cool water he listened to her ramblings with a heavy heart. Then she called out to him, "Alex, don't go away, don't leave me. What did I do? Why is he going away? I let Monsieur Manage touch me, that's why he's leaving. I tried to stop him. I stuck him with a needle. The captain made him stop."

"Alex, why don't you want a wife? Why don't you want me? Is it because Monsieur Manage touched me? Alex, help me! I'm sick. I'm going to die and Alex will never know. He won't look for me, he doesn't want a wife."

As she struggled against him, Alex held her, his tears wetting his skin. She rambled on about Prissy and Mrs. Barber and he fought to control his anger. No one should have had to endure what those two had forced on her. And Catherine knew, she had tried to tell him. He was as guilty as his housekeeper and the cook because he wouldn't listen. As he continued to bathe her with cool water and spoon Prissy's tea over her cracked and bleeding lips, he silently apologized, "Forgive me, Nichole. Forgive us all."

The evening hours crawled into night, and when she finally quieted down, he set about fixing some of the food Peter had brought. He got fresh water from the nearby stream and banked the fire. For the moment, Nichole seemed to be resting more comfortably, so he decided that he should try to rest himself.

He glared at the bedroll Peter had used and then at the bed. If Nichole got restless, or grew worse in the night, he wouldn't know if he slept on the floor. He crawled into the bed next to her and wrapped himself in a blanket. Once more during the night, Nichole grew restless, and Alex dragged himself out of bed. As he bathed her down, he wondered if she was truly cooler, or if she seemed cooler because he wished it so. He banked the fire and added water to both kettles; then he crawled back into bed. Soon, he drifted off to sleep.

The sun was warming him, and he was floating on his

214

back in a large, blue lake. Funny, he thought, only one side was wet, and if he was in a lake, he'd be wet all over. Instantly, he was awake. The side next to Nichole was damp, the bed under her was soaked and she was covered with moisture. Her fever had broken. Alex wanted to shout with joy. He looked down at her and realized her eyes were open and she was staring at him. There was no question: she recognized him.

Nichole studied Alex carefully. His face was covered with dark hairy stubble, there were dark circles under his eyes and he looked tired. She tried to sit up, but she couldn't move, she hurt all over. Where was she, and why was he lying in bed with her? She closed her eyes and tried to remember what she had been doing. Slowly, the events of the last week came back to her. She had left, needed to travel north to Pennsylvania, and then she got sick. Had her horse taken her back to Manor House? She opened her eyes and looked around. This looked like the cabin she had stopped in before she got so sick. How had he found her? Was he going to send her away now that he was here?

Nichole tried to ask him how he had found her and where she was, but her mouth would not obey her thoughts. Before she could make her lips move, Alex started talking. "Good morning, Nichole. You're all wet. We have to get something dry on you and some warm blankets on the bed. Don't try to talk just yet."

Nichole stared at him for a moment. Why was he chattering so? She tried once more to sit up, but she didn't have the strength. "Where am I?" was all she could manage as her eyes closed again.

"First, we must get you dry; then I'll answer your questions." Alex was rummaging through the things Peter had brought. He pulled a warm chemise over her head and tucked a blanket around her, then yanked the wet blankets from the bed. Spreading dry blankets on the bed, he rolled her back to the center and tucked another blanket around her. "You've got to have something to eat," he commented as he moved back toward the fireplace.

While some of the broth from Prissy warmed, he made fresh tea and brought them both to the bed. "I insist," he smiled as he held the spoon to her lips. She managed some of the broth and a bit of the bitter tea he said she had to drink, but she was fighting to stay awake. He set the broth and tea aside, and carefully spreading another blanket around her he whispered, "Sleep now, my love. We'll talk later."

Dazed with the thick clouds of unconsciousness, Nichole struggled to make sense of his words. "My love," he had whispered. Surely, he didn't say that she was his love. She could think no more.

Alex set about straightening the cabin. He felt great! Her fever had broken, she was alert, she was going to be all right. He wanted to sing, to shout. Thank God, Thank God, he murmured. He fixed himself something to eat, then checked on Nichole. She was still asleep, a deep healing sleep, so he went out to check on his horse and to dunk his own sticky body in the stream.

Refreshed, and elated with Nichole's improvement, he went back into the cabin. He leaned over the bed, she was still sound asleep. Sighing happily, he went back outside to chop more wood and think about the apology he had to give his young wife.

As he swung the axe, he planned his words. He would have to explain why he left her for the farm. Glancing back at the cabin, he stopped chopping for several minutes. Did she have any idea at all about men and women and married love? He could tell her that he was sorry he had hurt her, but was that what she wanted to hear?

While she was delirious she had mentioned over and over that she wanted to be a governess. If that was what she truly wanted, could he let her go?

His curiosity was getting the better of him when he realized that he had to know what had happened on the ship with Jacques Manage. She had mentioned a needle. Determined to get some of his questions answered, he went back into the cabin, but she was still sleeping soundly.

He added more wood to the fire and sank down into the only chair in the room to think about her recovery. Manor House, with the servants and Catherine, was where he should take her, but Prissy and Mrs. Barber couldn't be trusted. They might not be interested in her comforts. Even if they were sorry for what they had done, if Nichole didn't trust them, it wouldn't be good for her. Besides, he grinned to himself, he wanted to take care of her himself, he wanted to have time with her alone, before others interfered. "When she's strong enough to travel, I'll take her to Frederick. She can recover at the farm," he mumbled. Alex drifted off to sleep in the chair.

Chapter Eighteen

While Alex was caring for Nichole, Catherine agonized over her friend. If Alex and Peter couldn't find her, what would happen to her? She didn't know enough to survive in the wilderness by herself. If only she hadn't been so intent on spending the time with Robert, Catherine scolded herself, she could have prevented Nichole's departure.

By Wednesday morning, Catherine had to share her fears with someone. She would not, not in a hundred years, tell Prissy or Mrs. Barber how she felt. The whole thing was their fault, anyway. If they had given Nichole half a chance, she wouldn't be running away. With Peter gone with Alex she decided that Robert had to know. Seating herself at Alex's desk, she composed a note to Robert and sent it on its way.

Thursday afternoon, before dinner, Catherine heard the horse and raced for the front door. It wasn't Peter or Alex, she knew that the instant she saw the horse. When the tall man swung himself off the horse and limped toward the door, Catherine breathed a sigh of relief. Robert had come!

Catherine threw open the door and ran to the steps. "Oh, thank you for coming."

Robert's face was grim, and as he started up the steps

he pulled Catherine's note from his pocket. "What's going on?" He stopped on the top step, opened the envelope, and read Catherine's message out loud. "Nichole's gone. Come quickly."

Catherine glanced at him, surprised at the puzzled expression on his face. He couldn't have thought that Nichole died . . . But, of course! Nichole had been sick when he left and Peter never told either of them why Alex left. He thought—"Oh, Robert, I'm sorry. Nichole has run away. Peter and Alex are looking for her. Alex was so concerned about her, I thought you ought to know."

Robert took her arm and led her back into the house. "My dear lady," Robert said, grinning, "you have a flare for the dramatic." He glanced down at her, a little surprised by the sudden tears that glistened in her eyes. This was serious and Catherine was frightened. He really shouldn't tease her. "Catherine," he said quietly, "Alex is an excellent tracker. When he was in the army, he saved my skin a half dozen times with his skills. He'll find her. Don't worry."

While Catherine saw to his room and arranged for an extra place setting at the table, Robert read the note Nichole had left and talked to Maude. What could have happened to drive the French girl out into the wilderness? Robert wondered. Alex was moody, given to holding things inside, but Robert was sure that Alex had begun even before Christmas to seriously consider Nichole as a mate. Something terrible must have happened to send him back to the farm, to drive him away.

He questioned Catherine at dinner, but Catherine had nothing to add to what Maude had already told him. They had just finished dessert when another horse crunched across the gravel and headed back to the stable. Catherine, followed by Robert, raced for the back door.

Peter shouted the answer before Catherine asked the

219

question: "He found her."

"Well, where are they?" Catherine blocked his way, her hands clenched into fists and resting on her hips.

"She's—" Peter stopped, noticing Robert for the first time. "What's he doing here?"

"I sent for him," Catherine snapped. "Now, where is Nichole?"

"You remember that small cottage those settlers b . . ."

Catherine didn't let him finish. "What's she doing there? Is Alex with her? Has he apologized to her? When is he bringing her home?"

In exasperation, Robert grabbed her arm. "Catherine, give Peter a chance to finish."

Catherine glared at both men, then turned toward Peter, expectantly. Peter continued, "Alex took her to the cabin. Catherine, Nichole is sick."

"Sick? Then for God's sake, why didn't he bring her home? We can take care of her here."

Robert sensed that it was more serious than Peter seemed inclined to say. "Catherine, let Peter come in. He's probably hungry and if you give him half a chance, I'm sure he'll tell us everything he knows."

Peter frowned. He didn't miss Robert's word "us." Well, Alex didn't need to be concerned with his sister when his new wife might be dying at this very moment. He sighed and pushed past Catherine. He had to gather the things Alex needed and get back to the cabin. At the moment, he didn't want to tell the girl anything.

Somehow Robert understood the problem. "Catherine, while Peter gets something to eat, why don't you get some of Nichole's things together. I'm sure Peter intends to take some things back to Alex."

Peter smiled in gratitude. Catherine scurried off to see to some clothes for Nichole, and Robert followed Peter into the kitchen. Assured that Catherine was out of earshot, Robert asked quietly, "How bad is she?"

Peter scratched his graying stubble. "I didn't get a chance to see much of her. From the way Alex was carrying on, though, I'd say she was in a bad way."

"You're going back." It was more a statement than a question. Peter nodded his head and started for the pot of tea beside the fire.

Once he had his tea in his hands he turned back to Robert. "I'll leave as soon as I have the things Alex needs."

"I'd be obliged if I can stay until you return with a report."

Peter nodded his head once more, then grinned. "That just might keep Catherine from trailing after me. Yeh, you can stay, but I'd rather you didn't tell that young miss how sick Nichole is until I come back with some word."

It was Robert's turn to nod. Peter left to find Prissy, and Robert started off toward the stairs, scratching his head. Why was he more concerned with Catherine's feelings in all of this than for Nichole? he wondered.

In less than an hour, Peter was on his way, and Robert was left to contend with Catherine. Over tea in the study, Robert realized that Peter knew her well. Catherine stared at the fire. "I really ought to go to her. Alex doesn't care for her and if she's sick, she needs the care of a woman." She stood. "You can wait until Peter returns. I'm going to Nichole."

"Catherine," Robert said quietly, "it'll be dark in a short time. Alex is very capable of taking care of Nichole, and despite what you think, he cares for her very much. I don't know what happened, but lovers' quarrels often happen. We may never know what happened between them. He's found her and he'll take care of her." He whispered softly, "If he wanted you to help, he would

221

have asked Peter to bring you."

She sank back down into her chair. "You'll stay until we have some word? I don't want to be alone."

Robert smiled at her, "I'll stay," he said, and wondered at the twisted feelings that surged through his stomach at her words.

Robert wondered about that feeling all that night and again the next day. He and Catherine spent several quiet hours before the fire, and Catherine explained all the things Nichole had told her. She went on to tell him about the horseback riding and the work around the plantation. She even described some of the things she knew Prissy and Mrs. Barber had pulled on Nichole in their attempt to get Nichole to return to France. "She can't go back to France," Robert said in dismay. "People are killing each other over there."

Catherine brushed at her tears, turning Robert into soft mush. "You tell them that! Maybe they'll leave Nichole alone."

Robert considered saying something to Prissy and Mrs. Barber after Catherine sought her bed. Frowning, he admitted that it was Alex's affair, not his. Truthfully, he acknowledged that the only reason he wanted to tell the women was that Catherine seemed to feel that he should. He took himself into Alex's study and poured himself some of the whiskey Alex was so proud of. What on earth was happening to him? Catherine was the little sister of his best friend. And she was a child. She wasn't even that pretty! And here she was twisting him around her little finger. Obviously, he had to get back to the city. Staying with Catherine was not going to do him any good. He finished his drink and went to bed himself.

Early next morning, Peter was at the table with Catherine when Robert came into the room. Catherine glanced up, her eyes red-rimmed. "Peter says she's very sick. She may not make it." Catherine's voice sobbed and she ran from the room.

Robert stood in indecision. Should he comfort Catherine or find out what Peter had to say? He forced himself to turn to Peter. "Is she that bad?" Peter couldn't talk himself. He just nodded. Robert turned around and followed Catherine.

Later that afternoon, Robert sent a message to his office. He would stay at Manor House until Wednesday, and he asked his clerk to rearrange his schedule. He kept telling himself that he was staying to offer support to Alex if it was needed. There was no way he would admit to himself that Catherine might need him, too.

Peter gathered supplies, and the next morning he headed back to the cabin. Robert endured a long horseback ride with Catherine to keep her busy. Peter would return Tuesday, if not sooner. They should know one way or the other by then.

Peter cautiously opened the door to the cabin. Nichole looked deathly still in the bed, and Alex himself looked half-dead in the chair. For a second, Peter's heart lurched into his throat. Just then, Alex snored and Nichole rolled over. Peter sighed in relief.

Peter tapped Alex gently on the shoulder and whispered, "How is she?"

Alex stretched and grinned. "I think we both are going to make it."

Peter looked around the cabin, at the woodpile and at Alex. "Been busy, I see. I brought some of your whiskey in case you needed it. Want a drink to celebrate?"

Alex's wide grin was an answer in itself. Peter went to get the bottle, and in minutes the two men were sitting before the fire, talking and sipping the biting brew.

223

Peter left early the next morning, promising to come in a week with more supplies. Alex informed Peter that he and Nichole would travel to the farm when she was strong enough for the trip. "When you come back, bring a wagon and horses." Alex went on to list all of the things he felt he would need with Nichole at the farm. He even told Peter where to find the emeralds in his desk. Then he drafted a note to Catherine, asking her to pack some of Nichole's clothes, explaining that he was going to take them with him to the farm. He wrote that they would return to Manor House in two months and she wouldn't see them until then.

For the next three days Nichole did little more than sleep. Usually, she woke for meals, and she tried to stay awake for a short time each evening, but Alex made her stay in bed and sleep. He felt her health was much too delicate to talk about anything that might upset her, so he put off telling her how he had found her or why he had come back. His concern wasn't necessary, because Nichole asked no questions of him at all.

While she slept, he did the cooking, went hunting, and chopped enough wood to last for months. When she was awake, she was always pleasant but she seemed very distant to him and he was terrified that what he would say to her was not what she wanted to hear.

He practiced apologizing to the horse and the logs he was chopping, even to the trees beside the stream where he bathed. Nothing sounded right to him. As the days progressed and Nichole regained her strength, he still avoided talking about their relationship or what had happened before and after she ran from him, telling himself that he was afraid to harm her health. Finally, one afternoon, he admitted that he was a coward. Peter was due to arrive the next afternoon, and Alex realized that he and Nichole had talked about the weather, the hunting, the cabin, but neither of them had mentioned Manor House, or Nichole's reason for being in the cabin in the first place.

As Nichole slept and ate and gathered her strength, she forced herself to accept the inevitable. As soon as she recovered, she was certain Alex was going to tell her that it was time that they separated. She had no idea whether he was going to send her back to France or on to Mrs. Hutchinson in Carlisle. If he told her that she was to return to Manor House, she was prepared to bargain with him. She had already decided that she would not go back there, not even with Catherine there.

After the evening meal, Alex squared his shoulders and dragged the chair over to the bed. He plumped up Nichole's pillows, sat down in the chair and asked if she felt like talking. Nichole glanced at him and then at her hands folded in her lap. Her heart was in her mouth. She was nearly recovered. The time she had dreaded was here. He was going to tell her what her future held, and she was positive that it was a future without him.

Alex glanced over at his wife. He had never had to do anything so difficult in his life, he decided. All of the speeches he had been preparing for five days were suddenly forgotten. What if she wanted to go back to France or on to the woman in Pennsylvania? he asked himself.

He cleared his throat and looked at her again. She's as nervous as I feel, he told himself. He cleared his throat once more, "Nichole," he said, his voice sounding husky even to him, "I want to apologize."

For a second Nichole was stunned, thinking she should be apologizing to him. "There's no need," she started slowly; "I should be the one to apologize for taking you away from your farm. I know that is where you want to be."

Alex groaned; this was going to be more difficult than

he thought. He started again. "When you first came to Manor House, I told you why my father arranged a marriage between us, but I didn't tell you all of it." She raised her hand to stop him. "No, I want you to hear the whole story." He began by telling her about Catherine's part in Henry's scheme.

She did stop him. "You don't have to tell me any more. Catherine told me all about your father and his plans."

"Catherine doesn't know all about my father's plans, only a very little bit, just the part that concerned her. There is much more." He told her about his trips to Baltimore and his meetings with Robert. Trying to smile, he said softly, "Remember, all of this happened before I had even met you." Telling her about Catherine and the trip to the farm, he ended with his argument with his father. He stumbled over the next part. "Jacques Manage was supposed to . . . he was . . . he . . . Oh, hell! What you and I did the night I left you is what Jacques Manage was supposed to do. If you weren't willing he was told to force you. It's called rape!"

Nichole turned beet red and moved uncomfortably in the bed. Looking down at her hands, she muttered, "He didn't do that!"

A half smile played over his lips. "I know that."

She eyed him suspiciously. "How?"

Alex groaned. He knew that she had very little knowledge of the world; what did he expect? he asked himself. He would have to teach her about love, too. And her virginity was as good a place as any to start, he supposed. He took her delicate hand in his and explained to her how he knew Jacques had not succeeded with his father's directive. She alternated between a bright red and a pale white as he explained.

He also wanted to make certain that she never again blamed herself for what had almost happened. "Just because Jacques tried, and even if he had succeeded, it was not your fault. Men are stronger than women. If the captain had not stopped him, he would have hurt you, but it would never have been your fault. I fell in love with you before I knew that he had failed."

For most of Alex's explanation Nichole had sat watching the hand he held, her cheeks burning. With his last statement she gazed into his eyes. "You love me?"

Alex whispered, "Very, very much." He smiled from the chair.

Nichole was considering all that he had told her when he broke into her train of thought. "There is one thing I'm very curious about. The night of the attack, the captain said there were stains on the sheet, and blood on you. Did Jacques draw blood, before the captain arrived?"

Nichole's face turned crimson again. "I drew blood. I stuck him with a needle. When he jerked away, the needle cut his arm. There was blood all over his shirt sleeve and the sheets. There was even some on me." She glanced over at Alex. His face was red and she knew that he was angry, very angry.

When Alex regained some control, he commented, "Served him right!" He moved over onto the bed beside her. "Sweetheart, when Peter came after me, I had already started back to ask your forgiveness. When he told me that you had run away, and then I found you nearly dead in the woods, a part of me almost died. I didn't know how important you were to me until I thought that I might lose you." Alex paused, for it was now or never. "I want us to live together, be man and wife, raise a family, live happily ever after. I want you to come to the farm with me and be a farmer's wife. I want time to convince you that I truly want you for my wife. Will you come?"

Nichole gazed up at him. He looked so anxious. Did he really want her as his wife? He had changed his mind before, back at Manor House. Afraid that he might change his mind again, or that he might have forgotten why he left her for the farm, she murmured, "I didn't trick you. I didn't lie to you. I just didn't know . . ." Her voice trailed off.

"I know that now. I said some terrible things to you. I can't explain why I said them. I was confused, angry. You stirred up emotions in me that I couldn't deal with. That's what I was apologizing for, for all the things I said that hurt you."

Nichole sat looking at her hands again, almost afraid to commit herself to him. Alex sat waiting quietly, almost afraid to breathe. What if she turned him down?

"Alex, if I go to the farm with you . . ." A deep blush colored her face, and she glanced up at him. "Will you . . . will we . . . Can we make love again?" she whispered.

Alex smiled down at her. "I told you once, all night, every night. Do you remember?" She nodded her head gravely. He said softly, "If you were stronger, we could make love right here."

"Here?"

It was Alex's turn to nod his head. Nichole moved over on the bed and reached for his shirt. "Oh, I feel fine. I have almost completely recovered. I am very strong."

Alex raised his head to look at her carefully. "Are you sure? I don't want a relapse. I can wait."

Nichole cocked her head to one side and grinned up at him. "I can't!"

Alex chuckled and put his arms around her. As he lowered his lips to hers he wondered why he had ever thought to live apart. She was his life's blood, his days would begin and end with her and she would always be at

228

his side. He muttered into her soft, shell-like ear, "If you come with me, you'll have to clean the house." She nodded as she pulled at his shirt. "You'll have to cook my meals." He was nibbling at her ear as she reached for the waistband of his breeches. "You'll have my children." She was pulling his pants down around his legs. Alex started to chuckle as he reached for her chemise. "Oh, Lord! We'll probably have a dozen."

Chapter Nineteen

Together they sank into the thin mattress of the bed. Alex cradled her slender body against his and kissed her gently. "So sweet, so very sweet," he murmured against her lips. Nichole ran her hands over his shoulders and pulled him down against her, snuggling even closer to him. Even through his shirt, he felt so good to her. She let her fingers trail down his arms, up again and around his neck. Unconsciously she let her fingers twine through the curls at the back of his neck while she opened her lips to his exploring tongue.

He traced the inside of her bottom lip, and Nichole, hesitant, followed his lead, acquainting herself with the feel of him, the taste of him. She inhaled deeply and grew dizzy with the male scent of him. Suddenly his unbuttoned shirt was a hindrance she couldn't abide, and she pulled at the sleeves. "Take it off," she whimpered against his mouth. Instantly the shirt was gone, and she ran her fingers over the straining muscles of his back.

While Nichole was fingering his taut back, Alex reached for the fullness above her ribs. He held her breast, stroking the warm flesh, teasing it, squeezing it. He dragged his mouth from her lips to the firm nipple and attacked it with his tongue, his teeth, pulling, twirling until Nichole was squirming beside him. He raised his head to smile at her. "You like that, don't you."

"Oh, yes, yes, yes," she whispered as she reached up to push his head back where he could pleasure her more. This time she knew the thrill that was to come, and she arched up against him, wanting more, needing more. Without a word he seemed to understand, and he let his fingers trail down her ribs, past her tiny waist, over her hip bones and down her legs. She shook her head. That was not what she wanted and he knew it. He grinned up at her. "Tell me," he urged.

"Like before" was all that Nichole could manage, her voice a husky murmur.

"Like this?" Alex questioned as his hand drifted up the insides of her legs to the center of her. Nichole couldn't answer him. All of her senses were centered in that one spot as Alex separated the golden curls and teased at her pleasure. Nichole sighed.

Alex felt her quiver and he nudged her knees apart. With infinite care, he placed himself between her legs and thrust himself forward, slowly sheathing himself. When they were joined as one, he let his heartbeat slow as he stared down at his bride. "I love you, Nichole, my heart. You are mine, now and forever."

Nichole forced her eyes open and stared up into the face of the man she called husband. "I love you, Alex. I am yours, now and forever," she whispered in return. Alex leaned forward and brushed her lips in silent communication. Then he captured her mouth in a furious kiss and began to move, slowly at first, then more quickly, rocking her with him until she was spinning hopelessly in a world of brilliant lights.

Once again, she exploded, and she knew she cried out as wave after wave of pleasure engulfed her. Before she floated back to earth, Alex went rigid above her, a groan of satisfaction erupting from his throat. He moaned her

231

name and she knew that he had experienced the same fierce bliss. He held her tightly and she never knew when he moved to his side of the cot. She was sound asleep in seconds, happier than she had ever been.

Nichole awoke the next morning feeling marvelous. Even with her eyes closed she could sense that the cabin was filled with bright sunlight. She listened to the sounds around her. Obviously, someone was moving around the cabin, trying to make as little noise as possible. She opened her eyes and watched her husband as he gathered his clothes.

He glanced at the bed and seemed surprised that she was awake. "I'm sorry, I didn't mean to wake you."

Nichole looked at him, suddenly afraid that he was leaving. Her voice shook slightly and Alex saw the fear in her eyes as she asked, "Where are you going?"

Alex walked over to the bed and sat down. He stared into the soft green eyes that looked up at him in confusion. "There is a stream not far from here," he told her quietly, "and I'm going to take a bath. Then, if you promise to be good and stay in this bed, I'll get enough water so that you can bathe, too. But you, my love, will have to bathe in a bucket. The stream is too cold for you." He leaned over and kissed her soft lips, wanting to drown in them. He raised his head slightly, caressing her cheek with his large hand. "On second thought . . ."

Nichole pushed him gently, giggling a little. "Go bathe. Even a bath in a bucket sounds marvelous. I'll stay in bed. Just hurry."

"Are you anxious for the bath or for my return?" Alex teased, his lower lip protruding slightly in a fake pout.

"Both," Nichole spouted and then blushed a soft pink.

Alex grabbed two buckets and his clothes and started toward the door. "Be back soon. You stay there!" He was out the door and she could hear him whistling as he

232

walked away.

She snuggled into the blankets and let her thoughts drift. He wanted her to come with him to his farm. She would cook, clean and take care of her husband, just as Ma Mere had hoped she would. She chuckled; her husband would be surprised to learn that she was a good cook. He had teased about a dozen children. She frowned slightly. Did he have any idea how children came to be? No one had ever explained birth to her and she had never been around farm animals. Even the milk they used at the convent had been brought to them in buckets. Once, she had seen a woman feeding her baby, and Soeur Clare, embarrassed though she seemed, had explained that women's breasts filled with milk when a child arrived. Arrived from where, she wondered. If Alex didn't know, who would she ask?

As she thought of Alex, her thoughts drifted back to the night just spent. She blushed as she remembered all of the things Alex had done to her. Her blush deepened when she remembered what she had said to him. He told her he loved her and that she was his. She smiled, her body tingling just from the memory. She was not even aware that Alex had come back to the cabin and had been watching her from the door.

As Alex watched her, he could guess where her mind was leading her. Her eyes were half closed and her perfect oval face had such a sensual look to it that Alex abandoned the bucket of water and moved through the door. She licked her lips and turned her head ever so slightly. Her bath can wait, Alex thought, but I can not. Without a word he moved to the bed and drew her up into his aching arms. Slowly, they melted into the bed. Somehow his clothes were gone and he once more claimed the beauty that was his wife.

Much later Alex woke. Nichole was tucked firmly

against his body and his arm was holding her tightly against him. Lord, how would he ever get anything done? If every time he saw her in bed he had to possess her, they would never leave their bed. He chuckled; not a bad way to go. Of course the farm would fall apart.

The farm! Reality surfaced and Alex playfully swatted her behind. "Woman, Peter will be here soon." They hadn't eaten and she hadn't bathed. They wouldn't get away from the cabin for another week if he didn't get them started, he chuckled.

Nichole opened her eyes and rolled over. "Peter is coming?" she mumbled in her sleep. Then she sat bolt upright. "Peter!"

Alex laughed, "If you want a bath, you will have to hurry. Peter is coming with a wagon and your clothes and things for the farm. We'll leave early tomorrow for Frederick."

She scrambled out of bed. Suddenly she stared down at herself; she had forgotten that she was completely naked. Blushing, she grabbed for the blanket on the bed. Alex moved toward her and put his arms around her shoulders. "I very much like it when you have no clothes on. You're a very beautiful woman. You don't need to be embarrassed."

Nichole slid her arms up around his neck and pulled his head down so that she could kiss him full on the lips. She had never been so happy. Sighing, she grabbed for the slipping blanket. "Being this kind of married will take some getting used to."

While Nichole bathed, Alex fixed their breakfast. By the time she had finished, Alex noticed that she was visibly tired. He scolded himself for not adhering to his better judgment this morning and the night before. She should have slept, he admitted, rather than spending the night in his arms. After breakfast, he insisted that she

234

rest, and when Peter arrived she was sound asleep.

Everything Alex requested Peter brought, as well as a note from Catherine saying that she was delighted that Nichole was better. She added that she thought he was a selfish brute for stealing her off to Frederick for her recuperation. She also told him that Prissy and Mrs. Barber were so upset with what they had done that she almost expected them to start wearing sackcloth and cover themselves with ashes. "If you ever bring Nichole back to Manor House, and if you don't I may never speak to you again, she will probably be enshrined as a saint." She closed with her love and added that he could have Nichole to himself for two months. He chuckled at her post script: "Either you bring her back to Manor House by the first of May, or I'm moving to Frederick."

Peter told him quietly as he showed Alex where things were packed, "Robert Patterson came out again last weekend. He said he came to see Catherine. He seemed pleased that Nichole is getting better, but he sure seemed more interested in Catherine than he did in Nichole." Alex raised his eyebrows in concern. Robert and Catherine? Maybe he and Nichole should only stay at Frederick for one month.

Peter left before Nichole awoke. "Why didn't you wake me up?" she sighed when Alex told her the man had come and gone. Alex showed her Catherine's letter and she giggled.

"Peter also told me that Robert Patterson is visiting Manor House to see Catherine," Alex commented. "Maybe we should only stay at Frederick for a month." Nichole only smiled. She liked Robert and she loved Catherine, and they would make a great pair.

They feasted on the chicken pie and stewed apples that Peter had brought, and shortly after dinner Alex tucked her into bed. When he spread his bedroll on the floor,

Nichole gazed at him, her cloudy green eyes sparkling with questions. "I want you to rest. If I sleep in bed with you, you won't rest."

Nichole giggled and settled down in bed. "It will be lonely without you."

Alex replied firmly, "Until we get to the farm, I'll sleep on the floor. Then, dear wife, you won't ever again sleep alone!" As he uttered the words softly, a sense of foreboding crept over him. Could he keep that promise? Something told him he could not.

Catherine reread the note Alex sent with Peter. He and Nichole were going to the farm. Peter had already left with the supplies they would need for the trip and Nichole's clothes. She wandered out to the kitchen. Prissy and Mrs. Barber had been unusually quiet since Nichole had run away. Maude was living in fear that Alex would return and blame her for what happened to his wife. Catherine smiled as she patted the pocket of her dress. It was Thursday and her note from Robert said he would arrive late Friday afternoon. Had it only been four days since he left? It seemed like a month.

The hours dragged by as Catherine busied herself around the plantation. Friday morning, she went for a long ride, and Peter was back when she returned. "No, I didn't talk to Nichole, she was asleep," he answered her question. "Yer brother didn't say much when I told him about Robert coming to court you."

Catherine blushed. "He isn't courting me."

"What do you call it, then? He ses he comes to see you. In my book, that's courting."

Catherine frowned. If Robert was courting her and Alex didn't like it . . . "Oh, pooh," she muttered. Robert was not courting her. And Alex wouldn't object to his best friend visiting with his sister, would he?

Catherine didn't have time to worry about it, for a sixth sense told her the man she had been waiting for had finally arrived. Forgetting that she had been making every attempt to act a lot older than her seventeen years, she raced for the front door. Robert hadn't cleared his saddle when she flung open the front door and moved out to the steps. "Nichole and Alex are on the way to the farm," she told him excitedly.

Robert grinned up at her. "Then you will have to entertain me for the weekend."

Saturday they went to a party at the next plantation, and Prissy and Peter went along at Robert's insistence. "Without Alex here, I can't take Catherine without some kind of chaperone. What would the neighbors think?" Robert confided to Peter as they hooked up the team and the coach.

When Peter repeated the conversation to Prissy, especially the part about the chaperone, she bristled. "I should hope not," Prissy replied. "Peter," she asked quietly, "Do you think Catherine and Robert . . ."

"It's none of your concern, woman," Peter mumbled.

Sunday, before Robert left, he suggested softly that he and Catherine go to the study. "Catherine, I've given this some thought. I really don't think I should come again until Nichole and Alex are here. It doesn't look right."

Catherine stared at him, tears welling up in her eyes. "You aren't going to visit until they come home? They won't be back for two months," she wailed. Suddenly, she threw herself into Robert's arms. "I thought you came to see me."

Robert swallowed with difficulty. She was pressed up against him and he could feel the taut nipples and her full breasts pressed against his chest. Her mouth was inches from his, and he clenched his fists in a struggle to

237

keep them at his side.

"Catherine, I am coming to see you, but without your brother here, it doesn't look right," he tried to explain.

Catherine stepped back and looked at him. "What are you afraid of? Prissy and Peter are here. Everyone knows they are here."

He tried once more. "Catherine, if you won't think about your reputation, I must. Until Alex and Nichole return, I can't come back here."

Robert watched as she ran from the room. Perhaps it's better this way, he thought as he made his way out to his horse. "Lord," he mumbled as he hoisted himself up into the saddle, "I hope they don't stay for two months. I'll go mad."

Upstairs, Catherine watched him leave from her window. How could she have thrown herself into his arms like that? Peter's words, about him courting her, came back to her again. Well, she thought with a sob, I've ruined that. She sank down on her bed when Robert was no longer in view. How would she ever survive until Alex and Nichole returned?

Somehow, over the last two or three weeks, Robert had become very important to her. Was she falling in love with him? She sat very still. That would explain the way her heart did little flip-flops when he walked into a room.

Surely, that wasn't love. Oh, how she missed Nichole. She needed to talk to someone, and Prissy and Mrs. Barber were not yet over the scolding Alex had given them before he left. Her thoughts drifted back to her last stay with Martha Beal. Twice, Martha had forced her to sit with a friend of Martha's beau. He was a nice enough young man, but he kept trying to touch her, her thighs, her waist and once his hand had brushed the curve of her breast. At the time, she was disgusted with the whole thing, and Martha had criticized her unmercifully. What had she said? "You've never been in love, Catherine. When you fall in love, you'll want the gentleman's hands all over you."

Catherine remembered feeling sick to her stomach at Martha's words. Perhaps. She smiled grudgingly, Martha was not too far from the truth. Her breasts ached just from being pressed into Robert's chest. And she had wanted him to kiss her, too. Instead, he told her he wasn't coming to see her anymore. Catherine brushed at her tears. Of course, he wouldn't, not after the way she had thrown herself at him.

Chapter Twenty

Alex was awake with the dawn, and began to pack all the things in the cabin that he wanted to take to Frederick. He awakened Nichole, and they ate a hearty breakfast before they left the cabin where they had pledged their love.

They traveled slowly, with Alex stopping often so that Nichole could rest. Before sunset, Alex stopped at an inn along the way. They shared a relaxed meal in their room and once again Alex slept on the floor, insisting that she had to rest. "We'll share a bed when we get to Frederick," he told her softly when he kissed her good night.

Alex extended the two-day journey into four so that Nichole had a chance to rest often. They talked about weather, politics, farming and even Robert and Catherine. In spite of their slow pace, Alex was enjoying himself immensely, although part of him, he admitted silently, was more than anxious to get to the farm. He wanted her reaction to the place that would be their home, and he wanted her back in his arms.

Early in the afternoon of the fourth day, they reached Frederick. The house was spotless and the kitchen table was loaded with crisp fried chicken, loaves of homemade bread, tubs of fresh creamy butter and several kinds of pies. There was a huge basket of eggs, a sugar-cured ham, flour, cornmeal, and two bottles of whiskey. Alex smiled. Someone had been visiting.

They had gotten no further than inspecting the many items on the table when a rap on the door interrupted them. Alex answered the door, and his own foreman stood first on one foot and then the other. Nichole glanced at the man as he said quickly, "Peter came. The fixin's is for you and your bride. I hope you don't mind."

"Mind? Ben, this is a great gift. But come in. Come on." Alex dragged the reluctant man into the kitchen. "You have to meet Nichole."

Ben muttered, "How do." Alex grinned; Ben just stood there staring at her. She affected me that way, months ago, Alex thought.

Nichole smiled sweetly. "Thank you. I won't want for a thing. I'm looking forward to meeting your family and the other families. Please give them all my thanks." She looked at the overseer carefully. He was almost as tall as Alex, but twice as wide. Don't men in this country ever stop growing? she thought. He wore a shirt and pants of leather with fringe on the arms of the shirt and the legs of the pants. His hair was almost the color of the soft garment. It curled all over his head, and his twinkling blue eyes just stared at her. She wondered if there was something wrong with the dress she wore, and she glanced over at Alex, who was grinning from ear to ear, first at Ben and then at Nichole. She couldn't help it, she blushed.

Alex walked out with the man, still offering his thanks, and Nichole moved quickly from the kitchen into the next room of the house. It was nothing at all like Manor House. Alex had been right, it was much smaller, but there was a warmth about it that Manor House didn't have. She glanced back at the kitchen and sighed. It was a large room and had a fireplace on one whole wall. The wall next to it was covered with shelves, and on these were bottles and bowls, cups and cooking utensils. A large work table stood in the middle of the room, and Nichole grinned; there was certainly plenty of space to cook.

The second room and the third room shared a common fireplace. She glanced around at what was obviously the dining room. There were a large table and six chairs in the center. Several chests lined the outside walls and a hutch stood in one corner. She smiled as she thought of the fun she would have looking through those chests.

The third room, she decided, was like a parlor. In one corner stood a spinning wheel; a table and two benches occupied the other corner. A settle and two very comfortable looking chairs were grouped in front of the fireplace, and in the corner near the fireplace stood a harp. It looked suspiciously like the harp from Manor House, and Nichole moved closer for a more detailed examination. A soft smile lifted the corners of her mouth; it was the harp from Manor House and it had been restrung.

Alex found her there, and he questioned softly, "Do you think you can be happy here?"

She turned and walked toward him. "I'll be happy wherever you are!" Alex reached for her and drew her into his arms. He kissed her so tenderly that she felt tears sting her eyes. She thought her heart would explode with her happiness.

"Come on," he said, grabbing her hand, "let me show you the most important room of the house." He scooped her up in his arms and started up the stairway behind the spinning wheel. "This is our room." He put her down at the top of the stairs. "And"—he pointed to a doorway on the opposite wall—"that's the nursery when the time comes."

Nichole looked around and then at Alex. He seemed to

be waiting for her opinion. She glanced at the large bed in the middle of the room, at the two armoires standing side by side, and at the two chairs gracing the third wall. It was a much plainer room than any of the rooms at Manor House, but there was something warm and welcoming about the room. She couldn't decide if it was the pretty white muslin curtains billowing in the early spring wind from the two windows in the room or the brightly colored quilt that lay in the bed. Somehow she felt at home here, not like the guest she had been at Manor House.

She tried to put her feelings into words, and Alex nodded, then kissed her again. This kiss was even more tender than the one before, Nichole thought as she melted against him.

Alex led her to the other doorway and to a much smaller room. A smaller bed, a chest and a washstand were all there was room for. Alex grinned. "When Catherine came to visit, she stayed in this room, but now that we're married and living together, that won't do. I probably should add a room or two anyway." He winked at her and Nichole blushed yet again. He's always making me blush, she scolded herself. Then she smiled; somehow she would just have to get used to his teasing, she decided.

Alex led her back downstairs, and while Nichole fixed their dinner from the incredible assortment on the kitchen table, Alex built fires in the fireplaces. As long as she lived, Nichole was sure that she would never forget that night. They ate at their dining room table, and then Alex insisted that she rest in the parlor room while he cleaned up the dishes and heated water for a bath.

He carried her into the kitchen when things were cleaned up to his satisfaction. There, in their own kitchen, he carefully took off her clothes. He set her on the brass tub that had suddenly appeared out of nowhere and was now brimming with delightfully warm water and a scent of pine. Alex remembered the last bath he had given her and a sensuous smile lit his eyes. Deliberately, he took a bar of sweet-smelling soap and began washing her. Lingering over her breasts and moving slowly over her thighs, he remembered the pain he had experienced the last time he bathed her. He was about to tell her so when she interrupted him, "You once told me that husbands and wives bathed together."

"Ah, yes! I did say that, didn't I." He chuckled, delighted that she was remembering as well. "But I believe I also said that you would have to ask me to join you."

"Is this tub big enough for us both?"

"I do believe we can make do." Alex's husky voice shook.

Nichole looked up at him with sultry green eyes. "Shall we see if we can 'make do'?"

Quickly, his clothes joined hers in a pile on the floor, and he added another bucket of hot water before he eased himself into the tub. He allowed her to wash his arms, his chest and his stomach, but when she reached for his left leg, the play suddenly turned into something more.

He reached for her and drew her into his arms. She could feel his heart beating rapidly as she laid her head on his shoulder. Carefully, he rearranged her so that she was resting on his legs, her own spread out and around him. Slowly, ever so slowly, he drew her toward him so that his aroused manhood touched her. Then he kissed her. She thought her own heart would beat itself to death as hard as it was thumping. The kiss went on and on, as he tasted the sweetness of her mouth. Their tongues cavorted in the moist cavern, renewing their passions until they blazed as hot as the fire in the fireplace.

244

As his kiss deepened, he reached for her firm breasts, cupping the fullness in his hands, then running his thumb across the taut nipples. He lowered his head and teased at one of the stiff peaks, swirling his tongue around and around until she wanted to scream her pleasure.

He raised his head and kissed her eyes, her forehead, then traced her shell-like ear with the tip of his tongue. His voice was husky slur, he breathed in her ear, "I can't wait. I want you, now." He grasped her buttocks and raised her slowly, impaling her, piercing her with such a feeling of oneness that she gasped. As she clung to him, Alex pushed her away to gaze into her wide, startled eyes. In alarm, he asked, "Did I hurt you?"

Nichole was speechless, and could only shake her head. Alex gave her a chance to accept his presence, then he grasped her gently by the waist and picked her up and let her slide down his embedded manhood. Her whole body seemed to undulate against him, and he sighed in satisfaction. As the pressure built, he sought her lips, his tongue emulating the motion of his body.

As Nichole waited breathlessly for the explosion that she knew would come, she dug her nails into the rigid muscles of his back. She tried desperately to melt into his warm, wet torso. In that instant she was there, and the explosion that followed left her clinging to him, breathless, incapable of speech, her blood surging through her laden with pleasure.

Alex was just as speechless, and he held her close to him for long minutes, until their breathing returned to normal and their heartbeats slowed. He smiled to himself; even the water in the tub had begun to chill.

Without a word, he lifted her from the tub, wrapped a blanket around her and began to gently rub her dry. Nichole was stunned by the completeness of what they had just shared, and her tongue would not have worked if she had a coherent thought in her head. Quickly, he gathered her in his arms and carried her through the house, up the stairs to their bed. He laid her down in the center of the bed, pulled the quilt from the bed and settled her between the linen sheets. Carefully, he joined her there, drawing her body up next to his own, then covering them both with the quilt.

Nichole whispered in a husky broken voice, full of emotion, "You're still wet, you'll get sick."

Alex rested her head on the curve of his shoulder, planting light kisses against the damp curls on her forehead. "I have my love to keep me well." They drifted off to sleep.

Moonlight shimmered through the windows, waking Nichole from her slumber. She was still snuggled up next to him, his arms holding her against him. She moved her head slightly so that she could see his face in the soft silver light. He was such a handsome man. In his sleep he looked so at peace with the world. She couldn't resist the temptation to run her fingers over his jaw, so firm, so manly. She touched his cheeks, drawing the tips of her fingers across the rough stubble of his beard. Just touching him excited her. Her fingers traced the line from his nose to his lips. As her fingers grazed his lips he kissed the fingertips. Nichole whispered, "I didn't mean to wake you."

Alex chuckled, then captured one of her fingers in his mouth and sucked gently. Nichole stared at him, fire streaking from his mouth up her arm to the very center of her. What was there about this man that his very touch made her burn? She jerked her finger out of his mouth self-consciously.

As he brought her hand back up to his lips, he whispered, "I can think of nothing that pleases me more than to have my beautiful wife wake me." He kissed each finger in turn and then sucked gently on each one. Nichole was suddenly filled with such longing that she arched up against him. Once more they were lost in the thrill of the freshness of their love.

Sunlight flooded the room when Nichole awoke the next morning. At first she looked around her in confusion. She had forgotten where she was, but as she glanced at the full white curtains and the two armoires opposite the bed, she grinned in satisfaction. She turned her head and was disappointed that she was in the big bed alone. Alex was already up, and she strained to hear if any sound from the lower floor would indicate his presence.

She thought she heard noises and she dressed quickly. Slipping down the stairs, she walked through the parlor and the dining room. When she got to the doorway to the kitchen, she stopped.

Alex was covered with flour, and so, it seemed, was the entire kitchen. His face was screwed up into a grimace, and he looked so upset that Nichole rushed to his side. Before she could ask what was wrong, he turned on her. "What are you doing up?"

"I got up to take care of my husband. You did say that was what I was to do, didn't you?"

"But I want you to rest!"

"Alex, I'm not an invalid. I need to be up and I need to start doing things."

Alex grinned at her in a slow, seductive grin. "You can't make biscuits, can you? I've tried two batches and they are terrible."

Nichole grinned back at him and then glanced at the kitchen. "Yes, I can make biscuits. But you'll have to clean up your mess first."

In a short time, they were sitting down to a breakfast of sliced ham, a platter of fluffy scrambled eggs and hot

247

flaky biscuits that Alex declared melted in his mouth. "Are you any good at making other things?"

Nichole stated quietly, "I'm a good cook."

Before she could blink, Alex was at her side. He pulled her up into his arms and smiled down at her. "I'm going to love being married." He kissed her soundly.

"Because I can cook?" Nichole asked, slightly confused.

"Well, that has something to do with it, at least a little bit." His hands trailed down her back to cup her buttocks. "Maybe, just a tiny bit." He pulled her close to him and kissed her once more, holding her tightly against him.

She lifted her head slightly, pushing herself up against him. She giggled. "I really don't think the cooking has much to do with it." Alex made no reply. His head descended and he captured her lips once more.

The next three days were idyllic. Alex made love to her in the morning before they went downstairs to fix breakfast together. In the afternoon, he took her back upstairs on the pretext that she needed a nap. She slept in his arms after he loved her thoroughly. After a leisurely dinner, she would play the harp as he worked on his accounts, or read from one of the books that were stored in one of the chests in the dining room.

Twice more they bathed in the brass tub that was stored in a small barn outside the kitchen door. Each bath ended just as the first bath had ended, with Alex unable to wait until they were in bed. Both times, he carried her back upstairs, where they spent their time enjoying each other once more. Nichole told him, laughing softly, as he carried her up the stairs after their third bath together, "Now I know what a lustful man means."

Alex stopped on the steps, looking down at her for a second, then laughed as well. "And don't you forget it."

On the morning of the fourth day, Alex took her to meet his hired men and their families. Alex was delighted with how charming she seemed as she greeted each and every person, man, woman and child. Occasionally, when she thought no one was watching, he noticed a deep frown cross her brow. On the way back to the house, Alex asked her, "Nichole, do you feel all right? You're not getting sick, are you? You seem worried or upset about something."

"My back aches, and oh, I'm sorry, but Alex, I just don't feel well, not well at all."

Trying hard to cover his anxiety, he quickly took her back to the house, and put her to bed. Was she getting ill again? Should he send for one of the women? Concerned, he watched her carefully all night.

The next morning, Nichole was completely indisposed. She had stomach cramps, a headache and she knew immediately what was wrong. Trying to convince Alex that she was not ill but would be fine in several days without telling him what was wrong proved to be impossible. Finally, in desperation she snapped, "Surely, you know enough about women, especially with your own sister, to know what is wrong with me."

He stared at her for several minutes, trying to sort through the clues she had given him. Suddenly, he grinned at her like an idiot, Nichole thought. All he said was "Oh!" and came bringing her hot tea and warm blankets. For the rest of the day he was so condescending that Nichole wanted to scream.

"Please, just leave me alone," she begged, "I'll recover with no difficulty if you will just leave me be!"

Alex did leave her alone for the next several days, although whenever he was around he treated her like a fragile doll. He went about the work on the farm, but by the fifth day his curiosity got the better of him. "Nichole,

249

most women don't seem to suffer quite this much. Do you have this trouble every month?"

Nichole wanted to crawl into one of the cracks in the kitchen floor. This was only the second day she had been up to make his breakfast, and she still was not feeling up to par. She blushed a brilliant rose, turned her back to him and moved away.

"Sweetheart." Alex turned her around, and trying to be patient with her, he said, "Husbands get to know their wives' bodies as well as their own. You will know mine as well as you do your own. I will, on occasion, even have to relieve myself in front of you." She was now a vivid red. "My heart's desire, marriage makes two people one. You will know me, and I will know you. That's the way a good marriage is, and I want us to have a good marriage." He drew her into his arms and gently stroked her hair; then he pulled away from her slightly. "Now, will you answer my question? Do you get this sick every month?"

She was still fighting her embarrassment. "N . . . n . . . no," she stuttered. "But about two years ago, I had an ague that upset my stomach. I had a fever and was abed for a week. When, wh . . . when my time—" She swallowed hard. This was almost too intimate for her. She tried again. "I had cramps, a headache, a backache and was in bed for another week." She breathed a sigh of relief. "Usually, I feel fine, nothing more than an inconvenience."

Alex kissed her lightly and smiled down at her. "I've heard tell that after the first baby, those problems disappear."

Nichole went rigid. One could not be connected to the other, could it? She stared up at him, and she knew her ignorance was a shameful thing. She should confess that she knew nothing about babies, where they came from, how or why. But the conversation just past was still ringing in her ears. She could not ask, not yet. She stared up at him, a dozen emotions crossing her face.

Alex refused to admit that what he saw on her face meant anything to him, and he pulled her into his arms and held her lightly, kissing her on the forehead. "We'll just have to hurry up and make a baby."

She stood in his arms, more confused than ever before. How on earth were they supposed to make a baby when she had no idea how to even begin? She was disgusted with herself, with the nuns, even with Alex, just a little, she admitted to herself. Someone should have told her about this part of life.

Alex noticed the look of disgust that lingered in her eyes. Surely, his wife could not be opposed to having children. No, she was just embarrassed over their intimate conversation that morning. She wanted his children, she must want his children! He went back to his work trying to forget the look he had seen in her eyes.

Nichole threw herself into the housework that had been neglected while she was in bed. As she worked, Nichole considered their conversation, and then she tried to remember each reference to birth that she could think of. She had never wondered about it before and nothing she could remember gave her a clue as to how offspring arrived. She even dug out a Bible Alex had stashed in one of the chests. Even the Christmas story told her nothing. Desperate, she knew she needed to talk to someone, but Catherine was at Manor House and Nichole could not imagine herself talking to anyone else.

Alex watched Nichole, carefully. He saw her confusion, and could only guess at what was wrong. Working late each night, he managed to slip into bed when she had fallen asleep exhausted. She was usually up before him in the morning, fixing his breakfast. At first, he felt that her withdrawal was from her embarrassment, and he resolved to give her time to come to terms with her own feelings. After all, he reasoned, she had no idea that marriage demanded such intimate living conditions, but as another day progressed and she seemed as withdrawn as before, Alex lost his patience. Some of her ramblings while she had been so sick came back to haunt him. Obviously, she had been forced to marry him and now, she had decided that she wanted no part of him. The thought that she might be seeking some kind of revenge of her own even crossed his mind. The more he considered his future with Nichole the angrier he became.

By the end of three weeks at the farm, Alex was tense, frustrated and angry. Nichole was in no better condition and she could not bring herself to question Alex. For some reason, she decided, he changed his mind. He didn't want her as his wife. Her solution was to avoid her husband as much as was possible. They slept in the same bed, ate at the same table and shared the washstand, but they were barely talking.

One evening, after a silent dinner, Alex grabbed the plates and started for the kitchen. Nichole had just lifted the meat platter from the table, also on her way to the kitchen. They collided. Alex dropped the plates and they crashed to the floor. At that exact second, the meat slid from the plate Nichole was holding. Alex caught it as it slid from Nichole's hands and threw the juicy entree to the table. Instantly, Nichole started to sob, frozen in place. Alex couldn't stand it and gathered her close. "They're only plates, we can get more. Sh . . . sh . . ."

Nichole melted against him; it was the first time in two weeks he had touched her. She leaned into him, letting her tears spill down her face, wetting his shirt. Alex could not help himself. He lifted her face, brushed her tears from her face and then kissed her tenderly. Kissing her with all the hunger and frustration he had experienced, he drew her tightly against him.

She responded with her own desperation. The dishes were forgotten, the farm was forgotten, and she even forget that she desperately needed an education.

They made love all night long and once during the night, Alex asked her the question that had been driving him through his own hell. "Nichole, do you want children?"

He was holding her so tenderly, but as he said the words Nichole felt him tense. She looked at him in amazement, her soft green eyes glowing in the light from the burning candle by their bed. "Of course! Why wouldn't I want children? You did say we would have a dozen." This was the time! Nichole knew she must ask him now, but he was kissing her with such passion all thought fled from her mind. What was it she needed to ask? Something important, very important, but as Alex's work-roughened hands trailed up the inside of her thighs her mind ceased to function and she gloried in their love.

Chapter Twenty-one

As March blossomed, Alex watched his wife bloom with health and contentment. He found himself drifting back to the house, leaving the care of the farm to his men, or following her from one room to another as she went about her own tasks. He wanted nothing more than to spend his time at her side. She seemed to want the same thing, glancing at him shyly when he came into the room, then smiling at him as if she couldn't get enough of him.

As they studied Alex's rough plans for the addition to their home and talked about the spring planting that would begin in a short time, Alex wondered what his life would have been without her. He knew he was growing more and more in love with her. She filled a part of his world that he never knew existed.

One afternoon, in the middle of the month, Alex was interrupted from his work when a lone wagon came up the drive. Alex glanced up and was surprised to see Peter slumped forward on the seat. Beside him rode a small woman, her cap and the gray of her plain woolen garments crying her occupation. Damn, Alex thought to himself. Prissy had no right to decide that he and Nichole needed another servant. He wanted his wife to himself for a little longer. A servant in the tiny house would complicate their life. And he was sure that Nichole would not like it at all. She seemed to take great pleasure in doing for him.

Alex was already showing his aggravation when Peter pulled the wagon to a stop. He jumped down and said quietly, "Ya got a visitor, or leastways, Nichole has a visitor."

Alex watched as Peter helped the woman from the wagon. He was sure he had never seen her before. Her cap covered most of her hair, but brown and gray strands peeked from under the ruffles and strayed from the knot at the back of her head. She was short, much shorter than Nichole, and Alex guessed her age at about two score. Still puzzled, Alex stepped forward. "Mistress, I'm Alex Dampier. Let me welcome you to our home." Abruptly he added, "I'll get Nichole." As Alex led the way to the house, Peter hoisted a small carpetbag from the back of the wagon. My God, Alex thought, whoever she was, she was moving in.

Alex found Nichole in the bedroom, sorting through the clothing that needed to be scrubbed. "We have a visitor, and I have no idea who she is. I don't think I've ever seen her before. Nichole, I'm very much afraid Prissy has overstepped her grounds and hired you a servant."

"I don't need a servant," Nichole said, her voice carrying a hint of stubbornness. "If I felt I needed a servant, I would ask you to hire one for me."

"Well," Alex frowned, "the woman is downstairs. You'd best see to her."

Nichole tried to glare at her husband, but her bright green eyes twinkled with amusement. "Coward!"

When she rounded the corner of the kitchen, Nichole stopped short and gasped. Alex, who was directly in back of her, almost ran into her. And there was no question, Alex thought as he looked at Nichole's expression, that his wife knew this woman and that she was extremely embarrassed by the little woman's presence.

The woman spoke. "Child, I came as fast as I could. My brother had supplies to buy and he wanted to see about a bondservant. He took me to Baltimore. When I got to Manor House, this man agreed to bring me here." She looked over at Alex. "Is this your husband?" Nichole was speechless and only nodded. "If you've hurt this little thing . . ."

Alex sputtered, "Now, see here. I don't even know your name."

"Alex," Nichole said softly, "I would like to present Mistress Hutchinson, my friend, from the boat." Nichole regained some of her composure and flew at Nellie. "Oh, Nellie! I'm so sorry. Everything is all right now. I didn't think to write. Oh, and you came all this way."

The little woman patted her on the shoulders. "Now child, it's about time you said hello. Is he treating you all right, then?" Nichole brushed at her happy tears and nodded.

Nellie continued, "I needed a bit of a change. Your man," she directed her remarks to Alex, "said I could go back to Manor House with him in a day or two, if I'll not be any trouble."

Nichole didn't give Alex a chance to reply. "Oh, Nellie. Of course you'll be no trouble. Come! You must see my house. Oh, it is so good to see you." Nichole grabbed her hand and pulled her into the dining room.

Alex turned to Peter. "You're right, Nichole has a visitor."

"I'll see to the wagon." Peter started for the door, "Looks like you have a guest."

Alex frowned and glanced toward the parlor. He could hear Nichole's enthusiastic giggle. At least the woman wasn't staying long. Alex followed Peter out to the barn and asked for a report on Manor House and the women there.

"Something's wrong with Catherine. I'd say it was Robert Patterson, but it's not my place."

"Robert Patterson?"

"Yeh, I'd say you better not stay here until the end of May. I think you got problems at home."

Alex glanced at Peter; he wasn't joking. Good heavens, what was Catherine up to now?

Nellie stayed for five days and Alex made arrangements for one of the local merchants to provide transportation for Nellie back to Carlisle, Pennsylvania. Peter carried a message back to the brother that she was to have met in Baltimore. The Dampiers would see her back to his home.

When Nichole had tried to explain to Alex how Nellie had come to visit, Alex had listened quietly, still stunned by the cruelties of the people he trusted. That was probably why he had insisted himself that Nellie stay several more days than she had planned. She was a most pleasant woman, Alex decided as he watched Nellie work circles around his young wife. Nothing seemed beneath her, and Alex found himself wondering at her background.

He was sincere when he hugged the little woman and added, "We'll expect to see you again. If you'd like to come to visit, let us know and I'll send a carriage for you."

Nellie patted his hand. "A carriage? Nope, a wagon will do, and maybe in a few months, late summer perhaps, I'll come again."

When the small house was quiet again, Alex let Nichole tell him all about Nellie Hutchinson. He shook his head. He truly owed that little woman a great deal. Even if she had once been nothing but a servant, she was a good woman, the kind of woman that would enhance his home. His thoughts started churning. When the children started to come . . .

As March came to a close, Alex forgot Peter's message about Catherine and basked in the glory of his love. He found himself wanting to share all of his time with his wife. Often, he would pull her onto his lap after they had shared a peaceful meal and he would talk about his life at Manor House, his time in the army. One night, in whispered tones, he told her about Charles duPres.

The report Peter gave Alex was very accurate. Through the last week of February and well into March, Catherine wandered around the house, out to the stables, to the sheds that lined the property, restless, hurt and angry with herself. Many of the tasks she set for herself went unfinished, and she couldn't explain to either Prissy or to Mrs. Barber what was wrong with her. She wasn't sure herself, but she knew that Robert had much to do with what was wrong. In the three weeks since he rode away, she had not received a word, not one note, and she was devastated.

At night, when she prayed for sleep, Robert's blue eyes danced through her mind and she could almost feel the soft brown hair spreading through her fingers. "What is wrong with me?" She sat up in bed and glared at the dark room. "Am I going to waste away, dreaming of a man that considers me a child, the little sister of his best friend?"

The harder she tried to forget, the more frequently she remembered—his smile, the things they had laughed at together and the way she felt when she had thrown herself at him. That last day, the day she regretted with every bone in her body, played over and over again in her mind. Why? Why had she acted like such a child? Robert was probably glad that he had such a reasonable excuse to stay away.

The third week of March was drawing to a close, and Catherine went out to the stable to see her horse saddled. A long ride was what she needed. The long, boring weekend stretched before her. Weekday, weekend! What did it matter? Each day was like the next. Perhaps she was meant for the convent as her father had suggested once.

Even her two-hour ride failed to improve her spirits, and she meandered back to the house, stopping along the way to inspect the lifeless garden. "The thing looks as dead as I feel," she mumbled as she trudged through the kitchen door.

Prissy heard her come in and stomped up to her, her lips spread thin in disgust. "Where have you been? You have a guest and I'm getting tired of making excuses for you."

"A guest? Who?" Catherine asked, a little life sparking her dull gray eyes.

"He's in the parlor," Prissy said, and stomped back out of the kitchen.

Catherine looked down at her dusty riding skirt and her dirty hands. "I better clean up before I see anyone," Catherine stated to the empty room and made her way up the stairs. In fifteen minutes, she was cleaned up and had changed into a blue-gray dress. "It fits my mood," she thought as she glanced in her mirror. She started

259

down the steps to the parlor, her usual enthusiasm missing completely.

Her lack of enthusiasm changed to fear at the door of the parlor. Robert had his back to her, but it was Robert! He turned as she glided into the room. Holding his gloves in his hands, he glanced down, his expression guilty. "I couldn't stay away."

"You came to see me?" she asked softly.

Robert nodded his head. This time, when she flew into his arms, they gathered her close and held her tightly against him. He tilted her head back and touched her lips gently. "Just to see you."

By the end of the month, Alex admitted that they should return to Manor House, at least for a short visit. He had to see to Catherine. It took several days before he could bring himself to mention the trip to Nichole. One evening he broached the subject. "Nichole, I think we should go see how Catherine's faring."

She immediately grew tense and tried to explain. "I'd really rather have Catherine come here. I'm afraid if I leave, I . . . I won't come back."

Alex kissed her and explained, softly, "This is our home. Of course we'll come back. This is where we live. We are only going to Manor House for a visit and to see Catherine. I'll make sure that everyone understands that we are only guests." Despite her hesitation, Alex made plans. They would start for Manor House the first day of the next week.

Sunday evening, Nichole prepared a special dinner. Ever since Alex had said they were leaving she fought against a clawing fear. Some sixth sense told her that it would be a long time, if ever, before they returned to the

260

farm. Trying to ignore the terror that was building, she buried herself in her work.

Alex commented on her nervousness, and she had no explanation for him. How could she admit to her loving, practical husband that they wouldn't be coming back to the farm when he, only just that morning, had assured her they would be back by June?

After dinner, when the dishes were dried and packed in the hutch, Nichole went into the parlor and gazed at the harp. She let her fingers trail over the strings, remembering the hours of pleasure she had playing for her husband. Seating herself, she began to play. Unconsciously she plucked the old French ballad from the strings, the one she had played for Alex at Manor House.

Alex recognized the melody as he came downstairs. Why is she so melancholy? he asked himself. Was she afraid of what awaited her at Manor House? Her memories of that place were not happy, he knew, but surely she had to know that he would let nothing happen to her this time. Was she afraid that she would not share his bed? Well, she would learn soon enough that nothing would destroy their relationship.

He walked over to one of the soft chairs arranged before the fireplace and sat quietly, waiting for her to finish. When she stopped playing he spoke softly. "Nichole, come join me." He patted the seat of the settle as he moved over himself. She came to his side quickly and gave him a halfhearted little smile. He pulled her down onto his lap and put his arms around her. "You know that nothing will happen to you at Manor House, don't you? You are the love of my life. I won't let anyone hurt you. You are mine!" He kissed her tenderly, and she smiled up at him. "You'll sleep in our room there, and we'll visit with Catherine. I'll take you to Baltimore. Would you like to go to Baltimore?" She nodded her head, and for an instant her eyes sparkled. "We'll order a new wardrobe for you and get some nice furniture for the house and the new rooms. We'll spend some time with Robert Patterson, too. I'll have to spend a day or two with Peter, but, remember, we are only visiting. We'll be together just as much as we can."

She laid her head back on his shoulder and smiled up at him. I'm being so silly, she thought. Perhaps, unconsciously, she didn't want the real world to interfere with their own private one. She offered her thoughts to Alex as way of an explanation. He only smiled. A faraway look surfaced in his eyes. He agreed with her completely; they had been so alone and so involved with each other that the rest of the world had ceased to exist. Undoubtedly that was why she seemed so sad.

Alex lifted her off his lap and sat her down next to him on the settle. Standing, he went to the mantel and picked up a small chest that was resting on one corner. As he walked back to the settle, he opened it. Taking her hand, he gave her the chest and sat back down. "In there, you will find something that will mark you as mine for the world to see. I thought about waiting until your birthday in June, but I think I want you to have it now."

Nichole gazed down into the small chest, and her eyes widened in surprise. Nestled in white satin was a small broach in a flower design. The center was set with a dark green emerald. Tiny emeralds outlined the same dainty floral design on a pair of earrings, and next to them was a ring. It took was the same pattern, but the emerald in the center was much larger than the broach and there were a dozen tiny diamonds around it to make the ring look like a blooming flower.

Stunned, she looked up at Alex. She had never seen anything so beautiful in all of her life. Alex glanced at the ring and back at her, "If the ring is too big or too small, the jeweler said he could fix it."

Finding her voice, finally, she managed to gasp, "You bought this for me?"

Alex smiled tenderly. "Yes, just for you." He took the ring from her and, lifting her left hand, placed the band on the fourth finger. It fit perfectly. Staring into her eyes, Alex murmured, "With this ring I thee wed." Tears shimmered in her eyes as Alex reached for her.

It was very late the next morning when they were ready to start for Manor House. Alex had intended to start shortly after dawn, but Nichole was so enthusiastic about the jewelry and about thanking him properly that they ended by staying in bed two hours longer than he planned.

They had been on the road for over an hour when Alex became aware of the adoring looks she was giving him. He noticed that first she glanced at her ring, then at him, and then at the ring again. He chuckled. "If you keep looking at me like that, I'll have to stop the wagon and let you thank me again." Nichole only smiled up at him and pressed closer than she already was.

Alex grimaced; it was going to take them three days to make the trip, and Peter would rib him unmercifully. He knew that they would be stopping before dusk the way Nichole was pressing herself up against him. Where she was concerned, Alex thought as he pulled her even closer, I have no sense, no sense at all. He grinned down at his wife, his heart overflowing with his love.

Wednesday evening Alex and Nichole arrived at Manor House just as dinner was being served. Quickly, additional places were set, and Catherine, beside herself with happiness, hugged Alex first, then Nichole, then Alex once more. Dinner was a chaotic misadventure. Peter came charging in to see Alex, Maude arrived with tears streaming down her face and Catherine refused to stay at her place. All through the meal she continued to jump and and run to hug either Nichole or Alex. Even Prissy and Mrs. Barber hugged both of the young people time and time again.

From the reception they received, Alex felt like he and Nichole had been gone for two years, not two months. When the meal was finally over, Alex took Nichole into his study and closed the door. Even Catherine was ex-cluded. Alex left Nichole in the study and then went to the kitchen to see Mrs. Barber. She left him and grimly walked to the study. A few minutes later, she ran from the study, tears streaming down her face. Alex went back to the study and once more he left, again barring Catherine from the room. Minutes later a subdued Prissy made her way to the study.

Prissy and Nichole were closeted in the study for a much longer time, but finally, Prissy also left the study, wiping at her eyes. Catherine, watching from the hall and the parlor, looked at her brother, her eyes full of questions.

"They had to apologize to my wife" was all he said.

Later, when Nichole and Alex were in the large bed in his old room, Alex turned to her. "Was it so bad? I was right, wasn't I?"

Nichole sighed as she snuggled up next to him. "Well, Mrs. Barber didn't even give me a chance to say much. She begged my forgiveness over and over. Alex, I thought she was going to kiss my feet. When I told her it was all right, that I did forgive her, she started sobbing, and before I could say another word, she ran from the room."

Alex kissed her forehead and smiled down at her. "And Prissy?"

"Alex, she told me all about your father! She tried to explain why she and Mrs. Barber did the things they did. She was only trying to protect you, did you know that?"

Alex grinned. "I suspected as much. But I've made it very clear to them, I hope, that you are my wife by choice. If they so much as look cross-eyed at you . . ."

Nichole silenced him with a soft kiss which deepened quickly, and soon they were involved in sharing again their deepening love for each other.

The next week was almost heaven for Nichole. Alex rarely left her side, frequently dragging her into the study when Peter required his attention on a matter or two. By the end of the week, Alex explained that they would be leaving for Baltimore on Monday. He stated softly, "You need a new wardrobe, something that is a bit more practical than the silk and wool dresses you made."

Nichole was thrilled. "I never saw much of Paris or Le Havre, so just the prospect of visiting a city is exciting in itself." She paused, not wanting to hurt his feelings. "But Alex, I don't need to have my clothes made for me. I do sew, and if you'll just select the kind of fabric I should use, I'll make all of my own clothes."

"My wife will not have to make her own clothes," he growled, and then he grinned. "Of course, if you want to make a few things for me, I won't object."

Still, Nichole protested, "Alex, the money! Dressmakers are expensive, aren't they?"

"I'm not a pauper," he chuckled, "I live on the farm because I want to farm. The plantation, in spite of the demands, is one of the few that makes money, and at times a lot of money. We have more than enough for anything you might want."

"Then I have to go to the dressmaker?" she sighed in resignation.

"Yes, you have to go to the dressmaker. But don't worry, I'll go with you." Nichole could not help but notice the leer he gave her.

She laughed. "Now I know why you want me to go."

They left for Baltimore on Monday morning, and Alex told Catherine not to expect them back for two weeks. There would be the fittings, and Alex wanted to spend some time with Robert. Shortly after they had arrived at Manor House, Alex had sent Peter to Baltimore with a message for Robert. Robert responded in two days, writing that he would be insulted if Nichole and Alex did not consider the town house their residence while they were in the city.

Alex grinned as they moved away from Maor House. This trip was not solely for Nichole's benefit. The clothing was important, but he also wanted Nichole's reaction to the city before he asked Robert to find a piece of property on which he could build a town house for his wife. And he wanted to find out what exactly was going on between Robert and Catherine. He didn't miss the messages being sent and received every other day at Manor House, and he listened without a word to Peter's dry comments about their frequent visitor. He worried for his sister. If he knew Robert, he thought cynically, the poor girl was surely going to die of a broken heart.

Nichole, despite her enthusiasm for the trip, thought she knew why her husband was so insistent on traveling to the city. Already, she and Catherine had spent several hours talking, and every other word that Catherine muttered was something about Robert Patterson. The girl was besotted, Nichole thought, smiling, and her big brother was concerned. Realizing now herself just how glorious love could be, Nichole wanted only Catherine's happiness, for she loved the girl as much as if she was her sister by blood instead of marriage.

When they stopped for lunch at an inn on the way to the city, Nichole asked Alex quietly what he thought of Catherine's infatuation with Robert. Alex stared at her in surprise. "You noticed, also?"

She looked up at him with clear green eyes and said seriously, "I don't want Catherine hurt. I think she fancies herself in love with Robert. I only hope that Robert is as fond of Catherine as she thinks she is of him."

Alex turned away, and mumbled, almost to himself, "I thought perhaps I ought to talk to him about that very subject."

Nichole wondered if he was talking to himself, but he seemed to be waiting for her to comment. She gazed at him, her green eyes wide with concern. "Do you think Catherine will appreciate that?"

Alex grinned and took her hand. "Probably not. But won't you feel better knowing how the ground lies? I know I will!"

They reached Baltimore shortly after a brilliant sunset. Alex teased Nichole about Baltimore putting on her best colors for Nichole's visit. She smiled up at him. "Does she have something to hide?"

Alex and Nichole were up early the next morning. Alex wanted to lay the city at her feet, and as they traveled through the city, Nichole was hard pressed not to giggle at her husband. She loved the city and she told him so. Alex followed her around, watching her reaction to the merchants, the shops and even the docks. They

267

spent three hours at the dressmaker's, and by the time Nichole had been measured and fitted for her finery Alex wanted her back in his bed. He rushed her back to the town house, sighing gratefully. Robert had already told him he would be out of town for the day, and Alex and Nichole spent the rest of the day in bed.

Before the end of the first week, Alex told Robert to start looking for property for a townhouse. He explained that he wanted a retreat for Nichole in the boring winter months and that it would be useful, too, for extended shopping trips to the city. Something simple, he told his friend, that would require only two, or at the most, three servants.

Before dinner that night, Nichole complained to Alex that she was not feeling well, and right after dinner Nichole excused herself and went to her room. Before he joined Robert for an after dinner brandy, he went up the stairs to assure himself that his wife was not ill. She was resting comfortably, but she told him her back ached and she was sick to her stomach. Alex figured to himself quietly and made arrangements to sleep in the other guest room. Smiling at Nichole's continued embarrassment over her body's natural functions, he made his way back downstairs to join Robert in the library.

They talked about the situation in France for a while, and Alex was upset to learn that things were much worse for the aristocracy there. For a second he wondered about his aunt and uncle and their family. Just the thought of the duPres family made him tense. But the accident had happened long ago. Surely, they had forgiven him by now.

The conversation turned to Robert's pursuit of a town house for Alex. "You know, Alex, you ought to buy this house. It's perfect for you."

Alex glanced for at him. "Are you thinking of changing residences?"

Robert's face widened into a friendly grin. "You might say that I'm considering it."

Alex glared at his friend. "Why?"

"You must know. Peter has told you about my visits to Manor House. I *know* you've seen the letters coming and going between Catherine and me. Alex, Catherine intrigues me. There is something about your little sister . . ." His voice trailed off.

"I hate to sound archaic, but what are your intentions?"

At that moment, Nichole decided that she had to get something that would settle her stomach, for she was feeling worse by the minute. She descended the stairs with the intention of finding the kitchen as Robert answered, "I'm not really sure yet."

Alex was not pleased with Robert's honesty and decided to push him a little, just as Nichole was passing the partially closed library door. Alex commented, "She is very young. There are a lot of years between us." Nichole stood very still, her reason for coming downstairs forgotten in her confusion. Why would Alex be discussing her with Robert? She knew she shouldn't listen but for some reason she couldn't move.

Robert sighed, "I know!"

"She's led a very sheltered life, she really knows nothing about life yet, and she has very few friends, perhaps only one or two." Nichole smiled grimly; how well her husband knew her. Alex continued, "She's a bit selfish and too opinionated, though!" Nichole forgot her nausea. How dare he say those things to Robert!

Nichole heard Robert's angry reply. "You sound like you don't like her." Nichole smiled; she liked Robert, too.

Nichole strained to hear Alex's sarcastic answer. "I love her, I'm only concerned . . ." Nichole could not hear the rest of his comment, nor did she see his grin.

Nichole was so angry she was trembling. Starting back up the stairs, she paused on the landing for several minutes. She did indeed need something now. A cup of tea would calm her nerves. How dare Alex discuss her so freely with someone she hardly knew. It was almost beyond comprehension.

She started back toward the kitchen, with no intention of eavesdropping this time. Alex's angry words stopped her cold. "I don't care about the legalities. I say, send her back to France, where she belongs."

Nichole turned and ran up the stirs to her room, tears streaming down her face. She didn't wait for Robert's comment: "But she's such a trim vessel. And the fact that she was taken in the Caribbean by American pirateers . . . I don't know. Of course, the fee for the case is very good."

Robert and Alex were discussing a bill of sale on a stolen French vessel, but Nichole knew that Alex was telling Robert that he was not satisfied with her. Her sobs brought on a severe case of vomiting, and when Alex left the library, he was informed by one of the maids that his wife was very ill.

Alex raced up the stairs to his wife's side. She was curled up in bed, sipping on a cup of tea. She glared at him. "Just leave me alone," she whispered.

Alex smiled slyly and murmured, "You rest." Then he went back downstairs, a knowing smile flitting across his face. She would be fine in several days.

The next morning, Nichole woke feeling fine. As she lay in bed, she reviewed what she had heard the night before. Alex was obviously talking about someone else. He couldn't have been telling Robert that he was unhappy, not with what they had shared at the farm. No, he had been discussing someone else.

The maid came bringing breakfast and informed Nichole that Mr. Dampier and Mr. Patterson had gone out early in the morning. Mr. Dampier left word that she was to stay in bed for the day, and rest. She glared at the maid; Alex did not even have the courage to face her today. He must have been discussing her. And now he was ignoring her. The more she thought about it the angrier she became.

When the maid arrived with a supper tray and word that Alex and Robert had come and gone for the evening, Nichole was beside herself. What kind of man had she married? He had pledged his undying love to her when they were alone, and now that he was back in civilization, he dumped her in the house of a friend and ignored her. As she brushed at her tears she thought back to the first days of her marriage. Over and over, she remembered, she had been frustrated and angered because Alex declared her his wife and treated her like a servant. Now it was happening again.

By the time Alex returned, he was exhausted, and Nichole was so angry that she refused to even acknowledge him. What's gotten into her now? he wondered. Was she so embarrassed that she couldn't talk? She had to know that Robert, who also had a sister and was familiar with female problems, knew what was wrong with her. Then he remembered her convent training. "She's just embarrassed," he told himself, "and perhaps a little angry that I left without telling her good-bye." He kissed her on the forehead and commented, "I have several things to tell you; I've been busy today. Oh, and I

271

talked to Robert. When you feel more like yourself, I'll share what he said about Catherine."

He walked to the door and turned around. "You don't need to get up tomorrow, Robert and I will be out all day."

Nichole spent the next day in her room, but not in bed. She couldn't believe what had happened. Alex had completely deserted her. He was also avoiding her, which had to mean that what he had said to Robert was about her and now he was too embarrassed to face her. Nichole frowned; there was no way Alex could know that she had overheard his conversation. Perhaps he was busy securing her transportation back to France. A large part of her heart broke then. Silent tears streamed down her face as she stretched across the bed. It had all been a dream, a marvelous wonderful dream.

Chapter Twenty-two

When evening came, one of the servants brought Nichole a supper tray, and she merely picked at her food. Once more, she was truly indisposed. "I'm sick because of the situation here," Nichole told herself as she crawled into bed.

Alex checked on her himself, before he went to bed, but Nichole was curled up in the quilt, sound asleep. When the young maid told Alex the next morning that Nichole had been very ill again the night before he fought his panic; in a day or two, she would be all right. He stayed at the town house all the next day, and Nichole seemed distant, but there was no sign of illness until after a very strained meal between the two of them.

Alex waited up for Robert, who had gone to an evening meeting. When the young lawyer strode through the door, Alex met him, saying, "Nichole is ill. We have to get a doctor."

"She's ill? But she was fine this morning. What happened?"

Alex dragged his fingers through his hair. "Robert, something is wrong, very wrong. She won't even talk to me."

"Should I talk to her?" Robert asked in concern.

"Just give me the name of the doctor, and then you tell her I'm going for him."

Robert saw no reason to argue with the distraught man and hurriedly checked a list of names, writing one on a slip of paper. "You stay here. I'll send my man for him." Then Robert went up the stairs to speak to Nichole.

Robert knocked hesitantly; why on earth was he talking to Nichole? Alex should be the one to see to her. She was Alex's wife. He turned to go back down the stairs when Nichole opened the door. Even in the soft candlelight, Robert was more than a little disturbed by her ashen face. "Nichole," Robert said softly, "Alex has sent for a doctor."

Nichole stood frozen in the doorway. Her mother had been seen by a doctor, and then the woman had died. She didn't want to die, even if Alex didn't want her as his wife. "No!" she cried in anguish, "I won't see a doctor," and she slammed the door.

Robert ran down the stairs. "Alex, she won't see the man!"

Alex raced up the stairs, pounded on the door and then bounded into Nichole's bedroom. She was sitting on the edge of the bed, sobbing and gagging at the same time. Alex fell on his knees in front of her, terrified. "Nichole, you must see a doctor, you are sick."

She was hurting terribly over what she considered to be her dismissal from his life, and she sobbed, "I want to go home. I want to go home."

Robert's man returned and told him that the doctor had been called out of town on a carriage accident and was not expected back until late the next day. Alex looked at the stairs and then at Robert. "We're leaving

274

for Manor House first thing in the morning."

Dawn came and Alex saw to loading the carriage. He insisted that blankets and warming bricks were made ready for Nichole, even though the day promised to be pleasant. After a quick breakfast, he thanked Robert, escorted his wife to the carriage, climbed in beside her and ordered the driver to take his leave. "Carefully!" Alex shouted at the man as he glanced at Nichole.

Nichole felt fine but she had nothing to say to her husband. Alex tried several subjects but she wouldn't talk to him. After a tense lunch, Alex climbed up beside the driver and left her in the carriage. Except for her terrible depression, she managed the trip to Manor House without a problem. But no sooner had they finished a light supper than Nichole was truly ill again.

For a week, Nichole rested, but still her stomach refused to retain the evening meal. Breakfast was no problem, nor was lunch, but she could not get dinner to stay down. She was tired and slept a great deal, and the few times she ventured downstairs, someone or something would upset her and with tears streaming down her face she would retreat to her room.

Catherine watched from the sidelines that whole week, getting angrier and angrier, both with Nichole and with Alex. In spite of the fact that Alex was frantic she decided that he wasn't concerned about his wife. She promised herself that she would tell him just what she thought of his handling of Nichole. She waited impatiently to get him off by himself.

It took another week before she caught him alone one afternoon leaving the kitchen. Nichole, despite the rest, was no better. "She's killing herself!" Catherine snapped.

"Sis, she won't see a doctor. Every time I try to talk to her, she starts to cry and either mumbles something about going back to France or that her mother saw a doctor and then died."

Catherine looked at the lines of agony etched on his face. "I don't care if she won't see a doctor, you're her husband. Send for one anyway! What did you do to her in Baltimore?" Catherine watched the confusion on her brother's face; then she added for good measure, "If you can't take care of a wife, you shouldn't have one." She stomped off back to the kitchen.

Mrs. Barber grabbed her arm and forced her down in a chair at the big table. Clucking her tongue, she fixed a cup of tea for Catherine and patted her shoulder. "Now, lovey, don't be too hard on him. We'll just have to wait until she tells 'em."

Catherine stared up at the woman, as if she had suddenly grown two heads. "Until she tells him? Tells him what? She sick and he's not taking care of her!" Catherine watched in disgust as the woman grinned and went back to her work.

Catherine jerked away from the table, furious. Nichole was dying and no one seemed to want to do anything about it. "Well," she said, pushing her chair under the table with force, "if no one will do what has to be done, then I guess it's up to me."

Mrs. Barber grabbed her arm and forced her again to the table. "Now you listen to me, Catherine Dampier. We all have caused that poor lass enough trouble. She'll be fine in another couple of weeks. She'll tell your brother when she's sure, or he'll tell her when he figures it out."

Catherine, her patience gone, screamed, "She's sick, she needs care! And I'm going to see that she gets it."

The cook snapped, "You'll do no such a thing. Catherine, Nichole is going to have a baby, and none of

276

this is your affair. This time you will stay out of it." She looked at Catherine's steel gray eyes. "And you'll keep your mouth shut."

Catherine formed a silent "OH!" and sank down on the chair at the end of the table. "Alex doesn't . . ."

Mrs. Barber interrupted, "And you are not going to tell him. You WILL keep your mouth shut. Do you hear me?"

Catherine gazed up at the cook, stunned. "I heard you!" she mumbled.

A few minutes later, Catherine met Alex on his way to the stable. She grinned at him and went up the stairs to see how Nichole was feeling. Alex watched her mount the stairs, dumbfounded. Only minutes before, she had been screaming at him; now, she was smiling. "The whole household is insane," he gritted between clenched teeth. Thanks to Catherine's prodding he had just now insisted that Prissy give him the name of a doctor. She had chuckled and smiled at him as if he had just made the biggest joke of the year.

That evening, Alex noticed that Nichole ate hungrily. And she didn't get sick. In the next several days, he watched as she continued to recover. She was pale and a little thinner than she had been, but she was no longer ill. He couldn't understand why she was so distant. He tried to draw her out but she still refused to talk to him.

He considered taking her back to Baltimore. Her wardrobe was ready for the final fitting, but he was afraid that something in Baltimore had made her ill. He sought Prissy's advice, and she suggested, "Why don't you bring the dressmaker here? I don't think Nichole should travel yet." Alex thought about questioning her remark, but Peter was waiting for planting instructions that were needed at Frederick, so he let the matter drop.

The dressmaker arrived within the week, and many of the things Alex had ordered were finished. Arrangements were made for the gowns that were yet incomplete. Alex waited for Nichole to thank him, but she said nothing. He was also waiting for her to invite him back to his own bedroom and the bed he had given up when she was so ill. When they returned from Baltimore, he had taken the guest room, afraid that he would disturb her, but now he wanted to be back in his bed with her.

Nichole wanted nothing to do with Alex. She was convinced that as soon as her wardrobe was finished, she would be packed up and sent back to France. In spite of the fact that the terrible vomiting was gone for the most part, certain food still nauseated her, she was tired much of the time, and she found that she cried very easily. She frequently had to run to her room to hide the tears that flowed to excess. She attributed all of her problems to that conversation she had overheard in Baltimore.

Catherine was beside herself. As the week dragged by, she watched Alex and Nichole. It was evident that Alex did not know what was wrong with Nichole, and both Prissy, who had guessed herself, and Mrs. Barber threatened her with death if she said a word. Catherine mumbled, "How is she going to tell him something that she doesn't even know herself?" As incredible as it seemed, even to Catherine, she knew that Nichole had no idea that she was going to have a baby.

Catherine chuckled. "Robert can tell Alex." She sent an urgent message to Robert. She giggled when she wondered what Alex would think, two messages in two days. Robert hadn't been to see her since the weekend before Alex and Nichole had returned. She sighed as she remembered the argument they had over the time for the next visit. Robert wanted to talk to Alex before he came again. Since Alex hadn't invited Robert to Manor House while he was in Baltimore, Catherine wasn't sure what had transpired. Well, she could endure Robert's anger. He had to talk to Alex. She did something she knew Alex would be furious about: she insisted that Robert come for the weekend.

By the middle of the week, Robert had responded, and because of her reputation, he wrote, he had invited himself for that very weekend. Catherine was delighted. She hadn't seen him for weeks. After he talked to Alex, they would have some time together. In spite of Prissy's and Mrs. Barber's warnings, she just knew he would consent to talk to Alex, once she explained what the problem was. Of course, she told herself, Alex wasn't going to have an easy task. She herself had tried to talk to Nichole, but it was just too embarrassing. But men were different, she decided. Alex could tell his wife things that she, a sister-in-law, couldn't mention.

Catherine's biggest surprise came when she told Alex that Robert had written, inviting himself for the weekend. He seemed thrilled that Robert was coming.

Robert's impending visit was a godsend, Alex decided. He would be able to talk to someone who was sane. He wondered if Robert might even be able to tell him what was wrong with Nichole. The women of his household were driving him to distraction. Nichole appeared to be almost afraid of him, but Catherine alternated between a ridiculous grin and a look of consuming disgust whenever she saw him. He wondered if love had addled his sister's brain. His carefully ordered world was in chaos.

Even Prissy and Mrs. Barber were condescending, but Peter was the biggest surprise. He had counted on his old friend and overseer to retain his calm attitude. Instead, Alex found Peter gazing at him with such pity that Alex continually snapped at the man, "What's the matter now?" Peter would just shake his head and continue with whatever he was doing. Alex sighed. He definitely needed someone to talk to for a change, someone who was not totally mad.

Friday arrived bright and sunny. Robert was expected that afternoon, and Alex was praying for his arrival. Catherine herself was anxiously waiting. She was a little afraid that Robert would be angry with her, but she had a just cause, she decided. She had watched Alex try to talk to his wife the night before. Nichole had dissolved into tears and run from him before he had a chance to say anything. For most of the day, she had been in her room.

Nichole sat in her room, sick with dread. Robert was coming to take her back to Baltimore, she was sure of it. On top of everything, she had taken the time to realize that she had missed her monthly flow. In fact, she had not had that problem since the last week at Frederick. Something was wrong, terribly wrong, but what?

When the carriage was spotted late that afternoon, the entire household sprang into motion. Alex was on the steps outside the house before the carriage had pulled to a stop. Descending the steps, Alex laughed, "You started very early to get here so soon. Dinner won't be ready for an hour."

Catherine flew out of the house, but as the elegant man stepped from the carriage, Robert's name died on her lips.

Alex stood perfectly still before the arriving guest. The soft brown eyes, the curly brown hair and classic nose were very familiar. The family resemblance was unmistakable. Alex stared at the square chin that wavered just a bit as the man stepped away from the carriage. He noticed that the eyes were cold and the full mouth was hard. Was he seeing a ghost?

The man stepped forward. "You must be Alex." Shifting his gaze to include the girl, he looked back at Alex. "I'm Armaund duPres, Duc duPres and heir to the duPres estates." He looked at Alex accusingly. "You killed my brother, Charles."

Alex stared at his French cousin. Why on earth was he here, what could he want, and why, dear God, did he think that he, Alex, had killed Charles? Alex instinctively responded, "It was an accident. The gun exploded."

There was nothing to do, Alex decided, but to invite the cousin into Manor House. They could not stand in the drive and wrangle about an accident that happened almost fifteen years before. Suddenly, Alex thought about the impending arrival of Robert. He sighed in relief; at least Robert knew the whole story and could advise Alex on any legal claims the man made.

Trying hard to be the congenial host in the worst of situations, Alex offered some refreshments and then insisted that Peter take Armaund's trunks up to the room already prepared for Robert.

Alex made his way quickly up to Nichole's room. "We have an unexpected guest. With Robert arriving in about an hour, I'll have to sleep in here."

Nichole looked at him, her tension visible on her oval face. "I understand, there is nothing else to do. We wouldn't want your guest to get the wrong impression."

Alex stepped up to her. She looked tired, but when he tried to put his arm around her, she backed away from him. "Nichole," he said sharply, "cousin or not, you and I are going to have a long talk tonight. And I don't care how many tears you shed." He left to gather his things

281

from the room where Robert would stay.

Alex paced the floor in his study waiting for Robert. Armaund had refused Alex's offer of a glass of brandy, saying that he wanted to freshen up. A shiver ran down Alex's back. The Frenchman seemed to be antagonistic toward him, almost as if he wanted to do him in. Alex breathed a sigh of relief when he heard Robert's voice from the hall.

Even before Robert had deposited his cloak with Maude, Alex was dragging him toward the study. As quickly as he could, Alex explained what had happened. Robert's immediate reaction was quiet. "I can return to Baltimore first thing in the morning."

"No!" Alex snarled, "don't you dare." Alex stoppered the decanter he had just used to pour Robert a brandy. "I have a feeling that I may need a good lawyer before the day is out. He stood right out in front, right in the drive, and accused me of murdering his brother. Robert, his eyes . . . there is something about the man. I think he wants my blood."

Robert chuckled. "You may not need a lawyer, you may need a constable."

Alex glanced at him once more and then past Robert to the doorway. Nichole stood in the doorway, her face a pasty white. She had heard every word. "Alex, you aren't in any danger, are you?"

"I was just teasing Robert, I don't think . . ." He was at a loss for words.

Nichole was spared trying to sort through his comments when Armaund duPres made his appearance. Nichole welcomed him as cordially as she could and led the way to the dining room, where dinner was ready to be served.

The whole evening meal was a nightmare of unequaled

282

portions. Everyone at the table was convinced that Armaund was there for some reason other than to socialize. Nichole was already tense with worry over what Alex assured her they would discuss that night. Armaund's presence only aggravated the situation. Catherine didn't have a second alone with Robert, and she could tell that Alex was shooting sparks of anger in Armaund's direction, as well as Nichole's. And Catherine was sure that Alex would upset Nichole more than she was already. That wouldn't do, not until she had a chance to talk to Robert.

By the time the entree was served, Catherine was so subdued that Robert had to repeat a question three times before she finally answered him.

Alex was watching his wife, and he felt his concern lodge in his throat. He glanced at his cousin. Armaund duPres looked almost sullen. There was something wrong with the man. Clearly the meal was a disaster. Catherine and Nichole left even before coffee and dessert were served, and they went upstairs together.

For the next few minutes, the meal was almost pleasant, but when Robert pushed his coffee cup aside, Armaund turned and in a brisk tone said, "I have business with my cousin. I must ask you to excuse us."

Robert looked over at Alex in surprise. Alex stared at the uninvited guest, and then he snapped, "I think you forget yourself, cousin. Robert is my lawyer, my business agent, my friend and soon to be my brother-in-law. Anything that you wish to discuss can be said in front of Mr. Patterson. He was invited to this house. You were not!"

Armaund bristled, and slowly a brilliant red flushed his angry face. He got up from the table, snorting, "I can wait to complete my business with you." He left the

283

two men sitting frozen, watching him walk from the room.

"I may have been a bit hasty," Robert said quietly. "You may indeed need a lawyer. You may be tempted to spill his blood."

Alex shrugged his shoulders and then stared ahead. "You know, I don't think that man has full use of his faculties." Robert snorted but Alex continued, "No! I'm not joking. I really am concerned. He seems to be laboring under some great misconception. I have the strongest feeling that I should send Catherine and Nichole to the farm."

Robert didn't like Armaund's attitude, but he didn't think the man was deranged. "Alex, I think you're just unnerved by his appearance here and by his attitude toward you. That would upset anyone—which reminds me, I must see Catherine. I take it your answer is still yes. She seems very upset tonight and her note indicated that she was disturbed about something before Armaund arrived. Could I use your study for a few minutes? I'll ask Maude to get her."

"I must speak to Nichole as well. She was just starting to recover. This may bring back her illness." The two men stood, and Maude was summoned. Alex frowned. "I still think I should send Nichole and Catherine to the farm."

Robert cautioned, "Why don't you wait for a day or two. Let's see what he wants first."

Robert went to the study to await Catherine. He poured himself a brandy and sat down to wait for the young woman that he would ask to share his life. A good fifteen minutes passed before the little woman was closing the study door softly. She stepped forward and walked into Robert's outstretched arms. "I've missed you," Robert whispered, pulling her into his embrace.

Catherine turned her face up for his kiss. "I was beginning to think you planned this lengthy absence to torture me."

Robert sighed; Catherine always spoke her mind. "I talked to Alex, but with Nichole so sick, I didn't feel I could impose. I think, now that she's starting to recover, we can begin making our plans." He grinned down at her. She smiled back, and Robert couldn't resist the temptation to kiss her soundly.

The kiss was interrupted by a loud banging on the study door. "Mista Robert, Mista Alex, he wants you now. Mista Robert? You in there? Mista Robert?"

Robert swore, "Damn." He strode to the door and threw it open, glaring at Maude.

Upstairs in the master bedroom, Nichole had changed into a soft cotton gown and she was sitting in a chair, terrified by the conversation that Alex had promised they would have. Alex stood quietly at the door watching her for several minutes before he made his presence known. She looked so frightened to him, but surely, she could not be that concerned about the scene at dinner. As he walked over to her chair, he asked softly, "Sweetheart, what is wrong? Armaund is just visiting. He is a cousin. He'll be gone soon."

Nichole raised her chin and tried to still her quivering lips. Nothing he said had registered. "I don't want to go back to France," she muttered, before a fresh flood of tears burst from her eyes.

Alex stood stunned. Go back to France? Were all Frenchman crazy? He hadn't said anything about France since January. Her statement confused and frightened him. He asked, his voice a little sharper than he intended, "Go back to France? That is a crazy idea.

France is not safe. You are going to stay right here with me."

Nichole blinked back the tears; oh, she wanted to believe him, how she wanted to believe him. Alex read the longing in her eyes and quickly he picked her up and sat her down in his lap as he took the other chair. Cradling her in his arms, he tenderly caressed her cheek. "Sweetheart, you have been sick, very sick. I don't know where you got this idea but it is a very silly idea. You can't go to France, your home is here with me. We're going back to the farm in a few days and you're going to help me decorate the rooms we planned to build. Robert is going to sell his town house and I'm seriously thinking of buying it. When you get tired of the farm, we, you and I, will go to Baltimore to that town house. When you get your health back we may even travel to New York or Philadelphia, but that is as far as you are going, my love. And you won't go anyplace without me."

Nichole looked up at his anxious face. She wanted to believe him. She had to believe him or go mad. She leaned into his chest and sobbed. Alex stroked her head. "Why won't you let me send for a doctor? You don't feel good. I'm scared to death that you will get even sicker than you have been. Please, let me send for a doctor."

Nichole shook her head, then raised her tear-streaked face. "My . . . my mo . . . mother saw a doctor and then she di . . . died."

Alex enfolded her in his arms and rested his chin on her head. "If you're not better next week, I'm sending for a physician." His voice was barely above a whisper.

He lifted his head and set her from him so that he could see her face. "I never told you about Robert and Catherine, did I?" he asked, praying that a change of

286

subjects would stop or at least slow the tears she was still shedding. He dried her eyes, and then in a lively voice he commented, "I asked him what his intentions were."

"Oh, Alex, that's so old-fashioned," she offered quietly.

"Well, he had the audacity to tell me that he didn't know."

Nichole gasped.

"I told him that she was too young for him, that she knew very little about the world, had very few friends. It wasn't until I told him that she was self-centered and very opinionated that he got very defensive about her."

Something about his choice of words sparked her curiosity. "Alex, when did you and Robert have that conversation?"

Alex looked down at her, wondering why the timing seemed so important to her. "I think it was the evening you got sick. Yes, you went to bed and Robert and I retired to the library. Why?"

Nichole blushed a bright pink, and her mouth formed a small oh. Alex stared at her and suddenly it struck him. "You shouldn't eavesdrop like that."

"I didn't," Nichole snapped, then stopped, "At least, well — I . . . I didn't mean to. I came downstairs for a cup of tea to settle my stomach."

Alex looked a little unsettled. "You thought I was talking about you, didn't you?" She only nodded her head. Another thought struck Alex. He and Robert had also discussed the taking of La Bonne Mer that night. He remembered that he had very loudly expressed his own opinion about the sale of the ship. He looked at Nichole, very leery. "What else did you hear that night?"

Nichole tensed. Now that he knew she had overheard

his conversation, would his story change? She looked at him suspiciously. Let him try and deny it! She glared at him. "I heard you say that legalities be damned, I ought to be sent back to France."

Alex winced. He was afraid she had heard that. Would she believe his explanation? He felt her suspicion. No, she would not believe him. He set her on the other chair and went to the door. Opening it wide he bellowed for Maude. She came running. He said something to her about Robert, and Maude disappeared.

Alex walked over to one of the armoires and took out one of Nichole's new robes. "Better put this on, love. We are about to have company."

Nichole hadn't gotten the robe closed before she heard rapid footsteps down the hall. Alex opened the door even before Robert knocked. Alex yanked him into the room and said unevenly, "Nichole wants to ask you something."

Nichole was embarrassed and frightened. She wasn't dressed and she had no idea what on earth Alex wanted her to ask. Alex had said she should go back to France, not Robert. As the tension in the room began to build, she stared at first one man and then the other.

Alex was more than a little upset. How could she doubt his love after the farm? He snapped at Robert, "She overheard part of our conversation about La Bonne Mer."

"You dragged me up here for that. I was trying to . . . Damn it, man, you sure picked a poor time." Robert was obviously angry, too.

"Well, right now, my marriage is more important than one that hasn't even been agreed to yet!" Alex grumbled.

Robert mumbled something about not even having one at this rate, but he turned to Nichole and asked her in a level tone, "What is your question?"

Nichole stammered, "I overheard Alex say he wanted to . . . to . . . to send me back to France."

Robert looked startled. "When?"

Nichole was getting angry. "He didn't say when, I didn't hear . . ."

"No! When did he say he wanted to send you back?"

"The night I got sick."

"At my town house?"

Nichole nodded.

Robert stuttered, "The night you got . . . La Bonne Mer!" Robert smiled. "Nichole, I told Alex about a client of mine who had just purchased a ship from a man in the Caribbean. It had originally been stolen by pirates. Alex told me that I should forget my client and return the ship to France."

Nichole turned on Alex. "You were talking about a ship?"

Alex chuckled. "Listening to other people's conversations can get you into trouble."

Nichole turned away. She wanted to sink into a crack in the floor. Never had she been so embarrassed. Alex thanked Robert and closed the door softly. He walked to where Nichole stood, straight and rigid, her back to him. "Would you have believed me if I had explained it to you?"

"I don't know," came her soft whisper.

"Sweetheart," Alex turned her around and lifted her chin with his finger, "I didn't mean to embarrass you, but, if I'm not mistaken, what you thought you heard has made you ill. A little embarrassment is better than a lot of doubts and fears, isn't it?" Nichole fell against him, sobbing as if she would die. Alex held her close and whispered sweet words of comfort in her ear. Slowly, her sobs slowed and then stopped. Alex raised her head once more and began kissing away her tears. He crushed her up against his hard, masculine body. "I will never let you leave me, I will never send you away, never!" He picked her up and carried her to their bed.

Chapter Twenty-three

Alex carried Nichole to the bed and carefully placed her in the center. As he ran his hands over her ribs, he noticed that she had grown thinner in the last weeks. "You're getting too thin," he muttered.

Nichole had no desire to talk about herself, and as she pulled his head down to hers she whispered, "I'll eat tomorrow." She kissed him with complete abandon. Drinking from his strength, his love, she caressed him.

Slowly, with infinite care, Alex removed her robe, then her gown, and when she was completely naked, his own clothes joined hers before he lowered himself to his bed. He took her face in his hands and lowered his parting lips to drink of the sweetness he had thirsted for these many weeks. He raised his head to gaze into her eyes. "Nichole, I love you. You are my wife. I want you with me forever."

She surrendered to his words, wrapping her arms around his neck and slowly, so slowly, she pulled his head down so that she could touch his lips. She kissed his nose, his eyelids, his forehead and finally trailed her lips back to his, parting her lips in invitation. Alex accepted her invitation and rolled closer to her. Nibbling his way down her neck, he stopped briefly at the point where her neck joined her shoulders, and then he traveled to the tip of her breast. Gently, he cupped one soft mound and trailed his thumb across the nipple while he ravished the other with his tongue. Her breasts were fuller than he remembered, but he was too involved in his play to let the thought register.

Nichole was mindless. She ran her hands over his broad back and kneaded the muscles that rippled as he moved above her. She was on fire, and the more he touched her the higher the flames burned, until she knew that soon she would be nothing more than white ashes. Suddenly, his roaming hands cupped the center of her and she gasped. A thought, a single thread of consciousness forced its way into her mind and she trailed her hand down the light furring of his chest, across the taut muscles of his belly and lower still. She wrapped her fingers around his male pride and delighted in the gasp of pleasure she heard. Smiling to herself, she played through the dark hair, returning often to greet his male staff.

Alex pulled away from her touch. "Stop," he gasped. "I can't take any more just yet." He moved above her, and took her lips in a bruising kiss. Then, as if a voice told him to be more gentle, his kiss grew tender and he kissed her neck, her shoulders, trailing soft kisses down her chest to the valley between her taut breasts. Before she took a much needed breath, his lips were teasing the skin stretched over her ribs at her waist. He paid homage to her belly, and then moved lower still, until his kisses brushed through the soft golden curls between her thighs.

Now it was Nichole's turn to plead. In a husky, broken voice, she whispered, "Now, now!"

Alex strained for some control, but her begging voice ended his restraint. He pulled her under him, and positioning himself, he entered her slowly. For several minutes he lay motionless, kissing her deeply, waiting for a signal from her. As if she sensed his desire she wiggled under him, then pushed up. Slowly, wanting this exquisite joining to last for an eternity, Alex began to move. But they had been apart too long. In seconds, they both were writhing in ecstasy.

Alex wrapped his arms around his wife and rolled to his side, taking her with him. "I'll never let you go, never! You are mine." Still trailing soft kisses across her hair, over her eyelids, across her forehead, he held her tenderly. "Sleep now." She opened her eyes and smiled at him so gently that he thought for a second his heart had been torn from his chest. Lifting her hand to caress his cheek, she closed her eyes and drifted off to sleep.

Morning came and she was still snuggled up against him, her buttocks fitted snugly next to his groin. His arm was resting across her ribs and his hand was involuntarily cupping her breast. She gloried in his closeness. How foolish she had been, she scolded herself. If she had only asked him about that conversation, he would have told her that her fears were unfounded. She should never have allowed herself to react the way she did. Because of her own lack of trust, she had made herself sick. When twinges of hunger gnawed at her, then rumbled in the emptiness of the quiet room, she pulled away from Alex in embarrassment.

Alex's hand tightened on her breast for a second, and then he rolled toward her. He opened his eyes and grinned down at her. "I think my lady mistress needs some food." As she sat up, ready to leave his bed, he pushed her into the pillows. "You stay here. I'll go get

293

us something to eat." He chuckled at the surprised look on her face. "I'm not finished with you yet," he whispered.

Nichole said softly, "But we have guests."

"And they can fend for themselves for a while."

She lay back down and closed her eyes. In truth, they were his guests. For a few minutes she let her mind drift; then he was back. Nichole looked at the tray hungrily. There was tea and coffee and hot sugar cake. She licked her lips in appreciation. They ate in bed, and Nichole had three slices of cake to Alex's one. When the tea and coffee were finished, Alex took the tray, stripped out of his breeches and joined his naked wife in their bed.

Against his warm lips, Nichole mumbled, "We really should get up." As he kissed her deeply, Nichole gave up any thought of leaving her husband's side. If he wanted to stay in bed for a week, then that was definitely where she wanted to stay as well.

Down the hall, in the massive bed of the guest room, Armaund duPres was starting to stir. At first, he couldn't remember where he was. The rocking of the ship was missing, he thought. He raised himself up on his elbow and looked around. His clothes were in a discarded heap by the bed, and for a second, he wondered where Pierre, his private valet, had gone. Shaking his head, he tried to stem the ugly events of the last months that flowed over him.

Once more he was at the Chateau duPres, overlooking the River Rhone just south of Lyon, in the wine district of France. For hundreds of years the family of duPres had farmed the land, producing fruit and grapes and from the grapes, wine. Just last fall, the peasants who worked side by side with the family revolted. His father and mother had taken the three girls and fled with what they could carry to Bordeaux, and then to England to family friends. Charles Philipe had begged his son to go with them, but Armaund had refused. Charles finally told his son that the estate was in, as his father had put it, his capable hands.

Immediately, he began making changes. He made a list of regulations that would increase the chateau's profits, and he made sure that the peasants understood what would happen to them if they did not follow his directives. Within weeks, after he had posted the new working rules, the peasants had turned on him. Surely, he told himself, the two were not connected. They carried pitchforks and handmade swords as they descended on the chateau. The battle that followed lasted only minutes. Those few of the household staff that remained loyal to the family died at his feet. The peasants left the courtyard to bury their own dead, allowing Armaund the chance to escape.

He remembered standing in the middle of the carnage and staring at the unseeing eyes of his personal valet. Wave after wave of terror filled his body and he hadn't been able to move. Only the noise of the returning men seemed to shatter the ice that held his feet. He remembered running, screaming and pulling at his hair, with no direction in mind. His clothing was covered with spatters of blood, and as he ran he discarded what he was wearing and donned anything that was lying about.

He thought he ran through the vineyards and into the fields, and he did remember hiding. Several times in the days that followed he sneaked back to the chateau and gathered clothing, food, and a small bag of gold coins hidden in one of the bedrooms.

As he lay on the cold ground, fearing for his life, he thought about Charles. Charles was the firstborn.

Charles should have been the one to endure this shame, not Armaund. Charles had been the heir to the chateau, not Armaund. Charles should have been the one to fight the peasants. It was the responsibility of the first born to bear such indignities. Armaund, as the second born, should have been in England with his parents. It was not his fault that the servants died, it was not his fault that the chateau fell. Charles should never have died.

But Charles was dead. And, one bitterly cold night, Armaund remembered Alex Dampier. Charles was not defending the chateau because Alex Dampier had killed his brother! At that moment, Armaund knew what he had to do. He had to travel to that place called Maryland, and Alex Dampier had to die!

A frown crossed Armaund's face. He had gone back to the chateau and gathered his mother's jewels, then made his way to Nice. He had managed a place on a ship bound for Philadelphia. It was only a short trip to Baltimore. Now Armaund was actually in the home of Alex Dampier. Now Alex would die.

This wasn't the first time Armaund had wanted Alex Dampier dead, not at all. Five years before, on a clear spring day, his father had called him into the office of the chateau, and he remembered the scolding his father gave him, for his lack of interest in the vineyards, in fact, his lack of interest in anything that did not produce instant pleasure. I'm not like your firstborn, Armaund wanted to yell. He didn't want to work like the firstborn, either. With Charles dead, the family assumed that Armaund would continue the vineyards and the special skill that made the wine.

"But I don't want to make wine," Armaund tried to explain, but no one listened. He hadn't wanted to work at all. Armaund gritted his teeth. If his older brother had lived, Charles would have worked and Armaund could have spent his time in much more pleasurable pursuits. But Charles had not lived, Alex Dampier had seen to that. That was the day that Armaund decided Alex Dampier would pay for his crime.

Armaund straightened his shoulders. His day would come. He would make the vineyards yield more money than the family had ever dreamed possible. Then he would find Alex Dampier and end his life. So he started learning how to make wine, and every day he cursed Alex Dampier a little more.

With the revolt, and the flight of his parents, Armaund forgot his resolve. He even forgot about all the money he had spent to learn about his Colonial cousin. Then the chateau had fallen.

He frowned as he tried to remember just how he had met Jacques Menace. But the Frenchman turned Colonial knew the family of Dampier well, and he was as hungry for the coin as Armaund. Armaund stretched in his bed, grinning to himself. Jacques Menace certainly was hungry. Somehow, all the information that the little Frenchman had sold him would pay off. After all, he was in Alex's bed, and eating his food.

He shrugged off the bed linens and sat at the edge of the bed. Last winter's payment to Jacques had been healthy but worth every penny. Strange that Alex never wondered how he knew the Dampier heir was married. Of course, the honorable thing was a duel, Armaund told himself. Yes, the honorable way to kill the man was a duel, but according to Jacques, Alex was good with pistols and with swords. How could he possibly fight a duel with Alex Dampier? There had to be another way, and he would stay in the man's home until he found it.

Of course, if the stayed in the house, he would have

to apologize for his actions last night. He had never apologized to anyone before. Whatever had made him demand to speak to Alex alone? He didn't want that, not really. What he wanted was Alex dead, just like his brother. He would have to bide his time, and he would use whatever means he had to bring about Alex's demise. But now, he told himself, he would have to see about something to eat.

He dressed and went downstairs to the kitchen. "Why wasn't my breakfast served in bed?" he asked a stunned Priscilla.

She looked at him through narrowed eyes. "Sir, we are less formal here than in France. If you want your breakfast in bed, you should have brought a servant with you."

"Madame, my servant died at my feet. Tomorrow and henceforth, I want my breakfast served in bed." He turned on his heel and went in search of Alex. He had to get the bedamnable apology out of the way as quickly as possible. Unfortunately, Alex was still in bed. Armaund found Catherine in the study and using all the charm he could muster, he asked her to show him the house and the stable.

He seemed pleasant enough so Catherine, playing the hostess, showed him the house and then took him out to the stables. By the time the tour was ended, Catherine decided that her charming cousin had only been out of sorts from his long carriage ride from Philadelphia.

When Alex and Nichole finally came downstairs, Robert was waiting for Alex in the study. Alex winked at Nichole and whispered something in her ear. She chuckled and kissed his cheek. Then she went in search of Catherine. She found Catherine in the kitchen with Armaund, discussing the different ways to make coffee.

Nichole invited them both to join her for breakfast.

Minutes later, Maude came looking for Catherine. "Ya wanted in the study," Maude explained. "Mr. Alex, he wants to talk to ya."

As Catherine left the dining room, Nichole glanced over at her new cousin by marriage. She tried to overcome her apprehension at being left in the company of a man she didn't know and didn't think she liked. Armaund seemed to sense her distrust. "Madame, I must apologize. I had such an inconvenient trip by ship, and the carriage ride here was the worst I've ever endured. The roads are absolutely abominable. I was not myself yesterday."

Nichole smiled. She remembered all too well her own trip from Baltimore to Manor House and the more recent trips with Alex. "Yes, I must agree. The roads here are terrible. A great many people travel by boats in these parts."

With the ice broken, Armaund described his recent voyage and the carriage ride from Philadelphia. By the time Alex joined them in the dining room, Nichole and Armaund were laughing and joking like old friends. Alex felt just a touch of jealousy, then dismissed it. His wife was only playing the gracious hostess, he told himself.

When Alex strolled up to the head of the table, Armaund jumped to his feet, his face coloring slightly. "Sir, I must apologize to you. I have already done so to your charming wife. I endured a most uncomfortable trip to arrive here, and I was not myself yesterday. Please, excuse last night and let us begin again?"

Alex was astonished. But his mind was whirling. Why had the Frenchman come to Manor House? Granted, Alex told himself, they were relatives, but why here and why now? He didn't have a chance to question Armaund for just then, Robert came into the room, dragging Catherine after him.

Robert was grinning from ear to ear and Catherine's lips were dark pink and her cheeks flushed. Robert held Catherine about the waist, and he gazed down into her twinkling gray eyes. "She said yes!"

Alex quickly reached for the brandy, leaving Nichole to explain to Armaund, "Catherine and Robert are to be married. You have arrived at a most happy time." Nichole got up from her place at the table and hugged Robert, then kissed Catherine. "I wish you both much happiness."

Alex passed around the brandy, and all glasses were raised to toast the happiness of the couple.

For the next two days, Alex watched Armaund and complained to Robert that there was still reason for concern. Robert stayed until Monday, and he continued to tell Alex that his concern was a little exaggerated. Armaund was charming. The Frenchman told Alex that he had traveled to Maryland to meet his cousins and to bring them the news that the chateau had been destroyed.

Alex wasn't satisfied. He questioned Robert in the study after Armaund had retired. "Why did he come? The reason he gave is no reason at all. The chateau means nothing to us. It never has. A letter would have done as well. There is more to it, but what?"

Robert argued in Armaund's defense, "The poor fellow was probably so upset with the situation in France that he wanted to spend some time with relatives instead of depending on just friends."

Alex was tempted to tell him that there were other cousins in Philadelphia, relatives of the duPres family, relatives who had entertained his mother, father and himself when he was a boy. They were friendly, wealthy and decidedly more French then Alex and Catherine. No, if Armaund wanted to avoid being dependent on friends and be with relatives, the Philadelphia Bordeleaus should have been his choice.

Robert left early Monday morning, and Catherine spent the rest of the week trying to decide on a wedding date. She pleaded and argued that Nichole and she be allowed to travel to Baltimore for a visit to the dressmaker. Alex refused to even take it under consideration. Inwardly he cringed. The last time Nichole had gone to Baltimore she had come home so ill that he worried about her survival. Under no circumstances was she traveling to Baltimore until he was satisfied that she was completely over her disorder. But the reason he gave Catherine wasn't as forceful. He insisted, "Nichole needs to nap in the afternoon and recover her strength." Both Prissy and Mrs. Barber agreed with Alex. Nichole should not travel, not now.

To Catherine's horror, Nichole seemed to agree with Alex and she smiled at Catherine. "Alex is right. Until I completely recover my strength I'll stay here." Nichole tried to hide her grin. She was almost completely recovered now, although she still tired easily. She felt great and was eating like a field hand. She had started gaining weight. In fact, she was afraid to tell Alex that several of her brand new dresses were getting too tight in the waist. But if Alex didn't want her to go to Baltimore, then she wouldn't, even though his excuse was no excuse at all.

Before Robert went back to Baltimore, he promised Catherine that he would arrange a visit with his parents early in July, when they returned from an extended visit with his sister's family. And Catherine, pointing out that Robert had to be socially introduced to their neighbors,

301

succeeded in getting Alex to agree to a ball the first of August. "You and Robert can announce the engagement then. Of course, I'll have to have a whole new wardrobe for everything, the visit, the ball and all the things Robert says we must attend."

Alex groaned. "I hope Robert knows what he is getting into."

Catherine grinned and tried once more. "I want Nichole to come with me to the dressmaker. She has such good taste."

"No," Alex said firmly. "I've already said she can't go to Baltimore. She's going to stay right here. If you have to go to the damned dressmaker, then I'll take you myself; in fact, I'll take you the first of next week."

Catherine was beside herself. She was sure that Alex hadn't guessed that he was going to become a father, and the several hints she had thrown at Nichole had passed her by. Nichole didn't know she was going to be a mother. Catherine had never been so frustrated. The trip to Baltimore with Alex was the perfect time to explain the facts of life to her brother, but she was bound by her promise to Robert. She had to keep her opinions to herself. He had been very adamant. Nichole had to tell Alex about the baby. Catherine had sworn to say nothing.

Catherine remembered the conversation so plainly. Oh, how she had ranted and raved. "How can she tell him something that she doesn't know anything about? Alex will have to tell her." But it had done not a whit of good.

"Catherine," Robert told her quietly, "every woman, even one as innocent as Nichole, knows about babies, she's just waiting for the right time. You must promise to stay out of it! I want you to swear to me that you will say nothing."

She had nodded her head. Robert was usually so wise, perhaps he was right about this as well. Somehow, though, she had her doubts. But she had sworn . . .

Chapter Twenty-four

Armaund was very much aware of the tension in the house, and he took credit for it, decided that he was probably the cause. They don't trust me, he told himself. There was only one thing to do; he poured on the charm. He played his role and watched Alex carefully. If Alex was to be his victim, he had to know everything that happened in the house.

Armaund found himself furious over the affection between Alex and his French wife. Obviously they were very much in love. But what bothered Armaund was that Alex couldn't keep his hands off of her, frequently pulling her into his arms, no matter who was in the same room to observe them. And she never objected, Armaund thought in disgust. They seemed to gravitate toward each other, and Armaund thought it most improper. A Frenchwoman should never be so brazen in public. "It's in such poor taste," he muttered.

It galled him more that Alex should be so happy. He had no right to any kind of happiness, he mused, murderer that he was. While he watched Alex and Nichole an idea occurred to him. Perhaps he didn't have to kill Alex. No, in fact, perhaps death was not the ultimate sacrifice for the man. There could be another way. Nichole was the answer. Nichole would be the sacrificial lamb.

On the day before the trip to Baltimore, Catherine was beside herself. She spent the afternoon arguing with Prissy and Mrs. Barber. Promise or not, she was going to tell Alex about the baby on the way to Baltimore.

"Don't you say a word. Robert will skin you alive," Prissy hissed at her charge.

"But Nichole can't tell him, she doesn't know. I'll just have to try and explain things to Nichole!" Catherine's eyes danced.

"You'll do no such thing!" Prissy snapped.

Mrs. Barber looked up from her bowl of ginger cake. "I've been thinking about this and I have to agree with Catherine. I don't think Nichole knows. I know ya can't believe that, and I have trouble with it myself, except, there's kinda like a questioning look in her eyes, like she knows something's amiss, but don't know what."

Prissy said angrily, "You better stay out of it, too!"

"All right!" the cook shouted. "When she whelps right in front of him, you can explain why we said nothing."

Armaund was on his way to the kitchen for something to eat, and he arrived outside the door just as Catherine made her first comment. He stood glued to that spot until the discussion was finished. Tiptoeing as quickly as he could back through the dining room, he made his way to his room. He poured some of the brandy from a decanter that Alex had insisted that he take and sat down. Unbelievable! Catherine and the cook both were positive that the mistress of Manor House was expecting but neither parent knew. Now this was worth thinking about, this was something he could use. He grinned at nothing and thought about a plan.

Early the next morning, Alex helped Peter hitch up the

team. "I want you to keep a very close eye on Nichole. Don't let Armaund spend much time with her," Alex ordered.

"You're just jealous. Your cousin has been most charming. The only thing you don't like is that Nichole seems to enjoy his company. Of course, she seems to enjoy your company a whole lot more." Chuckling, Peter went on about his work.

Alex grinned himself. What Peter said was true. When they were together the rest of the world seemed to disappear. Whenever he put his arms around her, she usually turned her face to his, imploring that he plant a kiss firmly on her lips. Oh! she didn't say the words but it was in her eyes every time she looked at him. She was as madly in love with him as he was with her. The whole world could know for all he cared.

Shortly after breakfast, Catherine joined Alex, kissed Nichole on the cheek and stood impatiently while Alex told his wife good-bye. While she stood quietly off to one side, Prissy walked over with a lunch basket. Scowling at Catherine, she mumbled quietly, "Not a word. You hear?"

Catherine didn't wait for Alex to help her up into the carriage. She flopped into the seat, her anger rocking the vehicle. Alex climbed through the door, glaring at her, "My God, Catherine. Can't you wait until I've told Nichole good-bye?"

Catherine turned her head and stared at the drive. Sometimes Alex was so stupid!

Nichole wasn't upset by Alex's departure. She planned to spend her time trying to figure out what was wrong with her. Before the carriage was out of sight, she was in the library, pouring over the many books that mentioned diseases, infirmities, anything that she thought might

306

apply. There were over a hundred books lining the walls. Chewing at her lips, she admitted by the end of the second day, the information she needed was not in a book.

Armaund spent very little time in the house himself. Each morning, after breakfast, he ordered a horse saddled and he left the plantation, to ride, he said. He always returned by dinnertime, and Peter grinned in pleasure. Alex would be delighted, for the Frenchie and Nichole spent no time together, except for dinner.

The afternoon of the third day, Catherine and Alex returned. Nichole, Peter and Armaund, who gave up his ride that afternoon, greeted the master and his sister. Catherine was in a rage. "All he did was push, push, push. We left Robert's home at dawn. I didn't get a chance to spend any time with Robert at all!" She ran to her room to pout.

Alex chuckled and told Nichole, "They had their first lovers' quarrel. They were arguing about something the second day we were there. She is very angry at Robert about something. But she wouldn't tell me what it was."

Armaund drew in a quick breath. Somehow, he had to maneuver the household into position so that he could put his plans into motion before someone like Robert or Catherine spoiled the whole thing. For two days he listened carefully to every conversation on the plantation. Several times, he ducked out of sight just in time. Something he heard threw him into a rage. Alex was going to take Nichole back to the farm in a few days! Armaund shook his head; that would never do, not at all. He had already spent three days in preparation for what he had in mind. Alex was not going to ruin it, he was not!

Armaund paced his room that night. He had already exchanged some of his mother's jewels for fees and everything had gone so nicely. Alex was going to ruin it. There had to be something he could do. Somehow, he had to see the man gone for at least several days. Armaund had to get him back to Baltimore. No, that wouldn't do, for Alex would return much too soon. Perhaps the answer was that farm of his, but without Nichole. He had no illusions about accomplishing that.

Armaund wanted to shriek with glee the next day. He overheard Alex telling Peter that the someone had to travel to the farm to see about the place before he and Nichole arrived. Peter volunteered, and Alex explained that while he was at the farm Alex would take Catherine back to Baltimore for her fittings. Robert's parents had returned and were insisting on a small party the following Saturday so that they could introduce her to the family. Alex added, "I will leave her with Robert's parents and you can retrieve her on the way back from the farm."

Armaund smiled broadly. If he insisted on traveling along, he was certain that Alex would change places with Peter. "The man could not stand to be in a carriage with me for that many hours," he congratulated himself. He had been watching Alex as he observed his wife, and Armaund suspected that he was very close to guessing the truth. The plan must be put into action, quickly. Tonight, he would force Alex to the farm, after he secured a invitation to ride in the carriage to Baltimore.

Before dinner that evening, Armaund made his announcement: he was leaving for Philadelphia. Would it be possible for Alex to allow him to accompany him to Baltimore?

Alex stared at his cousin, wondering again why the man had come, and even more curious why the man was leaving. Not one more word had been said about

Charles duPres or the accident that had claimed his life. Alex dismissed his own questions. The man was leaving! That in itself was reason for Alex to rejoice. He had never trusted Armaund, and the sooner he left the happier Alex would be. And Armaund had been correct in his assessment of Alex's feelings toward him. Peter was immediately told that there would be a change of plans. He, Alex, would go to the farm, and Peter would take Armaund to Philadelphia; in fact, Armaund could accompany Catherine and Peter to Baltimore and Peter could continue on to Philadelphia and then return for Catherine.

Armaund smiled as Alex announced a change in plans to Peter, but the next part of his comment sent Armaund into panic. No! Peter could not take him to Philadelphia. That would never do. He wanted to go to Baltimore, and that was as far as he wanted to be taken. The only reason that he was leaving was to get Alex away from Nichole and give his cousin the impression that he was gone from Manor House. Armaund insisted, "If I can accompany Peter and Catherine to Baltimore, that is far enough. I want to see some of the fair city before I travel on to Philadelphia. You have been too generous. I cannot, in good conscience, allow you to arrange my travel to Philadelphia. I'll arrange that when I have tired of Baltimore."

Alex agreed so quickly that even Nichole shook her head. Perfect, she thought to herself. Just the day before, she had listened to Maude telling Prissy and Mrs. Barber about a young man who was doctoring in the area. "Why, he even saved two youngens who have the fever. And, if ya have a need he is right there." While Alex was at the farm, Peter and Catherine in Baltimore and Armaund gone from their lives, Nichole would see the man herself. Surely if the young man was as skilled as Maude said, he would know what was wrong with her.

After dinner that night, Alex made a halfhearted attempt to offer Peter's services to Philadelphia, but Armaund smiled broadly and told him firmly that it wasn't necessary. "You've done more than enough for me by allowing me to stay and share your home for five weeks. I have a desire to look more closely at this town of Baltimore; then, I can see my own way to my cousins' home in Philadelphia."

The plans were finalized at dinner the next night. Alex felt no hesitation in leaving Nichole alone at the plantation for the five days he would have to spend at Frederick. "I'd really like to take you with me, but there are several things that I must do and I would much rather leave you here than at the farm. As soon as I return," he assured her, "we'll pack and the two of us will return to the farm." He grinned at her. "I told you we'd be farmers."

Since Nichole had plans of her own to make, she encouraged her husband to leave, offering, "The sooner you go, the sooner you'll return." Nichole smiled; she had her own note all ready to be delivered to the young doctor in the village just five miles from Manor House. She had requested that she see him on Saturday afternoon. Peter with Catherine and Armaund were leaving Thursday early in the morning, and Alex would probably be gone at dawn.

Thursday was bright and warm. Alex didn't leave first but waited until the carriage had left with Armaund and Catherine. Alex whispered that she was to start packing. "Peter will be back Sunday afternoon with Catherine, and I'll return by Wednesday. "We'll have dinner, hear all about Robert's family, and Thursday, one week from today, woman, we'll head home." Nichole gazed up into his warm eyes. Home. The word held a special thrill for her.

After the confusion of seeing everyone off, Nichole announced that after lunch she was going for a nice, peaceful ride. Her statement roused little concern for, after her recovery, she frequently rode short distances with Alex. She decided that if she rode a little today, and more Friday, her longer absence on Saturday would not cause suspicion.

After lunch, she donned her riding suit and went to the stable. She was gone for about an hour and when she returned, Prissy was more than a little upset. "Where did you go? You shouldn't even be riding. I don't care if you rode with Alex and Catherine, you shouldn't be out there. Anything could happen. The horse could have problems, you could have problems. You should not ride alone."

Nichole felt like screaming. Prissy's attitude was going to complicate things. Now she couldn't very well ride off to see a doctor without the household getting up in arms. She tried to laugh Prissy's fears away. "I'll be all right," she said quietly. "I'll stay close and I won't do anything to hurt myself, or scare the horse, if that's what you're worried about. I do ride fairly well now."

Prissy clamped her mouth shut. She couldn't say more, not without admitting to Nichole something she didn't think she had any business admitting. The more she thought about Nichole riding around the plantation the more concerned she became. Finally, her expression grim, Prissy decided she couldn't keep quiet. "If you hurt yourself, Alex will have my head."

There seemed to be only one solution to Nichole.

311

"Would you like to ride with me, tomorrow?" she asked a bit belligerently. Prissy never had seemed fond of horses.

"Yes, I think I will. At least if you fall off the horse, I'll be able to bring you back."

Nichole tried to keep her anger in check. She wanted an excuse to travel to the doctor without anyone knowing, but, she reasoned, if Prissy went tomorrow, then perhaps Nichole could convince her that she was not needed for the expedition on Saturday. And maybe, just maybe, Prissy would decide not to ride at all.

The next afternoon, after lunch, Nichole dressed in her riding skirt and jacket and went out to the stable. Nichole scowled; Prissy had not changed her mind. She was waiting. Two horses were saddled and the stableboy helped the women mount. Nichole decided to travel north on the Baltimore road for a short distance, then move east through the pasture before they returned to the house. The ground was fairly flat and Nichole thought that would give them a sufficient ride to convince Prissy that she could ride without a companion.

They started out together, and in less than ten minutes Nichole almost turned back to the stable. Prissy was not much of a horsewoman, and her pain was printed plainly on her face. Nichole felt so sorry for the woman, after another ten minutes down the road she did offer to turn around.

"No, let's go on. You do need the exercise," Prissy muttered.

They rode on for another five or six minutes and Nichole decided to turn east over the pasture and head back to the stable. Priscilla's sacrifice was just too much for Nichole.

As they started across the field, Nichole spotted a lone

horseman coming down the road toward them. He looked vaguely familiar, and Nichole pulled up on her horse's reins and pointed him out to the other woman.

Nichole wasn't sure what happened next, whether when Prissy turned around she jerked on the reins, or whether the horse was spooked by a small animal, but the mare Priscilla was riding reared up screaming. Prissy slid from the back of the horse onto the hard ground, hitting her head. Her horse took off for home and Nichole slid from her own horse and knelt at the side of the housekeeper.

Prissy lay deathly still, and Nichole fought a lump in her throat. "She was so worried about something happening to me," Nichole mumbled as she felt for a pulse. The other rider was on top of them by then and Nichole looked up. No wonder the rider look familiar. She stared into the leering face of Armaund duPres.

"She's hurt, we must get her back to the house," Nichole said to her surprised companion.

"Oh, I don't think so, but it doesn't matter."

"What do you mean, and what are you doing here? Did something happen to Peter or to Catherine?"

Armaund smiled down at her, enjoying the moment. Ah, sweet revenge, he thought. "No, as far as I know Catherine's just fine." He swung himself out of the saddle and stood beside her.

Nichole tried to ignore a feeling of impending doom. What was he doing at Manor House? What did he want? Suddenly, she remembered Alex's original fears. She stood gazing at him, her fear an almost tangible thing. Was he planning to hurt her husband?

"Madame Dampier," Armaund leered, knowing he had to set his plans into motion before someone came, "did you know that you're going to have a baby?" Her

313

stunned expression told him that the women at Manor House had been correct. She knew nothing. "It is growing here, in your stomach." Armaund lightly caressed the bulge that made her dresses too tight. She tried to push his hands from her, but he grabbed her wrists.

"Most babies live inside their mothers for nine months, but sometimes accidents occur, something happens and they come too soon. Then they are too small to live and they die. If you fight me, your baby will come too soon and it will die." He laughed diabolically. "And, of course, if you fight me, I have every intention of killing both Catherine and Alex."

"A baby? A baby! I'm going to have a baby." She stood up in disbelief. Was it possible? She could only stare at the Frenchman beside her. She and Alex had made a baby.

Her jerked her toward her horse. Nichole slapped at him. "Here, what are you doing? I must get Priscilla back to Manor House."

"Don't fight me!" Armaund growled at her.

"Why? Why should I fight you?" she asked quietly.

"Because you are not going back to Manor House. You are going with me. I'm afraid that you might not want to leave with me. You will, though, because if you don't Alex and Catherine will die and your babe will die as well!"

"I have to tell Alex about the babe. I'm not going anywhere with you." She glanced at the tall man, still very dazed.

"Oh, you are coming with me, and now. Prissy's horse will go directly to the stable and they will come searching for you." Armaund pulled her toward her horse.

"Leave me alone," Nichole snapped.

Armaund slapped her across the face, hard. "If you

314

don't come and now, I'll hit your stomach and the babe will come. It will die! Do you want that to happen?"

Her eyes filled with tears as she gazed up into his feverish eyes. He was mad! She could see it. Would he hurt her babe? She knew the answer to that as she looked into his eyes. He would do just what he said. Could she stall for time? They would come quickly when they saw Prissy's horse. But Peter was not there and Alex was days away, at the farm. There were only the stableboy and the field hands to answer her call for help.

"Alex will never allow this. He'll know that I did not go willingly. He'll come after you. You won't be able to escape. My husband will find us and take me back." She stood before him defiantly.

"I think not. When he sees my note, he'll understand that you are doing this on your own. I have told him that you want to go back to France. I know about your wedding, and what happened when you got here. Catherine told me all about how you wanted to go back to France, that you even ran away. Alex will think that you finally found a way to fulfill those wishes." He took a folded piece of paper from his coat pocket and placed it in Prissy's motionless hand. Then he yanked her toward her horse.

"Alex won't believe THAT!" She pointed to the note. "He'll kill you. You're singing your own death warrant." She stood her ground; soon someone would come. They had to come.

Armaund looked down into her cloudy dark green eyes, looking at him so furiously. He reached for her, but she evaded his grasp for a second. He lunged for her and grabbed her arm; then he hit her hard, across the face, dazing her for a moment. "We've wasted too much time. We're leaving now." He pushed her toward her horse. She struggled with him, trying to claw at his face, but he grabbed her hands and none too gently threw her on her horse. Nichole tried to dismount but he grabbed her hands and pulled a piece of strap from his pocket. Quickly, he tied her hands and twisted the leather around the saddle. Breathing heavily, he mumbled, "Get off of that horse and you'll be dragged to your death."

For an instant, Nichole wondered if death would not be preferable to the company of a madman. As soon as the thought crossed her mind, she realized that Alex would come, he would rescue her. She had to take care of herself and the baby until he found her. She glanced back at Prissy lying so quietly on the hard ground. If the stable hands came quickly, she would be all right. As Armaund grabbed at the horse's reins, Nichole thought she saw Prissy's eye flutter, but she could have imagined it, she told herself. She looked back once more as Armaund led her horse toward the road. Prissy was still lying on the pasture grass. She had not moved.

Chapter Twenty-five

Still slightly dazed, Nichole clung to her horse. Her captor led her down the road toward Baltimore for a short distance, then veered off into the woods. As her head cleared, Nichole realized that it would be at least four days before Alex could follow and Peter wouldn't return to Manor House until Sunday evening. If she was carrying a child, then at all costs, she had to save the child.

She refused to give in to panic. Alex would find them, no matter where Armaund was taking her. After all, he had tracked her once before. Once, she had doubted him; she would not doubt him again. He would come.

She turned her thoughts to the possibility of a babe. That would certainly explain the queer fluttering she had been feeling. Did Alex know? she wondered. Bits and pieces of conversation, long ignored and never understood, filled her thoughts. Some of the things she'd read in Frere Francis's books began to make sense to her. She guessed at others. Had it been Armaund who said nine months, or had she heard that from someone else? She began counting from the time she had gotten sick at the town house. The babe would arrive in January, then. A small smile touched her lips; she and Alex had made a baby. When he rescued her he would be so pleased.

They traveled for the rest of the afternoon and late into the evening hours. She refused to allow herself to complain and glared at Armaund when he looked her way. When she thought she could ride no longer, Armaund stopped at a dilapidated farm. Nichole wondered how many miles they had gone and how many miles they were from the road. Could Alex find them in this wilderness?

"We'll stay here the night," Armaund explained, "but if you cause me the slightest trouble, I'll end the babe's life tonight." Nichole only nodded her head; she was much too tired to cause him any trouble. And if he was right about the babe, then she could not let him do any damage to her or the child.

Just after dawn the next morning, they were back on their horses traveling north. "We're headed for Baltimore," Nichole sighed in relief. Alex would be able to find them easily. She tried to relax.

When they had been traveling for over an hour, Armaund suddenly turned both horses west. Nichole cried out in alarm, "Where are we going?"

Armaund sneered in her direction and refused to answer her. He grabbed her horse's reins and forced her to hang onto the mane as he trotted along a narrow path. After another hour, he stopped and handed her the reins. "Just keep moving," he growled.

They stopped for lunch and Nichole asked softly, "Where are we going? I have a right to know."

Armaund glared at her. "You have no rights at all."

Nichole said nothing more, but she glanced around, her mind busy. Surely there was something she could do.

318

During lunch Nichole kept herself busy trying to devise some means of escape. She could think of nothing. Not yet, she told herself. In time, she would think of something that would not place her in a position where Armaund could hurt her. Then she would find her way back to Alex.

After lunch Armaund headed north again, but this time, he traveled on a road. Nichole kept praying that they would meet someone, anyone, but not another person passed them. Instead of stopping for the evening meal Armaund insisted they keep riding. "I can't go much further, I'm too tired," Nichole whined, hoping she could slow him down. But he just ignored her and kept riding.

When she knew she could go no further she screamed, "If you kill the babe, what will you threaten me with, and you will kill the child if I don't rest!" Armaund looked at her as if he just remembered that she was here. He led the horses deep into a forest beside the road and then pulled her down from her horse. Dragging her to a small bush, he tied one of her hands to the shrub and went back to hobble the horses. And she sat and watched him work, she scowled herself. Could she have gotten away from him before they stopped? He had been so surprised when she yelled. Had she missed her only chance?

Armaund started a small fire and opened a package wrapped in oilcloth that he had pulled from his pack. He glanced over at her. "Your trail will end here."

Nichole was suddenly terrified. Did he mean to kill her now? Surely, he was not going to kill her. He could have succeeded at any time during the past twelve hours, but he had never even come close to her. She tried to pull away from him but her bonds held securely.

Armaund watched her through dark, angry eyes. "Alex will not be able to trace you past that inn. I have our course all charted. You'll have to sleep on the ground, but Peter mentioned that you slept on the ground when you ran away and it was much colder then." He was laughing at her now. "Alex won't even know you're missing for days yet. By the time he leaves Baltimore, we will be safely hidden by some friends of mine."

Nichole took a deep breath; she had been right. He was not going to kill her. But Baltimore! Surely he didn't think she was stupid enough to think that they were headed for Baltimore. They were traveling west, not north. Nichole glared at him. "Alex won't go to Baltimore, simply because you want him to. He's a very good tracker, he'll find us."

"Oh, not true, my beauty. I have already seen to it that he will go directly to Baltimore. He'll believe that you are in Baltimore."

Nichole hinted, threatened, and pleaded, but Armaund would say no more. She thought about what Armaund had said. Alex was not to know where they had gone. Armaund must have seen to clues that would lead Alex to Baltimore. Well, not if she had anything to do with it. My trail will not end here, she told herself. When she was sure that Armaund had fallen asleep, she moved around the shrub. Eventually, she found what she was looking for, a small sharp stone. For an hour she worked until she had scratched her initials in the base of the tree next to her. She decided that she would leave Alex signs all along their route. Then she fell asleep, praying that Alex would not be led astray by whatever Armaund had arranged.

The next three days were like a nightmare, and Nichole wondered if it was worth the effort. Only the thought of the babe kept her going. "Alex will come, and he'll be so happy about the child," Nichole kept muttering as they traveled. Each night when they stopped, she found something that she could scratch her initials into, and she fell asleep praying that Alex would find them soon.

As she left her marks, she was driven almost to the point of panic. What if Armaund finds the marks, she asked herself. Was she endangering the life of her child? But Alex needed those marks to find her, she argued, and in spite of the fear she felt, she continued marking their course.

On the fourth day Armaund stopped once more, at a farmhouse. He secured them a place to sleep for the night; then he threatened her with the child's death, and to stress his point he added that he would see both Alex and Catherine dead. "I have told the lady of the house that you are my wife. Because of the horror you saw in France, you have not been able to speak. Defy me and you know the consequences," he told her quietly before he led her up to the cabin.

Nichole wanted to scream, but she held her tongue, telling herself that she was protecting her child. Nichole snarled at Armaund as he played the role of solicitous husband throughout the meal and for another hour before it was time to retire. At times she was afraid that she would be violently sick. Twice, she had to restrain herself from jerking away from him when he touched her. Only the glare in his eyes kept her from moving.

"Your sweet little wife will have to share a bed with my daughter," their hostess told Armaund.

He looked daggers at Nichole and started to protest, "She has such restless nights, since the revolution, I can't let you subject your daughter to her restlessness."

His hostess cut him off. "Oh, it will be fine. She's carrying a babe, isn't she? She must sleep in a bed. You can't expect her to sleep on the floor. No, my daughter is a heavy sleeper and she won't mind, will you, Martha?"

Martha dutifully shook her head and the argument was closed.

When Armaund tucked her in a short time later, he whispered in her ear, "Don't you try anything! I'll be watching." Nichole grimaced. It must look to this family as though he were displaying husbandly affection, and she wanted to vomit. She turned her back to him, her small piece of stone firmly grasped in her hand.

Long after everyone had retired, Nichole lay in bed, tense and waiting. When she was certain that the household was asleep, she began to scratch her message into the side of the wooden bed frame. Perhaps after they left it would be discovered.

Once again, after a big breakfast, they were back on the road. Nichole tried to indicate her thanks just before they left, but Armaund rushed her out of the house. And, of course, she didn't dare say anything.

On the next two nights Nichole found that she could leave no messages for Alex. Oh, Armaund found cabins for them to stay in overnight, but the women in those places did not offer Nichole a bed and she was forced to sleep beside Armaund on the floor. There was no way she could scratch out her message.

On the tenth day of their journey, Armaund told Nichole, "We are coming to the end of our travels. Tomorrow we will arrive in Philadelphia. We'll stay there until I can arrange for a ship to take us to England."

Nichole's heart sank. England? There were always ships traveling from Philadelphia to England, especially in the summer. In a matter of days she could be on a ship bound for the other side of the world. Her whole body sagged. She had watched so hard for some kind of sign that they were being followed, but there had been nothing. She watched the stars and prayed that Alex would be able to follow the zigzag course Armaund had taken. Would he follow her all the way to England?

Armaund chuckled at Nichole's grim expression. Almost as if he could read her thoughts he said quietly, "Alex is not following us. He wouldn't dare. I told him plainly that I was returning you to France and if he made any attempt to hinder our travel that I wouldn't hesitate to destroy you or the child."

"He'll follow," Nichole said with as much firmness as she could manage. "You just won't know it. One of these days, you'll turn around and he'll be there. He'll find us and rescue me. Wait and see," she announced with more confidence than she felt.

Priscilla lay dazed on the hard ground. She could hear voices above her, arguing. She tried to open her eyes and tell the people that she was all right. For several more seconds she tried to remember what happened to her that she should be lying on the ground. Slowly, the memory of the ride and Nichole pointing out the rider came back to her.

Once more she tried to open her eyes. The bright sunlight forced her to close her eyes even before she had them partially open. The man's voice grated against her nerves. What on earth was Armaund duPres doing there with Nichole? She was fighting with him about leaving. Leaving? Why would she leave with Armaund when Alex was going to take her to the farm?

The arguing stopped and then the ground started to move. After the ground stopped vibrating, Prissy tried to move. As she opened her eyes, the sunlight hurt. Never would she have thought that sunlight could hurt, but this brightness gave her a blinding headache. Or was the headache there before she opened her eyes? Everything was so confusing.

Help will come, she told herself as she tried to sit up. Her wrist was throbbing, and she wondered if it was broken. She tried to move her legs and sighed in relief when both limbs moved at will. Next she lifted one arm, and then the other arm with the aching wrist. Except for the pain, both arms seemed to work without a problem. Thank goodness, she sighed, nothing was broken.

Can I move my head? she wondered, and discovered immediately that even the slightest movement made her headache much worse. I must get up, she told herself as she raised herself onto her elbow. Suddenly, she was so dizzy, she dropped back to the ground. I can't lose consciousness, not now, she scowled. Lifting her good hand to her face, she shaded her eyes and tried to open them again. Just as she pulled herself into an upright position, the ground started to shake again. I must be in terrible shape, she admitted.

Someone was calling her name, and she turned carefully toward the sound. "Oh, thank God," she muttered. The stableboy and the new indentured servant were coming toward her.

"Mrs. Bentley, what happened? Where is Mrs. Dampier? Is she hurt?" The stableboy rushed over to help her to her feet.

"We must get help. Mrs. Dampier has been kidnapped," she explained as she struggled to stand erect. "Hurry, we must get help!"

Both men helped her toward the horse they had ridden from the stable. "Go, go! Get more help. Go tell Mrs. Barber, she must send for the neighbors. Run!" she pushed the stableboy toward the plantation. Before she got to the horse, the fellow was running toward the farm.

She grabbed for the reins of the horse and realized that she had a folded piece of paper in her hand. Now where did that come from? she questioned herself. She stopped for a fraction of a second. She knew she had had no paper in her pocket or on her person when they started out on the ill-fated ride. But there was no time now, she thought as she stuck the paper into her apron pocket. Later, much later, she would figure that out; now she had to get back to the house.

"Peter," she cried aloud. She grabbed at her head. Why was it hurting her so badly? And Peter? Then she remembered. Her husband was off in Baltimore with Miss Catherine. She had to get word to him, somehow, she had to let him know. He would know what to do. She crawled up onto the horse and glared down at the confused man at her side. "What are you waiting for? Get up here!"

"I'll walk." He lowered his eyes.

"Man, there's no time for that now. Get up here, behind me. And hang on."

He scrambled up behind Prissy, and as he gingerly put his arms around her full waist, she spurred the horse to a gallop.

Prissy was positive her head would fall off as the horse bumped and jostled her toward the stable. She gritted her teeth; there was no time for that now. Nichole needed help. And she was the only one who knew who had taken Alex's wife.

She yanked the horse to a stop directly in front of the big barn, and started yelling for the men before she had slid from the horse's back. The servant behind Prissy was a little green, she thought, but that didn't stop her from issuing orders like one of the king's own officers.

As the servants and field hands gathered, Prissy began ordering them in one direction or another, confident that they would follow her instructions. Two men she sent after neighbors to ask their help, one of the younger men was sent off to Baltimore for Catherine, Peter and Robert and two of the oldest indentured servants were sent to the stable. Prissy demanded, "Saddle one horse, take two more and ride for Frederick. Ride all night. Whatever you do don't stop. And change your mounts every couple of hours. If you kill the horses, it won't matter. Get Mister Alex. Just get Mister Alex and bring him back. His cousin, Armaund duPres, had kidnapped his wife."

Mrs. Barber watched the confusion and listened to the orders, her own heart sinking in her chest. "Do you think they'll come back?" she asked quietly as she pointed to the two men that were leading the horses from the stable.

Prissy yelled after the two, "You've only got a year or two to go. If I know Mr. Alex, he'll probably give you your headland and your bond, early, if you get to him and back here. Travel like the wind. Just get him back here and I'll talk to him." She rubbed her throbbing head and nodded to the cook. "They'll come back."

In less than an hour, burly, gray-haired Jake Morrison from the farm closest to Manor House arrived, and Prissy told him what she knew and what she suspected. "Will you organize a search until we get our menfolk back?"

326

Jake, tall and quiet, simply took over, directing arriving neighbors out in all directions. Prissy sighed and made her way to the house. At least she had been with Nichole and had seen who had taken her. That might be a help to Alex. And they might even get the girl home in an hour or two, even before Alex knew anything had happened to her. "I never did like that man," she said to the door as she made her way into the kitchen.

She made her way to the table. Now she needed to tell Mrs. Barber what all had happened on that fateful ride. Holding her hands to her throbbing head, she sank into a kitchen chair.

The cook silenced her. "Let me see to you first, and then you can tell me." Mrs. Barber looked her over and fixed a cup of herbal tea and an ice pack. Then she sat down to hear what had happened in the fields north of the stable.

"What will Alex say? The girl was bound to ride today. I tried to stop her, but she insisted. At least I was with her."

Mrs. Barber patted her hand in sympathy. "There was nothing you could have done. Alex won't blame you. Don't you fret, now. It wasn't your fault."

Daylight faded and more neighbors arrived to help with the search. All through the dark night, Manor House reflected in the glowing trails of lighted torches as searchers came and went. Words was always the same: "No sign of 'em yet."

By noon of the next day, Prissy admitted that Armaund had somehow managed to steal the young French girl away. What would Alex say? The trail would be cold by the time he arrived; where could he possibly look that the neighbors had not already searched? Prissy's head still hurt, but the ache in her heart was much more grave. Alex had just discovered the love of his life. Would he lose her so easily?

Before dinner, Robert, Peter and Catherine arrived. Prissy tried to tell them what had happened but before she finished her version, Robert and Peter were racing for the stable. Jake Morrison was still in the stable and he stopped both men. "Good to see you back here. Come on to the house and I'll tell you what I've done."

Peter stared at the man, but Robert was not speechless. "What the he . . . Who are you?"

"I've been directing the search until Peter got here," Morrison said, bristling.

Peter stepped in. "Robert, this is Jake Morrison. He owns the plantation southeast of here. He's a friend of Alex's."

Robert acknowledged the older man and said quietly, "Let's go to the house, the study. We can plan there."

All three men were deeply engrossed in conversation when Prissy came to the study door with a coffeepot and some cakes. Her red eyes left no doubt that she had spent many hours crying about the situation. When she saw Peter and Robert huddled over the desk with Jake Morrison, the tears started to stream again. When she reached into her apron pocket for her handkerchief, she pulled out a piece of paper. She looked at it in surprise. Remembering where it had come from she stepped forward. "Wait, this might be something!"

Peter took the folded paper from his wife and looked at her, his confusion clear. "Where did this come from?"

Prissy explained, and Peter handed the note to Robert. Robert broke the seal, gazed at the lettering and then read the note aloud. "Dear Cousin, Several years ago, I chanced to meet a Frenchman named Menace who knows all about you and your family. I paid him a great deal for the information he supplied. Recently, he told me how you were being forced to marry against your will. Such a wedding is not legal as you know. I'm eliminating your problem. Nichole is coming with me. I will wed her and return her to France. She does carry royal blood. A wife for a brother, not a bad exchange. Come after her and she will surely die!"

Robert lifted his head and frowned. "He must be mad. If he tries to go back to France, both he and Nichole will suffer." Robert took a cup of coffee and sat down. Where had he heard the name Menace before? He looked up at the man. "Jake, if your friends have found no trace here, perhaps they should move toward Baltimore. If he is going to take her back to France, he will need passage on a ship."

Peter added quietly, "We can find out about ships that have already sailed, before Alex gets here."

Robert stared grimly ahead. "I'll get some of my own men down to start the investigation." Standing up, he walked over to the big oak desk, pulled some paper from the center drawer and took the quill pen in hand. "Jake, ask the men who can stay awhile longer to question the innkeepers along the route to Baltimore." Jake nodded his head. Robert bent his head over the paper, and the others filed out of the room.

Robert was busy scratching on the paper when Catherine walked into the room. Her eyes were bright with her own tears. She moved over to the desk. "Robert, what about the baby? Nichole doesn't know, Armaund can't know. If he pushed her around or hurts her, she might lose it." The tears that were threatening to spill now streamed down Catherine's face. Robert laid the pen aside and gathered his love in his arms. "I know, sweetheart." He stroked the hair back from her face, tenderly. "We can only pray that we'll find her soon. Perhaps Armaund will not be too rough on her." The note Robert had started wasn't finished for a long while as he tried to comfort Catherine.

Chapter Twenty-six

A somber pall hung over the house as neighbors and friends arrived with their scant information. First, they reported to Jake, then to Robert or Peter. Weary men trudged back and forth, for fresh horses, something to drink and food. Robert finished his note to his office, requesting investigators and detailing where he wanted them to start. Notes were dispatched to local homes, Baltimore and the officials. Mrs. Barber and Prissy tried to keep busy, preparing food packs for the searchers and supplying hot coffee and sandwiches for the men who came to the house. By late night, the searching men returned with enough information to confirm Robert's suspicion that Baltimore was indeed the destination of the Frenchman and his captive.

Peter read Robert's mind. "But why can't we find 'em? We know where they're going and what he plans to do, but we can't find 'em. We should be able to walk right up and grab Nichole. Are ya sure we're looking in the right place?"

Sunday morning, one of the neighbors brought eyewitness reports that placed Armaund and Nichole west of Manor House, not north. That information conflicted with the information gathered the day before. Robert gave in to his frustration. "Where in the hell are they going? West of Baltimore? Impossible! It doesn't make any sense!" he yelled at Peter.

Peter shook his head in confusion and mumbled, "Suppose someone was paid to provide the wrong information? Maybe Armaund wants us to run off in the wrong direction. Maybe the new information is right and they aren't heading for Baltimore after all."

Robert glared at Peter and the overseer slumped down in his chair, promising himself that no matter what, he would keep his mouth shut. He could do without Robert's anger.

Afternoon came, and still more conflicting information came back. Robert paced the study. What was he going to tell Alex? He had been so sure that Armaund was headed to Baltimore to secure passage to France, as that damn note said. Alex would want his opinion. What was he to tell him? Somewhere, deep in his gut, he was positive that Baltimore was the destination, but what if he was wrong? How much precious time would they lose?

With little appetite, Peter, Robert, Jake Morrison, and Catherine sat down for the evening meal. The men speculated about Alex's arrival. "He'll come charging back, but he can't possibly arrive until late tomorrow," Peter stated quietly.

"If the bondsmen got there at all," Robert added quietly. Peter and Jake nodded their heads in agreement. Before the evening meal was finished, they all agreed that the entire household had to get a decent night's sleep to make up for the many sleepless hours they had all endured. They had to be ready when Alex arrived. Shortly after sunset, candles were extinguished and the household drifted into troubled sleep.

Peter was the first to hear the screams. He ran from his room at the back of the house, followed by Prissy, who was trying to don a robe to cover her worn chemise. Robert met him at the front door, his face white. "It's only twelve o'clock," Robert whispered. "How did he get here so fast?"

Peter didn't bother to answer and threw open the door for his young boss. Alex had a two days' growth of dark hair on his face and his eyes were wild. The black rings under his eyes spoked plainly that Alex Dampier had had no sleep for several days. His soft buckskin shirt and pants were covered with dust and mud, and he swore softly as he staggered through the door. "I killed one of the horses. Is she here? Did you get her back?"

Neither Robert nor Peter wanted to answer. Catherine's soft voice from the stairs brought Alex up straight. "No, we haven't gotten her back yet."

Almost immediately the house became a beehive of activity. That afternoon, Jake Morrison had moved into one of the guest rooms, and now he was summoned. Prissy woke the cook and a quick snack and plenty of black coffee were readied.

Alex paced the study floor as Prissy tried to explain one more time what had happened to her and what she had heard as she lay on the ground. Peter and Jake explained about the search, and Robert explained about the note.

Catherine stood by quietly, waiting. When the conversation died down, she stepped forward. "Alex, there is something else you should know."

All three friends tried to silence her; Robert muttered, "Not now, Catherine."

Peter yelled at her, "No, Catherine."

And Prissy grabbed at her. "No!"

Catherine raised her chin; Alex had a right to know. "Alex"—she glared at the other three—"they don't want me to tell you, but Nichole is with child."

Instantly the room was silent. Alex stared at his sister in the candlelight. "What did you say?"

"Nichole is going to have a babe!"

Alex frowned. "She would have told me."

"She doesn't know," Catherine said softly.

At that moment, Robert, Peter and Prissy started talking at once. Alex sank down in the closest chair and sighed. No, he thought, she would not have known.

Robert handed Alex a large whiskey and looked over at Catherine. "I don't agree with your sister. I'm sure Nichole would know if she was with child. She would have told you if she was."

Alex gloomily looked at his hands and the glass of whiskey. "She doesn't know. But I should have! The signs were all there." He turned pale. "If Armaund hurts her . . ." He didn't finish.

"Look," Robert urged. "There is nothing you can do tonight. We have already searched the neighborhood. We have people checking in Baltimore and on the road to Baltimore. Neighbors are out gathering information, and I've offered a reward. You need some rest. We can all start in the morning."

Alex shook his head stubbornly. "We can't let a minute go by . . ."

"You are in no shape to continue, not tonight. Let's get some rest, and then tomorrow we'll go over everything and you can decide what you want to do next. Alex, we have people looking, even as we speak." He helped Alex to his feet and aimed him toward the door of the study.

Alex moved in a daze. Without her, his life had no meaning. He had to tell Robert that without her, he couldn't go on. His friend pushed him toward the stairs. "Are you sure that . . ."

"Yes, I'm sure!" Robert interrupted. "Right now, you

need sleep. Tomorrow will be soon enough." Before another hour passed the household was once again quiet.

Alex made it to his bed and exhaustion claimed him. Before dawn, Alex stirred from his restless sleep. Instantly, he was awake, and he knew what he had to do. Dressing quickly he headed downstairs for coffee, before the rest of the household was up. Slowly, the others wandered into the kitchen and found Alex.

Peter and Robert took Alex into the study and went over the information they had gathered. "Something is not right here," Alex commented after Robert told him about the sighting of Nichole west of Baltimore. "I think we are being fed information about Nichole that's not true." He questioned Prissy once more and reread the note a dozen times. His heart felt as if it had been crushed. Where was his wife? Was she all right, and why, dear God, had Armaund taken her?

Once more Alex went over the information and then declared, "I think he took her west. I don't think he is taking her to Baltimore at all.

Robert was stunned. "Why west? Where could they be going? The port is in Baltimore!"

"I can't explain but I think he wants us to think about Baltimore. Oh, you keep some of your men in Baltimore, but we must send men further west and north, and perhaps southwest as well." Alex paced the study. He had already authorized an increase in the reward; there was nothing more he could do from Manor House. They would start in Baltimore. His insides where churning. He could not sit quietly in the house and wait for people to bring him the information. He had to take up the search himself. he left Manor House in Peter's care, and he and Robert headed for Baltimore to see what the men had found. Alex decided that if he found nothing in Baltimore, he himself would move north. With that in mind, he told Catherine and Peter that he would travel on, north to New York, if need be.

When they got to Baltimore Alex personally questioned several of the ship captains. Only three ships, he found, had left the port in the last three weeks, and none of them were sailing for France. No more ships were scheduled to leave for Europe for several months. Most of their trade would be up and down the coast until the cotton crop was in, and that was weeks away.

Alex spent three days in Baltimore, but still there was no word. The men searching the countryside to the west could find no trace of his wife, no word at all. Nichole seemed to have disappeared from the face of the earth. He traveled north, stopping in Philadelphia, then moving on to New York, but none of the ship's captains he talked to had received a request to take passengers to France. There was too much trouble in France. He traveled back to Baltimore. There was no news there either. Heartsick, he returned to Manor House. His beloved wife, his heart's mate, had been gone for two weeks.

Catherine met him at the door. "Alex," Catherine said, "something will turn up. It must! Nichole will get word to you, or she will send someone with a message. We just have to wait."

Robert spent the weekend, but there was little joy at Manor House. "Robert," Catherine told her future husband, "you won't mind if we skip the festivities until we find Nichole, will you? I don't even want to set a date for the wedding until we find out where she is."

Robert drew her into his arms. "I understand. Catherine, we'll hear. Someone will see something, or one of the captains Alex talked to will be approached by Armaund. It's just a matter of time."

How much time, Catherine wondered, and at what

cost?

Something Armaund said registered. Philadelphia! That was the end of their journey? Nichole was bone weary, but she glared at Armaund and at the malicious smile he gave her. "Why Philadelphia?" she snapped.

Armaund leaned forward in his saddle. "Let me explain some things to you. First, I know people in Philadelphia. Alex won't think to look here. And I have told the people who are hiding us that you are my wife. In truth, you will become my wife!"

Nichole shrieked, "Never! I will never marry you! I'm already the wife of Alexander Dampier. I cannot marry you."

"Oh, but you will!" he stated quietly. "If you want to raise that brat," he pointed toward her stomach, "you will marry me and you'll do exactly what I say, from this day on."

Nichole swallowed her terror. Now what would he threaten to do to her babe? she wondered. "Your first marriage was by proxy," Armaund pointed out. "All you have to do is say that you didn't understand what proxy meant. Of course, if you don't, or won't, then after the baby is born, I will take that child from you and give it away. If you want to raise the child, then you had better decide to follow my orders, every one of them. My orders for today are simple. You will follow me and keep your mouth shut. Do not say a word!" He turned on her. "Is that clear?"

She swallowed the lump in her throat and nodded her head. Her mind was in turmoil. Surely he wouldn't take her babe from her and give it away? She swiped at the tears that had gathered in her eyes. Armaund was mad, totally insane, and there was no reasoning with him. If he said he would give the babe away, then that was what he planned to do. Even in a fit of temper, he might carry out his threat. She must humor him and do exactly as he said. Alex would find her, or she would be able to get away from the crazy Frenchman, soon.

She felt the fight leaving her. Somehow, Armaund had kept them hidden for ten days. Was it possible that Alex had indeed gone on to Baltimore as Armaund said he would? Was he still looking for her? What if he didn't find her in time? Armaund said he was going to arrange passage on a ship for England. Would Alex sail halfway around the world to find her? She refused to search for answers, and her spirits fell. Her despair was so great that she couldn't even mutter the heartfelt prayers that had sustained her on their journey.

Armaund grabbed her arm, forcing her to look over at him. "I want your promise that there will be no trouble in Philadelphia. If not . . ." His words trailed off into nothingness.

Nichole stared at him through her moist eyes. "No trouble" was all that she could manage.

Summer was at its zenith and July was nearly finished as Nichole traveled through the streets of Philadelphia. They stopped at a trim white house, and Armaund led her to the door. "Remember what I said," he snarled.

When Nichole met the friends who were going to hide Armaund and her, she tried to be pleasant. Somehow, she wasn't surprised when the husband and wife turned out to be Armaund's relatives. Afraid of him now, she did exactly as he said, and smiled halfheartedly at the Bordeleaus.

Armaund was sickeningly sweet to her as he introduced her and he insisted that he see her up the stairs to her room. He personally ordered a bath and something for her to eat. Back in the parlor, he drew his cousin aside. Referring to the note he had sent weeks ago, he said, "We spent several weeks with the Dampiers. I really thought that Nichole would enjoy being with cousins more her own age. The trouble in France had alarmed her so." He paused. "But we couldn't stay. Nichole and I were treated terribly at Manor House. Alex Dampier behaved shamefully in my wife's presence. She is with child, as you can see, and he was much too forward. He appeared, at least to me, to be a little mad. She was so uncomfortable in his presence that I had to bring her here. You are sure you don't mind?"

Armaund waited for his cousin's sympathetic gesture. "I do have another favor to ask. If he or anyone representing him should contact you, I beg of you, please don't tell them we are here. I would have to challenge him, for Nichole's sake, but in her condition she would be so upset. I'm sure you can understand . . ." Armaund let his voice trail off as he watched Claude Bordeleau digest his information.

The older man frowned; he knew the Dampiers well. Henry Dampier had been an unscrupulous businessman, but word was that his son was more honorable in business. But Alex did have a reputation as a rake. To almost accost the wife of a relative albeit even one as beautiful as Nichole, was shameful behavior indeed, he thought. Perhaps Alex Dampier had lost his senses. No, Claude decided, he would not allow anyone from his household to say a word about their visitors. "No one will hear a word from my lips about you or your wife."

Armaund hid his smile. His cousin had bought his story completely. At least, Alex would not hear about Nichole from the Bordeleaus. "I want to take Nichole back to England before the babe arrives. She should be with my mother and sisters now. Would it be possible for you to help me secure passage on a ship bound for England as soon as possible?"

Claude put his arm around Armaund's shoulder. "We'll see to it first thing in the morning."

By noon the next day, Armaund had seen two ships and both ships were sturdy and well cared for, but the large vessel had more spacious cabins. It would take three weeks longer to reach England on the larger vessel, but Armaund was not traveling again on a ship that was small and cramped, he told himself. He chuckled; his cousin wouldn't appreciate his reasons, so the young Frenchman told his cousin what he thought he wanted to hear: "Nichole will enjoy the larger ship, I'm sure. The larger cabin will be better for her, and she'll have more room to walk around the deck. We have time before the babe is born. We'll arrange passage on the slower vessel."

Armaund spent a few minutes with the captain, then rejoined his cousin. "We sail in two and a half weeks. Now I'm afraid that I must ask you for one thing more. We left Manor House in such a hurry that we didn't bring any of Nichole's clothing with us. I refuse to contact Alex Dampier and request her clothing. I will simply purchase something new for her. I will need to take her to a dressmaker. If you could offer a letter of introduction I will see to my wife's wardrobe."

Armaund chuckled to himself; it would be a simple matter, with the letter of introduction, to have the dressmaker's bill sent after he and Nichole had sailed. Then he wouldn't have to spend any of the coins he had left on the girl. Things were working out very well, very well indeed.

Claude not only provided the name of a dressmaker but also insisted that Armaund accept the wardrobe for Nichole as a wedding gift. Armaund graciously accepted for them, for Nichole said next to nothing. Claude never knew that Armaund had said nothing to her.

Armaund left her alone most of the time, and for that she was grateful. She seldom left her room, preferring, she told Evelyn Bordeleau, to rest. Armaund told his relatives that Nichole had not really been herself since she had witnessed the destruction of the chateau. Evelyn, her eyes full of motherly sympathy, insisted that Nichole rest and read. Without saying a word to Nichole and thinking that she was providing the girl the best of care, she kept all of the servants away as well.

Nichole was petrified of Armaund. Both Evelyn and Claude Bordeleau seemed to be genuinely fond of Armaund, and Nichole was much too afraid to approach them. They'll not believe me, she sobbed to herself. There were no servants to ask for help, either, and Nichole wondered if Armaund had arranged that as well. Armaund did take her for walks each afternoon, and he took her to the dressmaker, but he said little and she refused to talk to him.

Every day she prayed hard that Alex would find her, but as each day drew to a close, and Alex hadn't arrived, she cried herself to sleep. Was he even looking for her? she wondered. Her mind screamed, Yes! Yes! And she tried to quiet the feeling of betrayal that tried to surface. She would believe in him. She could not doubt him, not now. He must find her, he wouldn't desert her.

In just ten days, the few things Armaund had ordered for Nichole were finished, and Armaund announced that they must pack. When everything was ready for the voyage, she stood with Armaund to thank his relatives for taking them in and seeing to her wardrobe. She kept telling herself that at any minute Alex would come rushing through the door and sweep her into his arms and her nightmare would end. But he didn't come . . .

Claude accompanied Armaund and Nichole to the

ship, and after Armaund saw to her trunk and his own possessions, he joined his cousin on the dock. "I can't thank you enough for all you've done. If Alex should approach you, I would appreciate your silence still. He has connections and I really would hate to have him arrive in England." Armaund looked at his cousin's suspicious glance. He wondered if he had said too much. He added, "For Nichole's sake. She has been through enough."

Claude left Armaund dePres on the dock. He shook his head. Something Armaund said caused him some doubts, but he couldn't put his finger on it. The man was probably just concerned for his wife as he said, but Claude couldn't brush aside the tragic look in Nichole's eyes as Armaund led her down the steps to her cabin.

When she was finally settled in her cabin, Armaund left her and went up on deck. He rubbed his hands together and chuckled aloud, pleased with himself. In less than twenty-four hours, they would leave the port of Philadelphia and head for England. In spite of everything, he had gotten even with his cousin. He had the revenge that he wanted.

Chapter Twenty-seven

Nichole stayed in her cabin the morning the ship sailed and Armaund smiled in amusement. She was not taking this separation from her husband very well. Thank God, there was available space and the captain had been very willing to give Armaund a second cabin for himself when he explained that he was afraid that he might hurt Nichole in his sleep. He could just imagine playing nursemaid to a weeping female. Oh, he would see to her meals, but at least he would have his own quarters and he was assured of many a good night's sleep.

He grinned at nothing. There was no question. Nichole was his and Alex would never find her.

His thoughts remained with Nichole. Now that he had her, what was he going to do with her? He ran his fingers through his hair as he considered his choices. He could do what he had told her he would do and marry the girl. But that would mean taking Alex's leavings. No, it would not do for him to marry that wench. She had been Alex's wife. However, she was beautiful, exquisite, really, and he wanted her. After the

343

child arrived, he would sent the child away and take Nichole to London. He could set her up as his mistress. He smiled in anticipation. Yes, that was what he would do.

He thought about his mother and father. Somehow, he knew they would never understand his need for revenge. And even before they found out about Nichole, he knew they would be very angry with him. After all, they had entrusted the chateau to him. But it was not really his fault that the place had been destroyed. That was the fault of the servants and the field hands. Their trusted workers had destroyed the chateau. He frowned; it would not do for his mother or his father to find out about Nichole. They would be even more angry with him. No, he must keep Nichole from his father and mother.

The first several days of their trip were pleasant, and Armaund took Nichole her meals from the ample supplies the captain provided. The weather was warm and his own cabin was as spacious as Nichole's. Everything was going well, very well, Armaund chuckled as he rubbed his hands together.

At first, Nichole couldn't bear to leave her cabin, as the waves gently rocked the ship. She couldn't cry any more, she had cried so hard these last two days. Alex had not come! She knew now, and she finally admitted that he was lost to her, perhaps forever. Somehow, her world was collapsing and she was falling to the bottom of a deep, black hole. Armaund had succeeded in tearing her away from her husband. And he said she had to marry him to save her child. The few tiny pieces of her heart that remained intact shattered with that thought. In her heart, she knew she could never marry again, not even for the babe.

Desperate, she even wondered briefly if Alex had

planned for Armaund to abduct her. Could he have wanted to send her away but been afraid to tell her himself? Armaund had figured out that she was going to have a child. Perhaps when he guessed that she was having his child, he decided he didn't want her and he paid Armaund to take her away. No, she screamed her denial. She refused to question her husband's motives. He did love her, he did! And he was looking for her, probably frantic by now! She had to believe that, to even continue to breathe.

By the third day, Nichole came to terms with her grief. She squared her shoulders and gave herself a scolding much more severe than any she had ever received from the nuns. Her despair was not helping her or her child. If she didn't accept what life had in store for her, she would make herself sick and she would lose her child. And it was her child. No matter what, the child had to survive, and she would make a life for herself and the babe. Somehow, she would get back to Maryland, and if she couldn't find Alex, she would get a job as a tutor, or governess, and support her little one.

Once she finished her lecture, she dressed in one of the two new dresses Armaund had purchased for her and brushed her hair. That afternoon, she ventured up on deck and took a brisk walk. Immediately, she felt better. The sun and breeze did much to improve her spirits, and she promised herself that come what may, she would escape from Armaund and make her own life. She had skills, she was educated and she remembered the bustle that had attracted her to Baltimore the first day she saw the city. Not only could she survive, but she knew that she could be happy. But without Alex . . . She scolded herself again. Her concerns now had to be her own life and the life of her child. She would not look back.

On the day that Nichole sailed, Alex was interrupted during a meeting with Peter by a tall lanky boy of about fifteen. "Mr. Dampier, Mr. Alex Dampier?"

Alex stared at the boy. He didn't think he had ever seen him before, and his heart skipped a beat. "Did Robert Patterson send you?"

"Nah." The youth shook his head. "But our neighbors in Pennsylvania says you should come. They got a message for ya and they wants ya to come as soon as ya can."

"Where are your neighbors?" Alex asked, almost afraid to hope.

"Southern Pennsylvania, not too far from here. My dad drew a map." The boy held the paper up as he backed away from the tall man.

Alex grabbed the paper and whispered in a broken voice, "Oh, please, dear God. Let this be from Nichole." With new determination, he strode toward the barn yelling for Peter, the boy forgotten. Before the hour was out Alex was on his way, his joy almost strangling him. Nichole was in Pennsylvania, he knew it. He didn't stop to reason why she had taken so long to send him a message; it really didn't matter. They would be together in only a matter of days.

Alex arrived at the prosperous farm on the map and introduced himself to Jonas Schultz and his wife. Looking around for his wife, Alex asked quietly, "Is she here?"

Jonas frowned. "Ain't no one here. We asked ya to come 'cause of a message scratched on Marthie's bed."

Alex turned away to hide his tears. She wasn't there; had she even been there?

346

Something the man said interrupted Alex's grief. ". . . Frenchman. We didn't think anything about it until I . . ."

"What did you say?" Alex asked.

"They came to stay the night, the girl and the Frenchman. We didn't think anything about until I found the scratches on the bed. Now, we's been a-wondering, perhaps it wasn't as it seemed."

"How did it seem?" Alex held his breath.

"We thought they was married, he said they was. And she didn't say a word, couldn't talk he said because of the trouble in France. But Marthie here says she mumbled 'Alex, Alex,' in her sleep. She thought the girl said something about Alex's babe."

"Where are the scratchings?"

"Come, I'll show ya. We might never found it, ifin I hadn't said I'd fix Marthie a new mattress." He led the way into the house and pulled a cot away from the wall. "Here, here's the side. See the scratches."

Scratched in the side were the words "Help A. Dampier, Manor House, Maryland." Jonas turned to Alex. "We figured you would know what it means."

Alex nodded, his eyes filling with tears. "How was the young woman? Did she appear to be well, was the gentleman kind to her?"

Anna Schultz looked at her husband in surprise. "She seemed tired but not overly so. She looked well enough. Course, she didn't talk, but her husband was kind to her. He took her her meals, helped her to bed, seemed to care for her greatly."

"Now, Anna," Jonas interrupted, "don't you remember? Marthie reminded you that he argued about her sleeping with our girl. He wanted her to sleep on the floor with him, and he seemed belligerent about it, too." Jonas rubbed his salt-and-pepper beard. "But

Anna told him pregnant women shouldn't sleep on the floor. He did seem taken with her."

Against all hope Alex whispered, "He didn't say where they were going, did he?"

"No." Jonas rubbed his beard again. "He only said they were going to visit with some of his relatives. I think he said they lived in Pennsylvania, too."

Alex stared at him, lightning crashed through his brain. "He said relatives?"

"Yeh," Jonas nodded his head, "he even told me their name, something real French, like his."

"Bordeleau, was it Bordeleau?" Alex encouraged.

"Yah, that's it!" Jonas shouted. "That's it!"

Alex smiled slightly. "Then I know where they were going. I can't thank you enough."

Jonas nodded and frowned. "Glad to help. Be she your sister?"

Alex's face lost its trace of a smile. "She is my wife!" The gasp was audible. He added, "The Frenchman kidnapped her." He thanked the couple for sending for him and left as quickly as he could. Now he knew where to look.

He forced himself to stop in a small village that he passed through shortly after he left the farm. After talking to the owner of the general store, he was able to hire two of the man's sons. He sent the oldest to Baltimore to Robert, and the other boy to Manor House to Peter and Catherine, explaining what he had learned and where he was going. In his note to Robert, he pleaded that he drop everything and meet him in Philadelphia, naming an inn. Listing the supplies he wanted, he wrote in his note to Peter the name of the same inn in Philadelphia and insisted that Peter meet him there in four days.

Alex covered the sixty miles to Philadelphia in two

348

and a half days. Robert had arrived only an hour before, and he was waiting at the inn Alex had suggested. Alex took time only to change his clothes and wash his travel-stained hands and face. The two men went directly to the Bordeleaus' home.

Claude Bordeleau refused to see either man. Rather than cause a nasty scene, Robert talked Alex into returning to the inn; then he returned to the Frenchman's white house on his own. He insisted to the stern servant that Claude Bordelau could see him now or meet him in court. The threat worked and Robert was admitted to the study where Claude stood waiting for him. Robert glared at the older man and demanded to know where Nichole Dampier was.

"Dampier? But Armaund said she was *his* wife! Oh, my God! What have we done?" Claude breathed and suddenly remembered his suspicions at the dock.

A short time later Robert was back at the inn. "I've accepted a dinner invitation for us. We're expected at five."

Alex glared at him and shook his head. "You expect me to dine with them? The bastard that kidnapped my wife is related to them. No, I won't break bread with them!"

Robert glared back. "Alex, they didn't know Nichole was your wife. They believed Armaund. He told them Nichole was his wife and Nichole never told them different."

"Why didn't she say something?"

"I imagine Armaund had threatened her. Look, I've already found out that Armaund is taking Nichole to England, not France. If you come with me, you'll be able to find out how she is and exactly what Armaund's plans are. And you're going to need help. This is not Maryland. I don't know too many people in

Philadelphia. The Bordeleaus have a good reason to help you. Damn it, man, take advantage of it. Alex, they didn't know Nichole was your wife!"

In the end, Alex left a terse message for Peter and went with Robert, back to the Bordeleaus' for dinner. They were received warmly, and both Claude and Evelyn expressed their regrets through the long evening. Alex asked dozens of questions, and either Evelyn or Claude answered each one. He discovered that Armaund had taken Nichole for walks each day, that she had eaten and rested and that Armaund had taken her to a dressmaker for a wardrobe. She seemed well enough, Evelyn assured him. "They didn't share the same room," Claude whispered when Alex asked about the sleeping arrangements.

Alex breathed an enormous sigh of relief. At least Armaund had not forced himself on her and she was well. Armaund had the decency to treat her with some respect, it appeared. It was all Alex could hope for now.

Late that night, they returned to the inn, and Alex had a hard time swallowing his anger, for Peter had not arrived yet. "He'll be here tomorrow. You did mention that you asked for the man to gather clothing and supplies for you," Robert said quietly, trying to keep Alex calm. "We have to see about getting you on a fast ship bound for England. At least the ship Armaund selected is a slower vessel, so that you should be able to find something that will bring you to England before he arrives."

Alex tried to listen, but his mind was trying to digest all of the things that Evelyn and Claude had told him. At least Claude had assured him that Armaund was concerned about Nichole's health. His depraved cousin was taking care of his wife, but for how long? What if they traveled through a storm? What if . . . Alex refused to let the questions surface, and he strained to hear Robert's words.

Early the next morning, Robert and Alex were at the docks, talking to the captains of vessels that were unloading and loading, those that had been at anchor for days and those just arriving. The first ship scheduled to leave for England was a large Dutch cargo ship. Alex was appalled. The vessel was large, cumbersome and filthy. "It will take that ship three months to get to England, if it makes it," Alex muttered as Robert dragged him away from the captain.

By the end of the day, they found what they were looking for, a sleek three-masted vessel of new design from Boston. It was sailing in five days and the captain claimed that if the weather held, with no storms to blow them off course, they would make England in four or five weeks. Alex and Robert quickly calculated that Alex could make English shores with at least a whole week before the ship carrying Nichole and Armaund arrived.

When they returned to the inn, Peter was waiting and so was a note from the Bordeleaus. Peter began to prepare a trunk for Alex's departure, and Alex and Robert discussed the note that had arrived. Claude and Evelyn were insisting that Alex stay with them until his ship sailed.

"Not a chance," Alex said quietly. "Robert, don't those people realize I've lost my wife? Can't they understand that I'd rather be alone? I have a lot of things that I must take care of and I sure as hell don't feel like socializing," he ended on an angry note.

Robert urged him to accept. "They feel terrible about what has happened. It's the only way they feel they can make it up to you. Accept their invitation. You will

351

have much to do before you sail, so you won't even be there except to eat and sleep. Look! I have to return to Baltimore. Unfortunately, you are not my only client. You never know but what you'll find out something else that might be very important, something that might help you deal with Armaund when you reach England."

"Deal with him?" Alex snarled, "I'm going to kill him!"

Robert packed his bag and said nothing more. He breathed a sigh of relief himself when Alex sent Peter with a note accepting the unwanted invitation. Early the next morning, Robert left for Baltimore and Alex and Peter moved his belongings to the Bordeleau home. There was a large room ready for Alex, and he set about putting his affairs in order.

Robert and Alex had already decided that Alex would stay in England with Nichole until after the birth of the babe and her laying-in time. When the babe was about four months old, Alex, Nichole and the infant would return to Maryland. He wanted the house at the farm finished by then, and he sent Catherine and his own overseer detailed instructions on what was to be done.

By the afternoon of the third day, Alex had everything accomplished, everything he could think of, he thought grimly. He was packed and ready to leave the following morning. Peter would see him to the ship, and then return to Manor House with Catherine's instructions.

Alex was extremely grateful that the Bordeleaus were so considerate. There was no socializing, and they met only for dinner each afternoon. It was a typically quiet group that met for dinner that last afternoon. Once more, Claude tried to apologize, and Alex accepted

352

politely and withheld his comments. There was little he could say.

When the bell rang to announce guests, the four people at the table jumped. The sound reverberated through the quiet room. In minutes, one of the servants was at Claude's chair. "There's a gentleman here to see you, sir. He claims to have a message from Armaund duPres."

Chapter Twenty-eight

The ship sailed away from Philadelphia carrying Nichole farther and farther from her husband, and she grappled with a desperation that kept resurfacing. No matter how many times she reminded herself that the life of her child made any sacrifice necessary, she still battled a deluge of tears. She missed Alex terribly, and she couldn't understand why he hadn't rescued her from Armaund.

She was grateful that Armaund seemed content to stay away from her, and she kept away from him. She saw him three times a day when he brought her her meals, and once more on the afternoons when he escorted her around the deck. He said little to her, but she noticed that his mood seemed to grow lighter and lighter each day.

As his mood improved, Nichole began to hope herself. Eventually they would reach England, and she began to make plans of her own. As soon as they reached England, she would seek sanctuary with the church. After the babe was born, she would find a job. The nuns could help her there, too, she was sure of it. When the child was old enough, and she had money for passage, she would return to Baltimore and find her husband. She began to watch the kinds of foods she consumed and started to exercise mornings and afternoons. The voyage was almost pleasant, with sunny, breezy days, and Nichole appreciated each one.

By the morning of the tenth day, Nichole felt much better. The sky was bright and the blue ceiling heralded another near perfect day. During her morning stroll Nichole noticed the white dots of other sails on the horizon but gave it little thought. As she walked she watched to see if the other passengers had noticed the sails, but it seemed no one on the ship was concerned.

After an early lunch, the white dots were visible as sails now, but still no one on board showed more than a casual interest. The ship was closing slowly and she stood with several of the other passengers, watching the slow advance of the craft. Eventually, she tired of standing and glancing at the position of the sun; she decided that it would be hours before anyone could see the colors of the speck on the horizon. Excusing herself, she retired to her cabin for her afternoon nap.

Nichole jerked awake just after the first boom of the cannon and splintering of wood. Terrified, she tried to get out of her bed. Suddenly, the door was thrown open, and Armaund burst into the room. "We're being attacked," he yelled at her. "You're to stay here. Do not come up on deck, no matter what you hear. When it's over, I'll come get you."

"Attacked?" Nichole asked, her voice trembling in horror.

"Pirates!" Armaund snarled as he left her room, slamming the door.

For what seemed like an eternity, Nichole cringed on the bed listening to the furious battle being waged above her on the deck. With every clunk of steel, every scream of pain, she sank down further into the mattress. Her problems with Armaund were forgotten, the pain of losing her husband and the fear for her child were pushed into the dark recesses of her mind and she prayed that somehow she would escape with her life. She had fought to live in the forest, she had struggled against giving up with Armaund. No sea vultures were going to deny her the right to live. She straightened her shoulders and prepared to fight for her life.

Suddenly, just as quickly as it had started, it was over, and Nichole held her breath waiting. The silence around her grew and grew until each beat of her heart sounded like an explosion of doom. She wanted to fly from her room, now a prison, but Armaund's warning kept repeating in her head and she sat quietly on her bed.

The minutes dragged by slowly, and then she heard a muffled scream, then several more screams followed by a scraping sound across the deck. Once more, she prepared to fight. She glanced around the cabin to judge what would serve as her best weapon. Scooting off the bed, she grasped the pewter mugs from the table and sank down on the bed linens to wait.

All at once, her door was flung open and a bloody Armaund glared at her from between two of the vilest looking men Nichole had ever seen. As Nichole gasped in horror, Armaund was thrown, cursing and swearing, into the cabin. Without a word, both men followed Armaund into the room.

They were both short, shorter by several inches than Armaund, and they had thick, greasy black hair. One of the men had a golden sash around the waist of his dark breeches, and a dark red shirt hung from his shoulders, parting down the front to expose the coarse black hair that covered his chest. He had a large gold ring hanging from his left ear, and in his hand he held a blade like nothing Nichole had ever seen. It was almost a yard long and curved, with dark stains on the glinting steel. Nichole decided she didn't want to even think about what those dark stains might mean.

She glanced over at the second man, who was even dirtier than the first. This pirate wore no shirt at all, and his breeches were held in place with a length of dirty rope. He held a long pistol in his clenched fist. He took a step toward her. "Captain says you be married to this one?"

Nichole glared at the pirate and then glanced down at Armaund, who was shaking. From cold, Nichole wondered, or from fear? He was pleading with her, just with his eyes. Nichole glanced at the pirate once more. Perhaps Armaund would live or die with her comment. "Yes, I'm married," Nichole muttered. Armaund relaxed slightly, but Nichole was much too concerned about what might happen to her to notice his reaction. "What are you going to do with us?" slipped from her lips before she had time to analyze what such a question might prompt.

The pirate stepped closer and laughed. "Be you with child, as this coward says?"

Nichole nodded her head, wondering if she had just signed her own death warrant.

"Then you be no use for our pleasure!" the other man snapped. He considered her carefully. "He say he have wealthy relatives in the United States?"

Nichole grimaced; she wasn't too sure what Armaund might have told these grubby men and she was not going to offer any more aid to any man. She returned the pirates' stares and closed her lips tightly.

The bare-chested pirate grinned. "You better hope he say true words! Ransom is what we want. If we get no ransom, then he die and you . . ." The two men backed out of the door, and above their loud laughs Nichole heard the key turn in the lock.

Armaund rolled over on the floor to his back and covered his face with his hands. "Pirates! My God! When will my life improve?" he shouted in French. Heaving himself up into a sitting position, he glanced over at Nichole's stricken face. "Well," he growled, "thank God you didn't contradict me. I would be dead now."

The words slipped out. "What will they do, what will happen to us?"

"I certainly can't answer your questions," Armaund snapped. "We will be held for ransom, it appears. If my idiot cousin pays them what they want, perhaps they will set us free. At the moment, I really don't care." He walked over to the bed, picked her up none too gently and sat her in the chair by the table.

"What do you think you are doing? Get out of my bed!" She reached over to pull him off of the bed.

He raised himself up, and at first Nichole thought that he was going to strike her across the face. Then he sneered, "What? My sweet *wife* doesn't want me in her bed?"

"Get out of my bed! If you don't move, I'll tell them just whose wife I really am. What will happen to you then?"

Armaund was off the bed and beside her in a flash. "You say a word and you'll find yourself without child."

"Armaund, things have changed now," she announced firmly. "From now on, you will threaten me no longer. You obviously have very little control over what will happen to either one of us now. I am not going to listen to any more of your threats."

"You dumb child!" he snapped. "If you do not do exactly what I say, I'll refuse to ransom you. After the child comes, I'll turn you over to the pirates, and you know what will happen then. With your delicate nature, I doubt that you'll live more than two or three days." Armaund leered at her.

Nichole took a deep breath. "If you fail to ransom me, they will know that you lied. What do you think your life will be worth then? You will not threaten me again, and you'll stay out of my bed."

Before Armaund could respond, the door was thrown open again, and the same two pirates stood grinning at them. Nichole glanced at Armaund; had they understood any of their shouting? Thank God, they had spoken in French.

Neither Armaund nor Nichole were given a chance to say another word, for the shirtless man grabbed her and yanked her from the room. "You will come with me. This ship is foundering and we don't want to lose our captives." He leered at Nichole.

She was pushed to the rail and helped down a rope ladder into a small boat. As she rested in the bow she watched the activity on the deck of her ship. Armaund was also being pushed toward the rail along with several other women and children. What about the sailors and the officers? Nichole wanted to scream. She glanced at the ship they were approaching. What would happen to her now?

She was taken aboard the pirate ship, and the sails were hoisted even before she was forced from the deck. Hunting for Armaund, she forced the pirate trying to drag her below to stop a dozen times. Finally, he yanked her to the stairs. "Your husband will be stowed in another cabin. You come with me now." He glared at her.

"If you don't, then I beat you."

Nichole glanced up at him. There was no question that if she didn't move he would do just what he said. She shivered and allowed him to pull her down the stairs to a stuffy little room on the third level of the ship. After what seemed like hours to her, a young boy brought her a bowl of something that resembled fish chowder. The smell almost made her ill, and she wondered if she dared refuse the food. Before she said a word the boy said quietly, "You better eat, lady. They only feed captives once a day on this ship."

For three days, Nichole stared at the four walls of her tiny room. Twice a day, someone from the ship came to bring her a meal, and she wondered if she was being treated differently than the other captives. There was no way she could tell, for she was afraid to question any of the pirates except the small boy and she only saw him one other time. All the rest of her meals were delivered by different pirates.

She surprised herself, for she was no longer terrified. So much had happened to her that, if anything, her present situation only annoyed her. The Bordeleaus would pay the ransom, and she and Armaund would be released; then she could get on with her own plans. She would have her babe. Somehow, she would get back to Alex and resume her marriage. This was just another happening that she had to endure. In the meantime, she could wait.

Sometime on the third day, the motion of the ship slowed, and Nichole wondered if they were anchored someplace. She had no window, and she could see nothing through the tiny cracks in the wall. Deciding that it would make little difference to her, she rolled over on her narrow bunk and went back to sleep.

Shortly after she awakened the next morning, the shirtless pirate she had named "Grimy" brought her breakfast. He handed her the tray. "As soon as you eat, you will be taken ashore. You will stay on the island until the ransom is paid." With that he turned on his heel and left her, locking the door behind him.

Nichole shuddered; could her fate be worse on shore than it was in this tiny room? At least here, on the ship, she was allowed to rest, and she was left alone. What would her fate be once she left the safety of this little cabin and the ship?

Before she finished her broth and biscuit, the door was thrown open and Grimy was back. He pointed toward the hall and snapped, "We go!"

"Is . . . is Armaund coming? Will he be joining us?" Even that despicable cur was better than facing what was on shore alone. Grimy said nothing, but pushed her toward the stairs. She was frightened and suddenly she was shaking. She wondered if she could negotiate the stairs.

Grimy seemed to understand what she was thinking for he snarled at her, "I'll carry ya if I has to." She moved up the stairs.

When she finally climbed the last steps, she was surprised by bright sunlight. Swallowing her fear, she looked around. The ship was anchored in a small bay, and on shore, a small group of pirates stood at the edge of a sandy beach that stretched for miles. They seemed to be waiting for something. Her unfriendly pirate picked her up and hoisted her over the rail.

"I'm being dropped into the sea" was Nichole's only thought, and she tensed and closed her eyes. She couldn't swim and she knew she was facing death. But strong arms grabbed her and placed her in a sitting position. Nichole opened her eyes. She was in a small rowboat with four of her questionable companions. Two were sitting at the rear of the boat and two were handling the oars. No sooner had she opened her eyes than they started moving toward the beach and the small cluster of men.

In minutes, one of the grisly men who stood on shore waded into the ocean, grabbed her and lifted her from the boat. Muttering, he carried her through the water and set her on the sand. Before she had a chance to look around another boat arrived and Armaund jumped out and headed toward her. She sighed in relief.

Without warning, the group parted and a tall man stepped forward. "Madame?" The man glanced over at Armaund and chuckled, "Armaund!"

Nichole looked up at the man. She could not believe her eyes. In front of her stood an older version of Alex Dampier! As she heard Armaund shout "Uncle!" the ground came up to meet her and the day turned black.

Out of a comfortable haze, Nichole became aware of soft voices around her and a soft mattress under her. Carefully, she opened her eyes and looked around. She was in a bedroom. Two black maids were busy with the curtains at the windows, and the man who looked so much like Alex stood at the end of her bed.

His deep rich voice sent a shiver through her. "So, you are going to join us now?"

Nichole only stared at him. When she finally found her voice, she muttered, just above a whisper, "Who are you?"

"I'm Armaund's uncle. Let me ask you, who are you?" The tall man leaned toward her.

Nichole tried to answer. "I . . . I . . ."

"Why did you faint? No one touched you!"

Nichole shook her head and glanced over at the soft curtains blowing in the morning breeze; in a choked voice she whispered, "You reminded me of . . ."

"Oh, *oui*," the pirate interrupted, "Armaund, and to think that rascal never even hinted that he was going to marry." He laughed softly and whispered, "What shall I give Armaund's pretty little wife for a wedding gift, eh, Madame?"

"Non!" Nichole cried, "Armaund is not . . ." Then, as he tears formed, she realized what she had almost said. "I mean . . . I . . . Oh, Monsieur." Nichole dissolved into a torrent of tears.

The tall man at the end of the bed was beside her in an instant, holding her in his arms as if she were a child. "I think," he said softly, "you had better tell me the whole story, *oui?*"

He ordered one of the black servants to bring tea, then sauntered to the door. "I'll be back with a bit of brandy and you'll tell me your story." Nichole tried to stop her sobs. Could she tell him? He was Armaund's uncle! Could Alex be related to the man as well? They looked so much alike. This pirate sounded as if he and Armaund knew each other well. Perhaps this uncle and Armaund had planned the kidnapping together. She remembered the night Alex told her about Armaund's elder brother, and she wondered if this pirate also blamed her husband for the death of Charles. He might want revenge against Alex, too.

Quickly, she decided that she would tell him a little, only enough to explain where she came from and what her future plans were. Somehow, she had to leave Alex's name out of their conversation, unless, of course, he mentioned Alex by name. Even that might be a trick. No, she must not mention the name of Dampier, not

363

ever.

In a few short minutes the older version of Alex was back with a crystal decanter and two glasses. He helped Nichole to one of the chairs in the room and poured her a small snifter of brandy. He handed it to her and sat down on the small chair opposite her. "Now, Madame, let us start with who you are, *oui?*"

Nichole took a sip of the liquid and let the warmth spread through her body. "My name is Nichole. I was born in Paris, and I lived most of my life in a convent." As she spoke the man sat quietly and sipped his own drink. She told him about growing up in the convent, about the man who came to pay for her education and the letter that told her that she would marry his son. Avoiding any names, she explained about her trip to America, and how Baltimore excited her. She skipped over the next part of her marriage to Alex and his reaction to her, saying only, "At first, my husband didn't want a wife. I was afraid at times that he was going to send me back to France. Then Armaund came and he took me away."

"You are married?"

She nodded her head. "But not to Armaund!" she said firmly.

Ivan looked puzzled. "Do you want to go back to your husband?"

She nodded immediately, then shook her head vigorously, and her voice broke as she tried to explain. "I don't . . . know. I . . . I . . ." If she said she wanted to be returned to her husband, she would have to tell this pirate Alex's name. At any cost, she must not mention his name.

The man stared at her, confusion written on his handsome face. "You husband, he did not treat you well? H does not want the child?"

Nichole tried, "He did not know . . ." She couldn't continue. Instead, she shook her head and gestured, trying to tell him that her husband didn't know about the babe, but she confused him even more.

"When will the child arrive?" he asked quietly. Nichole's tears slowed and she blushed. "I don't know too much about these things, but I think sometime in January." She smiled slightly. "I know nothing about babies. No one in the convent . . ." She stopped when she realized what she had almost said. She frowned as she rephrased her remark. "There were no babies at the convent." She glanced over at her companion; perhaps he would admit to his relationship with Armaund. "Now sir, who are you?"

"My name is Ivan Maison." He watched Nichole closely to see if the name meant anything to her. She smiled at him, hesitantly. He sighed; she did not know who he was. "I was called the Black Russian during my own pirate days."

Her eyes widened. "You—you are truly a pirate?"

"I was, and a very good one. I lived to spend my wealth. This island, the house and everything on it are a result of my days at sea."

"But, a pirate?"

He smiled at her. *"Oui,* Madame. During the war with England, the Americans made it very profitable to make war on certain ships. I made a great deal of money and I helped the Americans at the same time."

Nichole asked quietly, "You are an American?"

"Non, but like you I am French. I have a Russian mother. I left home when I was very young to make my fortune. My family did not approve of the way I made my fortune, so I settled here. I still rule a part of the

365

sea. Unfortunately, my men took the wrong ship several days ago. They sent the ransom note to Armaund's relatives before they came here."

Nichole looked around her. "Where is Armaund? Is he here in the house?"

He chuckled. "Do you want to see him? He has taken up residence in one of my cottages. He did not want to stay in the house."

"I would rather not see him. But, Monsieur, I am not Madame duPres. No ransom will come for me. What are you going to do with me?" She tried to keep her voice from shaking.

Ivan smiled. "I think we should contact your husband."

Nichole stiffened, *"Non,* I don't think you should do that. Perhaps he doesn't want me." The words caught in her throat. Oh, not true, not true, she wanted to scream. But, not knowing what existed between this Ivan Maison and Armaund duPres, how could she name her husband? Her eyes glistened with tears.

Ivan saw the tears and was confused even more. "I think perhaps we should ask him, *non?"*

"Non! Please, Monsieur. I would like to go back to Maryland. I will get a job as a governess or a tutor. I'm well educated." Nichole raised her chin into the air, tears glistening in her eyes. "If you will just send me back to Maryland, please?"

Ivan ran his fingers through his hair. "You must stay here, at least until after the babe is born. In the spring, we will decide what is to be done. Now, you rest. In about an hour, I'll send a young girl to you. She'll show you the house and help you with a bath. We'll have to see about some clothes for you, and perhaps I can find some linen and cotton for the babe. I will see you at dinner."

Ivan left Nichole's room scratching his head. He had the strangest feeling that his nephew, Alex Dampier, was the husband Nichole was not sure she wanted. And where did Armaund fit into the picture? He headed down the stairs to his study. For years, Catherine had written to him once or twice a year. He still had several of her latest letters. Right now, he needed to reread her last letter.

He made himself comfortable at the desk in his study and pulled the parcel of yellowing paper from the pigeonhole of the desk. Thumbing through the pile, he spotted the letter he wanted. He pulled the paper from its envelope and read Catherine's year-old message. She wrote that her father was dead, and that Alex had been married to a French girl. They were waiting for the girl to arrive, and he smiled at Catherine's carefully penned statement, "It's not a real marriage, but a marriage by proxy. Father's agent, Monsieur Manage, married her in Alex's name." And, according to Catherine, Alex didn't want her to know but he was planning to set the girl aside as soon as she arrived. Was this Nichole the French girl in question? Had Alex set the girl aside, and Armaund brought her with him? He hurried to the kitchen.

"Janelle? Janelle!" Ivan called. He found his housekeeper in the garden with her children. "We have a guest, someone that needs your help." Ivan smiled at the twin boys toddling toward him. He reached down and patted both boys on the head. "She is going to have a child, but I'm afraid that her knowledge is very limited. She was raised in a convent. It is all a little confusing." Ivan told her about the conversation he had just had.

"I don't want her to know anything about me, other than what I've already told her. Tell that husband of

367

yours, no tales, he is to say nothing." Ivan grinned. Donan had only been a cabin boy during the pirate days, but since he had married Janelle, become overseer, and fathered twin sons, his memory of the days at sea was too far from the truth. And he knew all about Ivan Maison and his family. Nichole did not need to hear about the adventures according to Donan, nor did he want her to hear about his American family, not until he knew what had happened in Maryland.

"I must talk to my nephew and find out why this girl was with him. In the meantime, can you help Nichole?"

Janelle turned her liquid brown eyes in his direction. "I will help her." Then she giggled, "But I say you tell Donan that he not talk. He not listened to me."

"She cannot know about me, Janelle. She thinks her husband does not want her. Until I'm certain that she is married to Alex, and I know what the status of the marriage is, we'll say nothing. I don't think she should be upset either. She says the babe is due in January, but she is very big. I'm not sure she knows when the babe will come."

Janelle watched Monsieur Maison walk away, scratching his head once more. Not know when the babe would arrive? Curious, Janelle hurried up the stairs to meet Madame Nichole.

Chapter Twenty-nine

Alex stared at the note in Claude's hands. Without a word, both men rose and left the table. Alex followed the man without an invitation, and Claude made no attempt to dismiss Alex as he headed for the study. He handed Alex the note while he lit the lantern on his desk. Without opening the letter, Alex gave it back. Claude glanced at him for a second and then opened the message. He stared at the neat pen of his cousin and then silently read the note. Quietly, he told Alex what the contents said. "It's from Armaund. They have been taken by pirates. They're both unharmed, but the pirates are demanding a very heavy ransom." He passed the note over to Alex to read.

The gasp from Alex alerted Claude to a problem, and Alex's white face confirmed his suspicion. "What is it, what's wrong?"

"It is signed Monsieur and Madame duPres" was all Alex could manage.

"They were traveling as man and wife, Alex. In her condition, they could not have traveled any other way. Her reputation would have been destroyed if she had not appeared to be his wife. That note doesn't mean they're married."

Alex could not voice his fears. He accepted Claude's

369

logic but he didn't like it, not one bit. The amount of ransom was not too unreasonable, and the procedures for payment were outlined in the note, but nothing in the note indicated that the pirates would return Monsieur and Madame duPres to Philadelphia after they received the ransom. Alex asked, "Without word of how Armaund and Nichole will be released, should we pay?"

Claude studied the note and stated, "Perhaps we should ask a few questions. I have some acquaintances that might be of use. Let's visit them in the morning. I'm sure you won't be sailing, will you?"

Alex glanced up at the man, his expression puzzled. In truth, he had forgotten all about his original plans. Mumbling, he left the room. "Sailing? I can't go anywhere until I know what's going to happen to Nichole."

The next two days, Claude introduced Alex to three different groups of sailors. One man even claimed to have some experience with pirates, and another told them that he personally knew the pirates that were demanding the ransom. "If they say they'll turn 'em loose, then that's what they'll do!" he assured Alex.

On the third day, Alex and Claude sent a message to the pirates explaining that it would take some time to gather the funds demanded and would they please make arrangements to transfer Madame and Monsieur duPres to Philadelphia after the ransom had been received.

October was two days old when a second message arrived for Monsieur Bordeleau, and it was exactly like the first, except for the last sentence: "You will be given instructions after the ransom has been paid."

Alex was almost sick with fear. Nichole was still in the clutches of the pirates, and what of his unborn child, if indeed she still carried the babe? There was nothing Alex could do but wait. One evening, Peter and Claude deliberately got him drunk, but the short space of time that he spent under the influence of the strong drink did nothing to deaden his pain. He cried into his whiskey until Peter, who had gotten sick of his moans, took him upstairs and put him to bed.

Alex wrote to Robert and asked what he thought of the situation. Robert fired back a note saying that the ransom should not be paid under any circumstances. "You don't pay ransom to thieves," Robert wrote, "unless you have ironclad assurances that the captives will be released at the time the ransom is paid." Against Robert's recommendations, Alex and Claude gathered the ransom, and sent it on its way according to the instruction they'd received. Again, they had nothing to do but wait.

For four days, in the assigned room of her Caribbean prison, Nichole slept almost continually. She insisted that most of her meals be brought to her as well. Only once did she venture out of her room, and that was to eat the evening meal with Ivan Maison, that first day on the island. On the way to the dining room, Janelle took her on a tour of the house, but Nichole wasn't very interested. It was a big house and spacious, pleasantly decorated, but Nichole was still exhausted from her adventure. Before the meal was finished she was struggling to stay awake.

When Ivan joined her for dinner that night, she gazed around her and then asked about Armaund. "Isn't Armaund coming to dinner? I thought he would be here, too."

Ivan smiled. "He is not being mistreated. He prefers to dine alone."

371

By the sixth day, Nichole felt completely rested and she was tired of her room. After her breakfast was served she asked Janelle if she could see the house again. After the tour, Janelle took her out into the gardens, and the two women sat and talked away a good part of the afternoon.

On the seventh day, Nichole awoke early, feeling better than she had felt in days. Janelle arrived along with several other black women and a dozen bolts of fabric. "The master says it's time for you to get busy. We have instructions to make you a wardrobe and you are to start the clothes for the little one."

"But I can't wear all of this," Nichole objected.

"Oh, yes you can. And Master Ivan wants you to join him for dinner every night. You will have to dress for dinner. You have to have a dozen gowns." Janelle laughed at her surprise. Ivan had given Janelle detailed instructions. Nichole was to be kept busy enough so that she would not get depressed and sewing for the babe, they both decided, would help. Janelle had pointed out that every woman likes new clothes. Dinner every night would make a perfect excuse for a dozen gowns.

Throughout the next week, Nichole, Janelle and two other women worked on Nichole's wardrobe, and while they sewed, Nichole and Janelle became friends. Quickly, Janelle turned the subject to having babies, and Nichole, hungry for information, asked the questions she had meant to ask Alex. The two women figured that Nichole would deliver in December, not in January as Nichole had originally thought, and Nichole threw herself into preparing clothes for the baby. As they worked on the gowns and dresses for the child, Janelle told Nichole about her twins and about their birth.

The twins often were allowed to spend time with Nichole as she and their mother worked. Nichole warmed to the boys instantly, and she started daydreaming about the child she would have. It will be a girl, she thought. I'll teach her how to sew and cook and she'll be able to read and write, Nichole planned. As the pile of baby clothes grew so did Nichole's confidence.

Even Ivan commented that she had grown more beautiful. "Your husband will be so proud. Why don't you tell me what his name is so that I can send for him?"

Nichole panicked. *"Non,* please, do not ask his name. I have already told you my plans. I'll make my own way." Silently, she wondered if her host was trying to lull her into a false sense of security and then get her to name her husband.

She simply didn't know enough yet about the man who bragged about being a pirate to trust him with Alex's name and his life. She asked dozens of questions about Ivan Maison while she and Janelle sewed, but Janelle merely shrugged her shoulders and commented, "I work here on the island. He comes, I go to work." But Nichole watched and listened as Ivan made daily trips and sometimes two or three to the cottage where she now knew Armaund was staying.

None of it made any sense to Nichole, and she couldn't help but wonder why Armaud was not staying in the house. And the master's visits, which happened so frequently, left Nichole with the impression that Armaund and Ivan Maison were planning something.

Ivan was even more confused. It wasn't that he doubted Nichole, but until she agreed to give him the name of her husband, he only wondered more. Armaund was no help, for Ivan realized after he had spent a few afternoons with his nephew that Armaund was mad. And yet, Ivan realized that often some reality surfaced

373

in the mind of his pathetic nephew. One afternoon he badgered Armaund for details on Nichole's life before they were married and Armaund told him all about the convent where Nichole was raised. Armaund admitted that his father's relatives in Philadelphia had been enchanted with his wife. There was enough truth to some of the things Armaund told him that Ivan wondered just who Nichole had married. Ivan left his nephew shaking his head.

Still not certain of the truth, Ivan continued his visits with Armaund. While Janelle and Nichole were happily sewing clothes for the babe, the Black Russian asked Armaund about Alex Dampier. Armaund's reaction left a twisted knot of suspicion in Ivan's stomach. Armaund's face lost all of its color, and he began to stutter and slur his words. Ivan pressed his point. "Did Nichole meet the Dampiers when you were in the United States? Did Nichole meet Catherine?"

From the look on Armaund's face, Ivan decided that Catherine was the key. Perhaps his original suspicions were correct. He glanced at Armaund. "Catherine and I have have corresponded for a long time. I've asked her to come for Christmas."

Armaund looked like he was going to pass out, and then he started jabbering about the chateau and wine and Ivan quickly left the man alone. Obviously, Catherine Dampier had a great deal to do with the situation, and Catherine would know just whose wife Nichole was. She might also know, if Nichole was Alex's wife, what happened to the marriage. The babe concerned Ivan, for if Alex had set Nichole aside whose child was she carrying? Ivan trudged back to the house and locked himself in the study.

Perhaps that was the only way, asking Catherine to

come for Christmas. There were serious problems with that, Ivan admitted. For ten years, he had hidden on the island and enjoyed his freedom. If he invited his niece to his home, it might bring more attention to the island than he wanted. And he certainly couldn't invite his godson. Alex was too well known and his arrival would bring too many questions. There were still a great many citizens in the United States who saw him as a criminal. They would think nothing of pressing for his arrest. He might find himself on the gallows.

If Alex and Nichole were married, as he suspected, Nichole would have to meet Alex in a neutral port, away from the island, and even at that, it would be risky. Ivan frowned; his crew of misfits could probably sail around enough to confuse Catherine, but not Alex. No, Alex could not come. He might accidentally lead the authorities right to the Black Russian.

Unwinding from his chair, Ivan thought of Catherine. If Armaund's reaction was any indication, Nichole and Catherine must have been close. Janelle would have to question Nichole, discreetly of course. He hurried to find his housekeeper and explained what he needed to know.

Janelle got little information for Ivan. "She has one friend, she says, a girl, but she will not tell me the girl's name. The girl and Nichole were very close. She cried a little when she told me about her. Is that what you wanted to know?" As Ivan shook his head, Janelle frowned. "Won't it help?"

"Not really. Did she say how she met the girl?"

"Why, yes, Nichole says her friend lives in Maryland, that the girl is related to her husband."

Ivan's face lost a little of its color and his suspicions grew. The whole situation was too coincidental to be anything but what he feared. But he couldn't have Alex come. Could he send for Catherine? Did Catherine know whether Alex still wanted the French girl for his wife? And, if she was Alex's wife, why in god's name had Armaund kidnapped her? Could Nichole have been in danger from her own husband and Armaund been trying to save her? The frown deepened on Ivan's face and he shook his head. There were so many unanswered questions, and he had so few facts on which to make a judgment. To make matters intolerable, Armaund was no longer sane enough to answer any of his questions. As long as Nichole refused to talk about it, Ivan didn't feel he could press it. With the baby coming, she should not be upset. He had no choice. He had to send for Catherine.

By the middle of October, Alex was very nearly insane himself. Try as hard as he could, he could not stop thinking about his wife, and what he thought she might be enduring. He growled at everyone. There was no more correspondence from the pirates, and Alex was sure that there would be none. There was only one course of action he had not tried. He sent an urgent message to Robert. Come to Philadelphia!

It took Robert four days to get to the city and when he called on the Bordeleaus, the first words out of Alex's mouth told Robert what turmoil he was going through. Alex yelled, "Where in the hell have you been? I said urgent. It doesn't take four days to get here!"

Robert just looked at him and shook his head. He had lost weight and there were dark circles under his eyes. Alex was past reason, Robert decided, and he made no attempt to tell Alex that it took two days just to get his message. Alex dragged his lawyer into the Bordeleau study to explain what he wanted.

Robert paled considerably. "You want me to find a buyer for the farm, the whole thing, and—and mortgage Manor House? My God! Why?"

"I have to buy a ship. I've found some rather questionable citizens who claim to the know the islands. They know where the pirates have their hideouts. I will find her, if I have to sail to every island in that sea."

"I can't let you do this. You worked hard for that farm. It' yours. You'll want it back just as soon as Nichole returns. If you go chasing off now, you'll miss her, for sure. Do you know how many islands there are? There are hundreds out there. You could search the Caribbean for years and not find her. This whole idea is ridiculous. I won't do it! Get another lawyer!" He turned to leave; then, remembering Catherine's note, he turned back to Alex. "Your sister sent this. She said to tell you to open it immediately."

Alex glared at Robert as he took the paper and tore into the message. He scanned the note and then let out a strangled howl, bringing the older residents and all the servants of the house into the hall. Alex raced from the study, throwing the note at Robert. As Alex flew up the stairs, Robert read the note himself and smiled. Quietly, he turned to the assembled group. "Ivan Maison, Alex's uncle, has her. She is safe!"

All of the servants, the master and mistress and Peter, who stood in the doorway, reacted with cheers as Robert followed Alex up the stairs.

Robert watched from the doorway for a moment as Alex threw things into a trunk. "Catherine says that she has been invited, but you have not been. She writes "— Robert glanced at the note in his hand—"That arrangements will be made for you to join Nichole at a later time."

Alex turned around, his face flushed. "If Uncle Ivan thinks I'll let Catherine go and not go with her, he's out of his mind! If Catherine sails, I'll sail with her even if I have to stow away. Now, help me pack, or get out of here."

Robert grumbled from the doorway as Alex turned around and continued with his packing. Peter came to the door and Robert read him Catherine's note. Peter only shrugged his shoulders. "You won't stop him, save your breath."

In less than an hour, Alex and Peter were on their way back to Manor House. Robert traveled along, still trying, as he put it, to talk some sense into his friend's head, reminding Alex that Nichole was soon to have a child. She didn't need to be excited. Alex could go to her at a later time.

Alex refused to talk about a later time, repeating each time Robert mentioned Catherine's note, "If she sails, I sail too!"

The pace Alex set was furious, and even Peter asked him to slow down. When it became obvious that Alex had no intention of stopping for the night, Peter started to rage, "That damn tub won't even come for Catherine for ten days yet. What's your hurry?" Alex glared at him. "Alex," Peter snapped, "we have to stop for the night. You want to kill the horses again?" Finally, Alex drew up before an inn and glared at his companions.

Robert sighed, "Thank God!"

Before dawn, Alex was up and ready to travel. Peter and Robert both got Alex to slow a bit for the horses sakes, and they got him to stop at night, again pointing out that the horses would collapse if he continued to

378

drive them the way he was.

In three days, they were back at Manor House. It was after ten o'clock, but Catherine was waiting. "I knew you'd be here tonight. I just knew it."

Alex wanted to know how the message had been delivered and by whom. Catherine showed him the original note and answered his questions, commenting, "Uncle Ivan says you'll have to wait."

Alex read the original message and glared at his sister. "I'm going with you. I don't care what he says."

"Alex, you can't. What if they won't take you? Uncle Ivan makes it clear that he doesn't feel it would be safe for him if you to come to his island. What if we are followed? Will you endanger Uncle Ivan's life? He might be arrested. People know he's a pirate."

"I'll stow away if I have to! The matter is closed. Not you, not Uncle Ivan, not the whole damn Navy will keep me from sailing with you. If you go, I go!" He marched out of the room, leaving Robert, Peter and Catherine looking after him as he went through the swinging doors and up to his room.

Later that night, Catherine dragged Robert into the study. "I hope you have nothing pressing in Baltimore. I can't handle him alone and Peter just shrugs his shoulders and does nothing. Robert, he can't come. If the pirates find him, they might not take me, and then what will Nichole do?"

Robert pulled Catherine into his arms. "I'm not sure I want you to go. What the hell do I know about Ivan Maison and his crew of misfits? At least if Alex is along, nothing will happen to you."

"Can you stay?"

"I think I better," Robert answered quietly. The next six days dragged by for both Catherine and Alex. Whenever anyone mentioned the trip, Alex walked out of the room. He assured Peter and Catherine that he intended to stow away. Catherine continued to beg first Robert and then Peter to talk Alex out of going. Robert reminded her, the few chances they had to be alone, that Alex would assure her own safety, and Peter, who was more realistic, announced, "There is no reasoning with him. We might as well help him get aboard without being seen. If we don't, those pirates of Uncle Ivan may just shoot him."

Finally, Catherine realized the truth of Peter words. "I'll have to keep him hidden on board the ship until we get to the island; then I'll just have to tell Uncle Ivan that Alex came too. There won't be much he can do after the fact." Catherine told Alex that she and Peter would help him stow away, so he wouldn't get himself killed. Alex only grinned at her.

With their plans made, Robert dragged Catherine into the study for a long good-bye. Robert kissed her hard. "I don't like this one little bit. The only reason I'm considering it is that if Alex isn't reunited with Nichole soon, I'll have to hire a lawyer to defend me — for killing my best friend. He used to be so reasonable."

Catherine giggled. "Do you suppose you'd act like this if someone kidnapped me?"

The kiss Robert planted on her lips told her the answer, and she leaned into him. "I'll come back right after Christmas," she murmured, her voice breathless. "We'll be married early in the spring."

Sometime during the night, the last day of October, a ship sailed up the Potomac and docked at Manor House. Catherine and Peter planned carefully, and the next morning Peter made his way to the captain of the ship. He carried an invitation with him. Catherine invited the entire crew to the house for a feast. While the staff was pouring wine and serving dinner, Peter and Alex slipped past the one guard left to stand watch. And that man was enjoying his share of the feast, a gift sent by Catherine.

Alex moved across the deck in the shadows without a problem. He found the room that had been prepared for Catherine and made himself comfortable. At dawn, Catherine arrived and the ship moved away from the dock and into the rising sun.

Ivan's instructions to Catherine were to stay in her cabin and her meals would be brought to her. Her uncle wrote that he could only insure her safety if she stayed out. That suited her admirably, for no one would catch a glimpse of the tall dark man who shared her cabin.

The voyage would take about seven days, Uncle Ivan's message said. The trip was pleasant enough for the first five days, but Alex complained constantly about traveling so slowly. On the afternoon of the fifth day, a knock on the door sent Alex into a closet. The captain arrived to tell Catherine that they were in for a storm. Alex crawled out of his cramped space in a rage. "Why in hell does it have to storm now? If the man was any kind of a sailor, he could have sailed around the storm." Catherine thought of Robert's comments about her reasonable brother and she giggled.

For twelve hours, the ship tossed as the sea churned. But as the waves were calming the captain again came to Catherine's door. He knocked on the door and then opened the door wide, not waiting for Catherine to invite him in after she acknowledge his rap. Alex couldn't get to his hiding place fast enough. The two men stood staring at each other. They were only six hours from the island, and the indecision on the face of the captain was clear, even to Catherine.

Catherine grabbed his arm and tried to explain. The pirate didn't want to hear her and screamed for his men. In seconds, Alex was dragged from Catherine's room, yelling obscenities at the short dark men. Catherine yelled at his vanishing back. "I promise tell to Uncle Ivan that you're here and why you came."

For hours, Alex paced the small space into which he had been locked. Periodically he pounded on the door, screaming that he wanted to see Ivan Maison. Above his head, on the deck of the ship, he heard the sailors preparing to dock. He heard Catherine leave the vessel, and he thought she yelled at him. With no porthole, he could only guess that they had arrived. His frustration rose as he waited and waited. If there were just some way he could get off the ship, he could at least try to find Nichole. But, locked up as he was, he had to wait. Looking up he growled, "If this is supposed to teach me patience . . ." His voice trailed off.

Chapter Thirty

Through the month of October, Nichole sewed clothes for the babe and enjoyed Janelle and her children. The few times Janelle asked about her husband, Nichole changed the subject. She knew that Ivan Maison visited with his nephew every day; Janelle had told her that much, and she saw the Frenchman walking toward the group of cottages where Armaund was living. She couldn't shake the suspicion that Armaund's uncle might be involved in some kind of a plot to destroy Alex. She liked the older man and he had been very kind to her, but he admitted that he was a pirate. He could be guilty of anything.

Nichole sighed. If Janelle was correct about the baby, she only had to wait two more months before she held her little one. Oh, how she wanted a little girl, a soft little bundle, with hair of dark brown and soft brown eyes like her father's. One lone tear crawled down Nichole's cheek. Watching Janelle and her husband, Donan, Nichole knew she and Alex shared something very special. She missed her husband so much. There were still nights when, in spite of her best intentions, she cried herself to sleep. There had to be a reason why Alex hadn't found her yet. She fought with her fear that Armaund might have somehow been able to get to Alex and hurt him.

She shook her head as if to rid herself of her depressing thoughts. At least she would have her child, and as soon as the child was old enough she would return to Maryland, and then she would find Alex.

On the last day of the month, Nichole went downstairs to breakfast a little later than usual. The night just past had been especially bad for Nichole. Alex's smiling face had grinned at her in her dreams and she had found herself reaching for him often. Early in the morning, before the winter sun announced another day, her dreams had turned to nightmares.

She had tossed and turned as she watched Armaund and Ivan Maison pursue Alex through the Caribbean paradise. She could never reach him; in fact, she was sure that as hard as she called to him in the dream, he never heard her. The vision had been so strong that she was still shaking as she went down the stairs. The only consolation she had was that Alex was not on the island. It couldn't come true because Alex wasn't there.

When she got to the table, Ivan was waiting for her, a wide grin spread across his face. He noticed her pallid complexion but refrained from asking her if she had slept well. Obviously, she had not. His eyes mirrored the thoughts that were running through his head. Even swollen with her child, she was a beautiful woman. The puzzle about who she belonged to, Armaund or Alex Dampier, made him confess to the plans that he was sure would solve his dilemma. This morning, she looked tired and very unhappy. Perhaps the surprise he had for her would answer his own questions and please her as well.

Once they were seated Ivan turned to the expectant mother. "Janelle told me a month ago that you had a friend in Maryland. This girl, would you like to have her

384

come here for Christmas? I could send her an invitation and a ship to bring her here."

Nichole's gasp gave Ivan pause. She was shocked, and she didn't look as though she liked the idea at all.

Nichole gave him a bittersweet smile. "She'll not come. She is planning to be married soon. She won't have time to come." Nichole couldn't help the sigh that slipped from her lips, thinking of the happy occasion she would miss. She stared off into space, thinking about Catherine and all the plans the girl had made before Armaund interfered. Had she missed the wedding itself?

Ivan couldn't hide his surprise. Catherine, getting married? Catherine's last letter had mentioned Alex's wedding but not one for herself. Dear God, had he made a colossal mistake? He gazed at Nichole, who seemed lost in her own thoughts. Sometimes she seemed to drift away from the conversation they were having to dwell in her own world. Just the thought of a stranger around Nichole, now, with the babe so close, caused some of Ivan's color to fade from his face. What would he do if he was wrong?

There was always the possibility that the husband was Alex and she was running from him. If his nephew was her husband and had hurt her, he might have to take the young rake in hand and teach him a thing or two himself.

Ivan shook his head, remembering the reason for his earlier remarks. It was too late now. "Nichole, I have a surprise for you. I took the liberty of asking a close friend of mine if she wanted to come to visit. I told her about you and the babe. I hope you don't mind." Ivan drew a deep breath; in a second, he would know whether he had guessed correctly or made the biggest mistake of his life. "This friend of mine lives in Maryland also. Her

385

name is Catherine Dampier."

Her reaction was not what he expected. She sat very still, the color draining from her face. Tears started at her eyes and she rose from the table, swaying as she stood.

Nichole was speechless. He knew! Somehow, he had found out about Alex. Her dream had been a premonition of what was going to happen. He was bringing Catherine to the Bahamian islands to make sure Alex followed. Then her nightmare would come true. Once more she swayed slightly, and she grabbed for the table to steady herself. What was Ivan Maison going to do to her husband?

Ivan was beside her in an instant. "I'm sorry, I know I should have asked you before I issued the invitation, but I thought you needed a friend. Catherine Dampier is your friend, isn't she, Nichole?" But what about Alex? he wanted to ask. Looking into her tragic face, he knew he could question her no more today. It was so clear, so plainly visible, that she was afraid, she was terrified of something. It was probably his own godson, Alex Dampier. His nephew had done something to this precious flower that had cut her heart into a thousand pieces. Perhaps he would never allow Alex to see Nichole again.

Nichole wiped at her tears. "It was a nice thought. I would love to meet your friend, but . . ."

"But you will!" Ivan interrupted. "She is leaving Maryland tomorrow. She is coming here, to see you, and she is coming for Christmas. She'll be here for the birth of the babe."

Nichole took a careful breath. In her mind, she could hear the words echoing, "What about Alex? And what will happen to him if he comes?" She tried to smile, but it was more of an effort than she could manage. Tears still falling, she turned to go.

"Don't you want to meet my friend?" Ivan asked softly.

"More than anything," Nichole choked. "More than you know."

"Good! It will take a week. My crew has to sail around in circles, so she won't know where she is being taken . . ."

Now Nichole interrupted, "Doesn't she know where you are? Don't people know about this island?" Her voice was barely above a whisper.

Ivan followed her thinking. "No one knows where my island is, Nichole. There are quite a number of people who would happily invade my paradise and drag me to the tallest tree. In the eyes of most, I am a criminal."

Nichole couldn't say a word; she was stunned. Alex didn't know where to find her. He couldn't come. He didn't know where she was. He was safe! She giggled; it would be wonderful to see Catherine, and her sister-in-law could tell her how Alex was and if he knew about the babe.

Ivan forced his own smile. He had just told her that her husband could not find her and for the first time since she came into the room she appeared happy. In fact, to Ivan's dismay, she was giggling. Her reaction to the news only confirmed his suspicions. She was terrified of Alex Dampier. Now that she knew she was safe from her husband, she could relax and enjoy Catherine's visit. Damn that boy! But that still did not answer the question about what part Armaund played in all of this.

Nichole sat back down at the table and they finished their breakfast. When Nichole went upstairs to her room, Ivan made his way through the fields to the cottage where Armaund was staying. As he dismounted from his horse, his troubled thoughts turned to the lad. There was always the possibility that he had accused Armaund of making trouble when perhaps he had only tried to prevent something more unpleasant from happening. He frowned. He was still left with the task of explaining to his own sister that her remaining son was totally insane, and would be for the rest of his life. God help Alexander Dampier if he was responsible for that as well.

Perhaps it would be better if he kept Armaund here and let his sister believe that the boy had died trying to defend that worthless chateau they had valued so much. He shook his head; there seemed to be no answer. He nodded to the guard who leaned back in a rough-hewn chair on the porch of the cottage; then he pushed the door open quietly and entered the living area. Armaund was curled up in a ball, sound asleep on the floor!

Ivan stood silently, watching the man/child sleep. His thoughts drifted back over the last four weeks and the visits he had made here. Since the day Ivan had said Catherine was coming, Armaund had changed, and it was not for the better. Ivan remembered the day he had asked about Armaund's marriage to Nichole. Armaund had looked up at him, shock written plainly on his face. "Why, Uncle, you jest! I'm not married. I have to go to France and fight for my title. I can't have a wife until I have a title!"

The next afternoon, Ivan found Armaund sitting on the bed, crying like a frightened child. Ivan had been concerned and asked what was wrong. Armaund's chill voice screeched, "Alex Dampier killed my brother and you know what? I'm going to kill his son!" As hard as Ivan coaxed, Armaund would say nothing more.

Ivan watched Armaund sleep for a time and then left

the cottage. Poor little French girl, a husband who broke her heart and a madman who wanted to kill her child. Some people were never meant to find happiness.

As he rode back to the house, he thought about Catherine's trip. Had he only made matters worse? Would Catherine's visit remind Nichole of the man she was so frightened of? He shook his head. He might never know if he had done the right thing.

All that day and the next, Nichole seemed very edgy to both Ivan and Janelle. It was obvious that she was not sleeping well, and Ivan blamed himself. "I never should have invited Catherine here. I should have waited."

Two days later, Janelle took matters into her own hands, insisting that Nichole take an afternoon nap. Ivan Maison and Donan were both told that Nichole was to have a short walk, one in the morning and one in the afternoon, and Janelle ordered Nichole to go. In three days, there was a noticeable improvement in Nichole. Some of her color returned and the dark circles under her eyes lightened. But she was still much too nervous to suit Janelle. "You must calm down and relax. You must rest and eat or your baby will be sick. Please, Nichole, you must take care of yourself."

Nichole was in bed, taking one of the naps Janelle was now insisting upon, when Catherine's ship was spotted. In a short time, the ship anchored and a long-boat was hoisted over the side. Ivan made his way down to the sandy beach, and Catherine ran into the waiting arms of her uncle as soon as the boat reached the beach. He swung her up into his arms. "Let me look at you." Laughing, he set her down in the soft white sand. "I haven't seen you for eight years, you know. Your eyes are still full of mischief."

"Oh! Uncle Ivan, I'm a lady now. I'm even going to be married in the spring. It's so good to see you. It has been years and years."

Uncle Ivan draped his arm around her shoulders, hugged her once more and started her toward the house. Catherine looked around. "Where's Nichole? She's here, isn't she? You can't imagine how awful the last months have been. We didn't know where she was or if Armaund had hurt her. Did you send him on to his family? Alex has been beside himself. Where is she, I must talk to her!"

Ivan stopped in the sand. "Catherine, one question at a time. Yes, Nichole is here. No, Armaund did not hurt her, and the pirates didn't hurt her. Yes, you can see her, but first, I must talk to you about Alex. Nichole is married to Alex Dampier, isn't she?"

Catherine squirmed out of his hands and stared up at him. "Yes, she is married to Alex. Alex! Oh, Uncle Ivan, I have to tell you something, something I don't think you're going to like. Alex, well he . . . I know what you said . . . but he couldn't wait." Ivan raised one eyebrow to stare at the nervous girl. She muttered, "He's on the boat."

Ivan backed away from his brown-haired niece. "You were to come alone."

"Let's go to your house," Catherine mumbled, trying to keep from feeling so guilty. "I'll tell you what happened. Alex had to come, Uncle Ivan, he just had to."

Janelle watched the man and woman approach the house. Her own heart sank. They both looked like they had come to attend a wake. It was obvious that Nichole's husband was the scoundrel Ivan Maison thought he was. "Poor little mother. Oh, men, you are so cruel," Janelle sighed.

When Ivan and Catherine were settled in the library, Catherine poured out her heart, telling her uncle all that she knew, from the time Henry had sent her to Philadelphia and Nichole was brought to America. "But they are terribly in love now. Do you know, Peter told me that he ordered Robert to sell the farm and mortgage the plantation just so he could buy a ship and go looking for her. I never thought my brother would find anyone, and certainly not fall this deeply in love, but he has. It's a good thing that Armaund isn't around. Alex is so angry at the man, I'm sure he'd kill him with his bare hands. If she is hurt, I think Alex would manage to cross the ocean on foot, just to get to him."

While Catherine told her story, Ivan looked pained, and the more she talked, the more his color under his bronze skin faded. "Oh, my God! I thought Alex had hurt her," he interjected at one point. What could he have been thinking? Ivan sat very still, trying to piece together a monstrous puzzle that still had missing pieces. He muttered as he tried to make some sense out of Catherine's story, "Why wouldn't she tell me her husband's name? Unless she thought with my visits to . . ."

Catherine interrupted, "She didn't tell you about Alex? Who did you think she was married to?"

Ivan admitted grudgingly, "Armaund at first, then I wasn't sure. Oh, no!" Ivan bolted from his chair. "Armaund is here. He's on the island. I have him under guard in one of my cottages."

Catherine's color faded to a pallid peach. "If Alex finds out, he'll kill him!"

"The boy is quite mad. He rambles on about France and the chateau, about Charles, about killing Alex's son. Alex can't kill him! He's insane."

Catherine stated firmly, "Mad or not, Alex'll kill him."

391

Ivan stared out the window at his property, as if looking for an answer written in the sky. "I'll have to send Armaund to England, to his family. I had hoped to spare my sister, but now I have no choice. Damn, and Alex is on the ship in the bay! Somehow, I'll have to send Alex to one of the other islands, immediately, until I can arrange to send Armaund on his way. Damn! I told you to come alone." He glared down at Catherine.

She sat up and glared back at her uncle. "You don't understand. There was no way I could have prevented him from sailing. He was coming and that was that. And I don't think Alex is going to sit on that boat and wait for you to get rid of Armaund. He's in love with her, Uncle Ivan, terribly, terribly in love." She leaned forward to make her point.

Ivan walked to the door. "Well, I have much to do. I cannot allow Alex to leave that ship until I get rid of my other nephew." He ran his hands through his hair in a helpless gesture. "I'll have to get a ship here from one of the other islands to take Armaund away, but before I do that, I must get Alex headed in the other direction. God, what a mess!" Ivan silently cursed his careful long-standing rules. Never did he have more than one ship in the bay at a time. At the time he made that decree, he was positive his orders about the bay kept him from being discovered, but right now, how he wished he had never made those restrictions.

He sighed; there was no hope for it. He had to send the ship with Alex to Nassau and another one of his ships must be signaled home. Then, flying the Union Jack, the ship could take Armaund from the island to England. Ivan grimaced; he supposed the first thing he had better do was to go out to the ship and see Alex. He needed to determine for himself if Alex was really as distraught as Catherine seemed to think. Dear God, if he man was truly enamored, how was he going to con-vince him to leave without seeing his wife, even for a few days? Then there was Nassau. The place was crawling with loyalists. If Alex so much as opened his mouth while they were in port, Ivan could not guarantee his safety. Ivan gritted his teeth. Pirating had been so much simpler.

Chapter Thirty-one

Alex tossed restlessly on his bunk. Damn bunk, he thought, it was too small for a tall man, and there was no way he could get comfortable. All afternoon, as he waited for his godfather to free him from his prison, he conjured up ways to escape. For one reason or another he rejected each plan. His thoughts kept drifting back to Armaund. Prissy said, from what little she could remember, that she felt the man was not a sane man. He wondered what had happened to Armaund. By now, he was probably safe in England with his family.

Alex let his thoughts drift back to Nichole. Could something have happened to her or to the babe? "Uncle Ivan had better come soon, or I'll not be responsible for my actions," Alex muttered to the wooden ceiling of his cabin.

His thoughts turned to Catherine. He jumped from the bunk and started pacing the small room. Perhaps they had not arrived at the island at all, and Catherine was at the mercy of the pirates from the ship. He slumped back down on the bunk. His mind was running away with him. He couldn't stand much more!

Until that moment, the ship had been deathly still but now he heard a scraping sound above him, then a pause, then more noises. Suddenly, he heard footstep moving outside his cabin. His door was thrown open. He stood frozen as he stared at five burly men, with pistols drawn. The tallest of the bunch said sternly, "You, the captain wants you!" Two of the men stepped forward and grabbed Alex by the arms. He was hauled out of the cabin and down the passageway before he had a chance to react.

At the other end of the passage another door was thrown open, and Alex was thrust inside. They're taking no chances, Alex thought.

He looked around the large cabin into which he was pushed. The captain and the first mate were standing beside a chair, and seated in the chair, staring at him, was an older version of himself. Alex gulped and stared at the man. There was no question. Before him sat Ivan Maison. Alex shook his head; no wonder his father had hated the pirate. But for the differences in age, he and Ivan Maison could have been twin brothers.

"Well, nephew," Ivan Maison drawled, startled himself, "I told Catherine to come alone. You don't obey orders very well, do you?"

Alex drew himself up to his full six foot four inches and glared at his mother's brother. He demanded, "Where is my wife? I want to see Nichole."

Ivan stood up and looked directly into Alex's yes. "I'm sorry, but you can't see her just yet."

Alex made what could only be a scoffing sound, but Ivan continued, "She is heavy with child. She cannot be upset. She has already been through too much. I will not see her hurt or abused. In several days . . ."

"Several days!" Alex yelled.

"In several days, if she wants to see you, I'll take you to her." Ivan sank back down in his chair. He watched the raw emotion flutter across Alex's face. There was no question, Catherine had been right. Alex was very much in love with his wife and obviously sick with worry. Ivan added softly, "It's for her sake, Alex, as well as the child. She can't stand a shock right now. Remember, we didn't know you were coming. Let her get used to the idea first, then you can see her."

Alex gazed at his uncle. "Is my wife all right? If she can't stand a shock . . ." His voice trailed off as fear registered in his face.

"She's fine, but the birth is only weeks away. She needs to stay calm and contented so that . . ."

Alex interrupted, "Do you think I'll upset her? Is that what you think?" He sank into a nearby chair and put his face in his hands. "Damn the man!" Alex roared.

"What man?"

"Armaund! He had no right. Where is that snake?" Alex growled.

"He is traveling to England." Ivan stretched the truth slightly. "Alex, the man is insane!"

"He's also going to be dead! I'll kill him when I find him."

Ivan shook his head. "You would sacrifice your future happiness to kill a man that may be forever dead to the world already? I thought you were smarter than that."

Alex left the chair and started to pace the floor. "Can't I just see her? She doesn't have to see me. She and Catherine could go walking on the beach. There must be someplace in the stern or in the bow where I could hide. I need to see her."

Ivan shook his head, wondering if the man was going to accept his suggestion. "I have a better plan. I ordered something from England several months ago and it has arrived in port, on one of the neighboring islands. You'll travel with Hank and Smithy here to bring it back. It's something I think Nichole can use, although I didn't order it for her. The trip there and back will take about thirty-six hours. It shouldn't take more than four hours to get the merchandise. When you return, Nichole will be waiting for you."

"And if I won't go?"

Ivan chuckled. "I've been told that you were a smart one. You'll go!"

Alex looked at his uncle. "Thirty-six hours?"

Ivan nodded his head. "Thirty-six hours' travel and whatever time it takes to pick up my goods, no more than forty-eight hours, two days. I will even tell Nichole how anxious you are to see her and that I made you go. She'll understand."

Alex glared at the older man. "I have no choice?"

"You have no choice."

Alex walked out of the door into the arms of three pirates. The ship's captain said softly, "Take him to the first mate's cabin." As the door closed Alex heard the captain say, "Don't worry, Ivan, we won't let him out of our sights."

Alex threw himself onto the bunk in the cabin of the first mate and looked at the rest of the area. This room was much larger than the cubbyhole he had originally occupied. Obviously, his status had improved, now that the crew knew that he was related to Ivan Maison.

He stretched out and put his hands behind his head. Uncle Ivan had said Nichole was fine and that the birth of the child was only a few weeks away. Their child, his child. He thought of the small creature that had been made in love and he wondered about Nichole. Would she be all right? His own mother had given her life for Catherine. Alex fought the chills that ran through his body. Could he find her once again, only to lose her to a child that he had never given much thought to until this moment? No, Nichole had to survive.

What about the child? Nichole had been so sick at

first, and with the kidnapping and the trauma of the pirates, could the child be deformed? What could he do then?

A knock on the door and a gruff voice announced that his meal had come. A large platter and a bottle of rum were presented to him by a burly-looking fellow who grinned through missing front teeth. He drawled, "Capt'n says you'll be needin' this. We'll be putting out in a few minutes. I'm to tell you that you got two guards. They won't think twice about knockin' you out for a day or two, so don't try nothin'."

Alex sarcastically offered his thanks and sat down with the food. After he had eaten his fill, he poured himself a mug of rum and stood at the porthole listening to the sea lap softly at the hull of the ship. The waves seemed to be whispering, Two days, two days!

Before too much time had passed, the soft sounds and the rum had the desired effect. Alex stretched out on the bunk and drifted off to sleep, muttering, "Two more days, two more days, two mo . . ."

In her sleep, Nichole heard someone calling to her. She struggled to awaken as the voice called again. "Nichole, Nichole? Wake up. Catherine's come." Nichole rubbed her eyes and tried to roll into a sitting position. Janelle was bending over her. "Catherine is here, and she's waiting to see you." The maid smiled down at her.

"She's here already?" Nichole asked hesitantly. Janelle nodded her head and helped Nichole to her feet. As she helped Nichole into a soft cotton frock and brushed her hair, Janelle chuckled; she had gotten much bigger in the last two weeks. She opened the door and called softly, "Catherine!"

With her usual exuberance, Catherine was through the door and hugging Nichole for all she was worth. Nichole laughed and Catherine giggled, "You have grown a little

398

since I last saw you."

Nichole patted her expanding belly. "I've not grown but my little one certainly has." She smiled, a soft pink blush tingeing her cheeks. "I'm going to have a babe." Together they sat down on the edge of the bed. Catherine launched into a myriad of questions, about her stay on the island, about the babe, and even about the pirates. Catherine and Uncle Ivan had decided that Armaund must not be mentioned, and Catherine had promised to wait a bit before saying anything about Alex.

Nichole's green eyes were bright and clear as she laughed at some of Catherine's reactions to the islands and the pirates on the ship that brought her. Soon, Nichole pulled out the gowns and blankets that she and Janelle had spent the past weeks constructing. For a time, the conversation whirled around the arrival of her baby, and then the girls discussed Catherine's wedding, planned for April. Nichole was afraid to confide her fears about Alex's safety to Catherine until she was certain that he was safe. Arm in arm the two girls descended to the first floor for dinner.

Ivan didn't join them for dinner, and Nichole immediately wondered why, but when Catherine didn't seem concerned, Nichole tried to relax and ignore her suspicions. She had to wait until she and Catherine were alone to share her thoughts abut the danger Alex might be in. After they finished eating, Catherine and Nichole went back to the bright rose-and-white room Catherine was going to use during her stay. Nichole asked Janelle for tea and while it was being served, Nichole felt Catherine's stare. After Janelle left the two girls, Catherine looked down at her teacup in her hands. "You haven't asked about Alex, Nichole."

The teacup in Nichole's hand rattled and she set it

aside. Standing, she tiptoed to the door, opened it, peered outside and sat back down. Catherine watched her, her face puzzled. "Catherine," Nichole whispered, "I'm not sure Alex is safe. Armaund is here and Ivan Maison visits him two or three times a day. I am terrified that those two are planning something. I suspect that they brought you here to force Alex's hand. I don't know how Ivan figured it out, but he knows I'm Alex's wife." She looked around the room, then back at Catherine. "I don't think we should be discussing this here."

Catherine's mouth dropped open and she stared at Nichole. "You can't be serious. Why, Dennis Ivan Maison is godfather to Alex."

Now it was Nichole's turn to stare. "Ivan Maison is Alex's godfather? Why would he want to hurt his own godson?" She shook her head to try to clear the confusion she felt. If Ivan was uncle to Catherine then he was uncle to Alex as well. None of this made any sense.

"Nichole," Catherine said quietly, "You better tell me all that has happened. I think there has been some kind of misunderstanding! Uncle Ivan asked me some strange questions and he wanted to know what Alex had done to hurt you so."

Nichole looked even more confused. "Alex never hurt me—well, not after Armaund came. Why would he think that?"

Catherine looked at her grimly and gestured with her hands. "The beginning, when Armaund kidnapped you."

Nichole explained how Armaund had dragged her across Pennsylvania, then to the home of the Bordeleaus, about the ship to England and the arrival of the pirates. She told Catherine some of her suspicions.

Catherine looked grim through most of Nichole's recounting, but when Nichole began describing her own fears for Alex's safety, Catherine giggled nervously. Quietly, she said, "Nichole, Uncle Ivan would never hurt Alex or me. It's common knowledge in the family that we are his favorites. Right after Charles duPres was killed, when Father was planning all the things he was going to do to Alex, Uncle Ivan came to see him. Uncle Ivan, Peter says, told my father that if one hair on Alex's head was hurt, Henry Dampier would have to answer to him. Believe me, Uncle Ivan would not do a thing to Alex."

Nichole sat quietly, trying to digest this information. Finally, she smiled shyly at Catherine. "Then tell me about Alex."

Catherine began by describing Alex's arrival just after she had been kidnapped. Just than a soft knocking on the bedroom door interrupted her tale.

Catherine walked to the door and glanced at Nichole. "That will be Uncle Ivan." Catherine opened the door and smiled grimly at the Black Russian. "I just told her about you and a little about Alex."

Ivan gazed at Nichole. "After you and Catherine have talked, I would like to explain, myself. If it's too late, we can talk in the morning."

It was late, very late, when Nichole told Catherine good night and went to her own room. Catherine had to stop a dozen times in her tale so Nichole could dry her tears. When she had explained as much as she knew about what had happened, she told Nichole about Uncle Ivan's letter and how Alex had stowed away on the ship, adding softly, "He loves you very much." Catherine frowned; she wasn't supposed to tell Nichole that Alex sailed with her. Uncle Ivan would be upset with her.

In spite of her elation at Catherine's words, Nichole fought her doubts. Armaund was still on the island and Uncle Ivan had disappeared during dinner. Finally, only an hour before the sun streaked the eastern sky, Nichole drifted off to sleep.

It was almost noon before anyone disturbed her slumber. She had missed the tall-masted ship that had graced the harbor for an hour and the struggle that had occurred on the beach as Armaund had been forced on board the vessel. After the ship sailed, Catherine made her way to Nichole's room. "You goose, Uncle Ivan has been scolding me all morning for wearing you out. He wants to talk to you. You can have your breakfast while I have my lunch," Catherine laughed as she pushed Nichole from her bed.

Nichole dressed slowly, trying to rehearse the words she had to say to Ivan Maison. In spite of everything that Catherine told her, she clung to her doubts. And no one had bothered to tell her that Armaund had left the island.

As she descended the stairs, she watched Ivan. He stood at the bottom step and looked so worried that Nichole leaned over and touched her lips to his cheek. "I'm all right. I didn't get that much sleep last night. Catherine didn't keep me up," she laughed. "I had a lot to think about."

Ivan still looked worried. "You are a little peaked. I want to talk to you, but it can wait if you don't feel up to it."

"No," Nichole stated firmly, "we'll talk after I've had breakfast. I need to talk to you as well." She moved awkwardly into the dining room for the meal that was being served. As soon as she had broken her fast, she asked for tea in the library and sent Janelle to find the master. She chuckled; it would seem strange, thinking of him as uncle.

He came quickly, and before she could word her first question, Ivan took her hand and smiled at her solemnly. "Nichole," he began, "I have something I want to say. Before I tell you the news, though, I want you to know that whatever you want, that is what we'll do. You are having a baby, my first grandniece or grandnephew. I want nothing to disturb you. You must understand that."

"You sound so mysterious. Will your news disturb me?" she asked quietly.

"Perhaps," he answered truthfully, his dark brown eyes, so much like Alex's, cloudy with concern. "Nichole, Catherine did not sail alone. Alex came with her." He watched as the color stained her cheeks. "You do not have to see him if you don't want to. Catherine told me that she believes you and Alex are very much in love. But I know that sometimes sisters don't understand the whole of it. If Alex has done something to hurt you, or if you are afraid of him, you do not have to see him. I sent him on an errand to a neighboring island so that you could decide what you want to do. If seeing Alex will upset you, then I will send him home."

Nichole looked at him in surprise. "Alex won't upset me." She looked at Uncle Ivan solemnly, "When Alex and I were first married, we had some misunderstandings, but I'm not afraid of my husband. I love him as much as he loves me. I thought . . ." Her voice trailed off.

Ivan smiled grimly. "Yes? What did you think?"

Nichole blushed. "I . . . I . . . Well, you went to see Armaund every day, and you or Janelle kept asking all of those questions about Alex, and—Oh, Uncle Ivan, I thought you were planning to do something to Alex, something terrible."

"Do something to Alex? He's my godson, I wouldn't . . ." Ivan threw back his head and started to laugh. "Oh, Nichole. You seemed so afraid, I thought you were afraid of Alex. I thought he had done something to you. I never dreamed that you might be afraid for him."

Catherine stuck her head in the door. "Can I share the joke?"

Ivan struggled for control. "Come in, you little minx. It would seem that Nichole and I have been at crossed swords. I thought she was afraid of Alex, when all the time she was afraid of what she thought I meant to do to him."

"Catherine told me that he stowed away with her and that he's here. How soon can I see him?"

Ivan glanced at Catherine, his brown eyes darkening with annoyance at his niece. "I sent him to Nassau. He didn't want to stay on the ship and he definitely didn't want to go on my errand. And it would appear that neither of my young relatives mind my orders very well. I told Catherine not to say anything to you."

"How long will the errand take?" Nichole asked, her eyes glowing and her cheeks bright with color.

Uncle Ivan grinned. "I believe they will sail into the bay early tomorrow. I'm to assume, am I not, that you will see him then?"

She nodded her head vigorously.

Chapter Thirty-two

Dinner that evening was anything but pleasant. Tension radiated from all three diners. Nichole was nearly beside herself. She picked at her food for she was much too excited to eat, and when anyone at the table asked her a question, she jumped a mile. In spite of the fact that she was anxiously anticipating the arrival of her husband, she also admitted to herself that she was scared to death. She was huge with child and she considered herself most unattractive. How could Alex still love her, as big as she was?

A dozen times, Uncle Ivan turned to her and said for her ears alone, "Nichole, this much excitement can't be good for you. Perhaps you should wait until after the baby arrives to see your husband. I'm afraid this is too much for you." But she only shook her head violently. She had to see her husband, and had to know if he still wanted her.

After dinner, Nichole waddled up to her room. She undressed and got into her nightdress without waiting for Janelle. She crawled into bed early, even for her. But she couldn't go to sleep. Catherine stopped in to tell her good night, and a short time later, Janelle arrived with a cup of warm milk. "Try to sleep, little mother." She smiled knowingly.

She did try, but sleep would not come. Several times

during the night she struggled out of bed, walked to the window facing the bay and gazed out at the water. Long after she went to her room, she heard footsteps in the hall and she knew Uncle Ivan had retired.

In the very early morning hours, she awoke from a restless sleep and rose from the bed to stand at the window overlooking the bay. She gazed out over the water, shimmering like molten silver in the rays of the full moon. It was a warm, bright tropical night made more beautiful because she knew that in a matter of hours, the man she loved above all else would be at her side. If only he still loved her too.

"This is ridiculous," she muttered. "I'm going for a walk." She thought of her special place at the edge of the beach where she had often strolled when she was full of doubts. A walk in the moonlight to that place and back would ease her tension.

She grabbed for her robe and then draped a shawl around her shoulders. As quietly as she could, she made her way down the stairs and tiptoed out the door of the mansion toward the stand of trees. She looked back at the house so silent and dark, thankful that no one had yet arisen.

Several yards from the main house, in the small cottage that was hers and Donan's, Janelle rose from a sound sleep and moved to the crib of her sons. She picked up one of the whimpering boys and sat down to rock him back to sleep. Her eyes drifted toward the bay and she watched the retreating figure of a woman close to her time, weaving her way toward the beach.

Nichole followed the familiar path through the trees to the sandy beach. As she strolled along she listened to the soft rush as the gentle waves caressed the glistening sand. She found the smooth stump of the pine tree she had claimed for her own weeks ago and eased her cumbersome frame down to watch the undulating motion of the water. She let her thoughts drift back to her days at the convent.

Once more she was standing in Ma Mere's drab little office, and she remembered the words Ma Mere had said. The mother superior had wished her much joy and happiness. She had been happy at the farm, but that had been for such a short time. Now, with the baby coming, she wanted above everything to be back in Alex's arms, to know again that special joy of being truly loved. Alex had to feel that way too. Then she would be truly happy and Ma Mere's wish and prayers would come true.

Something drew her eye to the end of the bay and she noticed, silhouetted against the dark sky, the white puffs of a sailing vessel moving around the end of the island. Her heart skipped a beat. It had to be Alex's ship! She watched as the sails were rolled up to rest against the invisible yardarms. They were preparing to anchor. It was Alex's ship! Sighing, she wondered if she would get to see him before morning was no longer an infant.

Above the hush of the waves playing over the sand, she heard a splash. The anchor had been let go—or had it? Against the silver stream of reflected moonlight she noticed a solitary figure moving through the water. It had to be Alex. Instinct told her that he couldn't wait. For several minutes she sat watching the swimmer, growing more certain with each second that her husband was coming to her. She stood and walked quickly to the edge of the beach. With her voice shaking, she called out, "Alex, is that you?"

Suddenly the figure in the water stood up and came toward her. In the soft light of the winter moon, Nichole recognized the familiar shape of her beloved husband. She forgot that she feared he would find her less than pleasing. Without a thought to her nightclothes or her condition, she stumbled into the ocean, one word on her lips, "Alex!"

She found herself staring into the wet face of the man she loved. "Oh Alex!" She moved into his outstretched arms.

Janelle watched the two figures outlined against the stream of sparkling water and smiled at her sleeping child. As she laid her own little one back in his cradle she sighed. All was well. Crawling back into her bed, she snuggled up against her man.

Alex gazed down into Nichole's bright eyes, noticing the glitter of tiny droplets of tears sparkling on her long lashes. He lowered his head and kissed her tenderly. After several minutes, he breathed in a husky voice, "Oh, Nichole. I couldn't wait another minute. I was afraid that Uncle Ivan wasn't going to let me see you. I have missed you so much. I jumped over the rail as soon as we got close enough for me to swim. I don't think they've even missed me yet."

She took both of his cheeks in her hands and pulled his head down so that she could kiss him again. Her arms slid from his cheeks to around his neck, as she leaned against him. She kissed him again and again. "Oh, Alex, I missed you so."

In response, Alex ran his hands through her hair, over her shoulders, up and down her back. He kissed her eyelids, her cheeks, then took her lips gently in another long, tender kiss. Against her lips, he whispered, "I love you so much."

Finally, his voice filled with longing, he pulled away from her. "I'm getting you all wet."

She laughed. "I'm already wet."

Without warning, he picked her up into his arms and started forward, whispering, "I want to get you into more light. Everyone says you're all right, but I want to see for myself. I'll sneak us into the house, if you'll tell me where your room is. Then we'll get some sleep."

She slid her arms around his neck and nuzzled his cheek with her head. "Through the front door and up the stairs. My room is at the top of the stairs, the first door." She giggled. "If you're going to bed with me, you'll have to take off your clothes. You're all wet."

He grinned down at her. "Madame, you're as wet as I am and when we have you changed, I intend to crawl into your bed. And I'm going to stay there today, tomorrow, forever." In answer, Nichole kissed him hard.

Nichole was amazed that they were not discovered, for twice, once inside the door and again on the stairs, Alex stopped to kiss her. When they got into her room, Alex tried to help her change to a fresh gown, but Nichole insisted that he turn around. She grew adamant when he wanted to light a lantern. "I'm fine," she kept reassuring him.

When she was changed, he picked her up, kissed her once more and laid her down on the bed. Then he saw to his own wet things. Before he removed his breeches, he stopped and turned, his expression solemn in the soft light peeking through the windows. "Are you certain that you're all right? Let me look at you. Is everything well?"

Intent on silencing him for the night, Nichole squirmed off the bed and stood before him, pulling her gown around her stomach. "The only problem I have is that I'm very fat," she wailed in a soft voice.

Alex reached for her. "Never fat, my love. Terribly dear and horribly missed, but not fat." He kissed her once more, softly, tenderly. He attempted to express his feelings: "Oh, Nichole! I wanted to die when I thought I'd lost you."

"Sh-sh-sh, my love," she whispered, "we'll talk in the morning." She eased out of his arms and pulled him toward the bed. "I'm very sleepy now. Come to bed with me, so that I won't be alone."

Alex chuckled. "I hadn't planned on sleeping in any other bed. You won't be alone anymore, sweetheart. Never again," he promised. He raised the covers and slid in beside her, sighing in contentment.

Nichole giggled, "Will you stay in my bed when I have the babe?"

"Especially when you have the babe!" Alex declared as he wrapped his arms around her and held her close. She snuggled up even closer and soon they were both asleep.

In deference to Nichole's delicate condition, Ivan slipped from his room as quietly as his rage would allow. He made his way, cursing softly under his breath, "Damn him, what is he trying to prove?" He sent for Catherine and paced his library as he waited. She was barely through the door when Ivan turned and glared at her. "He jumped ship!" he muttered through clenched teeth. "He's out there now. He has no idea where he is, and if some of my men try to grab him, he could get hurt. I'm tempted to just ignore the situation. I can pretend that I don't know a thing."

Catherine turned pale. "Armaund?"

"No! That stupid brother of yours. He couldn't wait, like I told him. You two don't know the meaning of the word 'obey'!" Ivan stormed from the house, trying not to disturb the one person who would suffer from this misadventure. He headed for the beach and his officers so that he could personally direct the search.

Catherine paced the same floor that Ivan had paced only minutes before, waiting for Uncle Ivan to return with some kind of news. When she felt she had waited long enough she made her way to the beach to find out what was happening. She stood at the edge of the group of men conferring together. When she discovered that they knew nothing more, she frowned. "I better go tell Nichole. If she wakes up and sees the ship, she'll wonder where Alex is. What am I supposed to tell her?"

Ivan shrugged his shoulders and went back to the group of sailors. He had no idea what Catherine should say. With a heavy heart she turned and made her way back to the house. Sometimes Alex didn't use good sense. Why hadn't he waited, like Uncle Ivan told him to? Now Nichole had to worry that one of those wicked-looking men would clobber Alex on the head, and perhaps hurt him seriously.

Creeping up the steps, Catherine listened for a sound, something to indicate that Nichole had arisen. "She'll think Uncle Ivan has done something to him for sure." She stood with her ear against the door, but when she heard nothing, she took a deep breath and reached for the door. Gingerly, she pushed the door open a crack, afraid that the slightest noise might wake the sleeping girl. She gasped as she gazed at the bed, then closed the door as quietly as she could and made her way down the stairs, an enormous smile gracing her lips. As fast as her feet could carry her and her long skirts would allow, she raced for the beach.

"Uncle Ivan, you don't need to search. Don't bother," Catherine shouted as she ran forward. Out of breath, she grabbed at Uncle Ivan's arm, trying to tell him that his search was no longer necessary.

"Not now, Catherine. We must find him!"

"I have," she grinned.

He looked at her, noticing her sly grin. "Where is he?" Ivan asked softly.

"You'll never guess!"

"Catherine!"

She was immediately contrite. "I'm sorry, Uncle Ivan. He's with Nichole. They're sleeping in each other's arms."

Ivan took off at a run for the house.

Whether it was a slamming door, Ivan's storming out of the house, or Catherine closing their bedroom door, something roused Alex from sleep, the first good rest he had had in months. He kissed his wife gently and watched her stretch then turn toward him. "Are you going to get up, sleepyhead, or do you want to stay abed?" he whispered softly.

He grabbed for his damp clothes and grinned at her as he dressed. "Come on, are you getting up?"

Before she could reply someone was banging on their door. Alex grinned at her. "Uncle Ivan!" he explained. He moved to her side and placed a tender kiss on her forehead. "I'll wait breakfast for you." He grabbed his shirt and shouted above the pounding, "All right, I'm coming!"

Nichole heard the low voices as she struggled out of bed. She hugged herself, for he loved her, and he still wanted her as his wife in spite of her full figure. She chuckled and dressed quickly. As she went down to breakfast, she thought of all the glorious days to come. Alex must have heard her coming for he stood at the bottom of the steps waiting for her. His eyes were full of a love that she could feel. She returned his smile, her own eyes gleaming with the depth of her feelings. Such happiness was truly a gift. If Ma Mere could only know . . .

Epilogue

Alex stood at the rail of the ship, staring toward the west. Six hours ago, he had helped Nichole to the cabin after a tearful good-bye with Janelle and Ivan Maison, and now they were sailing home. Home! Such a glorious word. After four months on Uncle Ivan's island paradise, they were going home. Alex grinned in anticipation as he thought of Prissy, Peter, and even Mrs. Barber. How those three would carry on over the small bundle he had left in Nichole's arms in their cabin just minutes before.

Marguerite Denise Dampier, named for his mother and Uncle Ivan, had arrived Christmas night. Without a doubt, that had been the most trying but the most joyful day of his life. He chuckled when he thought back over the events of that day. Early that morning, a priest from one of the neighboring islands had arrived for Christmas mass. After an enormous breakfast, and despite her size, Nichole had consented to play the guitar. Even the gravel-voiced Donan joined in the singing of Christmas carols. Early in the afternoon, while everyone waited for the feast that Janelle promised, his little daughter decided she had rested long enough. He still couldn't remember whether the feast was served or not. What he did remember was Catherine's rage when it became clear that he intended to be present for his daughter's birth.

"I don't care what you promised! It isn't proper," Catherine had almost shouted at him. Alex sat on the edge of the bed, his hand clasping Nichole's, his face grim. He reached over for the dampened cloth and wiped her forehead.

"Alex," Nichole muttered.

"I'm right here, love," Alex managed evenly.

Catherine stood with both hands on her hips, glaring at her brother. "Men do not belong on the bed of a laboring woman. Will you get out of here?"

Alex looked up at her, tried to smile and announced, "No!"

"Alex!" Nichole cried.

"It's all right, love. Janelle says it will only be a little longer. If you want to push, push!"

"I do, I do." She clutched his hand and gritted her teeth, moaning.

"Now we are getting someplace." Janelle looked over at Alex from her side of the bed and grinned. "Catherine, we are doing just fine. Why don't you go keep Uncle Ivan company? Everybody seems to have forgotten about him."

Catherine left the room in a huff. Alex heard her mumble as she went out the door, "I know when I'm not wanted."

His daughter arrived soon after that—the baby girl that Nichole had wanted. She had brown curls and soon had soft brown eyes, and Nichole delighted in telling him that she looked just like him.

He had not left Nichole, nor had he missed sleeping with her since he arrived on that hidden paradise Uncle Ivan called home. And with God's help he would never be forced to leave her again.

As he stood staring out over the water he thought back over the last four months. Catherine had been placated by being named godmother for Marguerite, and Uncle Ivan, duly named godfather, had seen that the same priest who came for the Christmas mass was sent for and the child

414

properly baptized.

Contrary to his orders, half of the fleet of the Black Russian arrived for the ceremonies and the party that followed. And what a party it had been. The hold of this ship was filled with gifts the pirates gave to his daughter. Nichole was gracious, but she let it be known that she would accept nothing for the child that was stolen. And those grim, world-weary men had agreed, explaining to Nichole as they presented their gifts where each item had been purchased. Alex laughed out loud when he thought of the shopping frenzy that must have occurred in the port cities of the islands.

Catherine grew very quiet after Marguerite's birth, and Nichole quietly asked Uncle Ivan to make arrangements for his niece to return to Manor House. After the party, Catherine took her leave and sailed back to Maryland on one of her uncle's ships to prepare for her wedding. The minx had even convinced Uncle Ivan that one of his cottages would make an excellent honeymoon haven. The ship that took her home would return at the end of April and carry Robert and Catherine back to the island to meet Uncle Ivan and enjoy his special brand of hospitality while they enjoyed their honeymoon.

Alex frowned, for not all the news had been good. Ivan Maison sent word to the duPreses of the condition of their son and how the boy had come to his island, adding that he was already on his way to them. He didn't mention Nichole or the harm Armaund had tried to do to Alex's marriage. Uncle Charles and Aunt Catherine had sent word that Armaund had never arrived in England. The captain of the ship Uncle Ivan sent told Charles duPres that his son jumped overboard near the English coast, mumbling something about the chateau and his titles. Alex wondered if he survived and if his destination was France. He shivered in the spring air as he thought about what awaited his mad cousin in the strife-torn country.

The same letter that carried such tragic news also brought word that the French aunt and uncle would be arriving for Catherine's wedding. Uncle Charles hinted that he felt that as Catherine's godfather he should give the girl away. Catherine took it all in stride, telling Alex, "Since you'll be Robert's best man, I think it will be nice." Alex wondered how Robert would react to an English duke at his wedding.

Alex thought of the surprise that waited for Nichole when they got to the farm. Even before Marguerite arrived, he talked Uncle Ivan into carrying a message to Peter. One of the vessels that came for the baptism brought the answer. Nellie Hutchinson had graciously accepted his offer. The little woman would be waiting for them at a completely refurbished Frederick farm as their new housekeeper.

Alex turned to glance across the deck. Moving toward him was his beautiful wife, their precious bundle in her arms. Since the birth of this child of love, they had grown so close. As he gazed at her, he was amazed that she was his. She was a wellspring of common sense, so intelligent and sensitive and with the most incredible sense of humor. He could not imagine a life without her.

He watched her in the golden light of the waning sun. She had lost her innocent beauty, and it its place was a more serene and mature elegance, born of pain and peace. She was like a rose, a perfect bloom, his own gentle rose. He opened his arms to welcome her and his daughter with her dark brown hair and soft brown eyes. Against the golden curls that crowned his wife's head he whispered, "I love you." He wrapped his arms tightly around her and the babe. "I love you both."